W9-CYT-288

MOROSE SWAMP

NORTH FORK HAMMOCK

CYPRESS STRANDER

OAK SENTINELS

TO LILLY'S ESTATE

CANFIELD FARM

CYPRESS BRIDGE

HOSTETTER FARM

CANFIELD HOUSE

DUCK

SOUTH FORK HAMMOCK

HOSTETTER CUTOFF

CANFIELD FOREST

LAKE

MOCKING BIRD ROAD

TO WINTER FREE

N

MONTOOTH

MONTOOTH

and the Canfield Witch

A CARTY ANDERSSON NOVEL BY

ROBERT JAY

Montooth
Press

Copyright © 2009 by Cloverleaf Corporation
All rights reserved including the right of reproduction in whole or in part in any form.
This book is a work of fiction. However, some of the historical characters who appear do so under their own names. Names, places, and incidents are either created from the author's imagination or are used fictitiously.
Montooth is a registered trademark of Cloverleaf Corporation.

Montooth Press
Publishing Division of Cloverleaf Corporation
1916 South Tamiami Trail
Ruskin, FL 33570

Cover artwork and chapter illustrations by Lauren Ireland
(www.laurenireland.com)
Text and cover design by AuthorSupport, LaGrange, KY
Author photograph in the Myakka swamps, FL by M. S. Christian
Book printed and bound by Berryville Graphics, Berryville, VA

Jay, Robert, 1943 -
Montooth and the Canfield Witch / Robert Jay.
p. cm.
1. Carty Andersson (Fictitious character) – fiction. 2. Montooth (Fictitious character) – fiction. 3. Florida swamps – fiction. 4. Witches – fiction. 5. Alligators – fiction. 6. Young adults – fiction. 7. Fathers and daughters – fiction. 8. Ybor City, FL – fiction.
I. Title
ISBN 978-0-615-29645-6
Printed in the United States of America

DEDICATION

This book is dedicated to my daughter and editor, Meghan Christian, without whose insistence and persistence it would not have been written.

From the time that she and her older brother, Matthew, were youngsters, I read to them nearly every night of their childhoods. But when he grew older and drifted away from the evening ritual, she usually implored me to put the book down and "tell a story from out of [my] head."

Shortly after Christmas of 1989, I was finishing a three-year assignment in West Germany while my family had already relocated back to Indianapolis. Over a couple of lonely evenings, I penned a short children's story "from out of [my] head" and mailed it to her. Nearly twenty years later, the little handwritten tale became the inspiration for *The Legend of Montooth*, which evolved into <u>Montooth and the Canfield Witch</u>.

Having inherited my pack-rat tendencies, Meghan had kept the little booklet for two decades. Last year, she presented it back to me with an order to make it into a book. After much debate and resistance, I acquiesced, but only under the condition that she took on editing and management responsibilities. With that agreement, this book and the publishing house, Montooth Press, took shape.

ACKNOWLEDGEMENTS

Though <u>Montooth and the Canfield Witch</u> is fiction, I sought to be historically accurate and need to thank several people for their assistance in this regard. There were more than a few re-writes to correct assumptions and memories that proved inaccurate.

First, Andy Huse, an historian at the library of the University of South Florida, has studied The Columbia's history in Ybor City from the time it started as a small tavern in 1905 through its present day status as the flagship restaurant in a multiple location chain. He kept me from overstating The Columbia's station in the early days.

Ken Breslauer, Communications Director and Track Historian at Sebring International Raceway, alerted me to the simple conditions of the first auto race at Sebring in 1950. I was heading down the road to overstatement until corrected as a result of his input.

Douglas J. Reatini, Director, Office of Worship for the Diocese of St. Petersburg, Florida delved into Church history to explain how Lent was treated prior to 1955, when Pope Pius XII extended the time of the Easter Vigil from noon to midnight.

Mr. Jules Baumer, S. J., my English instructor at St. Ignatius High School in Cleveland, Ohio, deserves special recognition. By the time we sophomores finished authoring long themes, each week, over the entire term, Mr. Baumer had us convinced that writing was not all that difficult. I have never forgotten that the demands he made on us in 1958 served me well in business and elsewhere during the decades since.

PRIMARY CHARACTERS

(March-April, 1950)

Andersson, Catherine "Carty" – Charter member of The Crew (group of friends), skilled archer, swamp expert, strong-willed tomboy, daughter of Michael and Bay Andersson, great niece of Lilly Andersson, fourteen

Andersson, Lilliquest "Lilly" – Wealthy descendant of a Florida sugar mogul, influential citizen of the town of Winter Free, philanthropist, aunt of Michael Andersson and great aunt of Carty Andersson, sixty-six years old

Andersson, Michael – WWII Army Ranger, decorated veteran, expert tracker, engineer, operator of family limerock mining operation, father of Carty Andersson, middle thirties

Canfield, Sally – Last descendant of ancestors driven from Salem, Massachusetts during the Witch Trials of the Seventeenth Century, recluse, mischievous, feared as a witch by most Winter Free townsfolk, upper twenties

Cruz Cruz aka "The Cuban" – U.S. Marine veteran, Tampa native, born to Cuban parents, emotionless, deadly behind-the-scenes power broker, superb military and operational mind, leader of the attackers of Sally Canfield, early to middle fifties

Dolder, Haywood – Fellow student and nasty rival of Carty Andersson, spoiled-rotten son of Winter Free's Chevrolet Dealer, devious but not particularly bright, thinks highly of himself, fourteen

Dredman, Damon – Possibly Ivy League educated, lazy, criminal, drunkard, get-rich-quick schemer, part of the attackers of Sally Canfield, late thirties

Elsmore, James – County Sheriff, WWII veteran, level-headed, fair-minded leader, principled, honest, early thirties

Holmes, Blake – Charter member of The Crew (group of friends), strong, courageous, gifted athlete, well versed in wilderness conditions, male, nearly fifteen

Hostetter, Clemens – Former neighbor of Sally Canfield, dim-witted, lethargic, easily led astray, lackey of Damon Dredman, part of the attackers of Sally Canfield, middle twenties

Montooth – Enormous alligator with large misplaced tooth, protector of ducks, denizen of Duck Lake, loyal, age unknown but believed to be well over one hundred

Stein, Maximilian "Mack" – Newly invited member of The Crew (group of friends), recent Jewish-German immigrant to Florida, well educated and cosmopolitan, committed to his adopted country, confronts intimidating wilderness conditions, fourteen

Wending, Hale – Charter member of The Crew (group of friends), leading student, from a large black family, good athlete, brave, resourceful, knowledgeable on wilderness conditions, male, fourteen

Zeller, Carey – WWII veteran of the Pacific Campaign, had difficulty adjusting back to civilian life, loyal to Cruz Cruz, shrewd, glimmer of a moral compass, skilled in combat, experienced in wilderness conditions, part of the attackers of Sally Canfield, early thirties

CHAPTER 1

Aunt Lilliquest

This swamp is a monument to death. Snakes, alligators,

quicksand, all bent on one thing: destruction.

EDWARD D. WOOD, JR.

By mere chance, or maybe because of confused directions, but certainly not intentionally, Carty came upon the witch's house at the edge of Morose Swamp.

The day that had begun poorly failed to improve as the hours passed. Before she got half way to school, her bicycle flipped the chain. So when she burst into Mrs. Tryon's eighth grade classroom, Carty was late and dirty from working the chain back on the sprocket. She arrived with her hands, slight freckles, and blond hair smudged with grease. Her upper lip, curved into a perpetual smile that exposed prominent straight white

1

teeth, betrayed her annoyance at the day's bad start.

Then Blake Holmes spent the entire lunch period teasing her about the "little dab of Brylcreem[1]" in her hair. Blake was a real buddy, but he had a way of being frustrating on occasion. Today, with him singing that silly radio jingle for hair goo, was assuredly one of those times.

As a youngster, Blake lost his mother to cancer just before he was to begin attending school. His sympathetic father kept the disconsolate boy home for a few days, then a week, then a month. By the time Blake was ready to go, he would have lagged far behind the other first graders. At that point, Mr. Holmes decided to hold him back until the next year.

Thus, he was a year older than Carty and his other classmates. She couldn't help but think that a boy of fourteen – "almost fifteen," as he was saying lately – should act more mature.

Already just a dash under six feet tall – even with his sandy hair in a short crew cut – he was framed with broad shoulders and thick arms that had propelled baseballs past the outfield fences even as a Little Leaguer. A couple of years before, he hit for the cycle against a St. Petersburg, Florida team that was good enough to reach the Little League World Series.

His engaging smile suggested "friend" to most anyone he met. Along with Carty, he was one of "The Crew," three lifelong buddies – the other was Hale Wending – who had grown up together on Periwinkle Street in the south central Florida town of Winter Free.

Actually, Winter Free had grown to city-size, but most locals continued to refer to it as a town, perhaps in a nostalgic desire to retain vestiges of the simplicity of their childhoods. It was so equal in distance from Sarasota and Tampa that residents often disagreed over which of those two cities' radio stations to listen to, department stores to shop in, and newspapers to read.

The next downward step in Carty's frustrating day occurred when Mrs. Tryon required her to stay after school to clean the blackboards as a gentle reprimand for being tardy. Carty often found herself in hot water for some small infraction or another. She was never intentionally mischievous, just too busy and distracted, and not sufficiently organized to stay fully on Mrs. Tryon's good side. It probably would have surprised Carty and most of the other students, though, to discover that the veteran teacher secretly regarded Carty as her favorite.

Carty really didn't mind the extra assignment, but her schedule these last several weeks was more hectic than usual. Besides school work, chores at home, and archery practice, she had taken on a new responsibility due to Aunt Lilliquest's accident.

Today's after school duty put her late to her father's aunt's home to help with the housework, though thankfully the bike chain proved reliable for that trip. Aunt Lilly had fallen and broken an arm and was still sporting a cast. She had toppled from a ladder while cleaning oak leaves from the roof gutters.

"YOU'RE sixty-six years old, Lilly," Carty's father had lightly reproached his aunt in Doc Brannigan's office on the day of the accident. "Why are you climbing on your roof?"

"I was not on the *roof*, Michael. I was on the ladder, reaching into the gutter. If that big old blue heron hadn't swooped to a landing right in front of me, there would have been no problem. As it turned out, we were both

3

startled and quickly jumped our separate ways." She laughed, even as she winced in pain, remarking with a twinkle in her eye, "Unfortunately for me, he was the only one with wings."

"That is not the point. You have more than enough money. Why don't you hire a handyman for the tough stuff? Shoot, if you get into a bind, you know I'll come over and help."

"Ha, a handyman. I'm lucky I can get a hold of the plumber, Joe Martin, and when I do, I am expected to adhere to his schedule. If he could figure out a way to get away with it, he'd make me take out the leaky pipe and bring it to his shop to be fixed. Michael, it's just easier to do things myself. As long as I am still healthy and able, I like to keep active.

"Seriously, I know I can count on you if I need anything, but now that the limerock business is really taking off, you don't have a lot of free time."

"You are right about the business, Lilly. It is growing like crazy, and I have you to thank. Your prescience was right on the mark."

IN 1945, Michael Andersson returned from duty as an Army Combat Engineer/Ranger in the European Theater. He had barely survived in the second wave at Normandy and was scheduled to be one of the first ashore in the invasion of Japan.

His vote for Harry Truman in 1948 was a direct thank you for the president's decision to end the War with the Atom Bomb. Almost none of Michael's immediate comrades had survived Omaha Beach. He recognized that Truman's tough choice in cutting the Pacific War short almost certainly saved his life and the lives of hundreds of thousands of other American servicemen.

"Ironically," he had explained to Carty, "Those two bombs likely also saved many more Japanese than would have been killed if we had stormed the beaches instead. Our fights to take the smaller Pacific islands were incredibly deadly for soldiers on both sides and on the local civilians."

Upon returning to Florida, he went to work for a road building contractor. He enjoyed the work, but disliked being away from his family for months at a time, moving from road project to road project. So he was in a receptive mood when Lilly talked to him about a proposed venture. It involved acquiring a multi-square-mile property with subterranean limerock deposits.

As an engineer, Michael knew that Florida's shifting, soft, sandy soil was poorly suited for roads and required especially thick road base before paving with asphalt or concrete. Limerock was the only suitable base material indigenous to the state, so any substitute would have to be trucked in from out of state – an expensive process.

He remembered her hauling out a series of U.S. Geological Survey reports showing that the raw material was located under the acreage that she wanted to buy. The deposit was one of only two such large supplies in the state. Old Man Hardy, who owned the mine and the surrounding untapped land, was ready to retire. He had offered the land to her at a favorable price.

"Lilly, this will be a terrific business in the next decade," Hardy had told her. "I don't need a lot of money, and I don't have any heirs worthy of more than a dime. I'm offering you a cheap price, because I like what your dad did with his sugar cane property, and I like you."

He gave her the necessary technical information and independent contacts to sort out the potential. "Take whatever time you need to come to a decision. I'm in no hurry, and I'm not going to offer it to anyone else unless you turn it down," he had told her.

After researching thoroughly, Lilly determined that Hardy was correct in his assessment and probably even too conservative – hence the call for Michael to pay her a visit.

"Michael," she had concluded after explaining Hardy's offer, "I can't run this type of business myself. It takes an engineer, and I don't want to sift through any number of incompetent managers before I find someone capable. I know I can trust you to operate it well. I'll put up the money. We'll share the profits equally, and I'll write you an option to buy me out at my original purchase price after ten years." Michael recognized that her offer was more than a fair deal; indeed it was largely a gift.

"Air conditioning," she had started out by way of explanation.

He often remembered how puzzled he was, standing at the table, looking at maps of limerock deposits, scratching his head. "What does air conditioning have to do with road base?" he queried.

"Air conditioning is the key, Michael. It will open up the entire South," she continued, "and Florida will benefit more than any other state. We are a large state, and we have enormous potential for coastal development. As the population up north ages, Florida will be the prime retirement destination in the east. Our most serious drawbacks have always been humidity and summer heat. Those Yankees can't handle either.

"Air conditioning is coming on strong in public buildings and retail businesses, especially since the War ended. The town hall, Dolder's Chevy dealership, and Doc Brannigan's new medical building all have put in air conditioning this year alone. Even Ensign Bank is adding it before summer, and that old tightwad Gardner Ensign isn't frivolous with the bank's money.

"The important point is that air conditioning is becoming so efficient and economical that individual homes are beginning to install it. As that becomes commonplace, it will encourage Northerners to move south and buy retirement homes.

"I've already invested heavily in Carrier Engineering, the air conditioning company," she added, "and I want you involved in the next step."

"Aha! I'm not as quick as you, Lilly," he recalled saying, "but I'm not a complete dunderhead. I'm beginning to understand. With fast-growing population comes demand for more and better roads. Hardy's mine has always made him a comfortable but modest living, but it will be like mining silver in Virginia City's Comstock Lode[2] if your ideas about a fast-growing population are correct."

They shook on the deal. Within a month, they had formed the corporation, signed their personal agreements, and acquired the property. Hardy stayed on without pay for six additional months to guide Michael through the early stages. Business had quickly taken off.

When Michael saw how fast sales were picking up, he asked Hardy if he regretted selling.

"Are you kidding? I'm too old to put up with all the headaches of a growing business. Besides, the bigger and more successful you get, the greedier and more jealous the politicians and bureaucrats become. Mark these words, Michael – before you retire, you'll find that you spend more time dealing with those non-productive leaches than with your actual business."

DOC Brannigan knocked on the door and came in for a final look at Lilly's cast. "You should be able to do some light one-handed activities by the end of the week, Lilly," he said. "I'll be out to take a look next week. Call me if you have a problem before then, but it was a hairline break so you should heal easily enough. In the meantime," he added, turning to Michael and looking at him over the tops of his glasses and through bushy white eyebrows, "See that she leaves flying to the Air Force."

Michael drove Lilly home in his new blue and white DeSoto[3]. The wide whitewalls took the bumpy county road smoothly. He brought up the business activity again.

"I was invited to the last State Road Commission meeting. Those guys are the major road builders in the state, and they pretty much run things. They usually don't invite mere mortals like me to their confabs," he chuckled, "but they have realized belatedly that your analysis of the coming demand for roads was right on the money. They were just a little slower than you were. One of them, Bill Brady, collared me after the meeting and tried to buy the mine property. He wasn't surprised when I said we wouldn't be interested, but he said he had to try.

"They had an economist from the University of Miami as a guest speaker. The gist of his comments was that Florida's population is already jumping upward. He estimates that it will accelerate and soon be growing much as California did in the last fifty years.

"As owner of the state's largest centrally located source of road base, we should be in for a long, successful run."

He paused for a few moments, and they watched a flock of orange-beaked white ibis rise from a grassy patch, spooked by the cloud of billowing dust following the car along the dirt road.

"Lilly, I've been thinking seriously about bringing Carty into the business after college. She has good math skills and thinks like an engineer. I'd hate to build up the business and then just sell it off when I get older. It might be tough finding an engineering college to take a female, but I'm sure you have enough influence at the University of Florida if we need it, Lilly."

"Ha, you're right about that. If they want another new building from me, they'd better find a desk in it for my great niece. But what about Purdue, Michael? You speak highly about the program you went through there."

"You are probably right, Lilly. Purdue has taken women into its engineering program since the Eighteen Hundreds. I'm just a little apprehensive about sending her that far away."

"Aside from where to send her, Michael, do you think she is suited for that kind of career?"

"I think she has the moxie to run anything. She can be tough as nails or as soft as a pillow, depending on the situation. She knows how to keep her mouth shut when it is more important to listen, and she has high ethical standards.

"During the War, women showed that they could handle most of what only men formerly did. She'd never get an opportunity to run Pan Am[4] or the like, but in a family business, I believe that she would blossom. What do you think?"

"I really can't say right now, Michael. I love Carty dearly and think of her as if she were my granddaughter, but I've never thought of her in that way. Do you think you could have her spend some time with me? We can say I need some help while my arm is mending."

"Lilly, you do need help while your arm is mending. The last thing I want is you trying to hang wallpaper with one arm in a sling," he laughed. "Seriously, that is an excellent idea. I'll explain it to Bay, and we can let Carty know that you need her assistance.

"Carty is growing up quickly. How is Bay taking that?"

"Carty is still very close to her mom. Once she starts to live away from home, it will be bad. I know Bay is dreading sending her to Sarasota Preparatory Academy next year. High school is bad enough, but a boarding school has her fretting."

"All the Bartlett women have gone to Sarasota Prep since my grandmother lived in Florida. I hope that you will prevail on Bay."

"Oh, Bay agrees with the plan. She just does not want to face it. However, we are going to an open house at the academy in a few weeks. You are invited to come along if you'd like."

"I'd like that very much. I haven't been back since a reunion almost... almost... gosh, almost fifteen years ago. It didn't seem that long until I thought about it."

THE day after Lilly broke her arm, Carty began a daily bike ride to Aunt Lilly's. Carty – Catherine was her given name, but no one had called her that since her Christening about fourteen years ago – scheduled time after school each day to help with the cleaning and cooking. She also picked Lilly's citrus – the oranges, lemons, limes, and grapefruit. There was enough to fill Lilly's fruit bowls with plenty more for neighbors, friends, and relatives who often happened by for a visit.

Because of arriving late today and because Carty ran into an unexpected snag while baking her aunt's favorite dessert, blueberry cobbler, she stayed longer than usual. Unfortunately, the baking effort moved well along before Carty discovered that Lilly's sugar bowl was almost empty. That oversight required a round trip bike ride to a distant neighbor's to borrow some sugar, and resulted in a long-delayed cobbler.

She had almost hoped that Aunt Lilly would send her home before the cobbler was done so she could make the seven-mile ride in at least partial daylight. However, Carty knew that working around the hot oven was not a one-arm chore, so she would not have left early even if offered. Anyway, she wanted to sample the cobbler.

"It will be dark soon, Carty. Would you like to stay here tonight?" Lilly knew that Carty would not like a long morning trip to school from the mansion, but she wanted to bring the late hour to Carty's attention.

Aunt Lilly had plenty of room in the large manor house. Her father, Sven Andersson, Carty's great grandfather, built the family mansion before the 1920s on several thousand acres of land he acquired for next to nothing. It was considered useless scrub land at the time, bordered on two sides by swamp and on the south by the Everglades, with no access roads.

Wealthy Northerners were flocking to the coasts of Florida at that time, but they had no interest in the sweltering, hot interior, occupied by, in their thoughts, all sorts of unpleasant creatures of both human and non-human form.

AS a young teenager in Sweden, Sven had been orphaned. He found work as an apprentice in a small factory in Göteborg. He possessed a natural aptitude for mechanics, hard work, and making people like him. In time, he became almost a son to the childless owner. When his mentor was ready to retire, he offered the factory to Sven at a very generous price and favorable terms. But Sven had a wanderlust that vied to be satisfied. He wanted to see a world beyond Sweden's shores.

On a frigid winter night, Sven handed a long letter to his benefactor, thanking him sincerely for all the old man had done to mold him into a good and capable person. Sven then packed a small bag with his meager belongings and a modest amount of money that he had saved.

He wandered the docks for two days looking over the ships and crews. He learned that the captain of an English steamer taking on Swedish cargo for the Caribbean route had a good reputation for fair treatment of his men. Sven talked his way on board and signed up as a lowly deckhand.

Three years later, he was first mate and appeared to be destined to have his own ship in a few years. But his contract happened to expire when the ship was berthed in the Bahamas. The balmy islands beckoned to Sven after all those years in cold, gray Sweden and on the high seas, so he turned down the opportunity to re-sign.

Leaving the ship, he found work on a sugar plantation. With his knowledge of machinery and ability with tools, he worked his way up into a small ownership of the facility. That led him to frequent trips to South Florida to deal with the plantation's customers there.

One of his better customers, a Sarasota bottler of a new carbonated cola drink, was also a real estate developer. The business mogul took a liking to Sven and convinced him to sell his interest in the island sugar plantation in order to partner in the Florida construction business.

For over three decades, Sven shepherded the construction of dozens of commercial buildings. However, his devotion to a real estate career waned prior to the Florida real estate boom of the early 1920s. At that time, he still supervised major hotel and resort projects in Sarasota and Fort Myers on the West Coast and in Miami Beach and Palm Beach on the East Coast, but he was phasing himself out.

Despite accumulating millions from his real estate career, he missed the feeling he got making living things grow. At that time, he bought vast primitive acreage in the Florida interior, stretching down to the Everglades. He cleared the land and built the manor house for his wife, the former Marie Bartlett of Sarasota. He planted sugar cane as he had in the Bahamas, and had his sugar refinery up and running the next year. By 1914, this part-time "hobby" was providing a major part of U.S. sugar production.

Demand for sugar boomed through WWI, causing Sven to concentrate his energies in the sugar business. By 1925, he had liquidated all of his other real estate holdings, missing the Florida real estate crash by a few years.

Sugar demand, however, stayed strong enough throughout the Depression years that Sven's operation continued to expand. When he died before WWII, having outlived his wife and both of his sons, he was one of the wealthiest men and the second or third largest land owner in Florida. Only his daughter Lilliquest and his grandchildren from the boys survived him. Carty's father was one of Sven's grandsons.

Like Andrew Carnegie[5] before him, Sven Andersson did not believe in passing on great wealth to later generations. He bequeathed most of his plantation land to the state for a wilderness refuge. He left the large house, a few acres of citrus trees, and a modest trust fund to Lilly.

He also apparently passed on to her the Andersson acumen for business and investment, because she soon built her modest trust fund into a substantial fortune. She had handled the company's finances almost from the beginning, when Sven recognized her expertise, and his training proved invaluable to her after he was gone.

"IF you'd like to stay," Lilly continued, "I'll call your mother so she won't worry."

"That's tempting, but I really can't be late for school tomorrow. We have an important math test in the morning. From here, Cross Creek[6] Elementary is a good ten miles, so I'd never make it in time by bike, and I'm already in trouble for being late today. Dad won't be back from his business trip until the weekend, so I can't get him to pop over here to give me a ride."

The cobbler was ready to come out of the oven. Carty's mouth was watering from the sweet berry scent wafting throughout the kitchen. She lifted the pan with thick pot holders and slid it on to the stone counter. Vivid blue-purple juices bubbled, popped, and oozed along the edges of the pan.

Aunt Lilly used her good arm and hand to pour two tall glasses of cold milk. She brought out plates, forks, a knife, and a large wood spatula.

"It won't be easy to scoop from the pan unless we wait a while for it to cool, Aunt Lilly, but I really should be leaving soon, so let's give it a try while it is still hot."

"I am really sorry about the sugar, dear. I should have remembered that I was nearly out. Then you would not be in this mess."

"Speaking of messes, just look at the way this cobbler spread out all over our plates. What a goopy soup."

"It looks good enough to me, Carty," Aunt Lilly responded. Taking a small bite after blowing it cool, Aunt Lilly marveled, "This may be the best cobbler that I have ever had."

"Flattery will get you another cobbler some day," Carty chuckled. "But it is good, isn't it?"

"I think we need a scoop of ice cream to top it off," Aunt Lilly suggested. Carty jumped off her chair and brought the box of vanilla to the table. Lilly preferred her homemade version, but the bad arm was boosting Borden's business lately. She added a generous scoop to each plate of cobbler. Carty took two tablespoons from a drawer and gave one to her aunt.

"The big spoon will work a lot better than the fork, Aunt Lilly, for both the ice cream and these sloppy blueberries."

Carty glanced out of the kitchen window at the rapidly sinking sun. "I really do not mind riding at night. It's that rutted dirt road that concerns me. If I can't see it well enough in the dark, you may be tending me for a broken arm," she laughed. "Oh well, fresh baked cobbler was worth any inconvenience," she said, wiping blued crumbs from her lips.

Lilly welcomed the comment about the condition of the road. When Carty had called from the school to say that she would be late,

Lilly seized the opportunity and was maneuvering to take full advantage of it. She did not want Carty taking the road or her bike home. Lilly had other subtle plans for her.

"Hmm, you are right about that. Your dad tells me that the county has this road in its long term paving plan, but that's a couple of years away.

"Carty, there is a shortcut to your house between Duck Lake and Morose Swamp. You would have to walk, though. It's too much of a tangle for a bike, but it would cut off a couple of miles or more and get you home before it got too dark. Swamp shadows can be intimidating as the sun sets, though."

Lilly knew that this last comment would have the effect she sought. During the last several weeks together, she had learned a lot about Carty's character, abilities, and intense competitiveness. Carty would take such a comment as a challenge.

Carty was not reckless. Nevertheless, while duly wary, she was not afraid of gators, boars, poisonous snakes, or most other swamp residents. The thought of bears gave her pause, but no one had sighted a bear in the area in this century. She had lived her entire life in and around the Florida swampland and knew how to avoid or evade the more dangerous creatures.

"Aunt Lilly, you know that Dad has been taking me camping and bow hunting in the swamps since I was little. It is not a frightening place if you understand it and are careful. Besides, we had a full moon a few nights ago, so it'll still be bright enough with tonight's clear sky.

"I have an old pair of blue jeans in your spare bedroom that I can change into. Back in a flash."

She darted away and swapped her skirt for the jeans, then tied her barely shoulder-length hair into a ponytail. She placed the skirt on a hanger and hung it in the closet.

Returning, she complained, "That long school skirt isn't suitable for hiking through the woods. It's not all that good for a bike either. I wish we girls could wear pants to school like the boys."

"Carty, you are getting to be a lady. You should be happy to dress accordingly."

"I know," Carty sighed. "It is just that pants are so much more convenient, especially if I'm facing a trek through a swamp. By the way, where is this short-cut? You've never mentioned it before."

"Go out past the old sugar refinery tool house to the property fence line. You'll see a path on the other side of the gate. Those old hinges have been rusted shut for as many years as I can remember, but I used to hop fences when I was your age, and I had to do it in a dress." With a glint in her eye and a smile on her face, she added, "So, you can see, we women have made some progress."

Carty scrunched up her face in response and then grinned back.

"Follow the path until the forest seems to hem you in. Then go for about another mile or so until you come to two large oaks that look like giant sentinels. Neither one has a branch lower than fifty feet off the ground, and the trunks are as straight as arrows. Between them and then angled to their right is a narrow hammock that runs between Duck Lake and Morose Swamp. During the rainy season, the hammock is occasionally under water, but this time of year, that hump of land will be dry and passable.

"With the lake on your left well off in the distance, you will come upon especially tall trees in a small bald cypress strand. It's surely dry now too. The area is not accessible by vehicles, so the loggers left those trees alone. They are hundreds of years old, dating back to the Spaniards.

"Look for a half hollowed-out trunk of one of the taller trees. Both the south fork in the path and the north fork circle around from that point for about a couple of miles or so. They end at opposite sides of the Hostetter's abandoned farm. The north fork avoids the Canfield property that borders the lake and swamp. The narrow dirt road in front of the Hostetter's old house leads to Mocking Bird Road."

"Oh, I know where the Hostetter Cutoff meets Mocking Bird. That spot should put me a couple of miles from home, right?"

"Maybe a little more, but yes, you are basically home at that point, as fast as you walk and run."

"It's strange that I haven't heard of this route. I thought I knew everything about the swamps around here."

"Your father takes you hunting in the opposite direction, towards his limerock mine. He's more familiar with the land over there. He probably never thought to take you into Morose Swamp.

"No one has occupied the Hostetter place since Cora Hostetter passed away years ago," she added. "Most of the people in Winter Free think that Sally Canfield, the woman who lives on the bordering property, is a witch."

"A witch? Aunt Lilly, that's silly. Who believes in witches nowadays? This is 1950!"

"Nearly everyone in Winter Free has heard that Miss Canfield is part of a long line of witches. At least they are afraid of her, whether they believe her to be a witch or not."

"Why are people afraid? Has she done anything to anyone?"

"The Canfields were almost certainly not involved, but people who have ventured around their property have disappeared. About ten years ago, Hoyt Whorton boasted to his friends that he was going to paddle up Spring River to Duck Lake to go duck hunting. The lake has borne that name as long as anyone can remember because of its reputation as a haven for an enormous duck population.

"He couldn't convince anyone to go with him, though, and he didn't return the next day. After waiting one more day, his brother and cousin paddled up to find him, and they disappeared too. No one ever found them, their canoes, or their shotguns, or came up with any physical clue as to what happened.

"The Canfields have lived in that area for hundreds of years. They arrived when the Spanish still controlled Florida. There were rumors of similar disappearances even long before Sally Canfield was born."

"Were they responsible for any of the disappearances? Do you think the Canfields are witches?"

"No, dear, I certainly don't. Sally still lived with her grandmother at that time. Our former sheriff deputized half the town and led them out to question the two women. He wasn't about to go out there alone. But nothing came of it.

"One of those deputies was James Elsmore, our current sheriff. He still chuckles at the large show of force they used to conduct an interview of one slightly-built elderly woman and a young girl barely older than you at the time. He is one of the few people I know who believes that Sally Canfield is not dangerous.

"Sally is the last of the Canfields, and some say she is the strangest of any of them, but strange does not mean she is a witch, nor does it mean that she is dangerous. I have seen her a few times in the last twenty years or so, and it seems to me that she only wants to be left alone. She visits town maybe three or four times a year to stock up on provisions, but otherwise stays on her farm all the time.

"People ease out of Homer's general store when she comes in, and they walk on the other side of the street while she is in town. The really fearful ones hide in their houses and peek through the corners of the windows. Whenever she glances around, you see curtains flashing in windows of every building.

"Homer himself looks like he holds his breath the entire time she is in his store. His face gets redder and redder the longer she shops. Sometimes she swirls around rapidly to pick out an item. Then old Homer turns white from fright. I think she makes the fast moves to amuse herself. One time I noticed the corners of her mouth curling into the tiniest smile when she glanced at him sidewise as she did the maneuver."

"So you saw her at Homer's, Aunt Lilly?"

"Yes. The first time I saw Sally was when she was a little girl. Her grandmother kept her close, and Sally stared down at the floor the entire time. I never saw her eyes. I was probably the only person in Winter Free to even say hello to them. They replied, but didn't offer any conversation. They were polite, and they certainly didn't 'hex' me as half the town expected.

"When I left Homer's, people stared after me as if I might float away, turn into a frog, or spontaneously combust. As uncomfortable as the town made me feel, I can imagine how hard it must be for the Canfields to be under constant scrutiny when they venture off of their property. It is no wonder they have been so reclusive.

"Since then, I've run into her a handful of times, almost always in the vicinity of Homer's or Ensign Bank, and the events were similar – never initiating a greeting, but polite hellos in response to mine. There was never any additional conversation. When Sally was grown, she did make eye contact. She has remarkably deep green eyes, not the dark eyes I had expected."

Lilly intentionally omitted mentioning one other more recent meeting.

"How old do you think Sally is?"

"Hmm, let's see now. The way she dresses and carries herself as an adult, it is difficult to estimate her age." Lilly paused a few moments and wrestled with the mathematics involved.

"She would have been about eight that first time I saw her – give or take a year. I recall that Rocco Barreldini had driven me to Homer's in his new four-door Graham[7] that day. On the way there, he told me all about the movie he had just seen, 'All Quiet on the Western Front.' That was showing around 1930 or '31, if my memory hasn't failed me.

"So that puts Sally around 27, maybe 28-years-old. She looks quite a bit older, though, but she's definitely not over 30."

Carty marveled at Lilly's detailed memory. "So what did happen to Hoyt Whorton and the others?"

"Hoyt never drank a drop of water unless it had at least six parts of gin mixed in. My guess is that Hoyt fell out of the canoe, or a gator or other critter got him. His two-man rescue crew was probably just as liquored up. Sheriff Elsmore believes there is an over-sized gator in Duck Lake that will take on most any small craft and is not intimidated by humans. Intoxicated boaters would be choice prey.

"Were there other disappearances?"

"There are many legends about missing Spanish Conquistadores and early trappers. Almost all of Florida was a large, untamed wilderness for hundreds of years under the haphazard rule of several different peoples. No doubt many early visitors were lost because of the harsh conditions, and subsequent residents probably embellished the mysteries of each preceding population. It is not likely that the Canfield clan had a connection with any of those lost souls."

"It is kind of exciting to live in a place with such interesting history, Aunt Lilly, even if much of it is myth."

"So, knowing about the 'Canfield Witch,' are you a little apprehensive about trying out a new way home, Carty?"

"Not me. Witch talk is silly. Anyway," she chuckled, "While I am keeping an eye out for the usual wildlife, I will be checking carefully for any flying brooms that might cruise overhead."

Aunt Lilly laughed. Her great niece was as fearless as she was level-headed.

"I want you to borrow Dad's old Bowie knife[8] for your trek, in case you do come across a belligerent critter." Lilly took Sven's large knife and leather carrier from a cupboard and handed it to Carty, who clipped it to her belt.

"Just remember to turn north at the hollow tree trunk, and you will avoid the Canfield house."

Carty spent a few more minutes washing dishes and vacuuming the upstairs bedrooms – not that they needed much attention, as Lilly lived alone. Some time earlier, she had asked Lilly why she stayed in such a large house by herself.

"Except for the years as a young child and at Sarasota Prep and college, I've lived much of my life on this property. A few years after Dad left the house to me, I realized I liked it here even if it is too big for me.

"I never found a man I felt comfortable to marry. Each time I began getting serious about one, he always gave me the impression that he was more interested in the Andersson estate than the Andersson gal."

Carty took down the clothes and linens that she had hung on the line earlier and tossed the wood clothes pins into a basket. The warm spring days were dry with the rainy season months away, so the clothes dried quickly in the sun-drenched yard. She liked the fresh smell of newly washed and dried cloth. Before saying goodbye, she folded the items and hung and stacked them in the closets.

"Are you sure that you don't need me to come back tomorrow, Aunt Lilly? I could finish vacuuming the downstairs then." She gave her aunt a hug and an affectionate peck on the cheek. Lilly held on to her for several seconds.

"No, dear, the cast comes off tomorrow, so I need to stop being so lazy. Using the Hoover[9] will be my first test.

"But you are welcome anytime. If I had known how much fun it would be to have you here every day, I might have broken an arm earlier," she smiled. "I have really got to know you well during this time. You are growing into a strong and delightful young woman. It's no wonder that your parents are proud of you."

"Aunt Lilly, you are making me blush. These afternoons have been fun for me too. I learn more from you about our part of Florida than from all of my school books. I plan to visit you all the time if you will let me, even after you heal."

Carty adjusted her ponytail and rubbed citronella on her hair, exposed skin, and clothes. The mosquitoes in the swamp were sure to be swarming, especially when the sun set. She had learned to put up without such aromatic protection when she went hunting, because the animals were capable of detecting the citronella scent well before she arrived. But she was not hunting tonight, so the repellant would be welcome.

"Say hello to your mother and thank her for lending you to me."

Closing the screen door, she called out, "Remember, north at the fork by the hollow tree trunk."

Lilly, a pensive look on her face, stared after her great niece as she rounded the corner of the tool shed and disappeared from sight. Lilly returned to the kitchen, stepped on to a small stool and opened a cupboard door. Using her good arm, she reached well back behind a tall stack of dinner plates. She felt around for a moment and then grasped her regular sugar bowl from where she had hidden it earlier in the day.

It was full to the top.

CHAPTER 2

The Witch House

*The suspicious mind believes more than it doubts. It believes in a formidable
and ineradicable evil lurking in every person.*

ERIC HOFFER

When Carty left the house, her canvas book bag did not seem all
that heavy, but as she moved farther into the swamp, the strap began tugging a little deeper into her shoulder.

The sun was moments away from setting as an enormous red ball.
The few long, wispy, white clouds had turned a brilliant pink against the
still blue sky.

This was the part of the day that Carty liked the most. It did not last
long, but it was inspiring – especially if, as today, the winds died down
and thorough calm settled in. Most of the night creatures were still rest-

ing. Only a few crickets began stirring. Quiet joined beauty in pleasing harmony.

The path along the hammock proved to be more tangled than she expected. Occasionally she had to climb over vines and around fallen trees and branches, always checking first for any poisonous snakes that might be making a home on the other side of the obstruction. So far, she had come across only a few harmless racers and a kingsnake, but she knew that every Florida snake would be more afraid of her than she would be of it.

At sixty-seven inches tall and a bit over 120 lbs, she was, in fact, quite intimidating to any snake she might encounter. As long as she was careful to avoid startling a snake and gave it an opportunity to escape, the slithery creature would always head away from her.

Alligators were more of a problem, but she knew how to deal with them. A full grown gator is faster than a horse in a short distance chase, so a human without a good head start would be out of luck trying to run away on a clear course.

Generally, though, a gator would run or swim away from a full grown human. Except encountering unusually large gators, only a small child would normally be at risk. Carty knew how to stay alert to avoid those large reptiles and to watch for available vines and trees to climb if all else failed.

Wild boars were nasty and fast. Their tusks were sharp and potentially deadly. Fortunately, those animals could not climb, so Carty always noted trees with low branches suitable for a quick boost up. Florida panthers, which were smaller than their western cousins, always shied away from human contact.

Bears, on the other hand, were better climbers than humans and potentially aggressive. So a large bear would be more difficult to evade, but bears had not been heard of in the area since Penny and Jody Baxter[10] took out Old Slewfoot[11] well north of Winter Free about seventy-five years earlier.

Carty knew that long shadows from the failing sunlight would cast strange illusions if she were to allow her imagination to run loose. Strands of Spanish moss hanging from tree branches resembled soldiers, ghosts, or dragons to a lazy mind. "Or even witches," she whispered to herself.

Many of the flowers were folding up for the evening. In the dark, colors were less vivid than during the day. She had always thought it was interesting that some plants slept, just like people and animals.

A grayish rabbit darted in front of her, and a family of armadillos ambled away when she neared. She spotted a skunk off to her right and paused long enough to let it move away unchallenged. The quacking from hundreds of ducks on the lake reverberated loudly.

"If people wondered how Duck Lake got its name," she said to herself, "They should listen to that din."

She passed along the edge of the lake as the last of the sunlight faded away, replaced by early hints of moonlight. She was correct about the moon. Its candle power was more than adequate to light the way, even beneath the swamp canopy. A short time later, the tall cypress appeared from the twilight as if on schedule.

She reached the nearly hollowed-out tree trunk and found it to be more of a marvel than Aunt Lilly had described. Only about a fourth of the trunk remained intact, but amazingly, the hollowed-out tree was alive and thriving. She peered at its branches and slightly swaying leaves high up against the sky where the first stars of evening were beginning to emerge.

A great horned owl looked down at her and issued its characteristic greeting, "Whoo, whoo."

"Just me, Bubo," she replied, using part of its scientific name. "I'm heading home. It's nice to see you." The stately bird swiveled its head to watch as she passed its tree.

The path improved beyond the majestic cypress – just a few branches and an occasional downed tree to jump over. She picked up her pace. Suddenly, she came upon an enormous house to her left, well beyond a farm pasture and a parallel finger of shallow wetland extending from the lake. Smoke drifted from the chimney in a soft swirl.

"That can't be the abandoned Hostetter farmhouse already," she thought, "especially with an active fire. I haven't gone far enough from the fork yet if Aunt Lilly's distances were accurate. Besides, its condition is too good, there is a nicely tended garden, and several farm animals are penned up."

Moss covered the north facing part of a lumpy roof, while moonlight glistened on the shiny smooth slate of the sloping roof elsewhere. The walls were mostly stone.

The part built with thick wood planking was unpainted. Having been cut from cypress, it did not need such protection. Early pioneers knew cypress as one of the slower growing trees, allowing the wood to accumulate a denseness that repelled both bugs and weather. The tree also developed a natural chemical resistance to wood-boring insects.

On the first floor, two small windows, about eight feet above the ground, bordered a formidable door. The shutters were open. The dark curtains that framed white sheers were pulled up and to the sides and held with red sashes. A pair of black cats lounged on the porch, one swaying its tail languorously, the other feline displaying even less energy.

Numerous larger windows on the second floor, edged by wide wood frames, suggested the presence of several bedrooms on that level.

Two large orange trees anchored the northwest corner of the house, their fruit offering the only bright color to the scene.

Carty stood still for a few moments to grasp the situation. Toward the east side of the house, a woman closed a chicken coop door and latched it for the evening. A rooster crowed a loud goodbye as she stepped down to the ground from the small building.

She wore a full-length, black, flowing dress of a slightly shiny material. The garment gathered above the waist and had sleeves slightly short of her wrists. Atop her head perched a wide, disc-brimmed, black cloth hat that coned upward except for the very top that flopped to one side. Long, stringy, black hair drooped from under the hat and draped atop her shoulders. Her medium-heeled shoes of supple appearing black leather laced up to mid-calf. Under the circumstances of the popular rumors of witches, it was an intimidating ensemble.

Carty blinked and focused. "I do not believe in witches, but if I did, I would say that I was looking at one right now. She has to be Sally Canfield, but I took the north fork, so how can the house be here? I am sure that Aunt Lilly told me to take the north fork to avoid this house. Oh well, either fork still gets me to Mocking Bird Road, so I can continue along this path even if I did take the wrong one."

Before Carty resumed walking, the woman stopped between the coop and the house to pat her cow on the head. She appeared to be speaking to the animal, which let out soft, satisfied moos. The two remained in apparent conversation for a few minutes, with the woman petting the contented cow's neck, and Carty watching.

"If she is a witch, at least she appears to be a nice witch," thought Carty. "Maybe her name is really Glinda[12] instead of Sally."

Before she was about to take a step to resume her journey, Carty took a careful look around for a bearing on the surroundings. She spotted unexpected movement in the tree line about two hundred feet ahead. Someone was standing off the path, positioned behind a tree in a way to be obscured from anyone near the house. As she concentrated her eyes in the dim light, she saw the hazy image of a second person behind a tree a few feet farther from the first. The two appeared to be watching the woman dressed in the black garb.

Carty was unsure what to do next. Instinctively, her hand dropped to the knife. Then she shook her hand away. She had no intentions of engaging in hand-to-hand combat with two strangers in a swamp.

It was too dark to make out more than height and body shape of the two figures. They were tall, probably men, but she could discern little more. One wore a fedora, odd head wear for a swamp, the other a baseball cap. She continued watching them as they peered at the woman.

Suddenly, Carty felt uneasy, a prickly sixth sense making another presence known. She swiveled her head slowly and steadily, seeking to be certain that no third man was watching her. In the watery swale that paralleled the path, a pair of red eyes reflected in the fading light just above water level and honed in on her.

"Oh, great," she thought, "This is not the time for a gator, and a big one, a really big one, at that." At the same time, the creature began slowly floating toward her, its long thrusting tail swishing in a deliberate, rhythmic, side-to-side, near silent motion.

Just then, the two men began to ease along the path toward her position. Fortunately, their attention continued to be on the house and on the distant woman. They showed no signs of sensing Carty's presence.

She wanted to avoid tangling with any alligator, and certainly that monster, but she did want to reveal herself to the two suspicious men lurking nearby.

Her dad had used his WWII Army Ranger training to teach her to be a skilled, stealthy stalker. "If you hunt with a bow and arrow," he explained to her early on when she was barely tall enough to carry a bow, "You must learn to be quiet and blend in with your surroundings, because you need to get closer to your prey than hunters with rifles do. If you are loud and awkward, your ramble through the wilderness will be enjoyable, but you won't be taking any food home."

Carty, it turned out, had a natural flair for stealth, and she took to Michael's lessons well. Normally, she would have no difficulty either concealing herself from these men or eluding the gator. However, the combination was complicating things.

The clumsy men, on the other hand, were not nearly as careful nor as quiet as she. Their noisy movements gave her the opportunity she needed. She was only a few feet from where she had crossed over a fallen tree trunk that rested on the path behind her. It angled sharply into the swale and perched mostly above the shallow water. She decided to retrace her steps and re-position herself so that the downed tree would shield her from the alligator.

She silently removed her canvas book bag and pushed it under a large fern – not well hidden, but the best she could do under the time constraint. She could not be certain that these two were the only stalkers, so she was reluctant to retreat and risk running into another man. Instead, with her eyes locked on the two, she stepped to the rear, moved over the trunk, and eased off of the path.

Using the tree trunk for visual cover from the pair and as a physical barrier from the gator, Carty slid slowly backward into the thick, slimy, black mud at the edge of the swale. She rolled on to her back and squirmed around to darken her jeans and white blouse. She quietly rubbed the black muck over her blond hair and exposed arms, shoulders, neck, and face, ignoring the worms and crayfish that she was unearthing.

She sensed that the gator was still heading her way, but was confident that the downed tree provided adequate protection both above and below water level. She rolled back on to her stomach to wait for the approaching men.

One man came closer, but she could not see him because of the tree trunk. He stopped on the other side, near enough for her to smell the cigarette smoke on his clothes. She heard a boot step on to the downed tree trunk. He clambered up to the trunk with his other foot and, shuffling along it to get a better sight line on Sally Canfield, continued edging closer to Carty. He stopped just above her head, oblivious to the massive reptile swimming toward him.

Carty resisted a strong temptation to look up. She was camouflaged well, but she had no way to darken the whites of her eyes. From above, she looked like a black hump of mud. She kept her breaths short and shallow to minimize telltale movement. Out of the corner of her eye, she spotted a blue Florida crayfish, about seven inches long, crawling toward her face. Normally, she enjoyed seeing these bright cobalt blue crustaceans, but not now.

Then the other man stumbled, splashed awkwardly into shallow water, and cursed.

"Quiet, you fool," hissed the man on the tree trunk, "She will hear you."

"I tripped over a canvas bag under that stupid fern," he said, pointing to where Carty had deposited her books. "What's that doing here?"

"Forget the bag and pay attention to the witch. We have to make sure she is living alone in that house."

"How many times do I have to tell you, Damon? She lives alone. This is stupid, hanging out in a swamp, getting eaten by mosquitoes and who knows what else. I'm grabbing that bag. Maybe there's money in it."

"It's not stupid; it's good planning. If we want to pull this off, we have to be careful and cover all the bases. So shut up and stop moving around."

The crayfish had reached Carty. She watched it from the corner of her eye as it paused against her face. It rose up and, with a startlingly quick thrust, snared Carty's earlobe with one of its pincers. It was all she could do to keep from ripping it away, settling for tightly clenched teeth to stifle surprise and reaction to the pain.

Just then, from the direction of the house, she heard a distant sound of a solid door closing. Apparently, the woman had gone inside.

In the next moment, an enormous geyser-like spray erupted from the other side of the trunk. Damon reacted instinctively, leaping away from the disturbance as a set of large white teeth flashed at his feet, and a scaly foot of claws slapped the top of the log. Damon's bent knees landed in the mud just inches from Carty's face, and he bolted away in a limping gallop.

Carty jumped to her feet, holding her arms high above her head in order to look larger and hopefully intimidate what she believed was at least a seventeen-foot, gargantuan gator. The blue crayfish still clung to her ear.

Concentrating fully on Damon, with its enormous head forward of Carty's location, the gator failed to notice her.

The reptile had snapped off one of Damon's boots with that first bite when Damon was in mid-air, knocking the man off balance. Hissing loudly now, the giant shook the boot from left to right and back again. Then he sent it flying deeply into the water. The enraged creature scrambled on to the path and raced after Damon again.

Damon's buddy was screaming, more from seeing Carty as a muddy swamp creature that had arisen from the muck than from the gator. Carty stepped briskly to her right, away from the gator and the men. In the meantime, Damon, like the gator, was facing away from Carty and too busy to notice her.

"Let's go, let's go!" the two men shouted to each other. The gator lost its chance at a huge meal because it had fussed with Damon's boot for too long. Before the gator resumed the chase, both men were on the path and running at full speed. They charged forward with the gator in belated pursuit.

Fortunately for them, there were enough downed branches and other obstructions in the path to impede the gator, as the slower but more agile humans leapt over the obstacles. Though fast, gators do not typically run far, and this huge one was no exception. Within twenty yards, it gave up the chase and slithered back to the other side of the path and into the swamp, seeking less difficult prey that was tastier than an old boot.

Carty gently pulled the crayfish from her ear, taking a small slice of skin, and set the brightly colored creature on the ground. She waited motionless for several minutes to make certain that the gator was long gone. Then she backed into the stagnant water, and used the malodorous liquid to wash most of the mud from herself.

She retrieved her book bag that the other man dropped during the excitement and silently thanked the gator that these two men had not taken it. Mrs. Tryon was not likely to believe, "An alligator ate my homework," she thought. More importantly, her name and address were in the bag, and she did not want those two to learn who she was, though she was curious to know who they were.

Damon and his pal had run in the same direction that Carty was headed. Nevertheless, she hurried along behind, confident that she was not going to run into them. They were not capable woodsmen, and with the gator to their rear, they probably would not stop running until they almost dropped.

Shortly before emerging from the swamp, she caught sight of them in the distance, but she was careful not to reveal herself. Something was not right with those two. She wondered why they were spying on that woman. She could think of no good reason, but many bad ones.

At the edge of the swamp she saw that several acres of cleared but abandoned farm land abutted the overgrowth. Farther ahead, she viewed a ramshackle house, a small dilapidated barn, and a small shed, all in dire need of paint and nails. "That must be the old Hostetter place," she reasoned.

Not wanting to emerge from the cover of the swamp, she paused to allow the shaken pair to continue moving ahead. She waited for them to reach the other side of the house so she could emerge unseen. However, they made a surprising move. Instead of continuing along the cutoff past the old farmhouse, they climbed the porch steps, unlocked the door, and went in. The door shut, and a dim light blinked on in the lower windows.

"Now what do I do?" she thought. She considered brazenly walking in front of the house, pretending that she knew nothing of the two men's existence if they came out and confronted her. That seemed a high risk plan. Instead, she stayed behind the tree line as she worked herself past the back of the house. It was a longer, more tedious course, but she could eventually get to Mocking Bird Road through the woods without showing herself on the cutoff.

Closer to the buildings, she heard a car engine sputter to a start. She hustled to a tree abutting the backyard of the house and spotted a Thirties vintage black Ford emerging from its parking place, belching purple exhaust. As the car bounced along the dirt cutoff toward Mocking Bird Road, she made out two men in the front seat. The passenger wore a fedora and the driver a baseball cap.

Probably she could take the easier dirt cutoff now. There might be others in the house, though. She paused for a few moments and then decided. It was too late to be fooling around in the woods when there was a perfectly usable dirt road to walk on. Besides, this farm was abandoned. It did not belong to these guys. She had as much right to be there as they did, she reasoned, and she could probably outrun them if necessary.

As she neared the house, curiosity got the better of her. She wanted to see what was going on inside. Impulsively, she retrieved a fountain pen and pad of blank paper from her book bag. With the safety of the woods left behind, she walked boldly up to the house and knocked. "Hello," she called out, "Girl Scout Cookies. Would you like to buy some cookies?" Silence. She knocked again, louder this time. Still nothing.

"Whew," she thought, "I'm really glad no one is home. This Girl Scout Cookie ploy was really a dumb idea. What was I thinking? Who sells cookies dressed in clothes dripping mud from head to toe? Besides, I don't even know the varieties. Maybe swamp fever got to me," she mused.

She returned the pen and paper to her bag and moved away from the door. Peering through a window of the front room, she saw typical pieces of furniture, though dusty, on top of a carpet that could have benefitted from the Hoover she'd used earlier in the day. Several prints of old English hunting scenes hanged askew from walls where faded wallpaper was beginning to peel away.

Carty circled the house, peering into each of the first floor windows. She saw nothing of note until she reached the kitchen. There were no soaps or cleaning implements evident and few cooking utensils, but piles of trash covered the floor, the table, and every other flat surface – days old newspapers, Shredded Wheat boxes, milk bottles, beer cases, Camel cigarette packs, ice cream containers, and more, including several empty Oreo Cookie packages. "Hmm, someone likes cookies; maybe the Girl Scout Cookie gambit would have worked. Glad I didn't have to find out, though."

The part that stood out was the grouping of newspaper articles and book pages thumbtacked to the kitchen walls. She really wanted to get inside to see what they said, but she did not feel right entering the house uninvited – it was bad enough spying though the windows – even though the mystery of these squatters intrigued her.

"No, girl. It is time to go home."

She hurried to the front of the house and broke into a trot as she hustled down the cutoff, hoping that the old Ford would not return too quickly. For once today, her luck turned positive. She made it to Mocking Bird Road uneventfully, and on to her own home. Dinner was almost ready when she arrived.

As she came through the screen door, she heard a Western on the radio, but couldn't remember if "The Lone Ranger" or the new "Hopalong Cassidy" broadcast tonight. Her mother called out, "I was almost to the point of getting worried. Aunt Lilly called to tell me you took the swamp route past the old Hostetter place. That must be a difficult path in the dark.

"Oh, my gosh, look at you! What happened, Carty? You're a mess."

"Oh, it wasn't so bad, Mom. I was careful, but I had to evade a world-class sized gator by spending some time in the mud."

Bay Andersson was more than a little concerned about the comment and Carty's condition, but she knew better than to verbalize it. Carty never gave her trouble and was nearly always in good spirits, but she could get really moody and defensive if someone hinted that she was not capable of handling herself in the wild. If Bay barely implied that, Carty might sulk for days.

"I hope that you didn't hurt the critter, Carty."

Carty smiled at her mom's way of expressing worry and replied, "You know I wouldn't hurt an animal unnecessarily. We just went our separate ways. By the way, I also made a wrong turn and came across the witch's house. In fact, I think I saw her at a distance."

Carty was about to mention the two men, but her mother interjected, "That is not nice, Carty. That woman is no more a witch than you are. She is a lonely person who just wants to be left alone. I'm surprised that Aunt Lilly didn't direct you to the south fork in the woods to avoid her house."

"I'm sorry I said that, Mom. I know she isn't a witch. I'll not call her that anymore. The south fork? I was sure that Aunt Lilly told me to use the north fork."

"No, dear, Lilly knows that south route from when she took care of old Mrs. Hostetter before she died. Lilly traveled that path almost daily for months. She couldn't have told you to take the longer north fork.

"You had better get cleaned up before dinner. Leave your horrible muddy clothes in the wash tub so I can get them soaking in Oxydol.

"Oh," Bay added, "Look at your ear. Bring some antiseptic so I can bandage up your earlobe. Don't tell me a gator did that."

"Ha, ha, no, that was a blue crayfish that nabbed me when I was in the mud. Gosh, did that hurt. I can't imagine why some girls poke holes in their ears just to hang silly earbobs. I'm probably going to have a scar as it is."

Hustling away, she called, "I'll bring the Mercurochrome[13] when I come down."

Carty didn't understand the confusion about the north and south routes, but she promptly forgot about it. There were far bigger mysteries. Who were those squatters in the Hostetter farmhouse, and what did they want with Sally Canfield?

She had difficulty finishing her homework and studying for the algebra test that evening. Her mind kept wandering to her adventure. Fortunately, math was her best subject, so she did not expect trouble with the exam. She just had to get up a little earlier to get to school on time. Because she left her bike at Aunt Lilly's, she would have to use her mom's fancy new three-speed in the morning, and its narrow tires did not handle dirt roads as well as her old wide-tired Schwinn.

Carty fell asleep listening to "The Shadow" that night. "Only the Shadow knows," she mimicked in a husky voice as her eyelids gently closed. "I wonder if the Shadow knows what is going on in the swamp around the Canfield house."

Around ten-thirty in the evening, her mother pulled the chain on the reading lamp and set Peale's A Guide to Confident Living on a chair. She stepped quietly into Carty's room, turned off the radio, slid a strand of hair from in front of the sleeping girl's eyes, and tucked the lightweight blanket around her. "Sleep well, dear. You are growing up so fast." She kissed Carty's forehead.

CHAPTER 3

The Crew Adds an Associate Member

A trusty comrade is always of use; and a chronicler still more so.
SIR ARTHUR CONAN DOYLE

The following day started out as well as the day before had been miserable. First, Carty discovered that yesterday the county had graded most of the dirt road between her house and the school, so her mom's bike performed marvelously. Using the speed gears, she zipped along effortlessly. With the cool morning breeze in her face and sunny sky brightening her mood, she temporarily forgot about the Hostetter mystery.

Arriving at school, she saw Blake and thought about it again. Motioning for him to come over, she said, "There's not enough time right now to talk about it, but I had a really interesting experience yesterday. I

41

think The Crew would be interested in the details. Would you make sure that Hale joins us at our picnic table for lunch?"

"Sure thing, Carty. It's been a while since we got together. What's the big mystery?"

"Hold your horses, 'Mr. Impatience' – we'll talk at noon."

The arithmetic test was a snap for her. She knew she had a 100% when she turned it in, and she had a head start on today's homework because she finished the test early. Mrs. Tryon no longer seemed to be upset with her tardy arrival the previous day.

Then, best of all, Mrs. Tryon explained the lab portion of their botany final exam. Although finals were two months away during the first week of June, Mrs. Tryon was going to have the class finish the lab portion of the course early because of weather considerations. Late May and June could be extremely hot in central Florida, and June 1 was the generally accepted start of hurricane season.

Since the lab final entailed quite a bit of field work, she wanted her students to work in cooler temperatures and when there was less chance for rain and high winds. Late March was a good time, and Mrs. Tryon had forewarned her students several months ago to keep this weekend open.

"This assignment represents fifty percent of your final exam, so you need to put a dedicated effort into it," Mrs. Tryon began. "You will organize into groups of either three or four students. You may decide on your own groups. Each group will elect its leader once it has organized.

"You will all be given the same list of native Florida vegetation. A few items on the list are ordinary and easily found, and some are very rare and difficult to find. Most are middle ground. Your group has until next

Tuesday to locate as many of the plants on the list as possible and to turn in a small specimen of each.

"Members of the group submitting the largest number of the correct specimens earn an A. Obviously, if your group finds all twenty-five specimens, the A is automatic since your group can be ranked no worse than tied for first place. Lesser numbers of finds qualify for lesser grades as shown on the back of the assignment page."

Mrs. Tryon was a firm believer that competition in this age group developed effective students in high school and beyond. To be successful later on, her students would have to compete with other adults, including those overseas. While the United States emerged on top of the world at the end of the War, she felt that it would not always be in such a preeminent position.

Questions came from several students. "What are the rules, Mrs. Tryon? Can we use plants in our yards? Could we buy specimens at Sweetwater Nursery or Stoney's Flowers?"

"I doubt that you would find many of these items at Sweetwater or Stoney's. Few of the plants are suitable as cut flowers, house plants, or for landscaping. For example, I know that Sweetwater does not carry water sundews, one of the listed plants, but if you want to spend your money for some of the other plants, that is your decision."

Mrs. Tryon knew that few students had enough loose cash to fritter away on items that could be found for free.

"The full instructions are on the back of the plant list. One major rule is that you cannot break any law, so do not appropriate any flowers or parts of plants from your neighbors' gardens or other private property.

If your neighbors are generous, though, you may accept specimens with permission.

"And of course, do not inflict any damage. Certainly do not dig up an entire plant. Take only a flower or enough of a leaf or frond so I can tell that you have the correct specimen. Don't try to trick me with so tiny a sample that I cannot identify the specimen. If I cannot determine what it is that you have turned in, I will not give you credit for it.

"You have tomorrow, the entire weekend, and Monday to identify and gather the specimens. This should be a fun assignment. You've all done extremely well in this class. I know that you will be able to put some of the book portion of your learning to work with this assignment.

"Use the sign-up sheets that I am sending around now to organize your group. Leave the lists on my desk when you are finished with them."

Though the students did not realize it, Mrs. Tryon allowed them to organize themselves as a learning experience. Friends might naturally gravitate toward each other. But some might go outside of their close associates to draft students who could offer special knowledge. She sat back to watch what happened.

The students buzzed like bees as they sought out each other in a quest for compatibility. They responded cheerfully to the relative freedom from the usual strict formality Mrs. Tryon normally required in the crowded classroom.

Two groups especially interested her. Carty Andersson, Blake Holmes, and Hale Wending joined together as she expected. They had been close-knit friends since before they started in the first grade in 1942.

The surprise came when Hale invited Maximilian (Mack) Stein, the recent German immigrant to join their group. Mrs. Tryon had been about to intercede and assign him to Eddie Marshall's team when Hale's invitation was extended.

MACK had been trying hard to fit in, even Anglicizing his nickname from Max to Mack. Mack had told her it was his father's idea. "Father," he had explained, "says that this country was kind enough to accept us, so it would be impolite to hang on to our old ways. We should show our thanks by becoming Americans through and through."

He was assimilating into the American way of life in other ways too, but he had not yet been fully accepted by the other students. Ironically, even though Mack was a Jew, his German background worked against him this soon after the War.

Barely five years ago, the fathers and brothers of many of Mrs. Tryon's students had fought and some had died in hard battles all the way to the Rhine River. A few students irrationally thought of someone with the Teutonic sounding name of Maximilian Stein as the former enemy, not as the victim that his Jewish heritage created.

MRS. Tryon was also interested in the Haywood Dolder group. Haywood was the biggest boy in the school, a little chubby actually, and rumored to be a bit of a bully. He thought more of himself than was probably warranted and had shown a penchant for deviousness when it suited his interest. She was not surprised to see that his little support group of born followers had banded together for the project.

Mrs. Tryon expected that the "swamp tomboy," Carty Andersson, would lead her group straight into the wilderness without hesitation, but she wondered how Haywood's group would approach the hunt.

She thought that Haywood's dad, the Chevrolet dealer and town Chamber of Commerce president, might try to purchase many of the specimens to help out his oldest son. Mr. Dolder was the only parent who consistently gave her trouble. In his mind, his son could do no wrong, but the more his father backed him up or covered for his mistakes, the worse Haywood seemed to get.

Carty was thrilled with the project. Instead of pouring over books to study for the final lab exam, she would be outside doing what she loved. Moreover, she would be with her two best friends and with Mack, who brought a different perspective. Nearly every person she knew was a native Floridian, so she found Mack more than a little exotic.

MACK had the peculiar combination of a slight British accent often with German syntax tossed in. When he got excited, he often peppered his speech with a random German word without realizing it. He read well in both languages, however. Though he seemed more sophisticated than everyone else in the class, he made an effort to avoid putting on airs.

Mack was tall and thin and looked more awkward than athletic. However, playing cricket in England had apparently prepared him well for baseball. Though a weak fielder, he became one of the school team's better hitters from the first day he picked up a bat.

Coming to bat in his initial inter-squad practice game, Mack was greeted with scorn from Haywood Dolder and his buddies. Dolder was the team's pitching ace.

"Come on, Nazi, see if you can hit a high hard one," Dolder taunted. Dolder's friends laughed and contributed their inane insults.

Hoping to make Mack look silly, Dolder instead threw a low curve about ankle high. It broke into Mack's strength. Unknown to Dolder, Mack's smooth arching left-handed swing was attuned to low pitches that are typical of cricket. Mack met the pitch squarely and whipsawed the ball well over the right field fence, a distant blow seldom accomplished with players at that age. As he circled the bases to the admiration, cheers, and laughter of most of the other players, he earned Dolder as a lifelong enemy.

At lunch following Mrs. Tryon's assignment, Blake shared his Moon Pie[14] and Barq's[15] Orange Soda with Carty. After a while, Hale Wending came over and brought Mack along.

MANY schools were racially segregated in Florida in 1950, but Hale was the son of the school custodian, so he became a Cross Creek student even though he was a Negro. No one in authority really made a decision on it. His father always spoke about how he would enjoy seeing his children at Cross Creek, and their attendance simply happened without any particular notice.

Hale's mother emigrated from the Bahamas where she had been a school teacher before meeting Mr. Wending. Their six children, of whom Hale was the oldest, all attended Cross Creek. The Wendings were often far ahead of the other students, because Mrs. Wending put all of her children through rigorous drills and additional lessons at home.

Mrs. Wending told Hale and her other children, "You can sit around,

47

play games, slack off, weep, and cry, 'woe is me, woe is me,' and be a failure. Or you can get to work and out-perform everyone else. If you do the latter, you will be a success. You may have a hard time and everything and everyone will not always be fair, but you will succeed. When you are grown, I hope that you will choose the latter. Regardless, as long as you are in this house, I'm making the choice for you.

Unfortunately, this was the last year the three pals would be together. Carty was headed for the all-girls boarding school in the fall, and the two boys would be split up. Blake would attend the white school in Winter Free, and Hale was destined for the Negro high school in the neighboring town.

BLAKE began scanning Mrs. Tryon's list and immediately shouted an alert. "Whoa. This isn't going to be as easy as we thought. Look at this list. Each of the plants is named by its scientific Latin name instead of the common name we might recognize."

"Oh, wow," Carty echoed, taking a close look at the list for the first time. "When Mrs. Tryon mentioned the water sundew, I was thinking we had clear sailing. Even though that is a really rare plant, I actually saw one during my adventure in the swamp last night. That is why I've already planned to take us into Morose Swamp for the search.

"Looking at this list, though, I don't even know which one is the sundew. We may have to spend a couple of days in the county library trying to figure out what these plants really are before we begin the search."

"Not necessarily," Mack interjected. "Let me see the list."

Mack scanned it carefully. "Here, Number 7, Drosera intermedia. I'm fairly certain that is the water sundew."

The others looked at him blankly. "How do you know that?" Hale asked.

"In school in England, we were required to study Latin, as we all will next year in high school. The first few years, it was the Gallic Wars, Caesar, the Roman Empire and all that. Later on, when we studied science, Latin just filled in without our really noticing it.

"Drosera includes insect-eating plants like the Venus flytrap and sundews. About all the items on the list, I'm not one hundred percent sure. But with a little research at the library, all of these scientific names I can match to a more common Florida name fairly easily."

"Ha, I knew there was a reason we drafted you into this group, Mack," Blake laughed. "Can I give you any help?"

"Oh, yes. If you come with me, you can scout out the reference books while I look through them for answers. I'm guessing we will need a couple of hours. I have to go right away after school, though, because my father is taking me to meet friends in Sebring for dinner about 7:30 – something about an automobile racetrack they are building. Can you do it so soon, Blake?"

"Sure, we can bike downtown from here right after our last class and finish up in time for you to be home when your dad needs you."

"Now, Carty," Mack said, "Tell us more about last night's big mystery."

Carty filled them in on the details of yesterday evening. They couldn't come up with a reason why two men would be squatting on the Hostetter place, or why they would be stalking Sally Canfield.

"You're certain that one of them said they wanted to be sure she lived alone?" Hale asked.

"Yes, and that sounds ominous to me."

Hale was not happy to discover that their assignment would require them to walk in front of the Hostetter place that was occupied by thugs who probably did not like Negroes. He was more concerned about the two in the house than the dangers that might await them in the wilderness.

Mack, on the other hand, appeared more apprehensive about the wildlife and discussions about a witch. "So in this swamp a witch actually lives, Carty – the swamp you are taking us to?"

"No, Mack. Sally Canfield is not a witch. People just think that she is. In fact, before yesterday, I didn't even know there was a big house in the swamp or that there was a Canfield family. Had you two ever heard anything like that?" she asked Blake and Hale.

Blake shook his head, but Hale spoke up. "Oh, sure, I've known about the swamp witches since I was a little kid," offered Hale. Grinning mischievously, he added, "Most of my people are afraid of ghosts, goblins, and witches, so we keep up on that sort of thing."

"Hale, you are the top student in our class. You can't tell us you believe in those witch fairy tales," replied Carty.

"I'm just funnin' you, Carty, but there is a lot of superstition in our community. Keep in mind that there is usually a little history involved with superstition – and some of it usually has more than a grain of truth mixed in with the legend.

The discussion had focused the four so intently that they did not realize Haywood Dolder and his cronies seated themselves at the next table and overheard the tail end of Carty's story.

"The guys in the house are probably witch hunters, Carty," interrupted Haywood. Dolder's buddies laughed.

"Seriously," he snapped, intimidating them into silence. "It makes good sense. If you got a bunch of witches running amok, there is no telling the havoc they could cause. You think we get hurricanes and droughts just because of bad luck. Wouldn't surprise me if there were some evil spirits involved. I'll bet those two guys in the house are from the government, probably the FBI, looking to scoop up the witch."

"Haywood," asked Blake, "How do you come up with this stuff? The FBI doesn't squat on someone's farm and make a mess of their house. They chase bank robbers and spies, not some poor woman living alone in a swamp."

"That witch isn't poor, buzz head. My dad says that Homer from the general store told him that she always arrives at his store with a really large wad of money. Her first stop when she comes to town is always Ensign Bank. So how does she make big money living out in the swamp? It doesn't grow there.

"What does she do in the bank? No one knows. Old Man Ensign won't tell my dad anything about her, even though Dad is the bank's biggest customer. Ensign claims it's confidential bank customer business. Says my dad wouldn't want him to tell her about my dad's Chevy dealership. Can you imagine? What business would Old Man Ensign have telling the witch about my dad?

I say she casts a spell to keep him quiet and tricks him out of the bank's money. I wouldn't be keeping my big money in that bank."

"Haywood, you don't have big money to put into the bank," Blake replied.

"Well, my dad sure does, and when I do get rich, my money is going under a mattress, not in the bank, that's for sure."

Carty turned an exasperated look at Dolder. "Under a mattress? Oh, you drive me crazy, Haywood. You're going to invest your money in ticking?" Carty turned to her group, "Let's take a walk. I can't handle any more from this shrewd businessman," she added loudly and sarcastically.

AS they walked away, Hale told them what he had heard over the years.

"The Salem Witch Trials began in Massachusetts in the 1690s. There were a few years of bad farm harvests, and the superstitious people of the time looked for reasons. In those years, people had little knowledge of science and figured that just about everything happened because God was ordering it done."

"Well, God does decide on things, Hale," Carty objected.

"Yes, yes, I know that. What I mean is that something like a hurricane occurs because the right wind and heat and moisture converge. Some years we get a hurricane, and most often we don't. It's not because one year we are bad, and the next year we are good. Sure, God made the wind and heat and moisture, but He doesn't wake up some morning in a bad mood and send a hurricane to Florida, like Zeus or Thor with a lightning bolt. That part just occurs naturally the way God put things in motion.

"Maybe once in a while God puts special influence into a situation, but in old time Massachusetts, people believed that God directly decided on everything, including bad harvests as punishment for misbehaving. Since no one looked upon themselves as the actual misbehavers, though, they figured things were going poorly because other people, their neighbors, were not acting right.

"Then on a Sunday morning, a couple of little girls were a bit out of sorts in church. Maybe they just had a fever or stomachache or something. Anyway, they were acting up. So someone came up with the crazy idea that the little girls were witches, and they, instead of God, were responsible for the bad harvests.

"The rumors started flying, and soon everyone just *knew* that these little girls were witches. Then it got worse. People decided that there had to be a great many more witches because the two little girls couldn't possibly be a strong enough evil force to cause all the problems that Salem was having.

Before long, most of the people in Salem and other towns in the area were in a panic, sort of like the "Chicken Little" story – no one looking at things logically, just acting on emotion. And the few sensible people were afraid to say anything for fear of being called witches themselves."

"Wow, Hale, it is a good thing that people aren't like that today," gasped Blake.

"What makes you think that people are different today? Back in the Thirties, most people thought that old Adolf Hitler didn't really want to take over the whole world and that he could be bought off with a country or two. That thinking didn't work out very well as wimpy Chamberlain found out. Next thing, Hitler is attacking everybody.

"Fifty years from now, people will come up with some other crazy idea, and thousands of people will dive in like a cult. It's just the way people are. My mom says that two of the most dangerous words in the

English language are, 'Everyone knows.'"

"Anyway, back in Salem, no one would listen to reason, and before long, people were being hanged or burned at the stake for being witches, and their property was being confiscated. If someone accused a neighbor, the accused was often convicted even though there was no evidence. Then some people figured out that accusing someone was a good way to get rid of rivals or competitors or people just different than themselves. So they began to manipulate the hysteria to their economic advantage.

"Others were just mean or stupid people who were jealous of those who did better."

"Kind of like what happened to your Uncle Eugene, Hale," Blake added.

Blake turned to Mack. "Hale's Uncle Eugene was a real war hero, Mack. He came back with a Silver Star and a bunch of other medals. Some of the locals – who had been too young to be in the service themselves – couldn't believe or didn't want to believe that a Negro could do all the things that qualified for the medals. They tried to pick a fight with him several times.

"Hale's uncle was a real gentleman and kept avoiding confrontations until those buffoons tried to set his house on fire after a night of drinking. He managed to put out the fire before it caused any serious damage, but that was the last straw. He went searching for them. If it hadn't been for Sheriff Elsmore, there would have been a lot of blood spilled. Anyway, the sheriff collared them before Hale's uncle got a hold of them, and they got eight years for arson.

"The sheriff has kept a lid on things ever since. My dad was worried that as a new sheriff, he took a real political risk sticking up for a Negro. But Sheriff Elsmore was re-elected without opposition that November. Most people in the county said, "Fair is fair," and they did not want rowdies running the town, regardless of race."

"Some people are always looking to blame others for what they do not understand, or what is different from them, or what someone else has," Mack agreed.

"We're kind of going off on a tangent here, Hale," Carty interjected. "What's all this Massachusetts stuff got to do with Sally Canfield of Florida?"

"Patience, girl, patience. I'm getting to that. The original Canfield was the richest and most successful farmer in Salem, but he was a rival to the neighboring farmer who was an important political figure. Even then, politicians were after the rich people.

"The neighbor saw an opportunity. He offered to buy Canfield's farm for half its value and threatened to accuse Canfield's wife of witchery if he refused to sell. Canfield might have fought it out, but his wife's life was at risk, so he took the deal and moved to Boston.

"He used the money from the sale to start a shipping business, and he proved to be as good a businessman as he had been a farmer. Before long, his ships imported the largest amount of tea from England and sent back the greatest amount of furs. But right about 1700, a prominent Boston preacher by the name of Cotton Mather started up with more witch stuff. He began to imply that Canfield's wife was a witch.

"By this time, witch-related hangings and property thefts had died out, but an accusation like this from a prominent citizen could have a bad effect on Canfield's business. So again he sold out, but this time, he made a bundle. Then he moved the family to New York City. There he eventually became a bank director and made a lot more money. After a few years, though, the rumors followed him to New York.

"So, Canfield decided to make a major move to try to break the rumor cycle. He took his extended family – by this time a couple of brothers, their wives, and kids joined him – by ship to New Orleans and by wagon train into Spanish Florida. He thought that such a major change would free his family of the witch rumors. They settled between Duck Lake and Morose Swamp, I guess where you saw the house. Except for a few Indians back then, they were the only people within a three-day ride. But as you know, the rumors caught up with them anyway.

"Ironically, while he was in New Orleans, one brother married a bayou girl. There is a rumor that she was involved in voodoo. So maybe they did bring some sort of spells into Florida.

"Many generations of Canfields have continued living there. They kept to themselves and didn't bother anyone. Even the Indians left them alone during the Seminole Uprisings in the 1800s. Sally is the last of the Canfields, and since she doesn't appear to be looking for a husband, it looks like the story will end with her."

Carty added, "My Aunt Lilly says that Sally Canfield lives all alone and never talks to anyone, except to conduct business in town. Even then, she talks as little as possible. People seem to be afraid of her, and everyone stays away. Gee, guys, she must be really lonely. I couldn't live like that, all alone, never talking with anyone."

"I understand what you are saying, Carty," Mack answered, "but there must be something to this witch thing if she wants to live that way. In Germany, the towns have old buildings with a hexenturm, which is a tall tower built to imprison witches. It seems to me that if the witch idea exists in countries all over the world, it has to be more than someone's imagination. And now she knows voodoo too."

He added in a hushed voice, "We aren't going to go near the witch's house, are we?"

"Maybe, Mack. We'll start out on the south fork in the morning and scatter into the swamp to look for specimens. There is a large forest between her house and that trail so we won't come close on that route. We want to end up at my Aunt Lilly's house around noon. By the way, if you want to stay on the good side of my aunt, don't refer to Sally Canfield as a witch.

"That water sundew specimen on Mrs. Tryon's list is one of the rarest. Hopefully, we will find one on the south fork in the morning so we can return by the same route. If not, we will have to head back via the north fork because that is where I saw the water sundew. It was growing next to the tree trunk I hid behind. I was really too busy at the time to look at the flora, but it was so close that I couldn't miss it.

"That northern route will take us past the Canfield house, but the path is not too close, maybe fifty or sixty yards away. Honestly, Mack, there is nothing to worry about. I was right there. I saw her and nothing happened to me."

"Except you were almost eaten by the world's biggest alligator and two assassins nearly hunted you down."

"Mack, I have no idea who those guys are, and I certainly doubt that they are assassins. And they didn't even know that I was there. Besides, none of those things is related to Sally Canfield being a witch."

Mack did not reply, but the look on his face suggested that he was not convinced.

CHAPTER 4

Gathering for the Assignment

Be wary then; best safety lies in fear.

SHAKESPEARE, *HAMLET*

They began gathering at Carty's house well before dawn, the heavy clouds making for a dark early morning. Her house, located on the edge of her father's limerock mine and processing facility, was the closest to Morose Swamp. More importantly, Carty's mom baked the best Toll House[16] cookies, and they had agreed that a long day in the swamp should always be followed with a large glass of ice cold milk and gooey cookies dripping with melted chocolate chips.

Blake arrived first, in the pitch dark of the early morning. His brown leather trousers, hat, and jacket were well suited for a trek through the swamp. They provided protection from thorny bushes and mosquitoes, and had the substance to deflect the fangs of a poorly aimed cottonmouth.

"Good morning, Mrs. Andersson," Blake said through the screen door in the back of the house. The kitchen smelled of freshly baked dough and bacon that he heard sizzling on the stove.

"Is Carty ready?"

"Come on in, Blake. She is just finishing her breakfast. Would you care for some bacon and eggs or a biscuit? I still have the range going."

"Oh, no, thank you, Mrs. Andersson. I ate already this morning. Well, maybe just a biscuit. I see your homemade raspberry jam."

"Hi, Carty. Ready for our field trip?" he asked, settling down at the kitchen table with her.

"Sure am, Blake. This will be the most enjoyable school project I've ever had. I am confident that we will get our A. We ought to be able to find the most flowers and other plants on Mrs. Tryon's list."

Bay brought a plate with three eggs, sunny side up, a generous slab of thick bacon, grits, and two soft, hot, golden biscuits. She set it down in front of Blake. Blake's father had picked up cooking duties after his wife died several years ago, but Bay knew that he wasn't very good at it. Blake probably had no more than a quick bowl of Cheerios that morning.

"Here's a little something extra, Blake. You're going to need a full stomach if you're going to be traipsing through the swamp all day."

"Oh, wow – thanks, Mrs. Andersson. You didn't need to do that. Just the way I like the eggs, too." He added his wide smile as she included a tall glass of milk to the feast.

She beamed back as he slathered a biscuit with jam, plopped a dollop of butter on his grits, and forked a slice of bacon messily into an egg yolk.

"Here come Hale and Mack," Carty said, peering through the screen door. "C'mon in, guys," she called as they reached the top of the porch.

They gave a wave to their partners as Carty introduced Mack to her mother.

"Isn't it a gorgeous day?" added Hale, the classic "morning person."

"Ever the optimist, Hale," Bay answered. "It looks to me like you might have rain most of the day."

"But it's warm, the early flowers are blooming, and the breeze is just brisk enough to keep the bugs from swarming. It won't be a hard rain in any event."

"A Saturday morning this early I usually do not wake," said Mack. "Even if it were sunny, it would be too soon in the day."

They all smiled at his garbled syntax. It always seemed more confused in the mornings and when he got excited, but he was getting better and beginning to grasp American idiom and slang.

"Have a seat, you two. You are stuck with bacon, eggs, biscuits, grits, and milk. If you want anything else, you are out of luck."

"'Stuck with,' Mrs. Andersson?" laughed Blake. "This is the best meal I've had in weeks."

The pair joined the others at the table and everyone ate until slightly short of bursting. Mack declined the bacon and generated laughs when he prepared his grits with milk and sugar. "That's not Cream of Wheat, Mack," Hale chided.

"Ach, you eat them the way you like them, and I will eat them tasting better."

Bay smiled and left them so that she could attend to her laundry.

While they finished the dishes, they chatted about the botany assignment.

"At the library, Mack was able to cross index each of Mrs. Tryon's scientific names with the common names familiar to us. He has it fully organized, but before Mack shows you what he did, wait until you hear what happened at the library after Mack left," Blake stated.

"Mack went home for his meeting with his dad, and I returned the stacks of books to their shelves. Then I stopped at the drinking fountain. That's when I noticed Haywood Dolder and his henchmen going through the card index. They were making quite a ruckus and getting noisier and more and more agitated as time went by.

"Eventually, one of the librarians came over to quiet them down. I moved between the bookshelves to hear what was going on. They were trying to find the same kind of botany books that I had collected for Mack, but they did not know how to locate the books through the card index."

"Not much surprise there," suggested Hale.

"Right, I'm amazed that they could even find the library. Anyway, Miss Cowden patiently walked them through the whole process and helped them find the books they needed. Then – you're not going to believe this – instead of pouring over the books the way Mack did, they checked out the lot: every book in the library that you need to look up the plants on Mrs. Tryon's list."

"So, with an armful of books each, they take off, laughing at how shrewd they are, because no one else will be able to do the necessary research. Apparently, it did not occur to them that Mack had already beaten them to the books."

"That will mean that only our two groups have a chance," Carty said.

"I want to win, but that is not fair. What's the fun winning a game where the other teams have to wear blindfolds?"

"Well," Hale added, "the others are not entirely out of options. They could get someone to drive them to Sebring or another city with a library. They will lose a full day, though, and there is not much extra time available."

"I don't like it," Carty insisted. "I'm sure that Mrs. Tryon didn't expect that the reference books would be hoarded. Look, what if we take Mack's list of the common names and write out a copy and leave it here. It'll take ten minutes. I'll ask my mom to call someone from each of the other groups to tell them that the list is available if they want to come over to write up their own copy."

"A little more 'do-goody' than I like," said Blake, "But it's not a big deal to me either way, Carty. If that's what you want to do, I'll write out the list and you give the names to your mom to call. It's too bad that they don't make home mimeograph machines. We could make a copy for everyone."

"What do you guys think of helping out the others? Everybody agree?" Hale and Mack shrugged their shoulders and nodded, expressing facially more agreement with Blake's attitude than Carty's, but willing to go along with Carty's sense of fair play.

Blake suggested, "While I'm writing the list, Mack, tell them what you did."

Mack straightened in his chair. His voice dropped an octave as he assumed an authoritarian tone. "From the reference books, I found each common name to match Mrs. Tryon's scientific name. With almost all of them from our class work, we have familiarity. You can see that I also sketched with colored pencils each one. That way we will know what we shall look for."

They scanned the pages of detailed color sketches. Carty arched her eyebrows and addressed Mack. "How long did it take you to draw these, Mack? These are works of art. I'd still be there working on the first one if I tried drawing these."

Mack blushed slightly at the compliment and answered. "It's just a knack I have. I can draw well, play music, and learn languages. The writing and math are what throws loops at me."

"You should have seen him," Blake added. "He drew the sketches as fast as we would draw a stick hangman."

They continued shuffling the sketches among themselves, awed at the detail.

"A problem that I thought about is that the books mentioned that several of these plants are really rare. And one, Chapmann's rhododendron, apparently only grows in the Panhandle – that's over 300 miles away. Do you really think we can find the others, Carty? I don't relish the idea of ten minutes in a swamp. An entire day is beyond reason, but it will be worth it if we locate all of these, or at least most of them."

The others smiled to each other knowingly at Mack's hesitancy. His family originated in Frankfurt, Germany. As Jews, they had escaped from Germany into Holland before the War and then to London shortly after Germany launched its invasion of Poland. The family was one of the last to reach England.

Mack's father was a mechanical and aircraft engineer. That was probably the only reason the British agreed to give them asylum. After the War, he was offered a position in Florida to design equipment for orange juice processing plants. An ex-Army Air Corps colonel he met in

England headed the machinery equipment company.

Mack had grown up in large cities and was not comfortable even with farm animals, let alone with less docile creatures native to a swamp.

"Blake, Hale, and I grew up in these swamps, Mack. We've seen nearly all of these plants at one time or another, but, to be honest, I doubt any of us has paid too much attention to vegetation. I was usually hunting for dinner among the animal population. Anyway, you've done more than your fair share for our group already, Mack. I think I speak for the others if I suggest that you can leave the next phase to the three of us."

A look of disappointment came over his face. "Oh, no. You mean that I stay home and the dirty work you three do? Just because I do not look forward to a day in the wastelands does not mean I shirk my duty. It was really generous of you to add me to your group. I am with you all the way."

The others clapped him on the shoulders.

"As you know, Mack, Carty saw a water sundew a few days ago between Morose Swamp and Duck Lake," Hale said, "That's why we're including that spot in the potential search area. If we can find that specimen and the rootless bladderwort, we should be well on our way to almost a complete sweep. Except for the Panhandle specimen, those two are the hardest to find. You'll be safe with us, Mack, and who knows, you may have fun."

"Nein," Mack replied, "Fun I will not have; safe I will gladly settle for."

"I'm not sure that your outfit is going to work very well, though," Blake added, giving Mack's attire a dubious eye. Those hiking boots are good, but why are you wearing shorts for a swamp excursion?"

"These are not shorts; these are lederhosen[17]. They are perfect for

65

walks," Mack replied indignantly.

"Maybe on well groomed paths and concrete sidewalks, Mack, but this is not a walk in a park. We will be slogging though water, mud, thorns, and bristle. Bare knees like yours will be scratched and bloody by the time the day is done."

"I thought the same thing," said Mrs. Andersson as she returned to the kitchen carrying laundry. Put this pair of Mr. Andersson's overalls over your lederhosen, Mack. They are a bit long for you, but you can roll up the cuffs, and I'll sew a few quick threads to keep them in place."

Mack stepped into the blue garment, hauled the roomy legs upward, and slipped the straps over his shoulders. He looked foolish in the baggy pants, but the others didn't laugh. They were afraid that he might refuse to wear the necessary protection if they made fun of him.

"Looks great, Mack," complimented Carty, though he looked rightly skeptical. "You are ready to go now. We will finish the dishes while Mom sews you up. We have to get moving if we are going to have a successful day."

Carty explained about the list of plants that Blake had drawn up, and her Mom said that she would be happy to call someone from the other groups. "Here is the list, and I've written out names and phone numbers for someone in each group, except for Dolder's. Since Dolder has the books, he doesn't need our assistance. I really appreciate your calling them, Mom. We will make our lunch stop at Aunt Lilly's around noon and see if she needs help with anything."

"She said she will have enough food to keep you alive for the afternoon," Mrs. Andersson said. "I called her last night. If you get going now, it should be daybreak about the time you reach the swamp. I'll take care of the rest of the kitchen. You'll be back before dark, I hope?"

"Oh, yes, Mrs. Andersson, there's no way at night I'm going to be in a swamp hanging around," Mack replied emphatically.

"We may not find everything we need today," added Hale, "but our plan is to return after church tomorrow afternoon if we need to."

Mack shuddered at the thought of a second day on the hunt, but smiled and nodded gamely.

Carty handed her canvas bag to Mack. "Hang on to that for our specimens, if you will, Mack. I'll carry my bow and a quiver of arrows. We aren't hunting for anything except plant life, but it's a good idea to have some protection if we are going to spend the entire day off the paths and deep in the swamp."

When she strapped Sven's old Bowie knife to her belt so she could return it to Aunt Lilly, Mack paled to an even more ashen shade.

CHAPTER 5

The Canfield Treasure

*Wealth hastily gotten will dwindle, but those
who gather little by little will increase it.*

Proverbs 13:11

In the Thirties, the Florida economy suffered from the Depression as badly as other parts of the country. Most farmers, especially the smaller producers, had a hard time finding markets for their harvests. WWII and the lead up to the War changed that.

European combatants demanded food and textiles for their soldiers. So even before Pearl Harbor, the American farm economy began to shake itself awake. Then the United States entered the fray, and the demand for production ramped up.

Cora Hostetter's husband had not chosen a good time to die. She did not have the business sense to take advantage of the expanding economy. Even if he had lived, though, he probably would have been called back into the service, given his pre-farm sailing experience. Either way, she probably would have had to run the farm by herself, and either way, "failed farm manager" was a likely entry on her resume.

Cora awakened to a tentative knock on her door and pulled the alarm clock close enough to see the large numbers. The hands showed a little after two AM. She hesitated to answer the door this early in the morning. She was alone. She was certain that the person at the door was not her son, Clemens. He had left yesterday with the little money she had accumulated from selling butter and eggs, and she never saw him for several days whenever that happened.

The farm was deteriorating under her management. She knew the basics about making things grow. Every farm wife picked up a lot of understanding just being there. But she had never given attention to the business side of agriculture, much to her sorrow now. She simply did not know how to manage it by herself, and everyone she hired proved to be lazy and inept.

Her son's performance was worse than that of any of the hired hands. Moreover, whenever she accumulated a small amount of cash, he would usually coax it from her with some outrageous sob story. When that didn't work, he simply stole the money as he had done yesterday.

The tapping at the door became more persistent, so she committed to see who was there. She pulled on a warm robe and slippers and descended the long staircase. Before opening the door, she turned on the porch light and peered through the front window. A thin, young girl, perhaps a young teenager, with flowing red hair stood at the door. Her striking green eyes were large and round and an upturned nose centered a long narrow face. She held a black silky cape tightly around herself in the cool night breeze.

Cora recognized the girl as Sally Canfield. Cora had occasionally seen her, because the only route between the Canfield house and town was along the cutoff in front of the Hostetter farm. The Canfields kept extraordinarily to themselves, but over the years, the two families could not help but encounter one another from time to time.

Cora had always been friendly, but she respected the Canfield's desire for privacy and never pried or forced herself on them. Conversation had seldom exceeded a "hello" or "good evening" and more often was limited to a basic form of sign language like a nod or a wave.

Cora opened the door and greeted Sally warmly. "Good evening, Sally. Come in out of the cold air. What brings you here so late?"

Sally hesitated. She was not accustomed to conversation with outsiders. And she had never been inside of a house other than her own.

Cora smiled and stood back away from the door. Sally tentatively stepped in and looked around. She was calmed by the pictures on the walls and furniture not unlike a few pieces in her house. She turned her large eyes to Cora and said almost in a whisper, "My grandmother ails, Mrs. Hostetter. I have tried to help her, but I know not what more to do."

It was not a request for help, just a statement of fact, articulated in an odd, almost old English accent and formulation.

"Would you like me to see if I can help?" Cora asked, her heart going out to the frightened, young girl.

"That would be so kind of you. I will show the way. When would it be convenient for you to initiate your call?"

"Just give me a few minutes to put on some warm clothes. Would you like a cup tea or some milk while you wait?"

"No, thank you, Mrs. Hostetter. I will wait here on the porch."

"Nonsense, Sally. Come into the kitchen. It is cold out there."

Cora set out a glass of milk and three ginger snaps on a plate. "You eat these while I go upstairs to dress. I'll hurry, and be back down shortly."

"How odd," thought Cora as she changed into a warm cotton dress and grabbed a shawl from her closet. "I lived barely a mile from the Canfield house for decades, and I have never seen it."

She was aware of the rumors of witchery and had initially been afraid to live so close when she and her husband purchased the farm. Years of proximity without incident had eased her fears. There was, to be sure, a moments' hesitation as she reflected on the old rumors, but it left more quickly than it had surfaced. Sally looked frightened, and she needed help. It was no time to be silly. She rushed down the stairs and called to Sally.

The walk along the dirt path was fast. Sally appeared to have no difficulty seeing in the dark. As they came upon the house, Cora was surprised to see a massive, mostly stone building. In her mind, she had always pictured the rumored "witch house" as a small, low level, one room cottage. This building, looking remarkably like a two story English manor house, loomed impressively.

The roof of large slate tiles was compatible with the rest of the stone architecture, except for the bumpy moss that covered part of the roof that faced north. Prominent shutters bordered the sides of all of the windows, most of which were on the upper floors.

A wide door of double thick cypress squeaked open on thick, sturdy hinges to reveal a large open great room with a tall stone fireplace. Cora did not recognize the type of stone as native to this area of Florida. The thick, rough-hewn mantle above the fireplace was high enough for a full grown man to stand inside of the opening, and the width would accept five-foot logs comfortably, the length of wood that was burning brightly this chilly evening.

An unidentifiably scented but not unpleasant concoction bubbled in an oversize kettle suspended from a strong iron hook hanging from the stone wall.

A sturdy table of what appeared to be oak was flanked by ten chairs of the same wood. The two windows were closed and covered with black curtains. The only light was that from the fireplace. Bookshelves covering an entire wall were filled with books from ceiling to floor. Cora saw two unlighted kerosene lamps but no electric lighting.

"Grandmother is in this room, Mrs. Hostetter," Sally said, leading the way into a ground floor bedroom to the left of the staircase.

Inside, Cora found a woman in a white nightgown. She was unconscious, and her breathing was deep and labored. The sheets and her nightgown were soaked with perspiration. Long red hairs, not unlike Sally's, escaped from her stocking cap – an odd sight for Cora, as she seemed to recall seeing Mrs. Canfield with black hair.

"Grandmother was bitten by a snake, Mrs. Hostetter. See the marks on her arm. Living out here in the swamp, we have all survived an occasional bite, but this snake was unknown to Grandmother and me. I have tried all of the remedies in the Canfield lore that usually work with snake bites, but nothing has helped with this one."

Cora looked at the woman's left forearm, and felt the heat radiating from the site of the puncture wounds. Even by the poor light of a small flickering kerosene lamp, the discoloration was readily apparent. A spider web of red lines radiated several inches up the arm from the two punctures.

"How long ago did this happen?"

"Late this afternoon as Grandmother was weeding the garden. She said that she saw what looked like a necklace in the beans, but it struck her as she reached for it. Snakes usually bite and quickly release, but this one hung on and seemed to chew Grandmother's arm. Grandmother seemed little affected at first, but after a few hours, she collapsed."

"Can you describe the snake?"

"Oh, I can show it to you. I killed it with a shovel when Grandmother pulled it off of her arm. We've seen many snakes colored like this before, but have never been struck."

Sally led Cora outside and pointed to an 18-inch-long snake that had been cut in two. Its alternating red, yellow, and black bands were a colorful contrast with the more sedate hues of most area reptiles.

"That's a coral snake," Cora said. "I recognize it from my childhood years in Fort Myers. I have never seen one around here, because coral snakes prefer sandy areas to our swampy environment. It ejects a stronger poison than many snakes much larger. Non-poisonous scarlet kingsnakes look very similar and are far more common. Your previous encounters have probably been with those benign scarlet kings.

"Do you have any small farm animals, like a goat or a young pig?"

"Both."

"How about a rifle or a pistol?"

"Both again, but the pistol has only one bullet."

"One shot is enough – get me the pistol and let's go find a goat."

Sally retrieved an antiquated pistol from a cabinet in the great room and asked Cora if she planned to kill the goat.

"Yes. Bring a large knife."

It was not unusual for Cora to be around butchered animals. She herself had killed and plucked many a chicken for a Saturday night feast. But killing this goat in the shadows of a house that many thought haunted was unnerving. It reminded her of the outlandish stories of animal sacrifice that had been attributed to the Canfields.

Nevertheless, the woman was dying, and Cora knew that it was impossible to move her to a hospital in time to help. She had heard of only one possible remedy, but had no personal knowledge of its effectiveness.

The goat looked up at Cora while Sally held it steady. Cora placed the gun next to the goat's head and squeezed the trigger. The old gun snapped back from the recoil, and the goat dropped over. Cora took the knife and sliced a long gash into the goat's underside. She reached into the bloody cavity and cut out the heart, liver, and kidneys.

"Do you know how to treat a carcass, Sally? It'll quickly draw attention from scavengers if we leave it here."

"Oh, yes, Mrs. Hostetter. Our family has lived on this farm for hundreds of years. Let me watch what you are doing with Grandmother. Then I will butcher the goat and store it in the smoke house."

Cora returned to the ailing woman. She washed the knife in a bowl of water on the nightstand and took the shiny blade to the fireplace. She held it over a bright flame for about a minute, then let it cool.

"Hold your grandmother's arm tightly, Sally, in case she awakens. I'm going to cut into the area where the poison entered."

Sally turned her grandmother's arm to expose the puncture wounds. Cora cut two slits into the woman's flesh, each about two inches long. A darker than normal blood spurted at first, then oozed from the arm. When the blood flow slowed, Cora placed the goat's heart directly on the cuts that she had made. She cut a strip of bedding and tied the heart to the arm. The woman moaned but did not awaken.

"I don't know what more to do. From what I have heard, this would have been better sooner. The organ will draw blood and poison from her arm. It may be too late, though, now that the poison has had hours to migrate into her system. In the morning, we will replace the heart with the liver and kidneys. We should know something by daybreak. I'll sit here with her the rest of the night."

After a few hours, Cora dozed off. Her head nodded and it jolted her awake. She stretched and got up to walk around the room. She noticed a tall stack of colorful documents on a roll top desk. She was not a financial expert, but her father had been a bank clerk in Fort Myers when she was a youngster, so she knew what she was looking at. She returned to her chair, perplexed.

Sally had completed her work with the goat carcass by the time that the sun was showing signs of rising. She was cleaned up when she entered the house. "Is there an improvement?" she asked.

"No, but there has been no deterioration, so I take that to be a good sign.

"Sally, I couldn't help but notice those documents over there. Do you know what they are?"

"Some kind of bonds, Mrs. Hostetter. Grandmother and I were going to cut out the small coupons to take to Mr. Ensign's bank tomorrow. He gives Grandmother money for the coupons."

"There are several hundred thousand dollars of bearer bonds in that pile. Do you know what bearer bonds are?"

"Not really, just some kind of investment that gives us money. Grandmother says most of the money goes back into other investments, and we only take a small amount of cash for what we need."

"Well, bearer bonds are also like cash in a way. Whoever physically possesses them can get paid for them. So it is kind of dangerous to leave them lying about. You should lock them up somewhere safe."

"Thank you for telling me, Mrs. Hostetter. I'll hide them with the others until Grandmother gets better."

"Others?"

"Oh, yes, Mrs. Hostetter. This is only a small part. Do you want to see where we keep the others?"

"No, dear, please don't show me. You should not show anyone, and whatever you do, never tell anyone about these bonds – except Mr. Ensign if you need money, of course. But keep this information to yourself. There are people who might try to steal them from you."

Though she loved her son, Clem, with all her heart, she saw his face flash into her imagination just then. She visibly shuddered.

"Are you all right, Mrs. Hostetter?"

"Yes, dear, I'm fine," she answered, trying to dispel the thought.

"YOU know," she said, changing the subject, "I am encouraged by your grandmother's condition. She is old, but I can see from her hands and muscles that she is a strong woman, and she is still hanging on.

"Why don't you make us a cup of tea for breakfast? Do you have any bread and butter?"

"Yes, Mrs. Hostetter, and I make a wonderful strawberry jam. There is plenty of bread we baked yesterday."

"Let's go and eat. I think we can leave your grandmother for a few minutes."

After breakfast, they returned to the sickroom. Mrs. Canfield had turned over on to her side. Cora spoke to her. "Can you hear me, Mrs. Canfield?"

The answer was just a quiet murmur, but it was enough to bring smiles to Sally and Cora. Cora removed the goat's heart from the arm. The organ had turned a sickly black color. "Look, Sally, the red lines are almost gone from your grandmother's arm. The heart did its job sucking out some of the poison.

"While I apply the kidneys and liver, take the heart outside and bury it deeply. Soaked in this poison, the heart could kill an animal that ate it."

It was another day before Mrs. Canfield regained nearly full consciousness and a day further before she realized that the bearer bonds sat exposed to Cora. Cora noticed the startled look on Mrs. Canfield's face as she looked at her pile of documents.

"Don't worry, Mrs. Canfield. I'm not a thief. My name is Cora Hostetter. I'm your neighbor to the west. You ride your horse and wagon past my house on occasion on your way to and from town.

"I've already told Sally that she needs to hide the bonds, but she has been so busy tending to you that she hasn't got around to it yet. Your secret is safe with me. I'm only here to help you get better. As soon as you are back on your feet – another day or two if you continue progressing so well – I'm off to my place again."

Mrs. Canfield relaxed and fell back asleep. When she awakened hours later, she was strong enough to sit up. Cora spooned her some steaming soup from a bowl while Sally tidied up in the kitchen.

"You must be curious about those bonds, Mrs. Hostetter," she mentioned after finishing the soup, "especially in this house of witches."

"It is not my business, Mrs. Canfield, and those witch rumors are just the talk of ignorant people."

"Actually, we Canfields encourage people to think of us as witches. Our family was chased out of Salem during the infamous "Witch Trials" in the 1600s. Morgan Canfield took the family to New York and elsewhere over the next several decades. Every place he ever went, he made a fortune. He had a remarkable knack for making money.

"However, jealous people with limited talent attributed his successes to witchcraft. Eventually, he became so disgusted with unjust critics that he brought the family here to this isolated swamp. The family, much larger in the early years, intermarried with early Spanish settlers, Indians, and trappers.

"My son, Sally's father, was killed by an alligator before Sally was born. Her mother died of malaria when Sally was a small child. She thinks of me as her mother.

"Morgan brought a large portfolio of investments with him. Each succeeding generation has expanded the fortune. They were also careful at choosing good banks. The Ensign Bank has been in the Ensign family for over a century, and the Canfields helped the Ensigns start it. The founding Ensign descended from a trusted banking colleague of Morgan's from when he worked in New York City. We are still silent investors. The bank survived the Civil War and the Depression."

"Morgan established our guiding family principle. If people were so gullible as to think we were witches, we should use their stupidity to our advantage. What better way to keep nosey people away from us? Since that early time, we have acted on that dictate, and it has served us well.

She paused, sighed, and fell back asleep. A look of satisfaction appeared on her face, as if unburdening the secret of the Canfield Witches gave her contentment.

Hours later, she awoke, strong enough to stand and walk several steps to the kitchen table. The three ate bread and cheese and drank steaming tea. "Mrs. Hostetter, I have a memory of talking to you about the early Canfield days and the family's wealth. Did I speak of those things?"

"Yes, it was a fascinating story, but perhaps one that was your fever talking," she suggested helpfully.

"You are kind to pretend that you do not believe it, Mrs. Hostetter. But you do know it is true."

"As I stated before, none of this is my business. Your secrets are safe with me."

"I do believe you, Mrs. Hostetter, and I plead with you to stand firm in that position. Sally and I rely on our isolation for our safety."

Cora nodded in agreement.

"Your husband died recently, didn't he?" Mrs. Canfield asked.

"Yes, Carl was my eternal love. It is hard living without him. I'm not a good farmer, but I do not want to leave our farm. There are too many good memories there."

"You'll not have to leave, Mrs. Hostetter. I promise you that."

AND true to her word, Mrs. Canfield always stopped at Cora's house with Sally on the way back from town and from Ensign Bank. The modest ceremony, performed about four times a year, never varied. Mrs. Canfield handed an envelope to Sally, and Sally stepped off the wagon, walked to the porch, knocked on the door, and handed the envelope to Cora. Each envelope contained more money than the farm had produced annually, even when Carl had been alive.

On the first visit, Cora protested. She opened the envelope while Sally walked away. Then Cora rushed to their wagon before they could pull away. "This is not right. You can't give me money. I've never seen so much money. You must take it back."

But Sally's grandmother insisted. "You gave back my life. It is the least I can do."

"Mrs. Canfield, I'm not certain that I did anything for you. Sally told me that she and you have had snake bites from moccasins and immature rattlers before. Those are lower grade poisons that can be easy to survive. Maybe those frequent bites allowed you to develop immunity to other venoms."

"No matter. Your kindness will be rewarded.

"We Canfields have always taught our children with intensity greater than that of any school. Sally and I spend at least six hours six days a week with reading, writing, arithmetic, history, physical science, and geography. You must have noticed the extensive library in our house.

"However, she has not yet studied the Canfield finances. So Sally is not prepared to live on her own. I need another year to teach her that, and I would not have had the necessary time but for your help. You deserve every cent that you will receive.

"I want Sally to hand you the envelope each time, because I want her to continue the practice throughout your lifetime, even after I am gone."

Whenever the Canfields returned from town, they did not stop on days when Clem Hostetter was home. They may have instinctively known that he was different than his mother, or perhaps they had heard or seen something that made them apprehensive. Perhaps they had been practicing their typical reticence at contacting outsiders. Regardless, they would bypass the house until a later time, that evening or the next day or the day after, when Clem was gone. Then Sally would return with the envelope.

A few years later, after Mrs. Canfield died, Sally did keep up the tradition. She told Cora, "You gave me Grandmother's life and my own life. I could not have survived on my own at that age."

Cora, mindful of the danger Clem could present to the Canfields, often told him stories to embellish their reputation as witches. Sometimes she reinforced the image by effecting odd but harmless changes to the house, such as re-hanging pictures upside down and arranging coffee cups in circles on the parlor floor. By the time Clem left for the Army, she had him convinced that the Canfields did cast spells, but even Cora's best intentions were not error free.

Just after Clem had signed on with the Army, and a day prior to reporting for duty at the Tampa marshalling yard, he found one of Sally's envelopes on the kitchen table. Cora had always been very careful to burn the envelopes and notes in the fireplace, but on this particular day she was on the phone with her sister in Okeechobee when her beef stew boiled over. By the time she finished cleaning the mess and looked around, Clem was sitting at the table drinking a beer. He was in the midst of reading a note that he found in the envelope that Sally brought earlier in the day.

In a flowing calligraphy she wrote, "Mr. Ensign tells me that the return has improved on our family's little treasure in the last year or so. I hope you find this helpful. As always, Sally."

Clem looked up just as Cora noticed his presence. "What treasure?" Clem asked, "And who is this Sally?"

Stalling for time to create a satisfactory answer about the treasure comment, she told him that Sally was a cousin on her husband's side who lived in Arcadia, but was moving to Miami because the Navy was hiring office workers at the port. She described in excruciating detail the fictitious type of work the fictitious cousin performed in the fictitious phosphate mine office in Arcadia, and how much better she would have it working for the Navy.

The more she rambled, the more Clem's eyes glazed over. Finally, he said, "Enough, I don't remember her, and I do not want to know anything about her," and he teetered through the front door on to the porch where he fell fast asleep on the swing.

The next morning, as Cora drove Clem to the induction center in Tampa, he asked again about the treasure. She had not come up with a story that would satisfactorily connect all the loose ends of that note, so she tried another tactic.

"Treasure? You must have misread all that fancy lettering that Cousin Sally writes in. She doesn't have a treasure."

"No, I'm sure she wrote about a treasure, and that a Mr. Ensign – I assume she means Gardner Ensign of the Ensign Bank, as he's the only one around here with that name – was upbeat about the return improving."

"Oh, no, dear. I think you misread it. She wrote that she had the *pleasure* of Mr. Ensign's company at dinner and that she hoped that he could *return* to take her out again sometime."

Clem looked skeptical, but his focus was on what his new life would be like in the Army. So he didn't argue anymore about it.

CHAPTER 6

Bringing in Dredman

It is a sin to believe evil of others, but it is seldom a mistake.
H. L. MENCKEN

It was more than a year after Clem was booted from the Army, while chatting with his new friend Damon Dredman, that he remembered the note from the mysterious Sally.

Dredman was a great storyteller. He had claimed to have attended an Ivy League college years ago – Clem could never remember which one; Clem wasn't good with memory – and, truthfully, Dredman was well read. He never found a productive use for his education, though, and was a drifter.

He regaled Clem with tales of his War exploits in the Navy. Dredman claimed to have served on a sub hunter between the Carolinas and Bermuda. He saw no actual combat, but to hear him boast, he almost single-handedly brought the entire Nazi U-boat fleet to ignominious defeat.

He was primarily a dreamer, reminiscing about the "treasure hunting" he did in Bermuda whenever he had shore leave. The several treasure maps he had purchased from island locals proved worthless, but he was insistent that there was pirate treasure to be found. That discussion triggered Clem's memory.

"I know about a treasure from back home in Florida," he bragged. "My mom, before she died, had a strange letter about a treasure. She told me I had not read the letter correctly, but the more I thought about it later on, the more I think she was hiding something from me."

"So your mom had a treasure?"

"No, not my mom. Someone named Sally. She claimed Sally was a cousin, but I hadn't ever heard of any Sally in the relations. The only Sally I ever knew about was a witch who lived in the swamp near our old farm. I think the witch has the treasure."

"A witch? Clem, you're crazy. There's no such thing. Are you sure it wasn't a leprechaun?" he scoffed.

"No, really. There is a family of witches that came to Florida hundreds of years ago from Salem. They probably brought the treasure with them. This Sally Canfield is the last of the witches. Maybe she took a liking to my mom and told her about the treasure. Anyway, I do know that Mom got regular money from somewhere, and it sure wasn't that lousy farm we owned. Maybe Mom found out about the treasure and made the witch pay her to keep quiet."

"That whole story sounds flaky, Clem. Maybe you shouldn't have that last Strohs," he said, grabbing away Clem's beer and guzzling the remainder down in one long swallow.

Though Dredman was not convinced, he tended to grasp at any straw that involved treasure. "Tell you what, Clem old boy, tomorrow we shall visit the main library in downtown Detroit and see if we can find anything about your witch. Canfield, you say?"

THE library had a surprisingly large collection of books on witchcraft and the Salem Witch Trials. Eventually, Dredman found references to Morgan Canfield and read that he and his wife, a rumored witch, had barely escaped the witch hunters. He traced the family's travels to Boston and New York.

At each stop, the size of Morgan Canfield's household expanded with brothers, sisters, and cousins joining an ever growing number of children. In each new location, he achieved further economic success. In fact, he made a lot of money. But at each stop, rumors chased them away.

The last references centered on the Canfields stopping in New Orleans, and Morgan selling large amounts of his property. He apparently bought a team of horses, filled several large wagons with farm implements and building materials, and departed for Spanish Florida. They also found two newspaper articles from the mid-1700s that referenced the Canfield emigration. Apparently, Canfield was a person of some note, so the wagon train attracted attention of news reporters.

Late in the afternoon, Dredman made sure that the librarians were not looking and stuffed the newspaper articles into his trousers along with pages about the Canfields that he ripped from the books. "We may need these as reference material when we land in Florida," he told Clem, without a care about the damage he had inflicted on the library's materials.

"We're going to Florida, Damon?"

"Indeed we are. I do believe that you may have stumbled upon something worthwhile. Besides, I've always wanted to visit sunny Florida. We'll stay at your abandoned farm and scout things out. I'll alert The Cuban in case this turns into something. We will never know how this will play out unless we give it a try, old boy."

Clem hated it when Dredman called him "old boy." He was younger than Dredman, younger by a lot. He hated even more the possibility of bringing in The Cuban with the odd double name. The one encounter he had – a bar fight in which The Cuban took a broken beer bottle to the face of a noisy braggart – was one too many. He wanted to talk Damon out of involving The Cuban.

CHAPTER 7

Hostetter and Dredman in Florida

Home of lost causes, and forsaken beliefs, and unpopular

names, and impossible loyalties.

MATTHEW ARNOLD

Mack and The Crew passed by the Hostetter place almost two hours before Clem Hostetter and his partner Damon Dredman awakened.

Clem, the first to rise, walked into the kitchen scratching his head and other less attractive parts of his body. He dumped a pile of Post Raisin Bran into a dirty bowl and proceeded to sort out all the raisins, tossing them in the general direction of a waste basket. He searched the Frigidaire[18] for milk. The bottle was several days out of date, but Clem used it anyway. "Looks like buttermilk," he thought, pouring in the remainder of the foul-smelling liquid and tossing the empty bottle where the raisins

88

had landed. He sprinkled several tablespoons of sugar on the cereal to sweeten the soured milk and began eating.

Dredman came in as Clem neared the bottom of the bowl. Dressed in a dirty undershirt and green polka-dotted boxer shorts, he yawned sleepily and stretched, exposing a hairy belly. "I don't know how you can eat that junk. It's for kids. Any beer in the Fridge?"

"I saw a few bottles of Tropical Golden[19] in the back. How can you drink beer for breakfast, Damon?"

"Beer is a great breakfast food. 'Nature's nectar,' I call it, but we could do a lot better than this Tropical Golden bilge water. It's sure not Stroh's. When we get back to Detroit, I'm going to call up Stroh and tell them they need to sell their beer down here. I'd almost rather drink water – almost, mind you – than the excuses for beer they have in Florida."

He retrieved a cold bottle, opened it, took a long swallow, and belched. "Ah, Hostetter. Here, try some on that cereal." Before Clem could say no, Dredman poured the remainder of the bottle into Clem's cereal and took another bottle from the refrigerator.

Clem looked at the concoction in his bowl and decided against finishing. He knew better than to complain to Dredman. His jaw still ached from the last time Dredman had punched him in a fit of anger. Since before arriving in Florida, Clem had been regretting partnering with Dredman. The guy had a good head for scheming, but he was as unpredictable a man as Clem had ever met. One moment he was as friendly as a long lost brother, and seconds later, smoke seemed to billow from his head. If he had to do it over again, he would never have mentioned the treasure to Dredman, but there was no way out now.

"I'm almost convinced you are right and the Canfield woman is alone in that house, Hostetter. But we'll give it a few more days of careful surveillance to be safe. I've got my old friend here," he continued, patting his loaded .45, "But if we are going to run into a husband or brother with any firepower when we go after her, we need to know that ahead of time."

"I'm telling you, Damon, when I lived here, she lived out there all alone. There was a grandmother, but she died years ago. This Sally is a hermit. She doesn't want anyone around. She never came over to visit us. From talk around, she's never spent any time in town except maybe a couple of days a year. She never even went to school. It is not possible that anyone else is in that house."

"Hostetter, you are an amateur. A lot of former buddies of mine thought the way you do and took short cuts. Today they are in jails or staring up at pinewood supporting six feet of dirt. You told me yourself that the woman and her kin have lived in that house for centuries. So there is no hurry on this. She's not going anywhere. We will take our time and do it right. Got that?"

"Sure, sure, Damon, don't get me wrong," Clem quickly answered. "I know you don't like crawling around the swamp any more than I do. It's your plan all the way. I'm just getting a little antsy hanging out in this dump. I hated living in this house as a kid, hated working the fields, hated the smelly farm animals, hated the summer heat, hated having a witch for a neighbor, and couldn't wait to join the Army and leave."

"Yeah, well, too bad the Army kicked you out. I guess you hated the Army too."

"All they wanted me to do was get up early and work like a dog. I couldn't figure out why the other guys didn't have a problem with all that crap."

"You think maybe they weren't as lazy as you are, Hostetter? This place is a mess, and it's like pulling teeth to get you to do swamp duty with me. You're the Florida native. You ought to be leading the way into the swamp, not me. But no, if I don't stay on top of you, you'd sleep all day and then try a break-in on the Canfield place with no planning.

Damon rose from his chair. "I'm going to add some oil to the Ford, Hostetter. It's dropping a quart a week. Why don't you clean the guns?"

Dredman opened the door to the porch. Instead of taking the stairs as usual, he turned right, intending to take a short cut by hopping the porch railing. After a few steps, though, he stopped and did a double take at the window sill. Puzzled, he continued to the next window and saw the same thing.

He rubbed one hand along the sill and the other along his unshaven jaw. He hopped the railing as he had originally intended but, instead of attending to his oil changing project, walked around the house. He stopped at every ground level window and examined each sill. All of them had muddy handprints. Dredman also noted that the ground under the kitchen window was clearly trampled.

A dark, gloomy look came over his face. He went back to the front of the house and looked closely at the porch. He noticed a set of muddy footprints all along the old wood. He looked around the rest of the house, but the other windows were too high for a nosy intruder to look into without a ladder. He slammed the kitchen door behind him with emphatic vehemence. Clem was so startled that he dropped the .38 he was cleaning on to the floor. Fortunately, it didn't discharge.

"We've got problems. I thought you said this property was deserted."

"It is, Damon. When Ma died, she left the place to me, but I sure wasn't coming back to run it, and I couldn't find anyone to buy it. I got a little money for the cattle, but the land is all played out, and nobody wanted it. You saw for yourself how empty the place was when we arrived. I think the witch living so close keeps the vandals away. Can you imagine what this abandoned place would have looked like in Detroit after all these years?"

"Well, someone isn't afraid of witches, Hostetter. We had a visitor, and he spent a lot of time here. He looked in the windows. There are footprints all around the house and handprints on all the first floor window sills. If you look closely, you can see several footprints on the porch."

"Yeah, I saw those footprints on the porch this morning."

"Hostetter, you idiot! You saw the footprints and didn't say anything to me about it? What were you thinking?" Dredman slammed a fist into Clem's nose and sent him head over heels into the broom closet. Mops, brooms, and old rags piled on to his prone body. Blood gushed from his nose. He was too stunned to answer.

Dredman continued ranting as he paced the floor, getting angrier with each step. Finally, he grabbed Damon's arm and dragged him from the closet, scattering the accumulated cleaning implements in all directions.

"Stop whimpering, you fool. First you tell me that no one will be here, and then when you see that someone was here, you keep it secret. I ought to plug you right now," he added as he reached for his gun.

"No, Damon, really," Clem cried, shying away from Dredman and scooting himself farther into the broom closet. "I wasn't keeping it secret. I thought the footprints were ours. We always track mud back from the swamp."

Dredman seemed to be thinking that over, so Clem pushed on, still sniffling from the blow he had sustained.

"We haven't seen anyone else, have we? Maybe the prints were ours."

That set Dredman off again, but this time not as violently. "The prints were not ours. You didn't circle the house looking in all the windows, did you? You didn't add muddy handprints to the window sills, did you? I certainly didn't. No, someone knows that we are here, and he has been snooping around. Now shut up with the whining so I can think, or I'll give you something serious to whine about," he growled, showing Clem a balled fist.

But Clem was relieved to see that Dredman had put the gun down.

After several minutes, Dredman said, "I've got an idea who it is. I just haven't figured out what to do about it."

"Who could it be, Damon, and why?"

"It ought to be obvious to even a dummy like you, Hostetter. Think. It has to be the witch. No one has been here for years. No one lives nearby. Everyone in town is too scared of the witch to come out here."

"Oh, no," Damon replied with fear in his eyes. "I knew she was a witch. She found out why we are here and is setting us up for some foul spell. I know she can call up mud monsters – I've seen that myself. Some say she can get the Seminoles to rise up again and bring the Conquistadores back from the dead."

"How do I get involved with such idiots?" Dredman asked rhetorically. "If the woman has witch powers, why would she be leaving footprints? Wouldn't she fly her broom to look in the windows? Wouldn't it be easier to first cast a spell on us and just prance around the whole house at her leisure? You still don't get it, do you, Hostetter? Witches are in fairy tales, not the real world. This is the real world. She is making footprints because she is only a woman like any other woman – just one who is a little weird. And nosey," he added. "And maybe rich."

He grabbed Clem's arm, lifted him to his feet, and dragged him out the front door on to the porch. "Take a close look, Hostetter. Those prints are from a smaller foot, like a woman's, not a foot like yours or mine.

"I figure she saw us spying on her place and followed us to the house so she could figure out what we were after. Judging by the trampled ground beneath the kitchen window, she spent most of the time there. She couldn't have found out anything just looking through windows, so we still have time. But we do not want to spook her into calling the sheriff."

"The sheriff, Damon? What are we going to do?" he moaned. "Let's give this up and go back to Detroit."

"No, you idiot, we are not giving it up. We've put too much effort into this to give up now. But we will have to move up the schedule, much as I do not like to rush things. Let's go to town. I've got to use the pay phone at Woolworth's to call in help from The Cuban."

"Oh, no, not The Cuban, Damon. The Cuban doesn't like me. You said we wouldn't need him."

"The Cuban doesn't dislike you, Hostetter. You are not significant enough to even register on his radar. I said we *probably* wouldn't need him. But that was before the Canfield woman learned about us. She may have help that we do not know about, or she may be about to ask someone to give her a hand. Come to think of it, Hostetter, didn't you say you found a canvas bag in the swamp the night we were chased by the gator? What happened to it?"

"I don't know. I dropped it and ran when I saw the mud monster with the big blue earring."

"Don't give me any more of that bejeweled mud monster crap either. I did not see anything but one massive gator, and I was right there with you."

"But you were looking the wrong direction, Damon. I'm telling you that a monster rose out of the floor of the swamp. It had to have been twelve feet tall," he exaggerated, "and it was coming after us. It only gave up because the gator got in between. I know you don't believe in witches, Damon, but I just know she conjured him up to get us," he wailed.

"Forget about the mud monster and concentrate on the bag. It must belong to someone – a real person, not a fictitious monster – who is helping Canfield. Could you tell what was in it?"

"No. It was heavy and hard and kind of square, but that's all I can remember. Maybe it was dynamite or an ammo box." Clem had not read a book since school, and he didn't do that very often back then, so he failed to recognize the shapes in the bag as Carty's school books.

"That's the first sensible thing you've said in weeks, Hostetter. She calls up the reserves and they bring in firepower. This is getting to be a good thing."

"A good thing, Damon? A good thing? How can that be a good thing?"

"Think about it Hostetter. Years ago you heard rumors about the Canfield treasure, but you didn't know if they were true. So where does our research lead us? On the one hand, the books we found, and the newspaper articles, plus the size of that mansion of hers suggest that you might be right.

"On the other hand, the Canfield woman surely does not live like she is rich. She doesn't even have electricity in that massive building. She pumps her water by hand and uses an outhouse. She grows most of her own food and milks that cow every morning, rain or shine. She doesn't own a car. She takes a horse and wagon to town. So we don't know if we are wasting our time or are on the verge of a windfall."

"But now we see that she is calling in help. She is sneaking around our place, and she's got people with armament involved. Why go to all that trouble if there is nothing of value to protect? So things are getting better, because we know that we are on the right track. And that is a good thing, because The Cuban would not like us to waste his time."

Clem nodded his head vigorously in agreement with that. The Cuban was the only man he ever saw that frightened Dredman. Dredman talked big when The Cuban was not around, but in his presence, it was, "Si, Señor, what can I do for you Señor, how are you feeling, Señor." Dredman never called The Cuban by his actual name, Cruz Cruz. Clem was afraid of Dredman, and Dredman was terrified of The Cuban. So Clem barely breathed when The Cuban was around. This whole project was spiraling out of control.

"When we do spying duty after lunch, show me exactly where you dropped the bag. I want to see what's in it."

CHAPTER 8

The Cuban

Insanity runs in my family; it practically gallops.
MORTIMER BREWSTER, IN *ARSENIC AND OLD LACE*
JOSEPH KESSELRING

Benito Cruz was the most prosperous man in Tampa in 1896. He did not achieve his status legitimately.

Alejandro Gomez, on the other hand, acquired his wealth honestly. A few short years earlier, he was the most respected member of the Cuban community in Tampa, Florida, personifying the dignified wealthy patrician of the latter years of the Nineteenth Century. His premier cigar factory, employing over two hundred expert Italian and mostly Cuban hand rollers, produced the best cigars in the city – some said in the world.

Sr. Gomez's cigar rollers were well paid professionals. They sat side by side on long wooden benches, the tables in front of them stacked twice daily with the best cigar tobacco leaf from the mountains of southeastern Cuba. These cigar rollers were highly skilled. They worked diligently and quietly, and daily each man produced several hundred of the most prized cigars of the era.

New York City was by far the largest volume producer of cigars at the end of that century, but Tampa was the center of the era's well-reputed cigar production. The premium cigar was the way big money was made. The Gomez & Cia. brand that also bore the name of the company was among the most sought throughout the United States and internationally.

When America moved into the Twentieth Century, factory work was still decades away from improving for most workers. Tampa cigar factories were the exception. They were among the more pleasant of any factories. No machinery banged, clattered, or disgorged noxious fumes into the atmosphere. The environment in a cigar factory was almost that of a library.

The Gomez & Cia. factory was located in Ybor City, Tampa's Cuban section. The first floor was about the size of half of a football field. Near what would have been mid-field, a tall mustachioed man sat on a tall chair, perched much like a lifeguard on the beach. However, his primary talent was not the breaststroke or the dead man carry, but the possession of a booming, deep voice that resonated throughout the vast room. He held the most prestigious position in the factory. He was the Reader.

In those days before portable radios and earphones, the Reader spent the entire workday reading aloud to the cigar rollers. At the time, Tampa boasted several English and Spanish language newspapers and one published in Italian. The Reader, always a multilingual, read them all and skipped nothing. Even the ads were included. About once a week he might read selected articles from Havana magazines.

BENITO Cruz started as the Reader at Gomez & Cia. barely two years before he took over the company. Benito's previous work involved smuggling between Cuba and Florida. He was always alert for opportunity – the more illegitimate it seemed, the more enticing. One such prospect was already germinating in his mind as he sat in the lobby bar of Henry Plant's Tampa Bay Hotel.

Plant, the Nineteenth Century railroad tycoon, ushered in Tampa's resort reputation when he completed the plush, minaret-studded hotel in 1891. Benito believed that if you wanted to seek out rumors involving money, you should frequent places where the money resided. In Tampa, you could not get any closer to the money than the silver-spired Tampa Bay Hotel.

The two men seated next to Benito at the bar that evening were building contractors. They were not conversing with him, but he was listening intently to their conversation while giving the erroneous impression that his mind was elsewhere.

"Yeah," one said, "Gomez bit off almost more than he can chew with his new hotel caper. We've had to stop all work until we can drain the land. It was a big mistake to start construction on that site before verifying the soil conditions. We have been pumping for sixty-some days and have lowered the water table less than two feet. I'm convinced we're going to have to build some sort of underground dam to divert the flow of water. It's almost as if there is an underground river. I'll bet it'll be a year before we can get going again in earnest."

"Can he stay afloat that long?" the other asked.

"If anyone can, he can. Gomez & Cia. cigars have to be pulling in a ton of money for him."

Benito dropped some coins on the bar, quietly slipped from the stool, and left the hotel. A few weeks later, after following up on the eavesdropped information, his plan was progressing nicely.

He approached Sr. Alejandro Gomez for the position of Reader, already confident that he would be hired. The previous Reader had only the day before been found floating face down in Tampa Bay, the victim of an apparent robbery attempt gone violent. In actuality, Benito had lured the Reader to the docks with the promise of cases of smuggled Scotch whiskey at half price and tax free. Instead, Benito greeted him from behind a large wooden crate with a sharpened ice pick.

With Sr. Gomez's primary Reader gone, he was desperate for a replacement to keep his employees happy and productive. Sr. Gomez himself served as his Reader's substitute the first day, but he knew that he could not continue as a long-term replacement. When Benito appeared at the office door before Sr. Gomez had even rushed a help-wanted ad into print, the factory owner thought it was his lucky day. In a way, he was right about that. Unfortunately for Sr. Gomez, however, the luck was to be all bad.

Benito started that very day. The workers appreciated his precise diction and that his booming, authoritative voice was louder and more easily heard than that of the previous Reader. Soon, he ingratiated himself with the rollers.

He joined them daily for lunch at a small tavern near the East 7th

Avenue site where a world class restaurant, The Columbia, would be born a few years later. In the 1890s, the small saloon was priced right for the factory's employees. Cold beer and a generous spread of complimentary cold cuts and Cuban bread made it a popular gathering place.

Usually Benito bought a bottle of wine for his table, always a good vintage from the private supply he had arranged for the owner to stock. Soon everyone vied for a place at Benito's table. Before long, he was included in the company grapevine. He missed no gossip or rumors, and he had an instinct for sorting out useful information from the trash.

Putting together several tidbits, he learned the extent of Sr. Gomez's financially overextended position. The cigar business was very profitable, but Sr. Gomez had indeed overly committed to the new hotel venture that was going every bit as badly as the bar patron had described.

Construction had been halted because the water table proved too close to the surface. Months and months of draining sucked up some of the excess water and nearly all the profits from the cigar business along with it. Though Sr. Gomez was not in critical financial distress, he could not afford an additional problem at that time.

Unfortunately for Sr. Gomez, he had already acquired that one additional problem. He had hired Benito Cruz.

AS Reader, it was not uncommon for Benito to arrive on the factory floor hours before everyone else showed up in the morning. He used that time to organize his papers and to look for any unusual articles that the rollers might find interesting enough for a second reading. He generally had free rein throughout the building during those early hours.

The Ybor City area was naturally humid, so it was friendly to cured tobacco. But occasionally a dry air weather front came through. So tobacco was always stored in large, dark, brick rooms to keep it moist and fresh, and then only brought out to the rollers' tables shortly before they reported in the morning or returned from lunch. Thus the tobacco was protected from dry air. There was no thought to protect it from poison. And that was the oversight that ruined Sr. Gomez.

Sr. Alberto Diaz was the inventory manager. His knowledge of cigar tobacco leaf made him one of the more valuable employees in the organization. Benito wasted no time befriending Sr. Diaz, and Sr. Diaz was flattered by the attention.

"In this room," Sr. Diaz pointed out proudly during a tour of the facilities, "We store the inexpensive leaf wrap from Connecticut. This the rollers use for the outer covering on the cigar." In the larger room over here, we keep the high quality mountain leaf from Cuba. The Gomez & Cia. brand uses only this rare variety for consistency and smoothness. The unique Cuban leaf is what makes the brand so successful."

"Why aren't the doors locked if this is such valuable tobacco, Sr. Diaz?"

"There is fear only of dry air, Sr. Cruz, not of thieves. The building is locked at night, and it would take a large vehicle to cart a significant amount of tobacco from here. Locks on these interior doors are not necessary."

Oh, but they were. Benito had no intentions of stealing tobacco. His plot was more elaborate and nefarious than that.

Benito could surreptitiously access the storage rooms in the early hours, because the building was mostly deserted at that time. He had to be careful, though. Like most entrepreneurs, Sr. Gomez was a hard-working individual who spent long hours in the business. He had run into Benito performing his plan's practice runs on a few occasions. Benito had a ready story for his pre-dawn wanderings.

"I like to take in the atmosphere of the factory before starting the day, much like an artist reviewing a scene before taking up the paint," he explained. "It gives me enthusiasm, and the men seem to sense the difference when I am inspired."

On a morning when he knew that Sr. Gomez would be visiting the hotel construction site, Benito put his plan into action. He entered the storage room and dabbed small amounts of poison on enough of the cheap Connecticut wrapper tobacco for a limited but significant number of cigars. He was careful to avoid contaminating the more expensive interior tobaccos stored in the adjoining rooms. He had chosen from his home country of Cuba a tropical poison made from two Brazilian sources that would be difficult for an American doctor to identify.

His supplier prepared a syrupy potion from curare roots and stems boiled for several days with the venom of jararaca snakes. The combination restricted functioning of a person's diaphragm and lungs, while encouraging internal bleeding. Benito was careful to lightly contaminate the leaves. He preferred widespread sickness to deaths. A few deaths were probably unavoidable, but too many deaths would bring too much scrutiny too soon.

Though tainted, the wrapper tobacco appeared unchanged to the rollers, and it was moved into production and shipped as finished product within days. Benito had timed the sequence to optimize the likelihood that the product would be included in local shipments, rather than mixed into product destined for distant customers.

Over a hundred people were sickened and a few elderly smokers with weak hearts died over the next week in Southwest Florida. Benito retrieved from the finished inventory the last contaminated cigar and smoked it himself. He emphasized to his doctor that he began feeling ill almost immediately after smoking a Gomez cigar. With that clue in hand, the doctor began making inquiries of other health care personnel.

Benito had prepared his scheme well. Doctors investigated the smoking habits of the sickened patients. Soon, Gomez & Cia. cigars were identified as the probable cause of the epidemic. But no contaminated cigars could be found to verify it, or to identify exactly the cause. All of the poisoned variety had been smoked.

Nevertheless, sales of the company's cigars came to an abrupt halt at precisely the time when Sr. Gomez had no financial reserves for such a calamity. Within weeks, he was bankrupt.

No competing cigar company had an interest in buying the business. The product name, Gomez & Cia., was now worthless, and the tobacco inventory was believed to be contaminated with probably no way to tell the good from the bad. Some even thought that the building might be infected.

Benito, with financial backing from smuggling contacts, had no competition buying the business out of bankruptcy for eight cents on the dollar. Upon taking over, he promptly gave the order to Sr. Diaz to destroy all of the wrapper tobacco in case any residual poison remained. It was inexpensive and easy to replace.

Of course, he knew that the expensive primary tobacco was untainted. So that inventory he put into immediate production. He changed the name of the cigar line to Rex del Sol and gave the company the same name. After a short time, the Rex del Sol cigar was selling as well as the old Gomez & Cia., and the new company prospered.

Benito intensified his smuggling activities now that he had acquired his own distribution outlet. He concentrated on sneaking in much of his Cuban mountain tobacco to Rex del Sol without paying the import tariffs that burdened his competitors. Because company profits were bolstered with smuggled ingredients, he was making higher margins than the others. Soon he was able to offer good prices to buy out most of the other cigar makers. Within a few years, he controlled well over half of the Tampa cigar production, and almost all of the premium market.

GRADUALLY, Sr. Gomez pieced together reasonably well the process that Benito had used to bilk him out of his business. A chance encounter with Benito's doctor had set off his thought process. The doctor happened to meet Sr. Gomez at a wine shop and remarked that he was the person who had discovered the relationship of the deaths to the cigars.

"Ironically, it was one of your employees, Sr. Benito Cruz, who had first complained of feeling ill after smoking a Gomez & Cia. cigar. It was his clue that led to my solution to the mystery."

Sr. Gomez immediately recalled the early morning meetings in odd places in the factory. In fact, he remembered that they had usually met near the tobacco storage rooms.

So Sr. Gomez began daily lunches with his old employees, listening as the company gossip moved among the tables. When his old inventory manager, Sr. Diaz, told him how Benito had immediately discarded the old wrapper inventory, but retained the quality tobaccos, he had the scam figured out.

Unfortunately, as an old man and now poor, and with no proof, he was without the energy or the finances to do anything about his beliefs. He was not quiet about voicing his grievances in the community, however, and Benito was becoming increasingly angry about Sr. Gomez's vociferous accusations.

When Sr. Gomez learned that Benito's wife had just given birth to a son, he remarked publicly, "Oh, no, not another Cruz." The comment spread throughout the Cuban community.

When it reached Benito's ears, he became irate. "So, Gomez doesn't want another Cruz," he told his wife. "In that case, we will give him two. We will not baptize our son Benito Cruz as planned. Instead, we will name him Cruz Cruz."

Sr. Gomez was an old man with a weak heart, so it was no surprise a few weeks afterward that he passed away of apparent heart failure. The attending physician, a young intern, knew nothing of the cigar poisoning epidemic that had occurred several years earlier. He assumed that his patient died of a natural heart attack and ignored a few unusual symptoms, symptoms not unlike those of the poisoned cigar smokers. No autopsy was performed.

CRUZ Cruz spent his early childhood years in one violent scrape after another. He was expelled from two schools for fighting, and he fractured the skull of a seven-year-old when he was a teenager. Only Benito's threats of physical harm to the young boy's father, bolstered with slashed tires and a torched garage, kept the frightened man from pressing charges.

Benito did not find Cruz's behavior particularly bothersome. In fact, it reminded him of his own childhood in Havana. When Cruz turned seventeen, his father signed a permission slip allowing him to join the Marines.

Surprisingly, Cruz blossomed under military direction. He forced himself to conform. The usual recruit accepted training to kill as a necessity to avoid being killed himself, not as a desirable activity. Not Cruz – he flourished as the violence quotient increased.

He could not learn enough. Unfortunately, he seemed to enjoy injuring his fellow Marines during training exercises. He actually alarmed some of his NCOs with his attitude, but every time there was talk about a discharge, he backed off into a temporary period of docility.

He managed, barely, to finish his tour of duty without an official blemish, and received an honorable discharge. As a mature young man, he had not grown tall, but had achieved enormous strength in his arms and legs from a daily regimen of lifting weights and distance running. He possessed the build of a fire hydrant, and his head seemed to sit directly on his shoulders.

His eyes were extraordinary. They stared out through such thin slits that occasionally people speaking to him thought he had fallen asleep. That along with the dark bushy eyebrows gave the impression of a Neanderthal dullard. Nothing could have been more inaccurate. He was, in fact, brilliant in the same dangerous manner as his father. He read so voraciously and pursued such a wide ranging subject matter that he was more educated than most graduates of the finest universities.

Benito brought him into the cigar business when he returned to Tampa after being discharged. Initially, Cruz learned only the legitimate operations, but he was too smart and more devious than his father to be kept from the secrets. He could see that the operation produced significantly higher profits than those of the competitors, for no readily apparent reason. Eventually, he figured out that the extraordinary profits were based on illegal smuggling activities.

Steadily he gathered evidence of the criminal behavior until he had enough to make a move. One evening after the other office workers had finished and left, Cruz entered his father's office.

"We need to talk," he started, thrusting a stack of papers toward Benito.

"What are these?" Benito asked, feigning innocence. He could see that a few of the documents near the top of the splayed stack were fake bills of lading for shipments of tobacco.

"You know what they are. They show how much Cuban tobacco we have brought in during the last six months. I know that we have only one source of tobacco, except for the small amount of Connecticut wrapper. Yet we have shipped out at least a hundred times this quantity in finished cigars over the same period. Given that some tobacco is lost during production as scrap, we should be shipping less than we import, not more. There is no question that you have another source that is off the books."

Benito beamed the smile of a proud father whose son had just scored the winning touchdown.

"Cruz, *I* don't have a second source; *we* have a second source. I am surprised and pleased that you discovered the secret to our success so soon. Employees with many more years of experience have not figured it out. Of course, they do not have access to the financial records that I have allowed you. Still, it is quite a feat for you to have found it in such a short time. Congratulations."

Benito knew Cruz well. He was confident that Cruz would not publicize the finding. Cruz enjoyed the power that money provided. They both sought power more than money. He would not jeopardize the source of the funds. In that assessment, Benito was correct.

But Benito had fallen into the same trap that had snared Sr. Gomez those several years ago. Benito had allowed someone into the company who would be scheming to take it away from him. In this case, it was not a stranger looking for a job. It was his own son.

"I did not come in here for a pat on the back. I want to learn how we are doing this, who our contacts are, how you keep the customs people off our backs, and on and on."

Benito noted the plural pronouns that Cruz was using, and that pleased him. Benito believed incorrectly that Cruz had been co-opted into the illicit organization to provide the support that Benito was seeking. Running the ever-expanding business by himself had become exceedingly more complex. He had to compartmentalize the staff so that no one person could comprehend the operation as readily as Cruz had. He could trust Cruz, he assumed, whereas a mere employee would be a risk to go to the authorities.

"All in good time, Cruz, all in good time. Tonight we celebrate, but not at the Tampa Bay Hotel. I will call Casimiro at The Columbia and ask him to prepare a private dinner for us. There is no better chef in all

Tampa. I keep advising him to expand his saloon into a restaurant, but until he does, we can take advantage of the best culinary secret in the city. All we have to do is supply the fish, and that is easy enough."

ONE of Benito's minor operations, Rex Seafood Distribution, Inc., was a wholesale fish market at the Tampa Harbor. Rex Seafood sold to walk-in customers, but most of its business involved dispatching its fleet of ice-cooled trucks to area cafeterias, restaurants, and grocery stores throughout the West Coast and central part of Florida.

Rex Seafood's best customer was the cafeteria at Rex del Sol Cigar Company. In fact, if anyone ever thought about it – but no one had access to the financial records to do so – the employee cafeteria seemed to purchase seafood in far greater quantities than it needed for the one meal per day that it served.

Rex Seafood acquired its fresh fish from independent fishermen who sailed into the harbor daily. The boat owners sold to the highest dockside buyer. That buyer was more often Rex Seafood than any other wholesaler. Rex paid the highest prices and charged customers the lowest prices. Other wholesalers, fighting over the leftovers on the ships, were never able to grow their businesses larger. They assumed that Rex was making its money on the high volume.

They would have been surprised to learn that each year Rex Seafood varied between losing a little money and barely breaking even. Benito did not care about making money on seafood. He wanted the appearance of a thriving seafood business that required a large fleet of delivery trucks, because he needed the operation to hoodwink customs officials.

After a superb meal at The Columbia, Benito and Cruz relaxed over Rex del Sol cigars and glasses of specially ordered Harvey's Bristol Cream. In the quiet of the saloon that Casimiro had closed to the public that night, Benito explained the operation to Cruz without the risk of being overheard. He held his cigar toward one of the lights and gazed appreciatively.

"These are the best cigars in the world, and we command a high premium price for each one that we sell. And we sell millions annually.

"The largest cost for any of us premium cigar producers is the high tariffs that the U.S. Government levies on imported tobacco. They want to subsidize the growers in Virginia, the Carolinas, and other southern states whose tobacco does not have to pay import duty. A Rex del Sol cigar cannot use any of that lower quality tobacco. The only domestic source we use is the wrap tobacco, but that is a minor part of the cigar.

"We own the plantation in the Sierra Maestra Mountains where we grow most of our tobacco. Most Cuban tobacco is grown in northwest Cuba, but our little corner in the southeast produces the best on the island. Sometimes the operation buys a little extra from bordering plantations if our harvest falls short. The main thing is that we control the source, so we can package the tobacco to our specifications. Packaging is the key.

"To keep up appearances, we periodically import tobacco from Cuba legally. This is a small fraction of the total we use, of course, but it is enough that no one will ever think it odd that Rex del Sol seems to get its tobacco from thin air.

"We hold our costs down here in Tampa by smuggling in duty free from Havana nearly all of the tobacco that goes into the Rex del Sol. Coupled with the premium price we get for our cigars, that is why we are so profitable and how we generate so much cash flow. It enables me to buy out any competitor who gets too big and who begins to cut into our market share."

"I understood the finances from those documents, Father, but how do you get the tobacco in under the noses of Customs?"

"We developed an airtight stainless steel container for shipping the tobacco. No air gets in, no water gets in, no odors get in, and the containers do not rust, so they are re-usable.

"The customs people seldom bother fishing boats. Fish is duty free, so there is little reason for customs to inspect. On occasion, they might give a boat a quick glance for contraband, but that is about the extent of it.

"You are aware of our Rex Seafood business. Almost all of the fishing vessels that supply us are independent outfits, but it is not known that we own two fishing boats through a Panama-registered company. These are legitimate fishing boats. We keep them in constant operation.

"The unique thing is that both were built with hidden holds to accommodate dozens of the stainless steel tobacco containers. To the typical customs inspector, the tops of the containers would appear to be the hull of the ship. We only have to make sure that Customs does not get tipped from a disgruntled employee so Customs isn't tempted to physically climb around the bottom of the ships.

"Our empty boats dock in Havana where we load aboard the tobacco filled containers. These we fill at the plantation and truck to the dock. Our contacts in Cuban Customs take long lunches when these are loaded. Moreover, we have led them to believe that we are shipping contaminated sugar.

"After accepting the tobacco containers, the ships set out on a fishing voyage. As the fish are caught, they are loaded into regular fish containers on top of the tobacco containers. When the ship docks at our Rex Seafood in Tampa, we unload both kinds of containers into our warehouse.

"Later, our delivery trucks bring fish to the Rex del Sol cafeteria at the factory along with the sealed tobacco containers. Only the manager at Rex Seafood is aware of the different cargo in the two types of containers.

"About every two years, we change the names of the vessels, re-register them in Panama, and paint them a different color to further obscure our activity. As importantly, we change out the crew at the same time so that no one gets too nosy. That is a problem with a ship's crew. They have few diversions on board, and can use their imaginations more than we like. Of course, the captains are in on it, but I pay them very well, like the Rex Seafood manager, and they know to keep their mouths shut."

"Thus few people know anything, and none know everything – well, except for me and now you.

"In other words, Father, you have compartmentalized the system to keep employees from understanding what they are part of. It looks smooth. I need to learn the operation in its entirety if I'm going to be helpful. I must get to Cuba right away, don't you agree? But I want to go incognito."

CRUZ began his education on the plantation. Benito sent him under the guise of being an auditor, a Sr. Marco Humberto. As an auditor, he was given free rein to go anywhere and look at anything without any further explanation needed. Cruz dedicated his efforts to learning how the tobacco plants were planted, harvested, graded, and most importantly, packaged.

However, to maintain his cover as an auditor, he did not ignore those job responsibilities. If anything, he was more zealous in his efforts than one could expect of a normal auditor. He soon realized that the assistant manager was stealing about five percent of the production and selling it to rival farms off the books. One afternoon, Cruz handed the man two fingers from his son's hand.

"You've been stealing five percent of our production, and those fingers represent less than five percent of your son," Cruz explained. "You should be thankful."

It was more effective than hiring a new man. The assistant manager was not tempted to skim anything further for his own account.

But it was the banditos that interested Cruz the most. Cruz noted that the volume of tobacco harvested from the fields was down the last two years from the previous norm, even accounting for the missing five percent. He examined the level of fertilizer used and found it to be identical. He checked past weather records exhaustively and found that, if anything, slight variations in rainfall and temperature in the past two years should have resulted in higher, not lower, production.

Eventually, he discovered that a small band of men, living off the land in the nearby mountains, was cutting tobacco from the plants just before harvest. Thus, yields were down. Cruz had so thoroughly interrogated the plantation workers that one of them happened to mention noticing that some of the plants appeared to have lost leaves before harvesting took place.

After Cruz conducted a short personal surveillance, he witnessed the banditos stripping small quantities from several tobacco plants. Instead of taking immediate action, however, he followed them to their base camp. He returned the next day and spent several additional days and nights reconnoitering. When he was satisfied that he had learned enough, he descended into the camp.

It was an especially dark night when he struck. Low clouds that blanked out the moon and stars generated a chilly drizzle in the high altitude. A sharp wind made the conditions miserable. Cruz could not have been more pleased with the environment, because he was at his best when his opponent was distracted.

A lone sentry huddled beneath the eaves of a small shed. He was more interested in staying dry than in guarding the camp. Cruz made short work of him and entered the tent of the commander, Ronaldo Cairo. With a seven-inch knife blade pressed tightly against the man's throat, Cruz spoke in hushed tones. "I assume that you wish to live. Thus, you will stay quiet and listen. Agreed?"

Cairo answered quickly but quietly, "You are surrounded by hundreds of my men. What makes you think that you can march in here and demand anything?"

Actually, Cruz knew that Cairo had only twenty-two men, not counting the now-dead guard, but still too many for one man in a pitched battle, even for a man of Cruz' extraordinary abilities.

"This may answer your question," Cruz replied. "Put out your hand." Cruz reached into a small container in his pack. He poured out two human eyes into the man's hand. "Your guards need to be more alert, don't you think? I believe this one's name was Cortez. He had no reason to lie to me while I was cutting."

In fact, Cruz had not cut out the eyes until after the man was dead. Cruz took no pleasure in hurting a foe. He was dispassionate about death and pain and used both only to achieve a goal. The horror of holding his man's eyes had far greater effect on Cairo than if Cruz had attacked with a force of twenty men.

Cairo shook his hand free of the eyes that splattered on the ground and attempted to shrink away from the knife blade. Understandably more docile at this point, he asked, "What do you want?"

"You have been stealing tobacco from the Rex Plantation. That will stop entirely. You have been stealing from other mountain plantations. That will accelerate slightly.

"Your group is not badly organized, and your methods are well thought out. I am actually impressed. Notwithstanding your former sentry, you have reasonably effective discipline for a ragtag operation – of twenty-two, by the way, not hundreds – and your personal command shows promise.

"However, you and your men need enhanced training, which I will give you. I will also provide you with the plan to better implement your thefts. Moreover, I will provide the outlet for the tobacco that you steal from the other plantations so that you will not get caught on the distribution side of the business."

The next day, Cairo introduced Cruz to his men as his new training officer, and a new branch of the Rex empire began to develop. For the next six months, Cruz introduced an iron discipline to Cairo's men and improved their ability to roam the mountains without detection. They learned from him that intimidation is always better than an outright battle. During the process, Cruz himself became an expert on the Sierra Maestra.

"Always seek to demoralize the enemy to the greatest extent while engaging him in the smallest way possible. This is not a game to determine who has the biggest bragging rights. It is a life and death battle where life goes to the boldest, who is also the smartest."

He taught them how to identify the best quality tobacco. They learned how to avoid taking too many leaves from any one plant to minimize the plantation owners becoming suspicious.

Whenever Cairo had accumulated sufficient amounts of high-quality purloined tobacco, he delivered it at a discounted price to the now loyal assistant manager on the Rex Plantation.

The Cairo operation resulted in slightly lower harvests on the other plantations, thus causing incrementally higher prices for other Tampa cigar makers who preferred to import the premium southeast mountain tobacco. At the same time, costs dropped even more for the Rex Plantation. Benito could not have been more pleased with Cruz when he returned to Tampa. He was not in the least disappointed in the methods Cruz used either.

THE fishing boats, Cruz's next area of interest, were not so easily handled. There were two ships, so both had to be examined. The Rex Group's ownership of the boats was secret, so Benito could not simply assign Cruz as a free rein auditor from the Tampa headquarters.

Fortunately, as a former U.S. Marine, he knew his way around ships. Since the captains were in the know anyway, he signed on as a "captain's assistant," an unusual position on a fishing vessel. However, the crew was hired new at the time Cruz signed on, so Cruz's unique job was accepted as the way this particular captain operated.

Both ships proved to be well run, and no one was lining his own pocket. Hiring entirely new crews periodically created certain inherent problems in running the ship, but seamen are seamen, so operations got up to full efficiency before too long.

Cruz thought that ships were especially well suited for handling discipline problems. The solution to managing any inquisitive malcontent was a meeting along the ship's railing on a dark, windswept night. No fuss, no discussion, no body. Fortunately, Cruz did not find it necessary to employ such discipline on either ship, since no one was there long enough to develop inconvenient curiosity.

He developed in his mind a back-up alternative to the stainless steel containers. At some point, customs people could always get lucky, or a new customs official might try to make a name for himself with extraordinary attention to detail. After all, he himself had a reputation for diligence that spurred others into discharging their responsibilities more effectively. There was always the risk that someone else might have similar dedication. But for now, he was satisfied that the chance was low.

Several voyages later, he was back in Tampa going over the land delivery system. He reported to Benito that, "I do not like the cafeteria connection. The same people are always unloading. Eventually, someone will wonder a little too much.

"From now on, personnel who unload the containers will be day shift, and people who open the tobacco containers will always be night shift. The day shift workers will always distribute the containers to the appropriate parts of the factory so that no one will make the connection. We need to take care that no worker ever gets transferred from one of these shifts to the other.

"Moreover, under the guise of efficiency, we will always arrange for the Rex Seafood trucks to stop at various supply houses on the way from the dock to pick up related items for the cigar operation like cigar boxes, aluminum foil, labels, etc. That way, if someone does make an offhand remark about the tobacco containers arriving with the fish, it won't seem unusual because that is how we get other supplies as well.

"Finally, we currently hire common carrier trucks to pick up the legal tobacco from the cargo docks. We need to use the Rex Seafood trucks to do it instead. This will reinforce in the minds of anyone too curious that we always use Rex Seafood trucks for tobacco deliveries."

Cruz sat back in his chair to give his father a chance to sift through the recommendations. Some people have such a high opinion of themselves that they refuse to see the value of another's concepts for improvement. Cruz, though, knew that his father was too results-oriented to let pride get in the way of progress. Thus, Cruz expected Benito to grasp the new ideas wholeheartedly.

Benito, like Cruz, had no reservations about receding into the background. It was not acclaim that drove them. It was power. Accepting an improved idea – no matter whose idea it was – contributed to achieving and retaining power. As expected, Benito offered generous compliments.

"Cruz, you have done a remarkable job in a few short years. I expected a lot from you, but not nearly as much as you have accomplished. In the next months, I will bring you into the marketing and distribution part of the business. These parts of the business are entirely legitimate. It is important to limit exposure to the authorities. Never invite scrutiny by upsetting your competitors or customers with questionable practices, because you do not want anyone lodging complaints either publicly or anonymously."

Benito introduced Cruz as his heir apparent to major customers at home and abroad. By the end of the training period, Cruz could have run the operation as well as Benito.

"You are a complete "rex" for Rex del Sol, Inc.," Benito concluded. "You know what I know, and if anything happened to me, I am confident that you can run things just as well. Tomorrow night we will go to The Columbia and enjoy one of Casimiro's private meals and a Rex del Sol."

"No, Father. Tomorrow the meal is on me, and we will go to the Tampa Bay Hotel's restaurant." Cruz wanted a location with the hustle, bustle, and noise of a large crowd.

That night at the restaurant, Benito sat back and finished his cigar. The meal was superb. Cruz experienced the slightest tremor of compassion as he watched his father set the remainder of the cigar into the ashtray with an unsteady hand. In Cruz's entire life, he had never felt a human tug on his heart, and he did not like the feeling. He shook his head to clear away the thought. His father looked at him and slumped deeper into his chair. Had any of the other patrons noticed at that moment, they would have suspected a guest who had imbibed a bit too excessively.

"I'm not feeling well, Cruz," Benito barely whispered in the loudest voice he could muster, his eyes almost closing.

"Don't fight it," Cruz replied. "It will be over in a few moments."

Benito's eyes widened ever so slightly, with a growing realization. They would have opened more had he the strength, but he was nearing the end. Nevertheless, he knew what Cruz meant.

"Was it the cigar?" Benito managed to gasp.

Cruz took the cigar butt from the ashtray and placed it into his pocket. "Yes, similar to the recipe you used against Gomez, but faster acting. I was told that it is painless because of its speed, and I am pleased to see that appears to be true. It is directed to the heart and is undetectable after twenty-four hours elapse. The symptoms give every appearance of a heart attack. Given your age, I am confident that there will be no rush to an autopsy.

Cruz looked deeply into Benito's watery eyes. "I want to thank you for your guidance, Father," he continued with complete sincerity, "and for your kindnesses over the years. I could not have asked for anyone better. It's just time for you to leave and for me to assume command of the family fortunes. I'm sure that you understand."

Oddly, Benito did.

CHAPTER 9

The Search Begins

I sink back shuddering from the quest.
ROBERT BROWNING

The Crew and Mack peddled their bikes along Mocking Bird Road. The two smooth, newly-paved lanes were a welcome improvement over the gravelly macadam roads more typical of the area. The Andersson limerock mine supplied nearly all of the Florida road builders south of Tallahassee, but most of that construction was concentrated in the larger cities like Tampa, Sarasota, and greater Miami. Except for a few state routes, most of the county roads were still dirt or gravel, but Mocking Bird was one of the first of many improvements to come.

When they arrived at the Hostetter Cutoff, they made an unexceptional effort to conceal their bikes behind bushy palmetto palms. The likelihood of theft was remote, but there was no reason to ask for trouble.

They continued up the cutoff by foot. That was preferable over trying to snake their bike tires through ruts and maneuver around gaping potholes.

The sun was still below the horizon, but its rays were lightly brightening the eastern sky as they neared the Hostetter farmhouse. The day was giving hopeful signs that the rain clouds would dissipate. It was already warm enough that they left their jackets on their bikes.

"Do you think we'll run into those guys from the swamp, Carty?" Mack asked as they began walking.

"I don't know, but don't let on that we even notice that they are occupying the house. Just keep your eyes looking forward so it looks like we aren't the least bit interested in them or the house. If they call out, just wave, smile, and keep moving briskly as if we do this all the time."

The tactics proved unnecessary, though, as the men were still sleeping off a beer binge from the night before. The expedition slipped past without notice from the residents.

"I watched closely out of the corner of my eye as we walked by," Carty said, after they were safely past, "and I didn't see any movement. The same car is parked on the side of the house that was there the other evening."

"Do you believe there are just two of them, or could there have been more in the house?" Hale asked.

"There is no telling. I saw only two drive away. There were no others in the house at that time. But maybe they went to pick up someone else. I didn't stick around long enough to find out if they came back with others."

As they continued, Hale pulled Carty aside and whispered in her ear. "You keep a close eye on Mack while you're in the deep scrub. He isn't familiar with much outside of a town and could easily get lost or injured. Just don't let on that you will be his guardian angel; we don't want to embarrass him."

Hale had taken to Mack. Perhaps it was their shared minority status in the school. It had been Hale's idea to ask Mack to join the group.

"There's no need to worry about Mack being reluctant to allow me to help," she laughed. "I've already offered my halo-headed assistance, and Mack has eagerly accepted."

"You bet I did, Carty," Mack piped in. "One thing I've learned is that if you don't know what you are doing, you'll likely do it wrong. I'll need all the help I can get in that horrible place."

"Really, it isn't all that bad, Mack," Hale added. "Just follow Carty's lead and do what she tells you. In the tall grass, walk slowly and look down before you take a step. There are a few dangerous critters, but nearly all of them will leave you alone if you don't startle them. Most of the snakes are not poisonous anyway. If you see a snake, stand perfectly still and call to Carty. She knows the good from the bad, and she will get you out of harm's way."

"All snakes are bad to my way of thinking, Carty," Mack replied.

"I understand your feelings, Mack," Carty said, "but few snakes are bothersome, and they are really interesting if you take time to learn about them."

Blake added, "You're talking to the world's biggest snake lover, Mack. In the sixth grade, Carty surprised us during speech class when she used an eight-foot eastern indigo snake as an exhibit. Old Miss Boxer almost dropped her false teeth on the desk when Carty hauled that monster out of the burlap sack. Of course, indigos are non-poisonous, but the sheer size of Carty's snake was really intimidating.

"While Carty helped the snake coil around her arm and body, most of the girls were squealing and the boys were laughing and cheering her on. Miss Boxer had lost total control over the class by that time, because she sat frozen in her chair with her hand over her heart and her mouth hanging wide open.

"Carty was oblivious to the wild commotion. She was concentrating on describing the snake and trying to explain to the class about its eating habits. No one was listening to Carty at that point, but she just kept rambling on in her schoolmarm voice."

That comment drew a sharp glance from Carty, but she avoided a rejoinder.

Hale added his memories. "Mr. Toth was the new principal that year. He came running into the classroom to see what the hullabaloo was all about. As he charged through the doorway at top speed, he hit the newly waxed floors and slid to a stop on his knees right in front of Carty. That startled the snake, and it struck out at Mr. Toth, catching him right on his neck.

"He began running wildly around the front of the classroom, yelling for help, and flailing his arms – with the huge indigo hanging on tightly just under his Adam's apple. The more he tugged at the snake, the more tightly it chomped down, so he gave up trying to pull it off.

"Finally, Carty got him to stop running in circles and sat him down on the floor. She began petting the snake and waving her other hand slowly in front of its eyes like an Indian snake charmer with a flute in front of a cobra. After about a minute, the snake released Mr. Toth, who by that time was babbling like a baby, and Carty re-bagged the snake. By then the room sounded like a stadium when the home team scores the winning run in extra innings.

"It was the most fun I've ever had in school."

Carty interjected, "Most people think that the Indian snake charmers mesmerize the cobra with music from the flute. But those guys are charlatans. Cobras, like most snakes, cannot hear. The cobras are actually attracted to the flute's swaying, not the sound. I just applied the same principle with one hand to calm my snake down.

"I've done the same thing in the wild many times. It's the easiest way to catch a snake if you don't have a tool to grab them with or a stick to pin them. Just wave your hand slowly, and when the snake is kind of mesmerized, quickly grab it behind its neck with your other hand. 'Course, it'd be dangerous to attempt that type of capture with a poisonous snake, so that I wouldn't try."

"No, thank you, Carty. I'll let all kinds of snakes have their freedom," Mack said.

"Anyway," Carty continued, "If everyone in the classroom had acted more maturely," glaring severely at Blake and Hale, "students and teachers alike, there would have been no trouble." Carty was clearly still miffed about the entire episode.

"Gee, did I hear it at home that night. Mr. Toth phoned my mom to schedule an 'emergency meeting.' My mom refused to go. She phoned my dad at work. She was still embarrassed about the wrestling match I had with Haywood Dolder in the third grade – which I might add was entirely his fault."

"Beat him good, too," complimented Blake. "He grabbed her from behind for no reason and she flipped him through the air as though it was a choreographed western saloon fight in a movie. She had him in a headlock and was pushing his face into the dirt. Dolder was whining like a baby, yelling 'uncle, uncle,' but Carty didn't know that 'uncle' meant you were giving up. So she kept grinding his face into the dirt until one of the teachers pulled her off of him.

"It took him weeks to get over the embarrassment of being bested by a girl. And Carty has been both admired and a little feared by most of the kids in class ever since – except for Hale and me. We know she is a softie at heart."

That last comment generated a small smile from Carty.

"So is that why Dolder seems to have it in for you?" Mack asked.

"I guess," Carty answered. "He is usually careful around me. He outweighs me now by seventy pounds or more, but he remembers that I knew how to flip him over. He is a big talker, but he is essentially a coward. He prefers going after the younger kids, although he backs off of even that when he sees me around.

"Anyway, Dad had to drive over to the school from his office that afternoon and take on the snake meeting by himself. When he got home, I got a serious tongue lashing. 'What were you thinking? You know that most people are afraid of snakes. Couldn't you bring in a piece of camping gear or some toadstools and mushrooms or uh, uh, uh, a needlepoint?'

"Gosh, can you imagine me doing a needlepoint? When Dad said that, I couldn't help but grin. Of course that set him off even more. As punishment, I had to rake all the oak leaves from the yard by myself, go to bed early on the weekend, and no 'Boston Blackie' on the radio that week."

"Late that night, I overheard uproarious laughter in the living room. I sneaked down and listened through the closed door with a drinking glass to my ear. A glass acts like a hearing aid, you know. Dad was telling Mom about his meeting with Mr. Toth and Miss Boxer.

"'Toth was still shaking,' Dad was saying, 'and Miss Boxer was nodding in agreement so vigorously to everything he said that I thought her head might snap off. It was all I could do to keep from slitting my sides with laughter, the more he blathered and she bobbed.'

"Dad continued his story, 'Of course I maintained a grave look and agreed that this was a serious situation, and told them Carty would be severely punished and admonished to avoid any further unacceptable behavior.'

"'Toth kept stroking his bandaged neck as he spoke, complaining that the snake might be poisonous. I assured him that if Carty said it was an eastern indigo, there was no doubt that it was an eastern indigo, and that's not poisonous, so he had no worries.'

"'Besides,' Dad added, 'If it were a poisonous snake, you would already be dead. You should have seen his face.'

"'You didn't say that, did you?' Mom gasped. 'You are an evil man, Mr. Andersson – funny, but evil. Maybe it is you, not Carty, who needs punishing,' and she must have given Dad a playful slap on his head, because he complained about her messing up his hair. But by this time, they were both laughing harder than I've ever heard them before or since.

"With that, I peeked through the door. They hugged and Mom got serious. She said she was worried that I might never grow up to be a lady if Dad kept treating me like a boy, what with snakes and archery and hunting. Dad told her not to worry. I would do just fine as a lady when the time came, but that since they did not have a son, he hoped that I would be strong enough to take over the business when he retired.

"I don't know if I want to take over the mine when I grow up," she interjected, "But I do not want to disappoint Dad. Anyway, after hearing that Dad wasn't really angry with me, the punishments were easier to take.

"So, Mr. Toth survived, but he did quit as soon as classes ended in June, the only one-year principal in Cross Creek's history. Before he left, he put in a new rule at Cross Creek – no animals brought to school – except for the horses of the kids who ride to school, of course."

"Funny story, Carty," Mack replied, "but that is one school rule that I can accept without reservation. So where did Mr. Toth end up going?"

"I'm not sure. I think Dad said that he went to work for the State Department in Washington."

THE search plan was pre-arranged. They started out on the south fork in pairs, Blake and Hale scouring the semi-submerged area to the north of the path, and Carty and Mack on the other, drier side. That kept Mack in easier and safer territory.

Mack carried Carty's canvas bag to hold the specimens that they found. When the searchers acquired a specimen, they took it to him to confirm the identification and for safe keeping.

Mack proved to be as good a searcher as a Latin scholar. He had an ability to differentiate from afar a correct leafy frond from an incorrect one that looked similar. He had no explanation for his knack, but Carty was in awe. The group had bagged eighteen specimens as lunch time approached, and Mack had accounted for ten by himself.

Hale and Blake were a muddy mess by then, having slogged though mostly swamp. They were tasked with the more difficult search of hard to reach plants, those that sometimes required wading into black-as-ink, chest-high water. They worked in tandem, Hale on the lookout for undesirable creatures, and Blake going for the plant specimen.

They had to wait out one mid-sized alligator and circle around a nasty nest of cottonmouths, but their search proved safe and successful. The six specimens the pair found were not uncommon, but were those that grew in more inaccessible locations, including an insectivore, a rootless bladderwort (Utricularia floridana).

Carty had found only two, but hers were among the rarer varieties on the list: a Florida spiny pod (Matelea floridana) and a Florida coontie (Zamia pumila). "Do you remember Mrs. Tryon telling us that in early Florida history, some of the coonties were used as food by Indians?" she asked Mack. "They don't look very edible to me."

"Actually, the part of the plant that we collected is not really useful as food. The Indians used to dig up the roots to grind them up into a kind of flour," Mack elaborated.

"How on earth do you know that?" she inquired in amazement, continuing to marvel at "city-boy" Mack's knowledge of the flora.

"Oh, just something I picked up looking through the books when we were researching at the library."

She was startled by that revelation. According to Blake, during the speedy search through those reference materials, Mack devoted little more than a minute to any plant, including the time to sketch it. It was amazing that Mack could have retained such detailed information in those few seconds. It was as if Mack had photographed the pages in his mind.

Spirits were high by the time the group crossed the ancient cypress bridge over the creek that connected the swamp to Duck Lake. As they approached Aunt Lilly's house, she greeted them with a wave and a smile from the expansive porch. Carty was happy to see her aunt waving with the repaired arm.

"OH, my, you four are a mess. Before you go any farther, take off your shoes and rinse off in the sprinklers," she ordered. She descended the steps and, using her good hand, turned on the faucet full strength.

"I'll find you some towels," she called as they ran into the spray.

The temperature of the water started out almost hot, because it had been warming in the sun-baked hose, but then it cooled off. The day's temperature had reached the low eighties by this time, so the romp through the lawn sprinklers proved good fun. Carty got the worst of it, since the boys naturally teamed up against her. But she was a good sport about it and held her own, including booting Mack in the rear and sending him face first into a large puddle at one point.

After a while, Aunt Lilly returned, and Carty took off for the house to change. Cleaner but wet, the boys took the large beach towels and clothespins that Aunt Lilly offered.

"Boys, you can change in the tool shed. Hang your wet clothes on the clothesline afterward. In the warm sun and nice breeze, they should be almost dry by the time you finish lunch.

Carty had a supply of clothes that she kept at Aunt Lilly's house, so she was already dressed when they sat down to eat.

The three boys sat wrapped in large beach towels at Aunt Lilly's picnic table. Aunt Lilly had thick slices of roast beef laid out and a pile of leafy lettuce and tomatoes for sandwiches. Her canned dill pickles were the highlight. The hot homemade chicken soup felt good going down, since they were still chilled from the soaking in the sprinklers.

"Wow, thanks, Miss Andersson. This really hits the spot," enthused Blake, as he spread a hefty portion of horseradish on to his meat. Blake was always passionate when it came to filling his stomach.

"And you make the best lemonade," Mack and Hale chimed in together. "'Lilly Lemonade,' Carty calls it."

"Well, if it is one thing I have on this property, it is citrus, and though the peak of the harvest season is past, this is still all fresh picked thanks to Carty. The key to Lilly Lemonade," she added, smiling, "is to add the juice from one orange for every five lemons. You are welcome to take home any fruit you can carry."

"We wish we could, Miss Andersson, but we do not have much extra carrying capacity," Mack pointed out. "We might take an orange to eat on the way, though."

"Tell me how you are doing. It sounds like a difficult assignment."

"Oh, it is not too bad, and it is actually fun, Aunt Lilly. And we've done really well," Carty added. She explained how Mack had got them past the first hurdle with the library research. When she told Lilly about Dolder's ploy of hoarding the reference materials, she gave full credit to the four as a whole for offering help to the other groups.

"That was really Carty's idea," Hale interjected, "and the more I have thought about it, the more I am glad that the rest of us agreed to go along. I have to admit that it feels good."

Carty went on, "We have well more than half of the assignment in our specimen bag already, with a lot of daylight ahead of us. Mack has been the star of the team. He can spot specimens that everyone else misses."

Mack added, "I don't think that we will get all twenty-five of the specimens, though. One on the list, Chapmann's rhododendron, also known as rhododendron chapmannii, grows only in the Florida Panhandle, according to the reference book at the library. Mrs. Tryon must have been sending a little trickery our way."

"Well, twenty-four specimens should be good enough for the A then," Carty surmised. "To get that total, though, I'm afraid that we will have to take the north fork on the way back," she said to Mack. "We have not come across a water sundew yet, and I know where one is on that path."

Turning to Aunt Lilly, Carty explained that Mack had hoped to avoid the Canfield house, but that she had seen that rare specimen during her walk home on the north fork. She also gave a short report on her adventure that night, including noticing the mysterious pair in the car at the Hostetter place. She omitted mentioning her encounter with them in the swamp and that she had approached the farmhouse after they drove off.

"I must have misunderstood you, Aunt Lilly. I thought you told me to take the north fork to avoid Sally Canfield's house."

"No, dear, you have to take the south fork to skirt her place."

Aunt Lilly noted Carty's confused look and quickly changed the subject before Carty could formulate a question. "One of the men whom you saw was probably old Mrs. Hostetter's son, Clemens. I had heard that he was back in the area. When I was at Homer's store, he mentioned to me that Clem and another man have frequented his place for the past several weeks.

"When Mr. Hostetter died, his wife had trouble keeping the farm going on her own. Clem was too lazy to be of any help. He joined the Army in 1945, but was booted out before he finished basic training. Even with the War still going on, the Army didn't want him, so you can imagine what kind of a person he was.

"In any event, he stayed up north and never returned, not even for his mother's funeral. Can you imagine? He contacted a lawyer in town to sell the cattle that he inherited, but the farm has never sold. He probably still holds title unless he hasn't kept the taxes paid up."

CHAPTER 10

Lilly Remembers

Gratitude is the most exquisite form of courtesy.

Jacques Maritain

After lunch, Blake retrieved their clothes from the line and doled them out. Carty helped her aunt with the left-overs while the boys went to the tool shed to change. The heavier items were not fully dried, but in the warm sun, the dampness in the cloth and leather was not unpleasant.

They tidied up the kitchen, waved their goodbyes, and expressed more thanks. As they headed toward the path that led to Morose Swamp and the southern fork, Lilly thought back to several years ago when she had made a similar trip.

LILLY had first learned that Cora Hostetter was ill while visiting Homer's general store. Lilly was searching the shelves without success for a bottle of Bayer aspirin to add to her purchases.

"Homer, have you moved the aspirin? I can't find them."

"No, Miss Lilly, I'm sorry, but I sold the last two bottles yesterday. Had to have the Baxter boy rush them out to the Hostetter place. Cora Hostetter called to ask for the special service."

"Two bottles? Is she ailing?"

"Appears to be. I haven't seen her in several weeks. She's usually a regular."

Lilly paid her bill and asked, "Homer, would you mind if I used your phone to call Mrs. Hostetter? I'd like to find out if she needs anything."

"Go right ahead. You know where it is."

Lilly went to the back of the store and cranked the phone. The local telephone operator answered. Lilly began, "Hello, Bertha. Can you connect me to Cora Hostetter, please? This is Lilly Andersson."

"I thought that was your voice, Lilly, but you aren't calling from home."

"No, I'm over at Homer's right now."

"I see. I'll connect you right away."

The phone rang several times. Lilly was about to give up when Cora answered in a faint voice. "Hello."

"Hello, Mrs. Hostetter. This is Lilliquest Andersson. I'm at Homer's, and he said that he thought you were not feeling well. How are you doing?"

"Not too well to be honest, but maybe I'll be getting better now that the cool front is coming through."

"I'm on my way home from Homer's now. One of my cousins gave me a ride today. After he drops me off, I can walk over to your place this afternoon if you need anything."

Cora's voice seemed to weaken as she spoke. "Oh, no, Miss Lilly. There is no need to put yourself out. It's so nice of you to offer, but really, it isn't necessary."

Lilly sensed that Cora needed help but did not want to burden anyone. The woman lived alone, and insofar as Lilly was aware, had no nearby relatives. She doubted that Cora's worthless son would come home to help. "Nonsense, I'll be there about two o'clock, and I'll bring some biscuits and soup. I made a fresh pot of beef barley last night."

On the way through the swamp that afternoon, Lilly avoided the Canfield house. She was not a believer in the witch tales, but did not want to intrude on Sally Canfield. She knew that Sally lived by herself, now that her grandmother had passed away. In any event, the more direct south fork was a shorter trip.

It took nearly a minute for Cora to answer the door after Lilly knocked. The woman looked haggard and drawn. "Hello, Miss Lilly. You really did not have to come. I'll be fine. But do come in."

"Thank you. It is no trouble, and the walk is good for me. If you show me the way to the kitchen, I'll warm up this soup for us."

Though the farm acreage was not being worked, the house looked in surprisingly good condition, and the kitchen was well stocked. Lilly had heard that the farm had been run down since Carl Hostetter died, so she had wondered about Cora's financial condition. She was relieved to see that money did not seem to be a problem.

As they sat eating Lilly's soup, she learned that Cora had felt quite weak for several weeks. She didn't call Doc Brannigan out to the house, because she did not want to bother him. "He's got lots of babies to deliver and really sick people to visit," she said, apparently but incorrectly not including herself in the latter category.

Despite Cora's resistance, Lilly had insisted that she needed to be looked at, and Cora eventually relented. Lilly called Doc Brannigan that afternoon. "Duffy," she said, "I don't care how busy you are. You find some time to get out here tomorrow," she insisted.

"I don't know what these doctors are thinking," she remarked to Cora. "It's the hardest thing to get them to make house calls nowadays. Why do they expect the sick people to do the traveling?"

Lilly cleaned up the dishes. After making sure that Cora was comfortable, she told her, "I'll stop by tomorrow evening to see what the doctor reports. You rest up and call me if you need anything before then."

SHE returned the next day as promised, this time with a tuna noodle casserole. Doc Brannigan was just leaving as she walked up on to the porch. She did not like seeing the cheerless look on his usually happy face.

"Good afternoon, Lilly. It does not look good. I'm suspecting cancer, probably stomach, and well along. I'm arranging for her to go to St. Joseph's Hospital in Tampa for tests, but I am reasonably certain that's what they will find. She tells me that she doesn't have anyone to look after her."

"That's probably right, Duffy. Her only child is up north somewhere and hasn't been heard from in years. But don't worry. The Ladies Society at First Baptist is set up to help out in situations like this. I'll call Pastor

Bullock and he'll get them organized."

"No wonder Duffy doesn't like to make house calls," she thought, as he chugged away, still coaxing along his old, sputtering pre-War Hudson. "I wonder if doctoring will ever pay well."

UNFORTUNATELY, the medical tests turned out as expected. Cora returned to her house later that week with the report suggesting that she had less than two months to get her affairs in order. Her actual time fell a little short of that. The Ladies Society performed admirably. Someone was always with Cora to see her through the ordeal. Lilly came every day as well, and the two women grew closer as the end approached.

Two days before she died, Cora said that she had something important to say. "I have been struggling with this story, because I promised to keep this confidential. It is only because we have grown so close that I know you can be trusted," she began.

"Have you not wondered how I seem to have sufficient money to live so comfortably on a farm that has not produced a crop in several years, and whose only productive asset is a small, bare bones herd of cattle?" she asked.

"It has seemed odd, I admit, but I assumed that Carl had left you with a sufficient nest egg, such as a large life insurance policy."

"No, Carl probably thought he would live forever. He was never sick – not even a cold – in all the years we were married until the day he dropped over. In any event, he never purchased any life insurance, so when he died, Clem and I were nearly penniless. Things were difficult, but then they got better, and how they got better is what this conversation is all about."

Cora told Lilly about the time she spent with the Canfields years earlier. She laid out why the Canfields came to Florida, why they were so secretive, and why they perpetuated the rumors about their witchcraft. She explained how old Mrs. Canfield and now Sally Canfield provided her with a regular supply of generous amounts of money. Then she came to the difficult part.

"I love my son, Clemens, dearly." She choked, sobbed briefly, and continued. "Lilly, he is my son, what can I say? But he must never know about the Canfield saga. I did whatever I could think of to make him believe that they were witches, and it worked. His only interest in them, especially after he heard about the Whortons' disappearance, was to stay away, far away. Unfortunately, I made one mistake that I have always feared might prove disastrous for Sally."

She detailed how Clem had found one of Sally's handwritten notes just before he went into the Army, and how she had maneuvered the discussion to mislead him.

"I have always been fearful that I was not entirely successful, and that he might figure out what he had read. However, he has never returned, nor has he mentioned the Canfields or their treasure in any of his letters, and those letters always included a plea for money. When I send him money, I always send him small amounts to avoid suspicion. I am afraid, though, that it must seem strange to him that I am able to send him any sum, given the condition of the farm."

She had to pause for a few moments to recover her strength. She took Lilly's hand and continued.

"I want to ask a favor. In the cupboard to the left of the sink you will find a large sum of money in a cookie jar. Please set aside thirty dollars and give all the rest to the Ladies Society. Those Baptist women have been wonderful, and me being an Episcopalian. I don't want Clem to know that I have several thousand dollars in that jar, but he must get the thirty dollars, or he may want to know why I didn't have some money. He will net something additional from the few cattle and a little when the farm sells. Whatever he gets will soon be wasted away in any event."

Her eyes fell closed for a moment.

This was a lot of information for Lilly to absorb in such a short time, and she had to think it through. But the Clem issue was paramount and easy to deal with. Cora's eyes reopened.

"That is quite a story, Cora. Of course, I will respect all of your wishes. Like you, I have lived near the Canfields for most of my life. They have their eccentricities, but they never once were a problem for me. I can't say that I would have taken the same route that they have, but now I understand their situation. Like you, I want no harm to come to Sally – so I will keep the secret – not only from your son, but from everyone else."

Cora sighed heavily, as if a burden had been removed. Lilly later reflected that Cora had probably clung tenaciously to life for the seven difficult weeks, seeking a way to offer this final service to Sally Canfield.

When Cora died later that week, peacefully in her own bed in the farmhouse she loved, Lilly was with her. Cora let out a deep breath, smiled at Lilly, and said simply, "Goodbye, Lilly." Those were her last words. Lilly called Doc Brannigan, who also doubled as the county coroner.

"I'll be out this afternoon to fill out details for the death certificate. I'll try to get Sheriff Elsmore to come with me. I doubt that the county will need an inquest, so that will speed things along," he said. "On my last visit, Cora told me she wanted a service at St. Mark's Episcopal and to be buried in the church cemetery. I'll call the church when the sheriff and I finish up."

The next day, Lilly walked through the empty house. She selected a simple white cotton dress and appropriate accessories for the burial. She retrieved the money for the Ladies Society, which would receive the cash anonymously. She could not risk that Clem might hear any rumors about his mother being its source.

Lilly would send the thirty dollars to him in his mother's name, agreeing with Cora that it was an appropriate sum from a poor woman on an unproductive farm. Lilly disliked sending anything to him, though. She had secretly written to him, requesting that he return to Florida to be with his mother during her final days. She had even offered to purchase a train ticket for him.

She did not show Cora his reply. He had written back that he would not have time, and that his busy schedule would not permit him to be able to make the funeral either when that came.

She sighed as she took one last look around, then closed up the house and locked the front door, placing the key into the envelope with Clem's thirty dollars. As she turned around, she nearly bumped into a black-clothed woman climbing the porch stairs.

"Oh, I thought you were Mrs. Hostetter," the startled visitor said to Lilly.

Lilly recognized the woman as Sally Canfield, though she was no longer a child and now had stringy, unkempt, black hair. "Hello, Sally," she said. "I'm Lilliquest Andersson from the other side of the swamp. I'm afraid

I have bad news. Come, let's sit on the porch swing."

Sally hesitated and looked around with anxiety. Lilly smiled softly, took her hand, and led the way to the swing. They sat, and Sally focused her bright green eyes on Lilly. "Cora passed away yesterday after a short illness. I'm sorry that no one thought to notify you, though surely that is my fault more than anyone else's. You should know that Cora was very fond of you and your grandmother, and she thought of you until the very end."

Lilly did not mention that Cora had divulged any of the Canfield story, or that Sally had been Cora's primary source of funds.

Sally had been holding a small envelope in her other hand. She slipped the envelope into a pocket in her dress and sobbed into a handkerchief. "I lost my grandmother a short time ago," she said between sniffles. "Mrs. Hostetter is the only other person who was ever kind to me."

Lilly's heart seemed to stop. She hugged Sally and said, "I live on the east side of the swamp. You can get there over the old cypress bridge on the hammock through the swamp. If you ever want to talk – if you ever need anything – you come to see me."

Mindful that the Canfield house had no phone service, she added, "You do not need to call ahead. I'm almost always there."

Sally nodded and asked about the funeral arrangements. Then she got up from the swing, went down the stairs, and walked slowly toward home. That sad, black-clad woman never would make such a trip to Lilly's house.

THE morning two days later was dark and gray, unusual Florida weather for the season, but wholly appropriate under the circumstances. The warm temperature and humid conditions created an atmospheric wet blanket.

Fog layered the surrounding farm fields and the cemetery adjoining St. Mark's Episcopal Church. Soft, damp, wispy fingers crept gently toward the church, urged forward by an undetectable breeze.

Outside the church, Lilly recognized several women from the Baptist Ladies Society, Homer, and Sheriff Elsmore. There were three others that she assumed were distant relatives and a few townsfolk she knew from the congregation. She was aware that Homer made it a practice to attend the funeral of all his customers. "Just one last service," he always said.

Sheriff Elsmore's presence there, on the other hand, was a bit unexpected. She caught up to him on the church steps. He had taken off his hat in preparation of entering the church, revealing his thick, wavy, dark hair with just a hint of gray near the bottoms of his sideburns. His dark eyes and eyebrows matched the formal uniform he wore today for the funeral. He was just beyond thirty and still the youngest county sheriff in Florida.

"Hello, Miss Lilly – not a good day, is it?" he said.

"You are right about that, James," she replied, shaking moisture from the brim of her hat. "In many ways. I didn't expect to see you here. Surely you don't suspect something odd about Cora's death?"

"Oh, no, Miss Lilly, nothing like that. I got to know Carl and Cora Hostetter over the years and really came to like them. That son of theirs, Clem, was always in trouble, and I spent many a night at their house trying to keep him from getting into more. It was never anything really serious, but how those two nice people ever had such a miserable child is beyond my understanding. The best thing that ever happened to Mrs. Hostetter was when he left."

"How long have you known her?"

"About an hour shorter than what I've known you, actually. I was a rookie deputy before the War when we investigated the Whorton disappearance. The sheriff and most of the town suspected the Canfields. Our posse surrounded the house in preparation for the interview, and he used a megaphone to call to them. They peeped out of a small window and waved. The sheriff was a firm believer in the witchcraft rumors and wanted no part of going into that house himself. Since I was low man on the seniority totem pole, the sheriff sent me in to 'negotiate' as he described it."

"All I found was an elderly frail woman and her granddaughter, a young woman. They were dressed in all black clothes that looked like witch costumes on Halloween, I will admit. But they were no more dangerous to me than you are standing on these church steps. They were respectful and had a dignity about them that was unexpected from their appearance.

"The daughter did not say much, but she served me tea and little strawberry cookie-like things they called torts. You should have seen the sheriff's face when I told him that. 'You ate their food and drank their tea? How do you know what kind of potion' – he actually used the word potion – 'what kind of potion they were giving you?'

"The Canfields explained that they had heard some screaming on the lake on the two nights that coincided with Hoyt's disappearance and with that of his brother and cousin the next day.

"They both attributed the screams to someone or something being eaten by an enormous alligator they call Montooth that lurks in Duck Lake.

They could have been lying or hiding something, of course, but even as a rookie, I felt that I was a good judge of character.

"I reported back to the sheriff that they were uninvolved and suggested that the investigation should expand to the sides of the swamp. The sheriff wanted to get away from that house, so he was quick to accept my analysis and recommendation. He may have wanted to get away from me as well, thinking the potion might have a delayed effect."

"That's when you and I first met, James. You came to my house to ask if I had seen anything."

"That's right, Miss Lilly, and I almost turned you in for bribery that night," he smiled. "That was the best rhubarb pie I ever ate."

"That was probably because it was the only rhubarb pie you ever ate, since rhubarb doesn't grow here. A cousin from Ohio brings me some every time he visits."

"After speaking with you, I drove around to the Hostetter's. They hadn't heard anything either. Clem might have been a suspect, but I never pegged him for being dangerous – just too easily led astray by the ne'r-do-wells he gravitated to.

"Anyway, in the past, whenever I had questioned him for petty thefts or vandalism or other indiscretions, he displayed classic characteristics of the guilty: sweating, stuttering, avoiding eye contact, gulping down his Adams apple before speaking. That night he showed no nervousness at all, other than a little just for being in my presence, so I knew that he was not involved.

"That case was the final straw for the sheriff. He had been toying with the idea of retiring for a year or so. Several townsfolk were still convinced that the Canfield 'witches' were responsible for the Whortons' disappearance. The sheriff wanted nothing to do with the Canfields, so shortly after that he announced his early retirement.

"If the War hadn't arrived and taken most of his deputies, he probably wouldn't have filled out his term. As soon as we all came back from our service commitments, though, he was ready to go.

"I was back on the job all of four months when you stepped in, Lilly. I still shake my head when I think of that phone call from you. 'The sheriff is retiring,' you said. 'I want you to run for the position.'"

"I was looking at the phone, speechless. I had been a deputy for less than one year before the War. Along with my Navy years in the Shore Patrol, those little experiences were hardly qualifying to be the county sheriff."

"You had impressed me, James, during your questioning that first night, but it was the next day that convinced me you were the person for the job. Most of the town believed witches were running amuck. The sheriff was cowering in his office from a small but growing mob that was pressuring him to take action against the Canfields. I was envisioning our own version of Salem breaking out.

"You were level-headed. You marched out into the crowd and calmed the town down with your explanation of what probably occurred. It was not likely that you entirely convinced many of them, but you damped down the passion, and that was enough. I remember you saying, 'Everyone go home where you can be safe with your families. They need you more than we do here. The sheriff has everything under control.'

"Actually," Lilly added, "I'm not certain that the sheriff even had his bladder under control at that point. But I really liked how you were loyal to the sheriff, even as he was fumbling about, and how you were handling the situation for him.

"You did make history as the youngest man ever to be elected sheriff in the state."

"That would not have happened without your help and influence, Lilly. I remain grateful and awed."

"Shoot, James, you are the best thing that ever happened to this county." Taking his arm, she asked, "Shall we go in?"

THE service was scheduled for nine o'clock, and it began promptly. By ten after, the assembled were aware of a loud, steady closing of vehicle doors and tail gates that lasted all the way through the final remarks of Rev. Father Edward Carpenter. Initially, everyone present had expected to see the door-slamming late arrivals join them in the church. Soon it became apparent, though, that something else was afoot. Vehicle doors kept slamming, but the church doors stayed shut. Through the stained glass windows depicting biblical events and saints past, the assembled detected continuous movement, but the distorted etched glass obscured the exact nature of the activity.

When the formal service ended and Fr. Carpenter led everyone into the church cemetery for the final reading, the assembly was astonished. The sun had burned through the morning fog and now beamed on an ocean of color engulfing the cemetery around the upturned dirt at Cora Hostetter's gravesite.

The onlookers gasped and pointed to the floral display as it was being arranged by Stoney's Flowers. They could not have missed it. The flowers, in every color of the rainbow, with dozens upon dozens of varieties, ranged out for forty feet on four sides of the grave, and yet the deliveries continued.

Those in attendance snaked their way through the flowers to get nearer to the coffin. They were surrounded entirely by the vast sea of blooms. A steady stream of men continued hauling more flowers from a long and continuous line of Stoney's Studebaker van fleet supplemented with an irregular assortment of pick-up trucks. The deliveries that began shortly after the service started showed no signs of abating.

It was now nearly ten-fifteen, and the delay continued. Those who had come to pay their last respects had already devoted much more time to the observance than they had expected. Yet there was not a murmur of impatience. They watched in awe and whispered to one another in confusion as the small army of workers filed forward, adding to the display. Fr. Carpenter was so overwhelmed that he had not yet realized the job he was going to face removing the flowers when they wilted several days hence.

Nearby gravestones and those beyond were swamped. Multi-colored azaleas ranged eastward, covering the headstones of Mortimer Maxwell, R.I.P 1836, along with Reginald Cavendish, Husband, b. 1800 d. 1835, and Mary Cavendish, Beloved Wife and Mother, b.1803 d. 1841.

Pink roses, dogwood, redbud, and Florida orchids swallowed the Randolph family grave markers from the Civil War era.

Yellows – daisies, daffodils, black-eyed Susans, forsythia, and sunflowers predominating – fanned west, toward the church, engulfing a line of internments dated from the era of, ironically, a severe yellow fever outbreak in the late 1870s.

Plumbago, dewdrop, and cape honeysuckle turned several markers from more recent times a vibrant blue. The monuments of Capt. Wayne Milton, b. 1881 d. 1918, and his wife Jane, d. 1948, along with those of several Rawlings and Wilitsons, were hidden by hibiscus of nearly every hue – reds and oranges primarily.

With everyone focused on the ever-growing display, no one noticed the solitary figure far back on the outside of the south side cemetery fence. She was dressed entirely in black, but did not stand out, as that was the standard attire for everyone that morning.

Glen Stoney himself drove the final delivery van and helped carry over the last of the flowers. He shook his head when asked who had donated the enormous display.

"I wish that I knew. That is a customer I would like to thank personally and profusely.

"Last evening, someone left a large cardboard box on the florist shop doorstep with stacks upon stacks of money enclosed – the most I've ever seen in one place outside of a bank – and a short note written in old fashioned calligraphy. I nearly stumbled over the box as I was closing up, and I nearly fell over in a faint when I saw what was in it. The note said to supply as many flowers for Mrs. Hostetter's internment as the amount of money would pay for.

"You cannot imagine what we had to do to make this morning's deadline. We emptied florist shops in a seventy-five mile radius and had to borrow trucks and hire drivers and send them out last night to a dozen distant nurseries so they could load up at daybreak. If anyone dies, gets married, or has an anniversary around here in the next several weeks, they will be out of luck. There is not a flower to be had.

"The letter was unsigned, but it instructed us to include this card with the flowers."

He passed around the card, which had been penned in the same graceful script. It read simply, "Your friend."

"We do not know who 'Your friend' is," he added.

Lilly smiled at his comment. She knew.

CHAPTER 11

The Search Continues (Encountering the Witch)

The witch's face was cross and wrinkled,
The witch's gums with teeth were sprinkled.

OGDEN NASH

The four explorers passed the old tool shed and hopped the fence. Blake took it like a hurdler, but the others jumped from a standing position with a hand on top. Mack earned a severe glare from Carty when he reached his hand out to help her. Then she relented slightly, "I'm sorry. I know you didn't mean anything by it, but I like to think I can do anything a boy can do. You can always open doors for me at school, though."

"You are the boss of this expedition, Carty," Mack answered, "Whatever you say is all right with me."

"OK, then, keep your eyes open. We might find some of what we need before we get too deeply into the swamp."

In fact, they added two more rather quickly, and then the swamp engulfed them. Carty said to Mack, "The area around the south fork this morning was really not a swamp. There were some wet areas, but for the most part those were isolated patches of marsh compared with what we will be seeing now. Morose Swamp is on our right, and a small point of Duck Lake will shortly be on our left – you can't miss hearing the duck quacking like earlier this morning.

"The hammock can be narrow at times, and sometimes the drop-off is deep, so stick near to me and don't go venturing too close to the sides. If you see a specimen, just point it out and give me a chance to make sure it's safe to go after it."

"You don't need to tell me twice, Carty."

As she and Mack approached Duck Lake, Carty spotted three moorhens facing one another in a circle. She grabbed Mack's elbow to stop him and spoke in a low voice.

Pointing, she said, "Mack, you've got to see this. Those are moorhens. They are really ducks, not chickens, but they are called hens because the shape of their feet resembles those of chickens. I call them Christmas ducks because of their coloring – not their black body feathers, but the rest. They have red bills and faces, and green feet and legs. If we get close enough, you will see small green tips on their bills. You can't see their legs yet, but you will shortly."

As if on cue, the three ducks leaned over backward so their green feet faced one another. Then each began kicking and splashing water toward the others. They made quite a commotion for several moments.

"You'd think that they were males fighting over a girlfriend, but I've been told that it is the opposite. The girls are fighting over a guy. I don't know what the story really is, but it is one of the funniest displays in the animal kingdom."

When the activity died down, two ducks swam away, and the third emerged from the water and walked toward Mack and Carty, who remained motionless. "It's amazing that they can swim so well. They don't have webs on those green feet. I think the long toes are built for walking on soft marsh and swamp bottoms. They have to lift their legs really high like a scuba diver walking forward while wearing fins."

They continued watching for another minute or so until Blake and Hale each returned with a find.

THEY managed to stay reasonably dry in the afternoon as the later-discovered specimens were more easily accessible than those on the south fork. They needed only the water sundew for the twenty-fourth, and they would be done, having given up on the idea of acquiring the Chapmann's rhododendron.

The four marched briskly along the hammock in single file with Carty on point. She was making a beeline for the fallen tree where she had seen the water sundew. As they got close, she cautioned, "Let's be extra careful around here. We are coming up on the area where the large gator was hanging out. Let's not be surprised. Mack, you and Hale watch right, and I'll watch left with Blake.

She drew an arrow from the quiver, just in case she might need it, but her intention was to avoid contact with the intimidating reptile. Anyway, she was not convinced that even one of her arrows would penetrate the thick leather skin of such a large creature, or do much harm if it did. Nevertheless, she had packed her deadlier heavier arrows in anticipation of heading into the large gator's territory.

After a few dozen yards, she put up a hand. "That log up ahead is where the gator came out of the water. Everyone stay here while I take a closer look."

She walked ahead slowly looking right and left. She had already pointed out a tree with low branches that they could use for an emergency escape in case they encountered the gator. When she reached the fallen tree, she beckoned them forward. They stood in a small circle bathed in sun, rare for a swamp.

"No sign of my friend," she said. Pointing overhead she added, "I did not notice this opening in the canopy that night when I was here before, but this warm spot is probably what draws the gator to the area. It's probably why the sundew grows here too. I thought it odd that a sundew would grow deeply inside a swamp, because they like a little sunlight."

Pointing parallel to the tree trunk, she said, "There's the sundew."

Blake descended from the hammock as Carty kept an eye out for an unwelcome intruder. Knee deep in black mud, he cut off a sample of the plant. He used a helping hand from Hale to extract himself, as the mud clung tenaciously to his boots. Ironically, Carty had an easier time escaping days before, because she had spread out her weight horizontally.

Mack was staring to the left as Blake placed the specimen into the bag on Mack's shoulder. Mack appeared not to notice.

"That is the house where Sally Canfield lives," Carty said when she saw Mack's trancelike demeanor. It did not rouse him. He continued staring. The other three looked at each other and shrugged in wonderment. While they were walking though the swamp this afternoon, Mack was understandably agitated and nervous. Now he was calm, almost catatonic as he stared at the Canfield house.

"Mack," Hale shouted, shaking Mack's shoulder, "What's wrong?"

Coming out of it, Mack replied, "Oh, sorry. Do you see what I see?" he asked.

"Sure, it's the witch's house, only she isn't a witch, remember?"

"No, I don't mean the house. Look to the left of the house, along the fence line that leads to the small shed."

"That's a chicken coop," Carty replied.

"OK, but do you see what is growing along the fence line?"

The three glanced from one another, shrugging in confusion.

"We've no idea, Mack. What's up?"

"Those are Chapmann's rhododendron, the Panhandle variety that does not grow here."

"Are you sure?"

"Absolutely, get my sketch out."

Hale reopened the bag on Mack's back and pulled out his sketch of the Chapmann's rhododendron. They looked from it to the fence line and back to the sketch. After a few more backs and forths, they began to realize the possibility of a major, unexpected discovery.

Finally, Hale said, "It sure looks like it, and if anyone would know for certain, it would be Mack."

"We need to get a specimen," Mack stated boldly. "Let's go ask if we can have one."

"Wait, Mack, aren't you the one who is afraid that Sally Canfield is a witch? Now you want to knock on her door. My Aunt Lilly cautioned me not to bother Miss Canfield, so I don't know about your idea."

"We won't be bothering her," he retorted with a single mindedness that they had not seen in him before. "We can politely ask. If she says no, then we will leave her in peace, but if she says yes, we have our full twenty-five and a guaranteed A. This would be a real coup. To tell you the truth, I want to get all twenty-five to insure that behind us Dolder's group finishes."

Carty smiled at Mack's excited slip in syntax and said, "Why Mack, I had no idea you harbored such a competitive spirit."

"Oh, yes, you did, Carty, especially where Dolder is involved, and you do too."

"You are right about that," she admitted.

As Carty kept scanning for the gator, they discussed it a little more. Finally they agreed to follow Mack's suggestion.

Carty surveyed the area and, farther along to the west, found a dry passage from the hammock to the house. No one was outside the building as they approached, and smoke from the chimney suggested that Sally was inside cooking. Gathering in front of the door, the boys stood back a few steps, and Carty knocked. It was not a lack of courage on their part. They had agreed that Carty might intimidate Sally less than the boys.

After more than a minute, almost two, and after a second more tentative tap on the door, there was no answer. Disappointment set in as more time passed. Mack looked longingly toward the rhododendron, knowing that they were about to leave empty handed. Then the door creaked open to a woman dressed as Carty had seen her several days earlier.

CLOSE up, Sally appeared taller, over six-feet including the high-heeled black boots and pointed hat. She glared at them from one to one. Carty noted the bright green eyes that Aunt Lilly had mentioned. After a few seconds that seemed like minutes to the apprehensive foursome, she spoke.

"Yeeesss?" she greeted in a gritty voice, stringing out the word.

All four took an involuntary, synchronized step backward. The look on Mack's face clearly showed that the rhododendron had dropped several places on his priority list.

Carty cleared her throat and began speaking rapidly. "My name is Carty," and pointing in order, said, "This is Blake, Hale, and Mack. We are on a school project that involves collecting various plant specimens. We have spent the day in the swamp and have gathered all of the samples we need, except for one. We saw that you have some Chapmann's rhododendron along your fence line over there by the chicken coop. That plant is the one we are missing. We were wondering if we could have your permission to cut a small specimen from the plant. We will be careful not to damage it."

Carty had managed to get all of that out without taking a breath, which she took deeply at that point.

Expressionless, Sally looked from one to the other once again, with a penetrating stare. Then she growled, "You will leave now."

The boys began moving back. Blake said, "We're sorry we bothered you. We'll be going now." He took hold of the back of Carty's shirt and pulled her back.

As she began stepping backward, she said remorsefully, "We are very sorry for disturbing you. That was not our intention. My Aunt Lilly told me many times not to bother you. Please accept our apologies."

As the door was about an inch from closing, it stopped momentarily and creaked opened again. Sally looked at Carty. "Your aunt is Lilliquest Andersson who lives east of here?"

"Yes, Miss Canfield. Really, we are sorry that we disturbed you. She told me that we shouldn't."

"You may come in," she announced abruptly, opening the door wider and stepping back so that they could pass. Carty stepped forward tentatively, but the boys stood still. "You too," Sally commanded to them.

"Yes, Ma'am," they said, as the four rushed through the door which Sally slammed shut behind them, dropping the latch. They stood on a well-waxed hardwood floor.

"Your aunt, Miss Andersson, was kind to me in a time of great sorrow," she offered by way of explanation.

"Remove your muddy boots," she instructed, and pointing to the large kitchen table, said, "and sit there." She went to the wood burning stove to attend to the whistling tea pot.

Blake gave Carty a look that suggested that they should make a run for it, but Carty shook her head slightly, unlaced her boots, and led them to the table. They folded their hands and rested them politely on the table edge. Carty looked around.

A mezzanine with a low railing fronted eight rooms on the second floor, probably bedrooms. The high ceilings, massive stone fireplace, and solid wood ceiling beams reminded her of the Ahwahnee Hotel lodge in Yosemite National Park where she and her father had once driven. It was the summer after he returned from the War when gas rationing was cancelled and East Coast residents took to US Routes 40, 66, and other roadways west.

While little light made its way through the shears that obscured the view through the two small first floor windows, ample light streamed from the many larger windows upstairs.

The kitchen where they sat opened to the large room dominated by the fireplace. A large bear rug and several conventional rugs covered most of the solid wood floors. Stuffed heads of various indigenous animals were mounted on the remaining walls. Only the impressive bookshelves, encompassing an entire wall, and battery-powered Crosley radio[20] failed to match that rustic scene.

An old foot-powered Singer sewing machine and several bolts of black cloth occupied a corner of the room.

The only downstairs bedroom was to the left of the fireplace. It appeared to be the room that Sally used.

Carty noticed the absence of plumbing and electricity. A small breeze flowing through screened windows kept the room comfortable, despite the heat from the cooking stove.

They waited nervously while Sally poured tea into the four cups that were already set on the table. After pouring the fifth cup for herself, she returned the pot to the stove and sat down with them. "There is sugar in the bowl and milk in the pitcher. The items on the plate are scones. Help yourselves."

No one reached for anything until Sally added sugar to her tea and drank from her cup. Then they added various combinations of milk and sugar to theirs. Sally reached for a scone and dunked it into her tea. After she took a bite, they followed her lead and each took one.

With slightly less cackle, Sally began, "I enjoy the taste of scones, but they are a little hard for my liking, so I prefer to soften them in my tea. Feel free to do likewise." Again they followed her lead.

"Tell me again what brings you to my house."

Mack surprised even himself by answering. He explained the lab portion of the project, the task of converting scientific names to common names for the plants. He showed her his sketches of the various plants, including the Chapmann's rhododendron. He noted that the reference books claimed that the plant grew only in the Florida Panhandle, so that he was surprised when he saw it growing along her fence line.

She got up from the table and went to the bookcase. She returned, carrying a dog-eared notebook. Inside, written in an old style of English from Colonial times, was a long list describing vegetation. She began in a voice that had softened further.

"The Canfield clan in Florida came by wagon train from New Orleans. Besides a large number of children, there were eight adult family members and two hired hands in that convoy, each driving a wagon.

"You can see that this house was built with a large amount of stone that is not native to the state. Much of it is New Hampshire granite that was transported by ship to New Orleans and included in the first wagon train. The Canfield patriarch, Morgan, could never let go entirely of his deep feelings for New England, despite the ill treatment that originated for the family there.

"They also brought several samples of plants from New England and the Eastern Seaboard, plus some from the Louisiana Bayous. They picked up more that looked interesting as they traveled across what are now coastal Mississippi and Alabama and the Florida Panhandle. That is how the specimen you are looking for came to our land.

"They had no idea what would grow in this climate and what would perish. This book lists all the species that they brought and shows a schematic of our property where each item was planted.

"Most, as you can imagine, died within a few years. You can see the date noted here in the margin whenever a plant died off. A few survived, including your Chapmann's rhododendron, though Morgan's book refers to it as a Panhandle Rhododendron. Of course, the plants that grow here now are descendants of the originals. Before you leave, you may take as many cuttings as you need."

"That is very generous of you, Miss Canfield," Mack replied. Each of them offered thanks in turn.

"I never went to a school or had an assignment like yours. None of us Canfields has. I often wonder what school is like."

That startled them. "But you clearly can read. You had no trouble looking up our rhododendron in the notebook."

"Oh, certainly. I did not mean to imply that we Canfields are uneducated. I have read nearly every book in those bookcases on that wall and on the walls in the bedrooms. They include mathematics, physics, and chemistry textbooks. We have a bible dated from the 1600s, which lists the Canfield history of births, marriages, and deaths, and other editions through one from 1948 that I read now. There are works by Shakespeare,

Adam Smith, Arthur Conan Doyle, Dashiell Hammett, Hemingway, and hundreds – maybe thousands – of lesser authors.

"Each generation of Canfields teaches the next generation. In the early days, there were no schools, so there was no choice. Later, when schools started up, we continued our previous practice of family teaching that had served us well.

"What I meant was that I wonder if it is more difficult to learn in a large group in a school instead of one or two at a time, the way we have done it."

Carty thought momentarily that it must be easier to learn the Canfield way without having to put up with the likes of Haywood Dolder and his ilk disrupting class with stupid comments.

"If you don't mind, Miss Canfield, I have a question on a different subject."

"Go ahead, Carty."

"When we sat down, your table was already set with our cups and saucers, a set for each of us and for yourself – precisely five in all. And you had enough tea already brewing for all of us. How did you know that we would be coming?"

With a voice more like that which she had used when answering the door, she cackled, "Don't you think that we know that sort of thing ahead of time?" A piece of burning wood snapped in the stove, the only sound in the house. Mack's eyes widened, and he spotted an oddly shaped old broom standing in a large round coal bucket. A black cat reclining on the hearth looked up and blinked. Blake examined the door as if planning their escape. Hale and Carty glanced at each other quizzically.

"On the other hand," Sally continued in a soft tone, the slightest smile crinkling the corners of her mouth, "Perhaps I saw you when you left the swamp and headed across the pasture for the house. I was not certain that I was going to let you in, but I wanted to be a gracious hostess if I did. In fact, Carty, I saw you out there one other time a few days ago – when those men were hanging about."

Carty went rigid. She prided herself on her stealthy abilities. It was almost inconceivable that Sally could have detected her.

Sally noticed the shocked look. "You are very good, Carty. Once you consciously went into hiding to avoid the men, I lost track of you entirely. Before that, though, you were more casual, walking along enjoying the surroundings, not attempting to conceal yourself. That is when I saw you. Of course, that clumsy pair is always easy to spot."

"You know that they have been watching you, Miss Canfield?"

"Yes, they have been stumbling and splashing around out there for a couple of weeks or so. Actually, they don't concern me as much as the other fellow. He arrived more recently and appears to be much more capable. In fact, when I did spot him, it was as if he wanted me to see him, as if he were trying to challenge me. I have a feeling that he has not been out there as steadily as the pair."

"Oh, my gosh, have you called the sheriff – oh, you don't have a phone. Have you gone into town to tell the sheriff?"

"No, Carty. I do not want to call attention to myself, and anyway, the swamp is public property. They have as much right to be on it as you do. From what I can tell, they have never trespassed on my land. So what could the sheriff do?"

Carty answered. "I heard the pair talking that evening, Miss Canfield. The one named Damon told the other one that they wanted to make sure that you lived alone. That cannot be for any good reason. My Aunt Lilly thinks that the other one is Clem Hostetter, in case you were wondering."

"I see," she said. "It isn't good to hear that Clem Hostetter is one of the two. Fortunately, they are noisy stalkers, so I should have ample warning if they do decide to venture near."

"I'll say. One of them almost solved the problem for you by lack of awareness. That evening an enormous alligator – it might have been over seventeen feet long – took off after the two of them. They just barely got away. The gator did get Damon's boot, but missed out on the meaty part of the meal."

"The alligator sounds like Montooth. Did you notice one exceptionally large lower tooth sticking up in the front of his mouth when it was closed – sort of like a crocodile's?"

"I noticed a lot of teeth, but they were flashing by me so quickly, I couldn't tell which were on top and which were on the bottom. From my location, Miss Canfield, they all looked exceptionally large, and I don't remember his mouth ever being closed."

Sally smiled at Carty's intensity. "Montooth seldom misses a catch, so these men were truly fortunate, and so were you. He exceeds twenty feet, Carty, and he took my father shortly before I was born. We have always been alert, but Father must have had a lapse in concentration trying to finish mending a fence late one evening. All that my mother and grandmother found were his hat, tools, and the grooved track on the ground where Montooth dragged him into the water."

"I am sorry to hear of your loss," Carty replied sincerely, then added, "I didn't know that a gator could grow as large as twenty feet. I'm lucky he didn't see me out there."

"Duck Lake is Montooth's territory. He keeps the lake population down, except for the ducks. He never eats ducks."

"That seems odd," Carty mused. "Ducks are easy prey for gators. Why wouldn't he go after them?"

Sally responded, "Mack, why don't you go out and get the cutting that you need while I retrieve some hot scones from the oven. When you get back, I'll read *The Legend of Montooth* to you."

Hale jumped up, knowing that Mack would be hesitant going out alone, especially having learned about Montooth. "I'll give you a hand with the cutting, Mack."

By this time, all four had noticed a discernable softening in Sally's voice. It was as if the more secure she became with them, the more comfortable her voice evolved. Carty followed her to the stove. "Let me hold the plate for you, Miss Canfield."

A short time later, Mack and Hale returned to the house, having secured the cutting of Chapmann's rhododendron in the canvas bag. Blake had refilled the cups with hot tea. Fresh baked scones were already on the table. A jar of homemade mixed-berry jam beckoned. With their quest completed, the four began to relax in the strange atmosphere that was becoming less intimidating.

Sally explained that *The Legend of Montooth* was a fable that had been passed down by the Canfield generations for as long as they had been writing the family records in Florida.

"I don't know if the Montooth of today is the original Montooth, or one descended from a long line dating to the original. Nevertheless, he is so much larger than the state wildlife officials believe to be possible for an alligator. I myself have measured his muddy imprint where he had slept at 20.5 feet. That is three feet longer than the largest on the records of the Everglades National Park, and that was several years ago. So there can be no question that he is very old."

Then she retrieved a small, well-worn, leather-bound book from the bookcase. There was no writing on its maroon cover. Sally paged to near the center of the book, moved the ribbon bookmark to that position, and remarked, "This book contains many of the legends that the family has passed down over the century.

"You are fortunate that I will be reading from this version. Grandmother spent many a long evening re-writing the older versions into more current language to make the stories easier to understand in these modern times."

Sally began reading.

The Legend of Montooth

PROLOGUE

The two mallard ducks swam together in slow circles away from the shore of a large Florida lake. The female hen's brown feathers and brown bill blended well with the surrounding marshy vegetation. The feathers of the male, the drake, were more colorful than hers. A thin white ring on his neck separated a dark green head from a deep brown chest. The remaining feathers were light brown, his bill a subdued yellow. Only the red-orange legs of both ducks, currently paddling beneath the black water, were similarly colored, though hers were less vibrant.

The mild morning sun felt good on their backs as they paddled away from the warm lake's reeds and cattails, arcing toward the middle of the lake. She would lay her eggs in a few days, and a new family would hatch later in the spring. This was a serene time before the heavy responsibilities of parenthood took hold. They would not have felt so calm, though, had they been more alert.

Several times, they swam past a long log floating among the reeds. Each swimming circle was slightly larger than the preceding one. Each orbit brought them closer to the log. On the previous loop, the drake swam less than ten inches from the log. On the next loop, the drake would come close enough to brush the end of the log with his feathers.

Because the ducks were concentrating more on each other than on their surroundings, they failed to notice that this log had eyes. For what appeared to be a long, floating tree trunk was actually a long, floating, and very hungry alligator. Each time the ducks moved away from the alligator, she blinked her eyes open, and allowed her mouth to part ever so slightly, barely revealing eighty large, white, and very sharp teeth. Each time the ducks turned to approach, however, the alligator's eyes and mouth closed to avoid alerting the ducks to the increasing danger.

Well out in the lake, the ducks made their final turn, and began heading for the alligator's stalking position. Slowly they swam forward. Unaware of the pending danger, their course remained unchanged.

All of the alligator's senses were alert. Few of theirs were. A very tasty meal was being delivered. She closed her eyes, except for the tiniest little slits. They were swimming straight toward her mouth. She took one slow deep breath and held it so there would be no movement. By waiting patiently, she could time her move perfectly in order to snatch both ducks into her mouth in one powerful swipe.

The drake saw some particularly tender grass under the water and slowed to grab it with his beak. He tugged gently, and its roots loosened beneath the lake. He pulled it from the water. He offered it to his mate. She stopped to savor the tender texture. She smiled a thank you, and they touched the tips of their beaks together. Then they resumed swimming toward the alligator.

The alligator continued exercising patience. The ducks were coming, and nothing would stop them – nothing but a set of very sharp teeth, she expected. However, the short stop to pick and enjoy the tender grass had ruined the alligator's well planned timing. When the pair stopped for that small bite to eat, it changed the schedule just a little too much for the alligator's plan. She had held her breath to match the time when the ducks would arrive according to the original schedule. Because of the delay, she could not hold her breath any longer.

"No matter," she reasoned correctly. "The ducks are too interested in each other to notice me exhaling." With the ducks only a few feet away, she exhaled ever so quietly. She was right; they did not notice, even as the drake reached the alligator's striking area. "Just a few more seconds to allow the hen to get into range as well," she thought.

At that moment, a slight breeze arose. It plucked a

downy feather from the drake's wing and lofted it toward the alligator. She opened her mouth widely to prepare for the bone-crunching snap. However, she had to inhale just as the drake's floating feather brushed her nose. The feather tickled her nose as she inhaled. Her mouth was fully opened, but instead of engulfing the ducks in her vise-strong grip of jaw and teeth, she let out a violent sneeze. "ACHOOOO!"

The enormous explosion of air hurtled the ducks out of the water. As they tumbled skyward, they noticed those eighty scary teeth and rough red tongue and huge bulging eyes. Up and away they turned and twisted until they were able to gain control of their flight and fly to the safety of the shore far from the alligator's lair.

"Paldine, what was that?" Danielle managed to gasp, once her heart stopped pounding.

"I don't know, Danielle – but whatever it was, it was something I hope we never see again."

CHAPTER A

The Babies are Hatched

In Central Florida, the lakes are numerous, and many creatures – some cuddly and others not so much – live in and around that water. The lake in this story is among the larger, so wide that if you stood on the muddy north side, you could not see the sandy bank across on the south side. And it would take an alligator most of a day to swim from the east side to the west side.

Nowadays, the animals living at this lake call it Big Lake, though parrots report that Indians have given Big Lake a different name: Duck Lake. Of all the critters living in the swamp, only parrots can talk to both people and animals. So when the parrots say that people have a different name for Big Lake, the other animals believe it.

This story explains why people call it Duck Lake. Even

175

though humans have their name for Big Lake, they seldom ever venture near. Part of the reason why there are so few visitors is nearby Big Swamp that people call Morose Swamp, a huge quagmire and marshy area adjoining much of Big Lake. There are few houses and no roads near Big Swamp, and in the dry season, humans cannot use boats on the dried up river, so people go elsewhere to more pleasant and hospitable surroundings. For the most part, Big Lake is only for the reptiles, the mammals, and especially the ducks.

The many wondrous creatures in and around Big Lake include some kinds that are more frequently seen in Florida than any other state. Pink flamingos and roseate spoonbills add color to the dark greens and browns of the trees and scrub. Viewed from a long distance, snowy-white egrets perched on tall oak tree branches look like snowballs.

Each of these three types of large birds walks slowly in shallow water looking for small fish, snails, and shrimp to eat. The end of a spoonbill's beak is even shaped like a spoon, so scooping snails and other shell creatures from the muddy bottom is as easy as using a large spoon to scrape out the last noodles from the bottom of a bowl of soup.

In some places, the ground rises slightly above the bordering swamp. In these dry patches of ground, called hammocks, land animals make their homes. Squirrels scurry from tree to tree looking for acorns and other nuts. Rabbits search the underbrush for berries and feast on grasses and occasional clover where a patch of sunlight penetrates gaps in the tree branches. Armadillos, hauling their heavy armor, root through dead leaves and fallen branches for insects and worms, while moles burrow underground looking for the same kind of food.

Raccoons, wearing their sneaky masks, lurk about after dark, stealing bird eggs and prying mollusk shells apart. Large turtles, frogs, and cottonmouth snakes inhabit the lake. Ducks troll Big Lake for tasty vegetation.

Fishermen seldom come to the lake because it is difficult to reach. Thus, the fish grow to enormous size in their old age, and they make an excellent meal for the enormous alligator in Big Lake.

Big Lake has many stories, enough to fill a library. This is one of those stories, one that happened a long time ago. The story is a little scary in some parts, so be wary. But many other parts are joyful and heartwarming. You will meet several of the animals already mentioned. The story takes place near a community of mallard ducks. The ducks call their home Mallard Village.

In late afternoon on a warm day, the mighty alligator laid her eggs in the sand along the edge of Big Lake. Every year, she chose the same place for her nest, near the largest and oldest cypress tree in the swamp. She always looked forward to seeing her young hatch, climb around the tree roots, and swim beneath huge overhanging branches.

The temperatures were unusually hot that winter and early spring, even for Florida, so she knew that she would have all sons. If her alligator eggs were kept very warm, boy alligators would hatch. If the temperature stayed cool, she expected the hatchlings to be girls. If the temperature were in between, there would be a mixture of boys and girls. She liked it best when she had a mixture, but all girls or all boys were always fun too.

Soon, she would lead her newest children on swims and teach them to hunt for fish, fowl, and other food. Hers was a quiet life, enjoying a new family every year. Alligators do not think far into the future as people do, so she never thought that this life might change. But, sadly for her, big change was on its way.

In Florida, the storms usually come from the west, and the hurricanes from the east. The worst storms are usually in the summer and early autumn, whether they are fierce thunderstorms or hurricanes. But this year, something unusual happened. Because the hot temperatures came early, a terrible late spring thunderstorm broke out. It began when a sudden thrust of cool air from the northwest crashed into hot, humid air resting near Florida's West Coast. At first, the mixing air stalled over the Gulf of Mexico.

Though that delayed the arrival of the storm on land, it made things worse. The longer that the cold and hot air kept merging, the stronger the storm grew. After two days, the storm began easing eastward. On a line from Tampa Bay southward to Naples, it picked up speed and intensity. Quickly, the wind and rain roared inland. This storm was to become the worst storm in fifty years, even worse than many of the hurricanes that swept into Florida from time to time.

At Big Lake, the dark clouds were off in the distant skies, but already the air smelled of moisture and electricity. Tree branches began swaying, and dry leaves blew in circles. Spanish moss swirled on tree branches like loose necklaces on dancers.

The animals took cover, for they knew that bad weather was on the way. Ground animals ran for their burrows, and birds sought the protection of the hollows in dead tree trunks. Only the fish were not worried, for they could swim deeply into Big Lake where even the worst wind would not affect the water.

Before long, lightning flashed brightly in announcement that the storm had arrived. Wind howled and rain whooshed down so hard that the drops were painful to animals not completely covered. Blowing debris forced the animals to keep their eyes shut. Waves from Big Lake pounded the sandy soil around the alligator eggs.

Fortunately, the alligator knew what to do. She had been in many storms in her long life. Carefully, she eased her body between the water's edge and her eggs. The water splashed over her from head to tail, but her long body protected the eggs beneath the sand from the relentless pounding waves. For hours, the windy, wet violence continued, but her eggs were safe.

After almost an entire night of howling, the wind died down briefly, suggesting that the worst of the storm had passed. The sun had already risen, though the clouds were so black with water, no daylight shone through. Then, without warning, the fiercest of all lightning bolts pierced the darkness. The brilliant flash struck the largest limb of the old cypress tree. For a few seconds, the entire swamp appeared to be lit with kerosene lamps.

The mother alligator heard the thunderous snap. She smelled the burning wood and electric odor. But the bright flash momentarily blinded her. So she did not see the huge branch as it broke away from the tree trunk and fell heavily on top of her.

The deafening noise from the fallen wood lasted but a moment. Then the rain let up and an eerie silence came over the swamp. Slowly, the alligator's limp, dead body slid into Big Lake and drifted away from the nest.

The storm seemed to realize that the alligator was no longer in the nest protecting her eggs, because the wind regained its strength and forced the attacking waves deeper and deeper into the sandbank. One by one, the buried eggs were exposed. One by one, they began breaking apart. In just minutes, all the eggs were destroyed – all but one. That remaining egg, slightly larger than the others, was partially protected by the roots of the same cypress tree that had taken the life of the mother alligator.

No matter how hard the storm tried to break through, the roots held firm. It was as if the tree wanted to save the last egg to atone for what its branch had done to the alligator. In the early morning hours, the storm tried one last violent assault, and then failing, blew itself out. The egg was safe from the storm, but the prospects for the egg were not promising. The egg could not hatch without the warmth of the hot sun on the protecting sand.

In a short time, the dark clouds lightened, then raced off to the east. The sky turned sunny and clear. Cotton-white cloud balls floated above. The air was clean.

Nearby, the mother mallard duck, Danielle, emerged from the thick reeds and cattails. Her brown feathers glistened in the bright sunlight. She shook her head to send a few water droplets flying. Danielle had been awake all night protecting her eggs, and she needed a short time to relax in the warm sun and a few bites of food to eat.

She swam out past the cattails to the edges of Big Lake where she found succulent plants. Slowly, as she continued enjoying her snack, she floated back toward her nest, past the old cypress tree. There she saw an egg snared in its roots.

"How did my egg get out here?" Danielle wondered. "I was very careful during that terrible storm." She paddled over to the egg. The old cypress tree that had held tightly to that egg during the storm was happy to loosen its grip for Danielle. Carefully, she nudged the egg with her beak along the sand, through the reeds, and into her nest with the other seven eggs.

Duck moms are gentle and caring. They are capable swimmers and graceful flyers. But one thing that they are not good at is arithmetic. So Danielle did not notice that her family of seven eggs had grown to a family of eight. In the weeks that passed, she kept all of the eggs warm until they began to hatch.

Then, on a sunny morning, tiny beaks began pecking away at the inside of the eggshells. Soon, little heads followed the beaks, and then wet little bodies climbed out and quacked for their momma. Within a few hours, Danielle had seven cute, fluffy, yellow ducklings. She also had one sharp-toothed, leathery, green duckling with one particularly long bottom tooth that showed prominently toward the front of his smile.

Danielle had never had a leathery green duckling before. Once she had a duckling with just one leg, and another time she had one with all white feathers. Though different, those children had been among her more loved. "A green-colored duck is just something to make life more interesting," she thought. "Besides, he matches his father's neck feathers."

Anyway, all of the eight ducklings liked each other. Oh,

sure, they had little disagreements once in a while, but they always made up afterward. Green Duck, being the biggest and the strongest, was always careful around his brothers and sisters so that he did not hurt them.

CHAPTER B

The Success and the Failure

One thing that all ducks are proud of is their swimming ability. Ducks can swim the first day after hatching, their little webbed feet acting as efficient propellers. Of course, it takes quite a while before a duckling can swim as fast as an adult. But in less than a week, Green Duck could swim faster than Danielle. No young duck had ever swum that well, but then, no duck had ever used a swishing tail technique.

Every morning, Danielle arranged her ducklings in single file and led them into Big Lake. Green Duck always stayed last in line to make sure none of his brothers or sisters fell behind and got lost, especially Millard, who was a little clumsy and the worst swimmer in the village.

Danielle grew to love Green Duck's shiny "feathers" as much as the soft brown and tan feathers emerging from her other ducklings. She thought it interesting that Green Duck liked to eat little fish and tadpoles instead of the plants that she and her other children favored. But most of all, she loved his huge, bright, white, toothy smile that her other children did not have.

Paldine was most proud of Green Duck's swimming ability. Green Duck sliced through the water like a bird through the air. In the summer duck races, he finished so far ahead of all the other ducks that he had time to turn around and cheer those who followed him to the finish line. No one had ever seen such speed. He was still very young, but now he was swimming faster, indeed much faster than all of the adult ducks.

His brothers and sisters were happy for him, but some of the other young ducks in the village were jealous. In particular, Drack, who always finished second in any race with Green Duck, loathed him. No matter how much Green Duck tried to be friendly, Drack always refused the welcoming gesture.

Occasionally, other duck moms would comment, not generously, that a green duck is an odd duck, especially when this big green duck won all the swimming races against their children. But Paldine's loud quacking and noisy wing-flapping always put a stop to such talk.

The day finally came that all the ducklings were waiting for, the day that they were no longer ducklings, the day that they would feel like grown-up ducks – it was flying day. They had studied hard for the past weeks and all were convinced that they could fly like their moms and dads.

One by one they tried, and one by one they lifted off the water – wobbly at first – but soon nearly as smooth as any adult duck. Even Millard, after several unsuccessful attempts, climbed awkwardly skyward. By day's end, all of the ducks were flying smoothly – all except Green Duck.

No matter how much he tried to flap his front legs, he could succeed in only churning up the water like a side-wheeler on the Mississippi River. Some of the other parents, those who had envied his swimming ability, rejoiced at his failure to fly. They were led by Drack's mother, Hannah, a particularly haughty hen. They laughed and jeered cruelly at his inability to rise even a few inches above the water surface.

Paldine gave Green Duck private lessons. In desperation, he suggested flapping all four of his limbs, but that succeeded only in churning up more water. After several days of intensive effort from both tutor and student, Paldine confided to Danielle.

"I have explained to Green Duck that his swimming speed seems to take away his ability to fly. He is destined to spend his life in the water, Danielle, not the air. He needs you to console him."

So she sought him out. He was resting under the old cypress tree. An unusual sadness darkened his face. His toothy smile was gone. Only the prominent bottom tooth showed.

She put a wing over Green Duck, and together they swam to a small cove to talk privately. At first they said nothing, content just being together. Then Danielle spoke.

"I'm afraid that you are not destined to fly, my son," she said. "Although you are a swift swimmer, you are too heavy to get into the air. I know that you have tried your very best. You have worked as hard as possible. Your father and I are proud of your efforts. But you will have to stay near our home instead of flying as your brothers and sisters do. It is important that you always remember that we all love you for who you are, not for what you can or cannot do."

Later, his brother Millard climbed on to Green Duck's back, gave him a big hug around the neck, and spoke with him.

"It doesn't matter that you cannot fly, Green Duck. Look at me. I am the slowest swimmer in Big Lake. You always had to cheer me on well after every other duck had passed the finish line. Some of us are good at one thing, and some of us are good at another thing. And some of us are not particularly good at anything.

"I wish that I could be the best at something rather than mediocre at everything. And you are the fastest swimmer in the village, maybe in the history of the village. Be proud of that."

Unfortunately, not all the other ducks were so loving and understanding. The mothers who had been so jealous about Green Duck's swimming ability were secretly pleased to find something to criticize.

Drack riled up the other ducklings who had lost swimming races to Green Duck. They joined in with crude remarks, first only whispering among themselves, but later, speaking more loudly and boldly so that Green Duck and his brothers and sisters could not help but overhear.

Several arguments broke out over the next several days as Green Duck's siblings rose to his defense. Millard especially fought to protect Green Duck's reputation, and he suffered the most. His flying was temporarily suspended after Drack and two others jumped him. They damaged his right wing, and only Green Duck's arrival and steely glare put an end to the melee.

CHAPTER C

The Leaving

Green Duck could easily have defended himself, for he was by far the strongest duck. But he had a gentle and forgiving disposition, and he rushed in to stop several other fights. "Please, no more fighting," he called to his family, "Come home with me." Over and over, the rabble-rousers laughed and chanted as Green Duck led his siblings away:

> "Green Duck is a land duck,
> but he cannot fly.
> Green Duck's good in water,
> but he can't reach the sky."

Though the nasty words did not bother Green Duck, he could not bear to see how the remarks hurt his family. That night he told them that he would go away to avoid further strife and bad feelings.

"No, no," they cried, "You stay here forever. You can't leave us." So to calm them, he stopped talking about leaving. But he had made up his mind. For the next several days, he spoke with all of his friends and family, reminding them of a good experience or funny incident that they had shared. Then one night, after everyone was asleep, he swam quietly away.

When the sun rose the next day, it was quite a while before the family realized what had happened. Millard noticed first.

"Momma, I think that Green Duck left us. He has not been here all morning. I have searched the cattails and the mud flats and all the other places where he could be, and there is no sign of him. I am so sad."

Everyone was shocked and had empty feelings in their stomachs that lunch did not help. The children sobbed. "Remember how Green Duck gave us rides on his cool back?" they recalled. Even as a youngster, he had been strong enough to carry them all on fast swims around Big Lake.

Paldine tried to keep up their spirits. "He is a big boy, and he is growing fast. He will be all right. Maybe we will see him on our flying trips someday. Then we can ask him to come back."

Danielle missed him the most, more even than Millard, but she kept her feelings hidden from the children to spare them more sadness. Still, on quiet windless evenings, if one looked at her closely, there often appeared tiny circles in the water where large duck tears fell.

Meanwhile, the nasty duck families smiled smugly and spoke among themselves. "The village is a better place with Green Duck gone," they assured one another, though no one could really think of a reason why this would be true. Drack was particularly pleased as he was now the fastest swimmer.

CHAPTER D

The Discovery

After a few years on the far side of Big Lake, Green Duck was lonely. He missed his momma and his daddy. He wished that he could let his brothers tickle his long red tongue again. One time he saw three of his sisters flying well above the treetops, but they were looking the other way and did not notice him.

As he swam along the bank, a frog jumped from lily pad to lily pad. He watched it leap on to a log. Then the log's eyes opened. For a moment, he thought he was seeing his reflection in the water. Slowly, he circled. No, this green duck was slightly larger and much older than he was.

He swam closer and called out, "Hello there, duck. My name is Green Duck. What is yours?" "Alex," replied the ancient alligator, "But I am not a duck. I am an alligator. Why

192

do you have a duck name instead of an alligator name?"

"Because I am a duck, not an alligator," replied Green Duck. "I don't even know what an alligator is. I have never even seen an alligator."

"Well you have seen one now," said Alex. "I am an alligator just like you. See, we both have sharp teeth, and ducks have none. We have four strong legs, and ducks have two thin legs and two wings. We have tough leathery skin, and ducks have soft fluffy feathers. We can't fly, and ducks can."

Green Duck was dubious at first, but Alex did make a lot of sense. "I can swim fast, but it is true that I can't fly. I do look a lot different than my brothers and sisters," he admitted. He decided that Alex must be right. He was not a duck. This was a shock, but it explained a lot.

"That's why I can't fly. I am an alligator," he shouted happily. He swam in rapid circles hollering, "I'm not a duck; I'm not a duck; I'm an alligator!" The water splashed wildly about, as squirrels and rabbits and a big red fox jumped up on trees and rocks to view the spectacle. Birds lost momentary interest in searching for food and turned to watch.

Alex was becoming a little embarrassed at all the commotion. "All right, all right, calm down. It's no big deal being an alligator. We have our way of life, and ducks have theirs; that's all. So please stop acting so crazy. We alligators have to maintain a dignified station, and you are not keeping up your end."

"I will, if you teach me what alligators do. Will you please? I only know what ducks do. Please, please, please."

"Yes, I will, I will. Just calm down."

"How could I be so confused, though? If I am an alligator, why did I think that I was a duck? And why does everyone in Mallard Village think that I am a duck?"

"Hmm, that is a mystery. Let me think about it." Alex swam away with a thoughtful look on his face. After a while, he swam back to Green Duck.

"Well, this is how I figure it. Alligators come from eggs, and so do ducks and birds. Sometimes I have seen a mother cowbird lay her eggs in another bird's nest. That way she doesn't have to care for her own child, because some other bird mom does the work for her. Maybe an alligator mom was too busy to take care of her own egg, so she laid it in a duck nest when the mother was away."

"What you said might be right," Green Duck replied. "There were so many of us hatching at one time – maybe Momma never noticed an extra egg."

Alex continued, "Anyway, I have been watching you for some time, Green Duck. You just never noticed me. That is one of the alligator things I will teach you. We alligators notice everything, but we are so quiet that other swamp critters often fail to notice us. But you already know some alligator tricks. I've noticed how silent you are when you go fishing, for instance.

"There are some things that you need help with, though. For example, your hunting skills are terrible. Many times I see you pass by a perfectly good duck meal. And turtles are tasty, and they are slow and easy to catch, though they are a little crunchy. There are lots of other good things to eat in the swamp and in the lake. If you would like, I will help you learn the things you do not know."

"You are very kind, Alex. Yes, please teach me everything. I love to learn new things, so I will be an excellent pupil. But one thing I will not do is eat ducks, and you have to promise me one thing – that you will not eat ducks either."

"Uh-oh, I don't think I can agree to that. Ducks are yummy and really fun to catch."

"I really want to learn, Alex, but if you will not grant me that one wish, I will leave."

Alex had been alone for many years since his mate died. He was old and lonely, and he liked this youngster with the funny big tooth. He thought for a long while. "All right. There is plenty of other food. I suppose I can do without duck from now on, but how about geese? They come every winter, and they are tender and juicy."

"Geese are fine, Alex."

"Oh, good. I love Canadian food. Then we have a deal. Let's get started."

Green Duck was a superb student. For the next few years, he studied under Alex's tutelage. Green Duck learned to be the quietest creature in the swamp, for that is the best way to hunt and fish. Sometimes, egrets and other swamp animals actually walked on his back, thinking he was a log or a rock. When that happened, though, it tickled too much, and his giggling gave him away. Alex always chuckled when the startled animals shot off Green Duck's back. "There is such a thing as being too quiet," Alex would say.

Green Duck grew to an enormous size as he feasted on many new types of tasty food. Soon he was heavier and longer than Alex was. Several years later, after Alex had passed away, Green Duck had grown into the largest alligator ever to swim in Big Lake.

CHAPTER E

The Terror

Meanwhile, Green Duck was only a distant memory for most of the ducks in the far away village. Besides, the ducks were thinking about other more important things – things like disappearing youngsters. After a night passed, a young duck was often missing the next morning. One day a duck was there; the next day she was gone. Another day a duck would swim into the reeds; that night he did not come home.

Every time a duck was reported missing, the ducks' Council of Elders sent out a search party. The searchers found no signs of what was happening to these ducks. Sometimes they discovered a few scattered feathers, but nothing more.

The mystery continued. The missing ducks were too young to leave on their own. Yet, night after night, day after day, another duck, and sometimes two, disappeared. The duck parents were terrified. Who would be next, and why?

Young ducks were warned to stay close to their nests, especially at night. "No one is to go out alone," parents told their young. But youngsters sometimes think that danger does not affect them – only someone else – so some young ducks still slipped away for nighttime exploration. And each night, another duck or two disappeared. Millard asked if human hunters were responsible. Humans seldom visited Big Lake, and certainly not for an extended period of days, but every idea had to be considered.

However, Matthew, the oldest and wisest duck, said that there is always a loud noise like a tree branch breaking when a hunter takes a duck. "And we have heard no noise like that. No, this threat is quieter, sneakier, and more sinister than when a human hunter is involved."

So the Council of Elders established the No Venture Rule. Under this regulation, no young ducks were allowed to venture out alone until the mystery was solved. By this time, even the youngest, bravest, and most foolish ducks were afraid. All were more than willing to comply with the rule. During the next week, no ducks ventured out, and no more ducks disappeared. The mystery had not been solved, but the new rule appeared to be working well.

Just when the ducks were beginning to regain their confidence, their worst fears became real. It began on a quiet spring evening. The wind died down and the hot afternoon passed into a foggy, warm night. The ducks were asleep – even the momma ducks sitting on their recently laid eggs. A few ducks began to stir nervously in their sleep, not knowing why, but instinctively on edge. Then, without warning, loud quacking and flapping noises spilled out of the reeds at the north edge of the village. An unseen danger, perhaps the cause of the disappearances, might now be known.

The lake water churned with wild splashing. "RACCOONS! RACCOONS!" came the cry from the young momma duck under attack, as a large group of raccoons swarmed around her, snapping their teeth and slashing their claws.

Now it was clear why the ducks had been disappearing. Raccoons had been sneaking into the village under the protecting darkness. Their eyes are especially suited for night vision, as they peer through dark masks. Night after night, they had been killing and eating young ducks. The raccoons were confident and strong, and they were hungry not only for ducks, but also for newly laid duck eggs, raccoons' favorite food.

The Council of Elders' new rule had cut off the raccoons' easy food supply, because ducks stopped venturing out of the village. That made the raccoons angry and greedy – so angry and greedy that they became receptive to the plans of Moosta, an enormous and vicious raccoon.

"We have had easy success attacking lone ducks at

night," Moosta had exhorted earlier that day, "And we can use tactics we have perfected making quick night assaults on the village. Just because the ducks are staying within the village is no reason for us to give up on good duck food."

Before the other ducks could even get their thoughts together, the raccoons killed the momma duck and dragged her away, scooping up all of her eggs as they raced back into the woods. Moosta stopped to cast an arrogant glance back at the shocked ducks that had witnessed the attack.

So, with Moosta's leadership, the raccoons became more brazen, certain that they could charge in unopposed. They no longer cared that the ducks had learned the cause of the disappearances. But that overconfidence was foolhardy. With this new information, the ducks could plan defensive action.

After the raccoons retreated, the ducks murmured among themselves, unsure of what to do. The Council of Elders gathered near the shore for an emergency meeting. When they finished, Matthew climbed atop a fallen tree. He motioned for everyone to quiet down and to gather.

"Based on prior actions, we are confident that the raccoons will not be back tonight," he announced. "They have taken enough to satisfy their lust for a day. Tomorrow, we will establish a plan for the defense of the village.

"Many years ago, when I was a young duckling, several raccoons attacked us. At that time, the Council of Elders devised a plan to defend the village. We do not have to worry if we follow that same plan. Raccoons do not work well together. They are too selfish. That is their weakness. By tomorrow night we will be ready to use their weakness against them."

Ducks had always been good planners. However, Moosta was soon to gain a secret ally to gain an unfair advantage.

During the night prior to the No Venture Rule, Drack witnessed an attack on a young duck who had strayed from the village. Drack's nest was close by, but he offered no help. As he cowered in the darkness, not moving a feather to help, he saw Moosta and two other raccoons slash the neck of his friend and drag the hapless creature away.

The next morning, Drack debated with himself whether or not to tell the Elders what he had seen. Instead, he decided to keep quiet to see if he could gain anything from his knowledge. Besides, he could come up with no excuse for being so cowardly.

As soon as Drack heard Matthew's report, he decided to make his move. Ignoring the No Venture Rule, he took advantage of the remaining daylight to fly into the interior of the swamp where the raccoons lived. For several hours, he waited on a tree branch above until he saw a raccoon on the ground.

Drack mustered up every bit of his limited courage and called out, "I have something important to tell your leader.

You would be wise to report my visit to him."

The raccoon was bewildered and had difficulty comprehending that a duck would risk himself by flying into enemy territory. He looked around to be certain that he was not in the midst of a trap. Seeing no other ducks, he debated sneaking up the tree for a quick meal instead of complying with the duck's request.

While he debated, Drack said, "I saw your leader in Mallard Village. Unless he speaks with me, he will run into serious trouble soon, and he will not like that you failed to alert him to my warning."

That settled the question. With fear of Moosta overcoming his lust for duck meat, he raced off to advise his leader of the visitor's presence.

After a short time, Moosta and two lieutenants, Dool and Mockhead, arrived, treading warily under the strange circumstances. "I see you down there," Drack whispered from his high perch. The two lesser raccoons jumped at the sound, but Moosta merely looked upward with practiced calm.

"Perhaps you do," he said, "But we can climb trees, and you are too large to fly through these low lying branches in the dark. You would be certain to break a wing. I would say you were not smart to alert us to your presence, but we do want to thank you, for we are always hungry."

His lieutenants nodded rapidly and said, "Yeah, Moosta, yeah, yeah."

Moosta backhanded Dool, the nearest one. "Shut up. Let's hear what he has to say before we eat him. By the way, what is your name?"

"Oh, you do not want to eat me, Moosta. I know something that can help you, but I want something in return. My name is Drack."

"Well, Drack, what could you know that would be more valuable than the good meal you represent?"

"You have had some success against us recently, but only because we did not suspect that you raccoons were the source of the losses. Now that the Elders have learned that you are behind the disappearances, they know how to stop you.

"With the new No Venture Rule, you will be forced to attack into the village, and you will face the defense the Elders design. However, I know their strategy, and I am willing to trade it to you."

"Let's eat him," Mockhead said, scrambling toward the tree.

With three quick steps, Moosta had him by the tail and flung him to the ground. "Hold up until I give the word. Let me think."

"If I agree," he asked Drack, "How do I know if the information is any good?

"If it is not useful to you, you can consider the agreement void. I cannot get away, so you have nothing to lose."

"Fair enough. But what is it that you want in return?"

"If I give you the information, you will be able to take the village. When it is over, I want you to allow me to select twenty ducks of my choosing to repopulate the village under my leadership. I will become Supreme Ruler and do away with the Council of Elders. I will keep you provided with a regular supply of ducks and eggs from that point forward."

"That is a plan I could like from a mind I could admire," Moosta replied. "Come down, Drack. We have to trust each other."

Drack recognized this invitation as the moment of truth. If Moosta allowed him to live, he would become Supreme Ruler of the village. Was it worth the risk? He flapped down to the ground, flanked by the three raccoons. "Now we eat him?" asked Mockhead, who was still smarting from the tail flinging.

"No, you fool. We have an agreement with our new friend here – provided the information is good. Let's hear it, Drack."

Drack explained what he had learned from the Elders. The duck safety strategy has historically relied on the lack of organization within the raccoon ranks. Raccoons were stronger than ducks and possessed more lethal weapons in their claws and teeth. However, as long as the raccoons worked in their small independent groups, the ducks could concentrate a strong force to fight them off. On the other hand, if Moosta could coordinate all of the raccoons into a combined, well-organized, and disciplined attack, the ducks would be overwhelmed.

Moosta acknowledged that the information was valuable. He agreed to allow Drack to return to the village and to support Drack's coronation as Supreme Ruler.

As the three raccoons turned to leave, Mockhead grumbled, "We got his information. I still think we should have eaten him."

With a sly smile, Moosta replied, "Oh, we will. We will."

CHAPTER F

The Raccoon Camp

The next morning, in the raccoon camp, the feasting was over, though not everyone had eaten his fill. They had retreated with only the one duck and without gathering enough eggs. "We should have killed more ducks and dragged them back here," shouted a still hungry raccoon, "Then all of us would have had enough to eat."

Moosta recognized his opportunity. He climbed up the side of a tree and called out for silence. He was about to get the raccoons under his complete control. "Eggs are the best, and duck meat is good too. Soon we will get both, and we will get so much that our bellies will be full to bursting. I have inside knowledge that will allow us to take over the entire Mallard Village."

General murmurs of support soon deteriorated into raging

206

shouts and demands for immediate action. "Let's go tonight; no, let's go now." A few raccoons started running wildly toward Mallard Village. The troop was on the verge of becoming a typically disorganized raccoon mob. Moosta jumped to the top of a tree stump. "Halt," he yelled. To get their attention, he smacked the closest raccoon, sending him flying across the field into a painful heap against a spiny palm.

"We achieved outstanding success in last night's attack, but only because the ducks did not expect us. Now they know who we are. We no longer are an unknown risk that has confused them and served us so well. To win the entire war, however, we need better tactics.

"For many years, we were held back because we were not yet perfectly organized. Nor did we train hard enough beforehand. These have led to the raccoon downfall throughout our history, but soon it will be different.

"I have been meeting with the two other raccoon camps in the swamp. They learned what we did last night, and they have agreed to band together with us to form a huge army. I will meet now with leaders from each camp at the hollow tree. I will establish a well-disciplined plan this time, and we will train for it and execute it under my direction. Does anyone have a problem with that?"

No one dared to object, for all the others feared Moosta, and besides, the idea made sense.

As the leadership of the three bands of raccoons began

congregating, they looked from side to side to be sure that no one could overhear their plans. All appeared clear. But the raccoons failed to look up, or they might have noticed Penny, a green parrot with a small splash of yellow on her wings.

Last night, from afar, Penny had seen the meeting between Moosta, his lieutenants, and Drack. She was not close enough to hear the conversation, but was intrigued that a duck managed to survive such a gathering. She made it a point to stay in the vicinity of the raccoon village to satisfy a growing curiosity.

For several hours, the group met and devised its sneak attack. Each army division would have its assigned position. They would encircle Mallard Village and charge in from three sides on Moosta's signal, then trap the ducks against the lake. Emboldened by recent success, and employing the tactics needed for a large attack, the raccoons expected to finish off Mallard Village in a surprise coordinated night attack.

The leaders returned to their camps and announced the battle plan. It seemed to make sense, though it was against raccoon nature to fight together as a large cohesive group.

After they departed, Penny lofted high into the night sky and glided silently toward Mallard Village.

CHAPTER 12

The Sermon

Waste not; want not.

EIGHTEENTH CENTURY PROVERB

Sally paused and looked out of the window. "It is getting late. The sun has nearly set. Perhaps we should pause here so that you four can go home. Surely you do not want to be in my house in the dark," she added mischievously.

By this time, even Mack smiled at her challenge. "I think that for us your house is safe, Miss Canfield. Hansel and Gretel we are not, and your oven is not large enough for all of us anyway. On the other hand, I am not too certain the night creatures outside are as harmless, so moving along at this point sounds like a good idea."

Carty added, "It isn't the wildlife we need to worry about, Mack. It's

209

riding our bikes and dodging auto traffic on Mocking Bird Road in the dark. That road gets busy in the early evening when people are driving home from work.

"Miss Canfield, we'd really like to hear the rest of the story, but you're right. We should get going while there is still some daylight. Could we come back some time to hear the rest of the story?"

"Would tomorrow afternoon be a good time for the four of you?"

They all nodded their heads emphatically, and Hale added, "Actually tomorrow is a perfect time. We had already planned to return to the swamp tomorrow afternoon if we still needed to find some specimens. Since you helped us with our last find, we have the entire afternoon off."

"Very well then, intrepid explorers, let's say about one-thirty. And Carty, may I ask a favor?"

"Certainly, Miss Canfield."

"Could you bring your bow back when you come? I'd like to see you demonstrate it when we finish the story."

"I'd be happy to, Miss Canfield. We can set up a target against your barn. I'll even give you a lesson."

Sally turned down their offer to help clean the dishes, so they gathered their belongings and the specimen bag, expressed their thanks, and departed. They half walked and half jogged to make better time in the failing light and were soon past the Hostetter house. The old Ford was still parked where it had been in the morning, but the house was dark and it appeared unoccupied.

Actually, it was unoccupied because Dredman and Hostetter were still in the swamp peering at Sally's house. Earlier, Carty had nudged

Blake and cocked her head toward the intruders as they hurried along. She did not want to make Mack any more nervous than he was already by alerting him to the two men.

At Carty's house, Bay had removed the first batch of freshly baked Toll House cookies from the oven and had them cooling on the window sill. The second batch, her special recipe, was not quite ready.

"Hi, Mom," Carty called, as they clomped through the door.

"Everyone to the kitchen, Carty. There are plenty of cookies and milk to spoil your dinners," Bay called wryly.

"Hi, Mrs. Andersson," the boys greeted as they lined up at the sink to wash their hands.

"We had a great time," Hale added. "Even Mack seems to like the swamp now."

"We must not so far go as that, Mrs. Andersson," Mack rejoined, "but with these escorts I did become by the end more comfortable."

As they sat around the table and enjoyed Bay's treat, she asked, "How did it go? Did you find what you needed?"

Carty described how the morning set up the successful day, heaping praise on Mack's ability to locate the specimens despite conditions that were especially intimidating for him. She mentioned their lunch at Aunt Lilly's, and how much the boys liked the homemade spread that she had supplied.

She explained that by early afternoon, they had snared the twenty-fourth specimen, the sundew, out of the twenty-five on the list. Carty commented that they found the sundew near where the north fork came upon the Canfield house.

"We thought we were finished. The last item is Chapmann's rhododendron. The books say that it grows only in the Florida Panhandle, so we were not even looking for it. Then Mack, our resident expert, spots some Chapmann's from half a football field away, growing right next to the Canfield house. We know that we aren't supposed to bother Miss Canfield, but we really wanted a sample of that plant. We are not allowed to pilfer a specimen, but we can ask for permission.

"With more than a little hesitancy, we approached the house and knocked. Wow, Miss Canfield was really frightening when she answered the door. She was dressed all in black, and she even had on a pointed hat that looks like the kind of hat the witch wore when she was scaring Dorothy in Oz."

Hale jumped in. "She was about to slam the door and send us packing when Carty happened to mention her Aunt Lilly. Gosh, that opened the door in more ways than one. Evidently, Miss Canfield recalls a kindness that Miss Andersson performed for her, so she let us in.

"What a house she has. There must be as many books in it as the county library has. Some looked to be hundreds of years old, especially the bibles and other religious texts and a first edition of Adam Smith's "Wealth of Nations" from 1776. And there are many recent books too. I even recognized a book on agriculture by Booker T. Washington that we have in our house. The house is built with New England granite and slate that the original Canfield – Morgan – brought in by wagons in the early 1700s.

"Miss Canfield could not have been nicer," Blake added. "She fed us some scones from an old family recipe handed down from the Scottish side of her family. Most importantly, she let us cut a sample of the Chapmann's rhododendron. Apparently, the original plant had been picked up by Morgan Canfield when he trekked through the Panhandle centuries ago."

Opening the canvas bag, he took out the wilting sample. "It's not much to look at, but it is just what we needed."

"You know," Mrs. Andersson interrupted, looking at the deteriorating condition of the plant cutting, "I am going to get you some wax paper and an iron so you can preserve all of your specimens. You can tell me the rest of your story afterward."

Carty arranged the boys into an assembly line to efficiently extract each specimen and press it under the wax paper with a towel-protected steam iron. Mack finished by neatly printing the name of the specimen and, with Elmer's Glue, affixed his sketch to the top right-hand corner of each page.

Carty motioned Hale and Blake aside, and they whispered briefly amongst themselves. Mack was so engrossed with final touches to the last specimen page that he did not notice the small conference or the three heads nodding.

Carty took a pen and paper and scribbled on it. "Here, Mack, print this out as our title page." She handed the following caption to him:

TWENTY-FIVE SPECIMENS
Rare Florida Flora
By The Crew

As he reached the "ew" in the last word, he looked up. "But I'm not a member of The Crew," he said.

"Well," Blake replied, "It's true that you are not a charter member, but we have just elected you as an associate member. Congratulations. We are proud to have you aboard." They shook his hand and clinked milk glasses together in a celebratory toast.

Bay slipped a fresh batch of Toll House cookies from the oven. As usual, Bay had formed each cookie into an oval shape for easier dunking into a glass of milk. For this batch, she added a generous supply of Sun Maid golden raisins to the chocolate chips. The Crew savored the delightfully different taste sensation while Carty resumed the narrative of the day's activities.

"Then Miss Canfield told us part of a story that she says explains how Duck Lake got its name. It is kind of a fable, and it kept us on the edge of our seats, especially since she has a way of telling it in a scary manner. Unfortunately, it got late and she could not finish.

"It may be hard to believe, but she actually invited us to return tomorrow to complete the story for us, so in a way we're glad that we ran out of time. We went from being afraid of being anywhere near her to liking her a lot.

"This has been quite a week. I learned about a huge house nearby that I never knew even existed. Then I learned that most people believe it to be inhabited by a witch. Then I found out her house is being staked out by three men, one of whom may be Clem Hostetter. Then I discovered that the so-called witch is a very nice lady with a wry sense of humor."

Bay's eyes widened and a grave look came over her face. "There are three men staking out her house? What is that all about?"

"Oh, I guess I forgot to tell you. It was Aunt Lilly we discussed it with. That first night when I walked through the swamp from Aunt Lilly's, I saw two men lurking off the path in sight of Miss Canfield's house. They were watching it from behind trees so that she could not see them. She told us that she has noticed them a number of times, though.

"Anyway, I managed to avoid the pair, and they didn't know I was there. Then tonight I spotted them again as we left Miss Canfield's house."

Mack and Hale looked at each other in surprise. "You saw them this evening, Carty?"

"Yeah, they don't hide very well. If you had been looking in that direction, you would have seen them too."

Blake laughed at that proposition. "Guys, take my word for it. Those two may be clumsy oafs, but in the failing light, none of us would have been able to spot them the way Carty did. The only reason I saw them was that Carty directed my gaze in the right direction. Even then I almost missed them. When it comes to stealth, leave it to Carty to outwit a nasty weasel.

"When we were kids, everyone hated to play Hide and Seek with her, Mack. It was like she was invisible until she wanted to reappear. And when she was 'It,' the game was over almost before it started.

"At one Independence Day picnic, Haywood Dolder thought he'd get the better of Carty. He hid in a refrigerated ice machine – one of those big bins that automatically make ice cubes. It was against the Texaco station that abuts the park, so it was technically out of bounds for the game. Within about two minutes, she had everyone spotted, and figured out from Dolder's trail that he was inside the ice bin.

"Instead of opening the bin, she suggested that everyone head back to the picnic shelter for hot dogs – without 'finding' Dolder.

"By the time he came out of the ice bin, he was almost as blue as the writing on the ice bags. And all of us were back happily munching on our picnic food. When the frozen Dolder arrived and complained that he had won the game, Carty held up her Coke and led us in a toast, 'To the frozen victor of Hide and Seek.'"

"I think he might still be frozen if the embarrassed flush on his face hadn't thawed him out.

"Anyway, Mack, I don't know anyone who would have spotted those guys tonight except Carty."

Carty blushed at the flattery, but she knew that he was right. "My dad is the only one who can find me if I don't want to be found, and I'm the only one who can find him when he hides. He told me the last time we tried it that I was almost equal to him. He jokes that he planned to avoid the mistake of teaching me everything he knew, but that I figured out the missing techniques by myself. If I had been a boy, he says, I would have made a great Army Ranger."

Carty's mother interrupted the byplay. "Do you know anything about the three men?"

"Miss Canfield told us that she has noticed two of them lurking about for several weeks. She is less sure about when the third one showed up. She did not seem too concerned until I mentioned what Aunt Lilly told us. Aunt Lilly thinks one of them might be Clem Hostetter from the neighboring farm."

Bay replied, "The Hostetter farm hasn't been worked for years, but the Hostetters have abutted the Canfield place for a long time. I don't see any reason for Miss Canfield to be concerned about Clem after all these years." Ever one to see good in her fellow man, Bay suggested that Hostetter might be thinking about offering to buy the Canfield place to join his land. "That might explain why he has been looking over her property. I'll give Lilly a call tonight to see what she thinks."

THAT night, Carty slept well initially, but later she dreamed of a large alligator with the face of a man. It wore a grey fedora hat and smoked Camels. The creature had trapped her against a thick bramble bush, and it kept licking her hand and telling her not to worry. As it pushed a sharp tooth into her hand, she awoke in a sweat, her left hand jammed awkwardly and "asleep" under her ribs. The clock had not yet reached three AM.

She got up, shook the feeling back into her numbed arm, and got a glass of water from the bathroom. Uneasy, she did not return to bed immediately. Instead, she sat on the window box of her second floor bedroom with her chin tucked between her knees and looked outside.

There was little of the moon to see that night, but it cast enough light through the thin clouds to illuminate the broad expanse of grass that led to the mine property. A line of fox tracks meandered across the dew-drenched lawn. Not one tree leaf was stirring. The night was as peaceful as she remembered seeing. She wondered why she felt so apprehensive in such a serene setting.

THE morning seemed to arrive too early. Bay had to call when Carty slept through the alarm. That was unlike Carty. She typically was awake and getting ready for the day well before the alarm went off. She stretched while still in bed and rolled sluggishly to her feet, but began moving quickly when Bay called again.

"Hurry, Carty. The Wilsons will be here before long to pick us up."

Breakfast was always light on Sundays before church, usually just toast or a biscuit and tea or milk. As she ate absently, she thought about her dad. She missed him these last several days, and was glad that he would be coming back this evening. She had a lot to tell him.

Rev. Carpenter spoke forcefully from the pulpit that morning. He pleaded with the congregation to gaze into themselves. "God has looked favorably upon us when we needed His help against Germany and Japan. I fear," he continued, "that too many of us are taking Him for granted now that the War is over.

"Our country is the world's leader now, and we have shown people that it is possible to be an unchallenged military power and yet resist all urges to take over conquered countries. As we take pride in how our country is turning our former enemies loose to govern themselves, we can only shudder to think how different it would have been for us if we had lost the War. We need only look at how those vanquished enemies and even one of our prime allies, the USSR, treated citizens of countries that they had conquered.

"However, we cannot rest on our past. We must also use our talents to maintain our position in the world. Each of us personally must discover the talents God has given us and work diligently to perfect those abilities so that we will be a contributor to ourselves, to our families, and to our country.

"I am reminded of Matthew 25:14-30, The Parable of the Talents. You will recall that a land owner was planning a long trip. Before he left, he entrusted individual sums of money called talents to three of his servants. When he returned from the trip, the servants reported to him.

"The first servant had invested the sum wisely and returned the original sum plus a large profit to the land owner, who appreciated his resourcefulness. The second servant also invested wisely and returned the same percentage of profit for the master. The land owner was pleased and he promoted both of them.

"The third servant reported that he did not invest the money because he feared that he might do so unwisely and lose the land owner's money. So he buried the money to await the land owner's return. When his master came back, the servant simply returned the exact same funds to him. Of course, the land owner was not pleased with such a lazy and uninspired effort and banished him."

Carty could not help but remember Haywood Dolder's boast of several days previous that he would put his "big money" under a mattress. She glanced to her right where the Dolders were seated to see Haywood's reaction to the sermon. She need not have bothered. His attention was focused on punching his younger brother's arm.

Rev. Carpenter continued. "It has always been interesting to me that in Matthew's version, 'talent' was the word for money in the country of the parable. Our definition for talent in English is ability or skill. I believe that God may have selected the country in this parable – the country where 'talent' was the word for its money – so that we in these times would think of that word in our context.

"God is not so much telling us to invest our money wisely in the literal sense of the story, but rather to encourage each of us to make the most of our talents, that is, our abilities. He wants us to develop to the fullest whatever aptitude He has given us. It is not pleasing to Him if we, like the lazy and fearful servant, allow our talents to lie unused."

CARTY was so quiet on the drive home with the Wilsons that her mother asked if she were feeling well as they entered the house.

"Oh, I'm fine, Mom. I was just thinking about the mine. Dad has suggested that I consider an engineering degree when I finish the academy in four years. He thinks that Aunt Lilly can persuade the University of Florida to let me into their engineering program if I can't get into Purdue. But Purdue has allowed women before, and Dad is an alumnus. And my grades are surely good enough.

"He says if I can handle living at Sarasota Prep during high school, I'll have no problem living away at Purdue.

"I know he would let me do something else if I wanted to, but he seems to think that I have the natural ability to eventually take over the business from him. Maybe that's what Rev. Carpenter meant this morning."

"Dear, you have four years to think about it. I was very hesitant about taking on the accounting duties when we started the business, but I ended up really enjoying the work. All your father is asking at this point is that you concentrate on the science track at the academy. He just wants you to be prepared in case you might have an interest later on. You know that he wants you to take a summer job at the mine this year. It'll give you a chance to see if you like the business."

"Yes, we have talked about it. He even offered jobs to Blake and Hale to help them out. I think Hale might work with Mack's dad on constructing the new racetrack in Sebring, though. Mack and Hale have really hit it off.

"I'd miss my old lifeguard job, but the mine pays a lot more. Anyway, Rev. Carpenter's sermon today has just about convinced me. If Dad had been here this morning, I would not have put it past him to have pumped up the reverend to use that parable on me," she chuckled.

"Well, Carty, Rev. Carpenter does have a telephone, you know."

"Hee hee! You are such a hoot, Mom. That must be why I love you so much. Nevertheless," she kidded, "I'm still going to tell Dad you said that."

With only the two of them at home today, Carty and her mother shared some soup and cold chicken instead of the large traditional Sunday meal. "I'll have a roast ready for us late tonight when your father returns. He will be anxious for a home-cooked meal after his long trip. Be certain to be home by seven-thirty. Dinner is at eight-thirty, because your dad still has quite a distance to cover. Is Blake still planning to eat with us?"

"Oh, yes. He said he wouldn't miss one of your feasts, even though it meant having to miss the chance to fight off his brothers and sisters for their meal of bread and water."

"I'm certain that Mr. Holmes serves more than bread and water, but I know that Blake does appreciate a hearty, hot meal. Hale and Mack didn't change their minds?"

"No. They both have family obligations, so it'll just be Blake. Speaking of whom, here he comes. Can you let him in while I change out of these church clothes?"

By the time Carty came back downstairs, all three boys were drinking lemonade and finishing off the raisin Toll House cookies. Mrs. Andersson had prepared a fruit salad for them to take to Sally Canfield. She covered the bowl with aluminum foil and secured it in wicker that fit snugly in the wire basket on Carty's bike.

Carty carried her bow and quiver as before. Mack cradled a small bouquet of daisies for Sally, having given a similar one to Mrs. Andersson earlier.

CHAPTER 13

Cigarette Smuggling

Change is one thing, progress is another.

BERTRAND RUSSELL

Cruz hung up the phone after getting Dredman's update. He was not ready to tell Dredman how much his involvement had grown and avoided offering meaningful comments during the conversation.

He took a match to his Rex del Sol and inhaled deeply. He never gave up the premium cigar, though he had not owned the company for decades. During the First World War, Cruz saw dramatic changes developing in the tobacco market that presaged a structural shift devastating to the cigar business.

When the first machine-rolled cigarettes came to market, most male smokers considered the smooth cylinders to be too sissified compared with self-rolled. Even stout Camel cigarettes, the first national brand, were looked down on when they debuted in 1913. But during World War I, the Army supplied Camels and Lucky Strikes to American soldiers battling the Kaiser in Europe. When the men returned home, many had become addicted. By 1919, for the first year ever, more tobacco was going into machine-rolled cigarettes than into cigars.

Within a few years, Cruz sold Rex del Sol, Inc. to a rival cigar maker. He received a premium price when his brand and cigars in general were still close to their peak in popularity. Afterward, secretly, Cruz continued selling tobacco to the new owners from his Cuban plantation. He sold at a below market price to mask the low costs that his smuggling operation had been giving him.

Six months later, though, the plantation created a fiction for those new owners about a blight that had wiped out the harvest and that Rex del Sol, Inc. would have to buy from other more expensively priced plantations going forward.

Without the benefit of the cheap tobacco, the higher costs bit deeply into company profits. At the same time, market shifts from cigarette competition caused cigar sales to begin a sharp decline. The double financial impact put the company into bankruptcy in under two years, though the premium brand survived under a series of owners.

Cruz understood that the popularity of cigarettes to the addicted masses presented politicians with far too great a temptation for gouging. Both the states and the Federal Government implemented and steadily raised taxes on cigarettes. Politicians of whatever era believe that they can spend the taxpayers' money in more enlightened ways than the taxpayers can themselves. Moreover, each politician believes that he becomes ever more astute in this regard the longer he stays in office.

Cruz soon realized that in some states, high taxes opened up an opportunity. Michigan was a particularly good location for a scheme to take advantage of the high tax movement. The state's large population made for a strong market for cigarettes, and taxes there were among the highest.

He reconstituted his Cuban plantation as an island distributor of American cigarettes that he imported from the major producers in the Carolinas. Cigarettes exported from the United States are exempt from state taxes, and Cruz had only to be concerned with corrupt customs officials in Havana. Once again, the fishing fleet proved useful.

Capt. Luna had worked for the Cruz family for almost thirty years, except when he was in the Merchant Marine during the war years of 1942-45. Today he watched the loading of the last of the stainless steel containers into the bottom of his ship's hold as he spoke with the Savannah freight forwarder. The young man waited for him to sign the bill of lading.

"You are correct," Luna told him. "The Cuba Sea Reef was originally a fishing boat. But when the fish market turned down in the Thirties, we converted to a cargo ship. We are taking these cigarettes to Havana after we stop in Miami for additional cargo."

In fact, there was no additional cargo in the plans, nor was there a stop in Miami on the schedule. Moreover, the fishing operation would resume in a few days as always. The inquisitive clerk from the forwarding agent needed to be satisfied, though. Capt. Luna's ship was heading out to sea to add fish to the tops of the cigarette containers. It was a repeat of the original process with a different wrinkle. This procedure had been put in place in the Twenties.

When the fishing operation was complete, the ship docked at Rex Seafood as before. Once again, all was unloaded there. A few days later, Rex's expanded fleet of refrigerated trucks took fish and cigarettes to Detroit. There his wholesale food business specialized in ocean seafood and both legal and illegal cigarette distribution. Legal cigarette sales on which taxes were paid went to stores and restaurants.

Meanwhile, a group of Cruz's "runners" distributed illegal, tax-avoided cigarettes. Originally, these were sold to speakeasies and other outlets established to avoid Prohibition that started in January of 1920. These customers, already selling illegal alcohol, could be counted on to keep their illegal suppliers' identities confidential. That included Cruz's cigarettes. Cruz needed only a little time to get his tentacles around shady Detroit law enforcement – police and judges.

State revenue officials were tougher to infiltrate, so he used a different approach. The tax revenue agents were always on the lookout for trucks from around the Carolinas hauling contraband cigarettes. To help out, once a year or so, Cruz, under an assumed name, would hire a down-and-out trucker in Raleigh or Charlotte. He would have the small truck load up with cigarettes at a North Carolina plant.

Usually, Cruz instructed the driver to deliver the untaxed cigarettes to a fictitious Detroit destination. On occasion, Cruz would designate an actual destination of someone he did not like. That way, the unsuspecting individual would suffer along with the innocent trucker. Cruz always knew the trucker's route, approximate time of arrival at the Michigan border, and the description and license plate of the truck. Thus, it was easy for Cruz to tip off the state revenue officials anonymously.

Every time the tax people caught another trucker crossing the state line with untaxed contraband, they were lulled into believing that they were doing a good job. So they patted themselves on the back and relaxed their vigilance for a while. Cruz concentrated the timing of his real deliveries to follow these busts. The orchestrated loss of a small shipment from the Carolinas was worth reducing the likelihood of the authorities stopping his many large shipments from Tampa.

By avoiding taxes, it was cheaper to sell North Carolina cigarettes in Michigan through this elaborate, black market scheme than to acquire them legitimately. The higher the taxes became, the more profit Cruz's operation made. Soon Cruz befriended and supported every high-tax politician in the legislature in Lansing, and he became well-known as a major contributor to the state's pro-tax Democrats.

When Prohibition was repealed in 1933, Cruz cut back on the cigarette running, and by 1950, his cigarette operation had been reduced to little more than a hobby. Its post-Prohibition operation was a small fraction of his Prohibition Era business, and barely profitable.

Cruz had no financial reason to keep the cigarette smuggling going. If a man like Cruz could be thought of as being sentimental, that might be the explanation. He started in tobacco and was most comfortable when a related scheme or project was underway.

OVER THE YEARS, he invested much of his wealth in commercial real estate in Cuba. He had developed a cozy, if behind the scenes, relationship with the Carlos Prio Socarrás Administration, but he had learned to keep his options open in the fast changing politics in Cuba.

In the Twenties, Cruz had been a trusted supplier of contraband cigarettes to Detroit colleagues of Meyer Lansky, the Las Vegas' gangster. Two decades later, when Lansky wanted to expand his casino operations in Cuba, he could not get past the then current administration. He looked up Cruz and sought advice.

Cruz suggested that Lansky should work with a former Cuban strongman, Fulgencio Batista. Batista had been president from 1940-44, when Lansky started out in Havana, but Batista lost power when he was ineligible to run for consecutive terms. Cruz correctly believed that Batista might be interested in instigating a bloodless coup. With Lansky's financial backing, Batista had real prospects of success.

The three came to an agreement. Lansky would get a big cut of an expanded Cuban gambling business. Batista would get financial support for his takeover of the government. Cruz would be rewarded with a healthy share of the income, but he would stay behind the scenes. Though the project was still a year or two away, it was moving along steadily. Cruz was involved in the scheming, but the plan was intentionally progressing slowly and carefully at this stage, so he had time on his hands.

"Frankly," Cruz thought to himself, "I'm bored." The cigarettes were little more than a game to keep him occupied. Cruz certainly did not need the money. That's why Dredman's original call interested him more than he had let on.

CRUZ had not been in a swamp since his "auditor" days in the Sierra Maestra, under the alias, Marco Humberto. When his project with Cairo's group of banditos was in its earliest stages, he suspected that Cairo's second in charge, Manuel Tovar, was an informant for the government. However, Tovar learned of his precarious position and escaped only hours before Cruz could apprehend and execute him. For the next week, it became a cat and mouse game with Tovar seeking to elude and Cruz pursuing.

The chase began at Cairo's base camp in the Sierra Maestra. Cairo wanted to send out a squad of men to track the traitor down, but Cruz would not allow it.

"I will get him myself," Cruz said. "Sr. Tovar will regret hearing the name Humberto."

Tovar had more in-country experience than Cruz. He was native to southeastern Cuba. Moreover, he had the incentive of saving his life to spur him on. The one thing he lacked was the unyielding resolve that Cruz possessed when pushed or slighted, and Cruz took the news of the informant as a personal insult.

For six days, Tovar led Cruz on a trek through some of the wildest terrain on the island. What began in the cool night in the mountains wound down through the deep forest and along the swift flowing upper reaches of the Cauto River. It then flowed into the steamy hot Biramas Swamp, home to some of the more inhospitable land in the tropics.

The soft, deep mud could suck a human waist-deep and provide little chance of escape without help – help that neither man would offer the other. Indeed, to be so caught would be a death grip if the other found out.

At times, the mosquitoes were so thick that they created the look of snow flurries on a windswept night. Leaches dropped on the men from branches and slipped from leaves as the two brushed past. The slimy creatures sucked blood in greedy streams from the men's arms and necks. There were so many that the men gave up trying to remove them. The crocodiles were aggressive, but the human rivals were even deadlier. Any reasonable person would have been in an agitated state. Cruz could not have been happier.

His senses were at their peak. Tovar was more than capable of giving Cruz a good run, and the surprise that Tovar had arranged made the contest more exciting yet.

Cruz had nearly caught Tovar on several occasions, but the prey barely escaped each time. Enmeshed in the swamp a few miles from the safety of the coast, Tovar rested against a tree, his rifle at the ready.

Tovar was pleased that he had lured this man, Humberto, to this spot through a series of starts and stops that kept him close, but not close enough to strike. Tovar smiled ever so slightly. His plan had played out perfectly. He uttered to himself, "Humberto should have brought some help if he thought he could get the better of Manuel Tovar."

Suddenly, a knife appeared at Tovar's neck, cutting gently into the skin, and Tovar's arm was pinned painfully to his upper back. Cruz spoke for the first time in a week. His voice sounded gruffer than he had expected. "Sr. Tovar, you led me on quite an adventure. I truly did not expect to require almost full week to complete this job. You are to be commended for your professionalism. Now drop that rifle."

Tovar complied. He was surprised, but he showed no fear. He was a naturally brave man, and he knew something that Cruz did not.

"Before you get too aggressive with that knife, Sr. Humberto, I must tell you that you appear to be quite the master of the wilderness for a mere auditor. However, I am the Cuban Army's premier wilderness scout, and I would not allow myself to get caught so easily without backup. You see," he boasted triumphantly, "You are surrounded by a squad of nine of my most capable men. I have led you into a trap. Drop the knife now, and I may allow you to survive."

Tovar was surprised that Humberto did not flinch at the news. Neither did he comply with Tovar's order.

"I do not see your men, Sr. Tovar," Cruz replied calmly. "One might believe your boast to be an empty threat."

"You do not see my men because they do not want to be seen. These are the best wilderness fighters in the army."

With that said, Tovar called out, "You may come out now, men. Approach and disarm this man." Tovar was surprised that Cruz showed no intention of looking around for approaching men.

An unseen animal stirred in a nearby tree. Gnats and mosquitoes buzzed. Otherwise, all remained quiet. Tovar called out more loudly a second time, a trace of concern catching in his voice. Cruz pulled the knife slightly tighter, allowing a small stream of blood to flow down Tovar's neck.

During the previous days, Tovar had intentionally allowed the man he knew as Humberto to get close to keep him hopeful. Unfortunately for Tovar, he was unaware that Cruz played the same game. Cruz could have caught Tovar on several occasions, but allowed him to slip away at seemingly the last moments. For Cruz wanted Tovar to stay confident and he needed time to deal with the squad of nine.

"Your men do not appear to be following orders, Señor, or perhaps I should say Col. Tovar," Cruz quietly stated to a no longer calm captive. "Do not be angry with your men. It is difficult for dead men to obey orders."

"Dead men? You killed nine of my best men?" Tovar gasped in shock.

"It did not take me long to realize that you were playing with me, Colonel. On a number of occasions, you could have put more distance between us if you had wanted to. It became obvious that you had something more interesting in mind.

"The swamps are ideal for quiet searching and killing. Actually, I needed only to kill four of your men. Your sergeant was the first. The other five deserted you when they could not figure out who was killing their comrades. My life's motto is, 'Always intimidate rather than confront.' It is not difficult to frighten untrained and uncommitted men. Your men were not trained nearly as well as you believed, nor were they as committed to you as you thought."

"So what are you going to do with me?" a resigned Tovar asked. "A man of character would give me a chance to fight one on one," he suggested hopefully.

"That is true, Colonel. And as you are not nearly as capable as I in this environment, I doubt that you would have a one percent chance to take me in hand to hand combat.

Tovar began searching his mind for some method he could employ to defeat this man who had taken four of his best. He need not have bothered. With a quick move, Cruz sliced deeply into Tovar's throat and dropped him to the ground.

"However, I am not willing to take that one percent chance, and I am most definitely not the man of character you were hoping for."

Tovar heard none of Cruz's last comments.

CHAPTER 14

The Cuban in Morose Swamp

People thought I was ruthless. I was.
ALTHEA GIBSON

Speaking by phone, Cruz continued to keep Dredman from knowing of his growing involvement and exploration around the Canfield house. "It doesn't sound like something of interest to me yet, Dredman, but if anything more substantive develops, let me know."

As he smoked the Rex and drank his Scotch, his mind gravitated to his thoughts following the first conversation he had with Dredman about the prospects of a Canfield treasure.

"TREASURE is worth my attention," he had thought. "And dealing with a witch could be interesting. I haven't been involved in anything like that since running into voodoo in the Sierra Maestra with Cairo. And since those years, I haven't been anywhere wilder than a sandy beach in Clearwater. I do believe that I'd really appreciate a run around a swamp."

By that evening, he had talked himself into it. "If it turns out to be a wild goose chase that Dredman has put me on, though, he will regret it."

Just after midnight, he had driven from his Tampa estate south and eastward for a few hours. When he reached Mocking Bird Road on the outskirts of Winter Free, he continued past the Hostetter Cutoff for about a mile. Eventually he spotted a place to park his car well off of the road where it could not be seen by anyone motoring past. He passed only a few residences as he walked back to the cutoff and proceeded along the dirt road, noting the surroundings with eyes out of practice but still capable. That first inspection geared up his interest.

A couple of weeks later now, and after several forays to the Canfield property and surrounding areas, he was ready for more active participation.

He had gained only about five pounds since the days in the Sierra Maestra, and he was as fit as a man twenty years younger than his chronological age. He ran or swam daily regardless of weather, and bench pressed the same weight as he did in the Marines.

That day he had dressed in dark clothes and wore boots suitable for a rough environment. He inspected the Hostetter house. He took in the dilapidated condition of the property and the car.

Unlike Carty's lackadaisical approach, he left no clues for Dredman that he had been there. When Carty was focused on stealth, she was remarkably capable, but her lack of experience caused her to neglect to apply the principles at all times. Cruz suffered from no such shortcoming.

In Morose Swamp, Cruz was as thorough as Dredman and Hostetter were not. He viewed the Canfield house from all sides, not only from the north. The forest was dense to the south of the house with branches of the closest trees nearly brushing the walls. From the house, two thin pathways angled southwest and southeast for a half mile until they joined the south fork that ran between Hostetter's and the Andersson place. Cruz had scouted out the distance to Lilly's to be certain that help from that direction would be unlikely if he chose to conduct an operation.

He noted the size and number of windows in Sally's house, the sturdy shutters, and the one massive door facing north. He saw that the house had no outside stairs or fire escape from the second floor. He could not categorize the odd shape of the roof's north face where a short wide gate appeared to anchor an unlikely storage area of bumpy moss on the pitched slate roof.

This time he toured each out-building quietly, thoroughly, and expertly. Even the chickens failed to awaken when he entered the coop. Only the cow made any noise, and that just a gentle murmur. He examined the grounds around the house and around the other buildings.

Satisfied that he had a good understanding of the structures, he plucked an orange from one of the trees and entered the swamp, verifying that a previously located dry passage remained and that no new obstacles had developed. Throughout, Sally was unaware of his trespass. Somewhat out of practice, Cruz was nevertheless the complete opposite of the two awkward buffoons with whom he would soon associate himself.

He spent the entire night in the swamp, alert for any unwanted creatures that might venture past. For breakfast, he munched on the slimy raw meat of a rattlesnake that he caught and sliced into bite-sized chunks. He recalled his Marine drill instructor saying that rattlesnake tasted like chicken. "Yes, Sergeant," Cruz remembered telling him, "If you like your chicken slathered in phlegm."

Before dawn, he watched Sally milk the cow and toss cracked corn to the chickens. She gathered some eggs and took the pail of milk into the house. This time she saw him, but only because he wanted her to be aware of his presence. "It is better to intimidate than to confront," he reminded himself.

HE returned to Tampa that afternoon and briefed Carey Zeller. Zeller headed Cruz's Detroit cigarette runners and was in Tampa to recruit a few new men. Cruz preferred to hire out of town men for Detroit so the local police did not recognize them so quickly. Detroit cops were upgrading quality in recent years. Cruz trusted Zeller as much as anyone in his employ.

A tall, lanky contrast to Cruz, Zeller was twenty-some years younger and nearly as deadly. He wore his dish-water blond hair slicked straight back, which drew attention to his beak-like nose, sharp chin, and narrow forehead.

Discharged from the Marines in 1946, Zeller started as a Detroit cigarette runner for Cruz the next year. Zeller had tried more conventional jobs initially, but had trouble accepting slower paced life after the violence he experienced on the Pacific islands. After Nagasaki finished off the Japanese war effort in 1945, he was one of few Marines unhappy to learn that he would not be storming the beaches of the Japanese home islands.

His best buddy died at the hands of a Japanese soldier whom Zeller thought he had killed earlier. Unfortunately, the Japanese warrior had been wearing an experimental bullet proof vest. He was unconscious after the barrage of bullets hit him, but survived.

As Zeller and his comrade passed by, the man came to and struck with his knife. Zeller's head shot finished the enemy soldier, but it was too late to help his friend. He stripped the vest from the Japanese soldier and put it on under his uniform, wearing it for the remainder of the conflict.

ZELLER rose to the challenges given him by Cruz in the new job. Though Cruz had ratcheted down the operation by the War's end, he still enjoyed the challenge of beating out competitors. He welcomed the intensity and solid judgment that Zeller brought to the operation. Two upstart competitors tried moving in on Cruz, one a particularly clever Canadian who trucked cigarettes over the border on an unguarded hunting trail between Rainy River, Ontario and Baudette, Minnesota.

When Zeller discovered that he was losing business, he personally tailed one of the Canadian's runners on the return trip to Canada. Anonymously, Zeller informed U.S. Customs generally of what he had found out. He agreed to provide more details when he learned more. This enabled Customs to be prepared, despite not knowing the precise crossing location or the Canadian's schedule.

Zeller rigged two miniature explosives on the tire-rutted trail about two miles inside the United States. After waiting eight days, he was beginning to fear that the Canadians were smarter than he gave them credit for. He feared that they were using multiple crossings instead of this one that he knew about. He hoped that he was wrong, as that would require a far more elaborate plan. On the ninth day, however, his patience was rewarded.

About three in the morning, the same truck that he had tailed a few weeks earlier swayed along the dirt trail like a ship in choppy water. As it reached the point of attack, Zeller set off the small electric charges. The left tire blew off and the right front wheel rim suffered an irreparable fracture. The charges were intentionally small to confuse the driver into thinking that the tires had blown out after hitting some sharp obstacle.

Customs people were located several hours drive from this isolated location, so Zeller needed the driver to abandon the truck and seek repair help. He did not want the smuggler hauling the inventory by hand back into Canada. About the time that the driver realized that he was not in a position to repair the damage, Zeller drove up in his Jeep, fully outfitted as if he were on a hunting trip. He had shot a small buck earlier in the day and had it draped over the vehicle's hood.

Zeller got out of his car and approached the distraught truck driver. "Looks like you did some damage on this crappy road," he greeted sympathetically.

"Sure did, and I can't figure out what happened. I've been on this road before. It's not so bad that I should be blowing out two tires at once."

"Used to be an iron mining road," Zeller lied. "There's so much metal in these ruts, it's amazing you haven't run into a problem before. I always carry two spares when I come hunting up here, but my tires won't fit your truck. Never had to use both at once, but I've changed more than my share.

"Want me to take a look?"

"Sure, anything you can do to help."

After a few perfunctory pokes, looks, tugs, and sighs, Zeller told the man that he needed a tow truck.

"Closest one is in Baudette, a little south of here. Pointing to the deer on his Jeep hood he said, "I was planning to pop over to the Canadian side to see if I could get something bigger than this runt, but I wouldn't feel right abandoning you out here. Hop in and I'll drive you to Baudette so you can get some help."

"I really appreciate that, Mr. ...?"

"You can call me Smitty," Zeller replied. "Everybody else does."

"I'm Bill Mellingham."

After an hour or so of unexceptional chitchat, Mellingham said with mild suspicion, "Smitty, you are remarkably uncurious about what I was doing up there on a hunting trail in a box truck."

"Yeah, I kind of expected that you'd appreciate my ignoring it," Zeller replied. "'Course deer huntin' out of season without a license tends to keep me from getting too nosey, if you know what I mean. In fact, you can help me unload Bambi right here on the side of the road before we get to town."

Mellingham laughed and said, "I understand."

Several minutes later, Zeller pulled up to a Texaco station that advertised a mechanic and tow truck. He dropped off Mellingham with a wave and a smile and drove a block away to a phone booth. By pre-arrangement, and continuing in his pose as an anonymous tipster, he called his Customs contact at International Falls.

Within fifteen minutes, three Customs agents were on their way to the trail crossing that Zeller pinpointed for them. By the time the tow truck arrived with Mellingham at the disabled vehicle, the agents were already in position. As Mellingham approached, they sprung from the trees and placed him under arrest. Under intense questioning, he revealed detailed information on the operation. Working on U.S. Customs' information, Canadian Customs closed down the smuggling scheme later that week.

Cruz recognized that Zeller's elaborate planning was more intimidating than a frontal assault would have been. A direct attack might have inspired retaliation. Instead, U.S. Customs appeared to be the all-knowing Feds to the Canadian intruders.

ZELLER continued to grow in Cruz's estimation as he increasingly relied on him. Zeller proved to be a skilled administrator. He kept tight control over the runners to make certain that they did not fall for a ruse similar to his border crossing trick.

On two different occasions, Zeller tailed a pair of his runners to the same down and out tavern where he spotted another pair of men whom he figured to be undercover Federal agents. Zeller took care that those runners were never seen again in Detroit. Cruz appreciated Zeller's commitment and attention to detail.

Moreover, Zeller was a veteran of jungle warfare in the Pacific and more than capable of handling himself in the Florida swamps. Cruz wanted more backup in that environment than Dredman and Hostetter were capable of providing, so he had Zeller join him.

WEEKS later, about the time when Carty and the boys ate their lunch at Lilly's, Cruz and Zeller climbed into Cruz' black Cadillac and drove to

Hostetter Cutoff. As Cruz turned the big sedan on to the dirt road, he asked, "You noticed the bikes behind those palmettos, Carey?"

"Yeah. Four of them. One's a girl's. Look to be in running condition. I thought your man said things were isolated out here."

"That's why you're here. Dredman is book smart. He can quote Shakespeare and Chaucer, but he couldn't walk down a lighted street in a fancy downtown without getting mugged. The other guy, Clem Hostetter, I think would better be named Clem Kadiddlehopper after the Red Skelton character. He is about as valuable as Dredman, but he can only quote from beer bottle labels. This is really a lark for me, but they better not be wasting our time.

"Do you really believe that this is for real? I thought treasure maps were tricks for tourists."

"Yeah, you're right to be skeptical. In this case, there is no map. It may take some strong-arming to find anything, assuming anything does exist. But Dredman is good at research, and from what he told me, this has a feeling of authenticity.

"He established that the witch's family was really wealthy, at one time anyway – of course that's no guarantee that through wars, depressions, or stupidity, the money wasn't lost. This witch woman, who apparently lives alone, is the last of her family, so she might be the only one alive who can lead us to whatever loot there is. So her we have to keep alive.

"In addition, Hostetter read something she wrote years ago that apparently mentioned a treasure, so that may indicate that the wealth is still intact. It could also mean that the crazy old witch lost her mind.

"If there is a treasure, we don't know what form it takes. The original rich guy had interests in pre-Revolutionary War shipping, so there is always a chance that he was involved in piracy. Perhaps he had to escape down to these swamps in Spanish Florida to avoid the British navy. That might mean gold and jewels instead of cash, which would require truck transport. Anyway, we can deal with a problem like that when we get to it.

"Unfortunately, it looks like some kids may be hanging around, given those bikes."

There was a moment of quiet before Zeller responded. "I don't mind knocking off a crazy old woman, but I don't like the idea of hurting kids, Cruz. You know I'll do what has to be done, but I'd like to work around the kids if we can."

"You're such a softy," Cruz joshed. "You can leave the kids to me if it comes to that. Kids are just short, noisy adults as far as I'm concerned."

Zeller stared out of the windows without responding. He knew that he would not hesitate to back up Cruz. He did not like hurting children, but if that were necessary, there would be no discussion about it.

They approached the Hostetter house slowly. Unlike the motor in Hostetter's beat up old Ford, the big Caddy engine purred almost noiselessly as Cruz eased around to the back of the house. Zeller jumped out and opened the door of a small barn, more like a shed, that Cruz previously reconnoitered. Cruz pulled the car inside to conceal it.

They proceeded on foot east along the dirt road toward Sally Canfield's. As they came around a curve, the massive structure came into view. Zeller commented, "Cruz, that's an imposing building: two stories, huge, and in nice condition. There sure was money involved when it was built. Maybe there is something to this."

"I thought you would be impressed."

"No wires, so she doesn't have a phone. That helps. However," Zeller added apprehensively, "a building that size could house a lot of people."

"It probably held a big family at one time, but I have watched long enough to satisfy myself that the witch lives by herself now, so we should not have to worry too much about finding others inside. She may have visitors from time to time, though," Cruz added, pointing to the ground around their feet.

"I see what you mean. Fresh footprints of four people here," he said, "probably the kids from those four bikes. These car tire tracks are a few days old and don't belong to that old Ford next to Hostetter's. The Ford's tires are nearly bald, but these were made by tires with good tread."

"Did you notice our two clowns at the edge of the swamp who think they are hiding?"

"Yeah, the one with the fedora looks like he's going to the horse track or Edward Hopper's diner[21]."

"That would be Dredman. Hostetter is the skinny one. I'll spend some time with them in the swamp and bring them to the farmhouse later. Why don't you check out Hostetter's place in the meantime? We don't want any surprises there."

ZELLER returned to the farmhouse and picked the old lock in less than ten seconds. He checked each room on the first floor and then climbed the stairs. As a Detroiter, he also looked for a basement, but, this being Florida with its low water table, there was none.

He found several guns and was surprised to see that they were well cared for and operable. Satisfied that the house was empty and that the normal contingent consisted of two residents, he began the task of cleaning up the kitchen.

Neither he nor Cruz were planning to stay long, but they were not going to live in a hovel no matter how short the time. They could handle the most dismal conditions in the field without the slightest complaint, but they would not abide with filth in their living quarters.

CHAPTER 15

The Plan

*Repudiating the virtues of your world, criminals hopelessly agree
to organize a forbidden universe.*
JEAN GENET, *THE THIEF'S JOURNAL*

Dredman and Hostetter were unaware that Cruz had joined the quest several weeks earlier and that Zeller came aboard today. When Dredman initiated the most recent phone conversation, Cruz continued to voice only the slightest interest. Dredman believed that he would have to come up with something more convincing than what he and Clem had discovered thus far, so their late day began with another scouting mission.

The afternoon warmth that felt good to most of the area's residents wore heavily on the two hung-over hoods as they trudged through the treeless farm field en route to their watch over Sally Canfield's house.

Sweat dripped from the tips of their noses and soaked their shirts before they had reached the end of the clearing. As much as both despised the dreary swamp, today they welcomed the comparative comfort of its cooler temperature.

As they approached their vantage point, Dredman warned, "Let's take it easy, Hostetter. We don't want to scare up another visit from our reptile friend, no matter how important the task at hand."

Hours passed uneventfully. Dredman commented idly on the lack of activity. "She isn't doing much today. She must be home, though. Chimney smoke on a warm day like this means she is cooking."

"Damon, you have to agree that she is alone. We've never seen anyone else, no matter what time of day we come. If anyone has been here, they ain't around now. We should make our move ourselves instead of bringing in The Cuban. He's just going to take a big share anyway, when we have done all the work."

Before Dredman had an opportunity to reply, the massive door creaked open and the four young visitors filed out of the house. They appeared in good spirits and hurried along the dirt road in the direction of the Hostetter farm. Both men were silent, but their reactions otherwise were quite different. Hostetter looked apprehensively at Dredman while Dredman seethed.

Hostetter was the first to speak. "I don't see anyone else, Damon. I think she's alone now," he added hopefully.

"Idiot. 'No one else is ever there,' you said. 'She never has visitors,' you said. 'Everyone is too afraid to go near her house,' you said. Well what do you think those four were? Ghosts?! Goblins?!"

Hostetter managed just barely to duck under a wide, wild swing from Dredman's right fist. "They're just kids," Hostetter pleaded. "They can't be a problem."

"You fool. Every witness is a problem, and those four aren't toddlers. One of those kids is taller than you are, and he looks like he could pop you a good one if he tried. Even the girl looks athletic enough to make a run for it. And the numbers are a real predicament. Rounding up five people would be impossible for the two of us."

"Then let's do it now, Damon, while the kids are gone."

"Hostetter, your light bulb has no filament. They are gone now, but what if they come back? And how do we know there aren't more in the house? We've never seen anyone before, and all of a sudden, four pop up from nowhere. For all we know, she might have more of them in cages in there."

"I guess you are right, plus we have to worry about the bag."

"The bag? What are you talking about, Hostetter? What bag?"

"Didn't you see the canvas bag that the kid in overalls was carrying? That's the ammo bag I found in the swamp when we outran the gator and the mud monster. I recognized the red strap."

The impact of what Clem had just revealed made Dredman overlook another of Clem's references to the mud monster. "So these kids have been out here in the swamp too. They may have spotted us. That does it. This is too big for the two of us. I told The Cuban we might be calling him again if things developed. Well, they have developed, but not the way I wanted. Either he joins us or we're out of it."

Clem's heart sank at the thought of The Cuban joining them, but it was too late to back out, and he had to admit that they needed help.

"I guess you're right, Damon. Are we going back to the house now?"

Before he answered, a deep, resonant voice came from behind them, "I assuredly suggest that you return to your farmhouse so we can discuss how we are going to handle this situation."

Clem tripped backward into a shallow water trough and came up blowing water from his nose. Dredman backed into a thorn bush but recovered his balance soon enough to prevent serious pain.

"Señor," Dredman managed to say, "I did not expect to see you here already. I thought you were going to await further developments."

"I have been here several times over the past few weeks, Dredman, including last night. Your comings and goings have been quite comical at times. If the witch doesn't know that you two have been stumbling around out here, she would have to be a city girl. But she knows the wilderness, so I expect she has had you spotted for some time, supernatural powers or not.

"Let's move out now before she comes out of the house."

When they arrived at the farmhouse, Dredman and Cruz found that it was considerably cleaner and tidier than they left it. Clem was about to ask Cruz if he had cleaned the house, but thought better of it. As he put the thought into the back of his mind, he jumped again at the sound of another unexpected voice.

"Don't expect me to be your maid service," Zeller growled. "From now on, you two have domestic duty." He handed Hostetter a wad of cash.

"Take that heap of yours into Winter Free and get some decent food and S.O.S. pads and Bab-O^{22} for cleaning this place. I want steaks, pork chops, a bag of potatoes and fresh salad ingredients, and a big bottle of vinegar. Bacon and a couple of dozen eggs. You're almost out of coffee too. Get Maxwell House. And milk for the cereal. There's no milk in the house – what do you put on your cereal – beer?"

Clem, recalling the breakfast of a few days ago, cut a sideways glance at the equally shocked Dredman. "Anyway, there's already too much beer in the house, so don't get any more."

Cruz added an amused introduction. "Gentlemen, this is Carey Zeller. You will know and love him as you know and love me. Dredman, I'm sure that Mr. Zeller has some chores for you in the house. Before that, please bring me all the information you have collected on the witch, her family, and the treasure."

With that said, he sat at the kitchen table. "Get going, the two of you," he barked, "and Hostetter, don't talk to anyone in town."

They jumped at his voice. Damon approached Zeller, who directed him upstairs to begin cleaning the bedrooms after he gathered the information that Cruz wanted. Clem ran out the back door and then sheepishly returned for the car keys before trying again.

Cruz and Zeller read through all the material that Dredman had presented.

"You're right, Cruz. There is every reason to believe that there was big money involved. Whether it is still around or not is the prime question, plus where it is actually located, of course."

"After watching the witch, Carey, and examining the property closely, I strongly believe that there is still a lot of money, despite the weirdness of the woman. The house, which is an impressive structure, is in excellent repair. A lot of that has to do with its original solid construction, but you can see steady improvements. For example, the windows are not originals – probably replaced in the last twenty years – and they are an expensive variety.

"The farm stock is small but in excellent condition, and she has a perfectly tended vegetable garden. The seed that she uses has to be good, professional quality, not something she raised herself.

"At one point, I thought she was just a crazy woman who doesn't like modern things. Or maybe she was like the Amish. The next day I heard a radio inside the house, so there went that theory. The house has no electricity, so it had to be battery powered.

"Anyway, her wagons and tools are in tip-top condition. That takes maintenance from a well-equipped shop, so she must be paying someone in Winter Free to do that premium work, and it wouldn't go cheap.

"So, I'm leaning toward a lot of original wealth, at least some still in existence and probably hoarded in the house. I've decided to bring in a truck in case the treasure is heavy and requires a lot of capacity to move.

"Of course, she might have it in a bank. That would complicate things, but we'll find a way to force her to withdraw it. We'll have to use our two clowns if it comes to that. We don't want our faces to be associated with this. She won't be around to identify us, but if the banker and several townsfolk see us, that could be trouble."

"You're not planning to keep these two around as witnesses then?"

"No. If the cops start questioning Dredman, he would turn us in for a cup of coffee and a philosophical discussion. Hostetter is so dumb, you can't tell what he might do. The witch, of course, has to go. If we can work around the kids, we'll do so for your sensibilities. I've no interest in making this any more complicated than it needs to be. Besides, the authorities would spend a lot more effort on the case if kids got killed. An old recluse and a couple of losers from out of town won't generate nearly as much interest.

"In that regard, we should strike fast. I've never seen kids in the place before, and apparently they are a new occurrence for Dredman and Hostetter as well. If we get this done right away, it'll improve our chances of getting in and out before the kids decide to pay another visit.

"They were high tailing it past the house shortly before the three of you came back," Zeller noted. "They are big kids, but nothing we can't handle if necessary. The girl was carrying a bow, if you can believe that, but I don't think we need to worry about her as long as she doesn't upgrade to a rifle. From a distance, the bow did look like the real thing though – not a toy."

"Let's not be complacent just because they aren't adults," Cruz warned. "These are country kids, and any one of them or all of them might be good shots if they have a weapon. Dredman said something on the phone about finding an ammo bag in the swamp. Frankly, sometimes kids are even more dangerous than the typical grown man because kids haven't learned true fear yet.

"Tomorrow is Sunday, so it'll be a good day to strike. They'll probably be in church and with their families. Let's work this out tonight and get organized tomorrow morning. The longer these two losers are hanging around here, the more likely they will attract attention and ruin this operation. We need to strike quickly and get out even faster. Let's plan to be ready to go by early afternoon.

THAT evening Zeller took over the cooking. He prepared fried steaks, salad, baked potatoes with slabs of butter, and Wonder Bread dipped in the steak pan drippings. Clem and Dredman did not even mind having straight vinegar on their salads. It was the first decent meal that they had since arriving in Florida.

Cruz ordered, "After you two clean up the kitchen and brew some coffee, let's gather in the parlor to go over tomorrow's plan. Mr. Zeller and I have a part for everyone to play."

A short while later, after Dredman poured the coffee, they sat down to hear what was expected of them.

Cruz took over. "We'll get rolling about one PM. First we have to determine if those kids are involved or not. They have only been around once from what you are telling us, so we are going on the assumption that they will not be here tomorrow. However, we have to be sure and react accordingly.

We know where they park their bikes, so it'll be a quick matter to check that out. The first order of the day will be for us to drive down to the end of the cutoff to look for the bikes. That'll be your job, Dredman. If the bikes are there, we'll drop you off to flatten their bike tires and to hide in the bushes to make sure none of them escapes.

"With five people, there is always a chance of one getting away if they all make a break for it at one time. A stray gunshot out here will not attract attention. This is hunting territory. However, we cannot restage the OK Corral or we risk drawing in some curiosity seeker. We are expecting you to stop any kid that gets as far as the bikes. You have a gun, but try not to use it. If a kid goes for his bike, stop him and march him back here. Understand?"

"Sure thing, Señor. You can count on me."

Cruz and Zeller cast doubtful looks at one another, and then Cruz continued.

"On the other hand, if there are no bikes, we'll position you within view of their parking area to see if they come later. If you see them coming, hustle back to the witch's house to alert us before they get here.

"Hostetter, the witch probably knows you from when you were her neighbor. She may not like you being here, but she is at least going to open her door to tell you to scram. You are going to knock on the door so we can force our way in with a minimum of fuss. We do not want to have a long-term siege. We could eventually break in, but living out here, she probably has some kind of gun to make it tough."

Clem did not know what frightened him more, knocking on the witch's door and speaking to her, or telling Cruz he didn't want to do it. He settled for sitting there quietly and hoping the day would pass by quickly.

"Mr. Zeller and I will position ourselves on either side of you when you knock. When the witch opens the door, the three of us will rush against it and force her inside. Once inside, Hostetter, you guard the door. Don't leave your post. No matter how many we find inside, we have to make sure that no one leaves. Mr. Zeller and I will take charge of the witch for questioning."

"If the kids show up while we are in the midst of the operation, we can handle that well enough. Dredman will warn us ahead of their arrival. When they knock, we will force the witch to tell them to leave. It may take a little effort, but we will make sure that she is persuasive.

"When they leave, Mr. Zeller will follow at a discrete distance to make sure that they actually depart. We cannot rely on you for that, Dredman, because even kids would probably spot you following them, whereas Mr. Zeller will be invisible to them.

"If the kids are in the house when we arrive, things get a little trickier, but we can handle that too. We'll keep them confined to the house, of course. If they are too much trouble, we'll tie them up, but probably it will be sufficient to herd them together and cover them with a gun.

"Hostetter, you take a position on the path next to the chicken coop. That path leads southeast to the east-west fork between your place and a house on the other side of the lake. If anyone wants to escape eastward, this is the route they will take. It is the most direct and offers cover of the woods almost immediately.

"To get to the north fork, they'd have to run across a large open pasture and then have the longer and more difficult fork to the next house east of here. Anyone going that way does not intend to run for help, at least not immediately, but intends to hide out in the swamp. I can take care of that situation.

"Hostetter, you'll handle anyone you confront the same way as Dredman. If someone gets out and tries to take the path, stop them and bring them back. Try not to fire your weapon, but do so if you have to. Can you handle that, Hostetter?"

Hostetter nodded enthusiastically and said, "Oh, yes," with enough conviction that both Cruz and Zeller believed him. They mistook his relief that he would be far away from the witch for a feeling of confidence.

"OK, good."

To both Dredman and Hostetter, Cruz added, "Under no circumstances are you to kill the witch. If she tries to escape, grab her, tackle her, or aim a shot to her legs. Don't let her get away, but don't kill her. We need her to tell us where the treasure is located.

"We would prefer not having to deal with the complication of the kids, but if they become involved, it is not all bad. Sometimes people can hold out a long time when they don't want to tell you something you want to know. However, most people cave in if they believe that you will take out their stubbornness on a kid if they don't talk.

"Mr. Zeller will be taking my car to Tampa shortly to exchange it for a truck. Since we do not know how big the treasure is or what form it takes, we need to have adequate transport in place. That'll put the start of our operation around early afternoon. OK, let's check our weapons and get some sleep."

CHAPTER 16

The Story Resumes

*The fable, which is naturally and truly composed, so as to satisfy
the imagination, ere it addresses the understanding, beautiful
though strange as a wild-flower, is to the wise man an apothegm,
and admits of his most generous interpretation.*

HENRY DAVID THOREAU

A while after noon, The Crew concealed their bikes behind the palmettos at the corner of Mocking Bird and the Hostetter Cutoff, and
walked to the Canfield house. Once again, everything was quiet at the
Hostetter house as they passed by. No one stirred inside, and the old Ford
remained in place.

They arrived at Sally's house and knocked on the door, not nearly
as nervous as the first time, but still slightly apprehensive. They did not

257

need to be. Sally opened the door and greeted them with a slight smile, but a smile nevertheless. Though she was still dressed entirely in black with the tall witch's hat prominent on her head, she did not seem nearly as intimidating today.

"Come in, come in. Oh, are those for me, Mack?" she asked, taking the flowers he had thrust toward her. "Aren't you the flirt? Thank you, young man."

Mack blushed and managed to get out, "You are welcome, Miss Canfield."

Blake took the fruit to the table and told Sally that it was from Carty's mother. Sally arranged Mack's flowers in a vase that she placed as a centerpiece.

"I have set up a little target area against the barn so you can show me how to use a bow and arrow, Carty. The family records mention that passing Seminoles carried them, and I've always been interested in learning more."

Fingering a metal arrow head, she said, "This is sharper than the stone arrow heads I've found on the grounds, and the arrow is lighter than I thought it would be."

Carty answered, "The Indians did not have the benefit of the engineering that goes into equipment nowadays, so their arrows and their bows varied from piece to piece. They were not nearly as accurate as modern marksmen. It has always amazed me that they did as well as they did with such primitive equipment.

"Bows are more important than arrows. The Indians were limited to whatever wood they could find that would give their arrow adequate velocity to do damage. Now, bows are made from layered combinations of woods and designed for consistency from bow to bow. I'm talking about this type of recurve bow here. It is not a backyard toy that more or less floats an arrow.

"This bow is a Hoyt Professional model with 70 lb weight. Dad has an old Army buddy at Hoyt who got him this test version of the 1951 model they are coming out with next year."

"When we hunt, usually for deer, we use arrows heavier than these to be sure that we do not merely wound an animal. The last thing we want is to wound our prey and have it run off and suffer a slow, agonizing death. An arrow is actually plenty sharp and every bit as deadly as a conventional bullet if it hits a vital part.

"The heavy arrow is more lethal, so I was carrying heavy arrows yesterday for protection when we were in the swamp. The down side is that the heavier arrow tends to be more affected by gravity and is a bit less accurate than the lighter models, except in high wind where the heavier arrow is actually better. Today is absolutely windless, so light arrows will be fine.

"One problem hunters face in the field, especially when the animal is far away, is that the arrow tends to fly high. There are a number of theories for that, but I subscribe to the 'spring theory.'

"Beyond, say, fifty yards, the animal hears the bowstring and has a small fraction of a second to react. Most attempt to spring away from the unexpected sound. In doing so, their muscles tense and they scrunch down ever so slightly. Before they can spring away, however, the arrow arrives. Sometimes it overshoots altogether, but more often, it hits the animal a little above where the archer targeted. Experienced archers usually make a mental adjustment for this, depending on the distance.

"Target practice is a lot easier," she laughed. "The targets don't move."

Picking up the bow, Sally remarked, "Seventy pounds? It does not feel anywhere near that heavy."

"The 70 lbs doesn't refer to how heavy it is – as you can feel, the bow is really light to carry – but to the tension weight on the bow string. Pulling to that maximum 70 lbs. requires more upper body strength than you would have without training. It is why the boys kid me about my Charles Atlas[23] biceps and shoulders.

"That tension is the best for hunting large animals. Its thrust usually gives even light-weight arrows sufficient speed and velocity to penetrate flesh and bone of any mammal in these parts.

"Anyway, I'll be proud to give you your first lesson. I brought some light-weight arrows today. They are easier to learn with, and you don't need to use the full weight of the bow for your lesson."

As before, the table was already set. There was a selection of cheese and sausage on two large plates and a loaf of freshly baked bread.

"I make the cheese with the same process that Elisabeth Canfield, Morgan's first daughter, handed down from the earliest days. The pork sausage that I grind, though, is my own recipe. The Creole spices give it a little bite. My pepper plants were brought from New Orleans in the second of the wagon trains. Like your rhododendron, they survived the climate here.

"If you don't mind, I'd like to show you some of my ancestors while we eat," Sally said as she placed a large photo album on the table. Paging though the book, she explained that the older images were small paintings. Around

1890, the pages turned to sepia-toned photographs. Photos of more recent vintage bore the name of a photographer from town. She pointed to a photo near the end of the album.

"Those were my mother and father. I have no memory of them. Father was killed before I was born, and Mother died less than a year afterward. My grandmother, here on the previous page, was both mother and father to me. I truly do miss her."

Tears welled up in her eyes, and she choked back a sob. Carty instinctively stood and placed her arm around Sally. They stood together while the boys watched silently.

Carty finally spoke. "I can't imagine how horrible it would be to lose one of my parents. It must be terribly difficult for you."

Sally held her breath momentarily. Then she regained her composure and sat in her chair.

Blake was the first to speak. "When our mother died, I was young, but old enough to know what it meant. I missed my entire first year of school mourning her. Not a night goes by that I fail to think about her. I always say a prayer for her as I fall asleep. I think it is worse for the littler ones. They can't remember her at all. What really makes me sad is that as the days go by, my memory of her is fading, and I can't seem to stop it from diminishing. My dad does his best for us, and we love him for it. But he cannot give us a mother's love the way that Mom did."

Carty looked at Blake with wonder. She thought of him as a solid brick wall that nothing bothered. The sensitivity he was displaying now was uncharacteristic of anything she had seen of him before. He had stepped up a rung on her ladder of respect. She had always admired him for his fortitude, but it was good to see that he cared too.

Silence gripped the room. A chill enveloped them despite the Florida heat.

This time it was Sally who gave an arm in comfort, surprising all but Blake, who welcomed it more than he thought about it. He rested his head on her arm. After a few moments, Sally broke the mood.

"Well, enough of that. Let us eat."

This time, she bowed her head and said grace. At first, Carty wondered why she hadn't said a prayer yesterday. Then she realized that Sally was no longer performing her witch act for them. Instead, she was showing unexpected vulnerability and naturalness. They had come a long way in a short time.

As they ate, Hale said that he mentioned Sally's story of Duck Lake to his grandfather the previous night. "He told me that he vaguely recalled hearing something like it from his great grandfather a long time ago. He could not remember the details, but says it was well-known during slave times. He says he cannot wait for me to bring the complete story home."

"I believe," Sally began, "that when we left off, Penny, the parrot, had learned of the raccoons' plan to band together in a joint operation."

CHAPTER G

The Escape Plan

Penny circled above and swooped to a soft landing near Matthew. The short limb on the sapling barely drooped under her slight weight. "I have news that you will not like hearing. The raccoons are planning to attack again tomorrow night."

"We will be ready for them," replied Matthew. "The ducks from years ago knew how to confuse the disorganized attacks of raccoons. We will employ those same tactics. After a brief battle, the raccoons will look out for themselves as individuals and retreat. We will suffer, perhaps greatly, but our village will be saved."

"You don't understand," Penny persisted. "These raccoons are not like the raccoons of years past. Their leader, whose name is Moosta, has recognized their past weakness.

263

He is organizing all three of the swamp's raccoon camps into a single unified and disciplined fighting force. They are training together as we speak. I do not know if their plan will work, but I do know that you will be facing an enormous and well-trained raccoon army. Those raccoons have an organized plan designed by an evil and fearless leader."

Matthew replied, "From time to time, I have heard rumors of a strong leader among the raccoons, though I had not previously heard his name. Your news could be catastrophic."

Penny whispered to Matthew that she had something else to tell him. As she spoke, the gloom on his face deepened further. "Are you certain?" he asked.

Penny nodded solemnly. "I do not know what the meeting was concerning, but I saw Moosta and Drack in a long conversation just a few nights ago. At the time, I thought it odd, but I did not believe it to be important. However, it is clear that Moosta has a source for the information about your strategy."

Matthew thanked Penny for her help and was distraught at the idea that a duck from their village might be a traitor. Helping the enemy in any way was the worst possible betrayal.

Matthew quacked a young duck over and instructed him to notify the other council members of an emergency meeting. Soon they gathered together where Penny and Matthew were speaking. Matthew flapped up to a mound of dirt.

"I have learned from our parrot friend Penny that all the raccoons in the swamp have banded together under a single leader. It appears that they are organizing a combined plan of attack. This is the worst possible news. Our safety has always depended on the legendary inability of raccoons to cooperate with one another. Raccoons have always had the attitude of 'everyone for himself.' As they are now working together, our village may be doomed. Tonight we will try to come up with a solution. We welcome anyone with an idea. Tomorrow morning we will meet here again to announce the plan that we develop."

No one slept well for the rest of the night. The cloudy morning draped more gloom over the village. Surely they could not fight an army of raccoons, especially not so many in a huge organized attack. The Council of Elders convened what they considered to be their final meeting. Following a light breakfast, Matthew announced the decision at a village meeting.

After explaining what he had learned and what they would be facing, he gave them the bad news, keeping back only information about Drack. "We will have to abandon the village. Today will be for organizing the move. Before dark, we must be ready to leave for a safe location far away."

But to move away in such a short time would mean abandoning the newly laid eggs. Many of the duck moms refused to leave. "We must let them hatch first. We need to wait several more days. We'd rather die defending our children than let those ravenous raccoons have our eggs."

"Be reasonable," the Elders implored. "We can fight disorganized rabble, but we cannot fight off an orderly army. It is better to save ourselves while we have a chance. Next year you will have new eggs and new baby ducklings."

Drack saw that this discussion was not moving to his advantage. If the village were abandoned, his plans to become its Supreme Ruler would be ruined. There would be nothing left to rule. He spoke up, "I agree with the ladies," he shouted. "We need to fight. We have a chance. We can win. We cannot leave our village."

That is what Matthew was waiting for. Drack had never shown any streak of courage before. He was little more than a loud-mouthed bully at best. Of all the ducks, he was among the least likely to voice such strong sentiments. "What do you think that Moosta will do next, Drack?" Matthew asked.

"He will probably try some hit and miss attacks as he has in the past. If we defend in mass, we will scare Moosta and his horde back to where they came from."

"Tell me, Drack, how do you know who Moosta is? I did not identify him just now as a leader of the raccoons. No one in the village had ever heard the name Moosta until Penny reported to me and only to me. I didn't share the name with anyone else, not even with anyone on the council. The logical reply to my question would have been, 'Who is Moosta?' Instead, you knew exactly who Moosta was. How is that possible?"

Drack was speechless. Every time he thought of something to say, he realized that the excuse would not make sense. The villagers muttered among themselves in confusion. Finally, Drack said, "It doesn't really matter. Soon, with Moosta's help, I will be Supreme Ruler and you will be taking instructions from me anyway."

"Until then," Matthew answered calmly, "Tie Drack to the oak tree. We certainly do not want him getting in our way during the battle."

Danielle said to the Elders, "Battle? Does that mean that you will stay and help us protect our eggs and our village?"

Matthew replied, "Of course we will. I am sorry that we appeared ready to abandon the village. I arranged this little drama to make it look like we Elders were running away. It was the only way I could think of to flush out Drack's treachery. We have no intention of leaving you here on your own. We will stay and fight with you."

Unlike the fervor expressed at the raccoon camp, however, here there were no shouts or wild displays of enthusiasm, just grim thanks and recognition that there might be no survivors.

Later that evening, Penny reported back that the attack would come the following night.

CHAPTER H

The Battle

For the ducks, the night of the expected battle seemed to come more quickly than normal as the continuing heavy cloud cover sent the sun away early. The moon and the stars did not make an appearance as this frightful night wore on. The darkness was near total, an advantage for the sharp-eyed raccoons.

Despite the late hour, only the youngest ducks were asleep. The others lay with ears alert, straining to hear any unusual sound. Rustling pine needles alerted ducks on the north edge of the village that the attack was imminent. There was not much noise, but enough to suggest that the raccoons were even more numerous than the ducks had feared. And the ducks knew that the army was sneaking toward them on all three land sides.

The uneasy calm was broken by a clam shell splashing into the lake. That was Moosta's signal. Simultaneously, the attack came from all directions. Near the water's edge, on the north front, a loud commotion arose. Two large raccoons attacked Danielle. Violently, she beat her wings at the oncoming bandits, nipping at them with a sharp but toothless beak. One raccoon fell backwards, breaking its leg on a rock. It crawled away as quickly as it could. The second raccoon sunk its teeth deeply into Danielle's leg, pulling her away from the nest. They fell together into the water.

Paldine jumped on the raccoon's back and pecked him about the eyes. Two other raccoons joined the skirmish. They dug their teeth into his wing and pulled him away. He fought fiercely, but Danielle was on her own for now.

In the deep water, Danielle gained some advantage. She could hold her breath under water longer than the raccoon. So she feigned weakness and allowed him to drag her under, and then became the aggressor and struggled to keep him there until he drowned.

Elsewhere other attacks were underway. All of the ducks, including the Elders, joined the fight. In the beginning, the attack showed some hopeful signs of breaking down. A few raccoons stopped fighting to break open eggs and suck out the yellow contents. Others scooped up a few eggs and ran off with them. The ducks thought that they might have a chance if raccoon discipline continued to dissolve.

Then Moosta grabbed Dool as the underling was fleeing with a pawful of eggs and thundered, "All ducks to the death – no raccoon may leave the battlefield until victory is complete, or they will have to answer to me when the war is over. I am watching everyone." With that said, he bit through Dool's neck and left him in a lifeless heap.

Instantaneously, the direction of the battle shifted in the raccoons' favor. Out of fear of Moosta, the others resisted their instinct to operate independently. They banded together once again into a cohesive battle unit. Seeing this, the ducks sensed that their cause was lost, but they continued to fight valiantly.

Another wave of raccoons launched westward into the center of the duck's line of defense. If the raccoons could push through at this point, they would split the ducks' position. Then the raccoons could wheel right and left into the backs of the ducks fighting the northern and southern assaults. It would be the most effective way to defeat the ducks. But there the Elders held the line courageously.

Though no longer as strong as the younger ducks, the Elders were more experienced. Matthew liked to tease the youngsters during the summer duck Sports Games that age and cunning would always overcome youth and enthusiasm. This was not a game, however, but the Elders knew how to make the best of their situation. They always worked in pairs, selecting one raccoon to attack. Even if they were being hit from the back themselves, they ignored that threat and concentrated on the raccoon they had pinpointed.

The tactic achieved initial success as many of the raccoons were injured and limped away. However, the Elders suffered greatly by ignoring attacks on their own backs. Moreover, the raccoons' sheer numerical advantage was overwhelming the rapidly tiring ducks. They were holding their line against a breakthrough, but its center was sagging farther and farther back toward the lake.

The defensive line reached the tree where Drack was tied. "Let me go," he pleaded to Drennan, an embattled duck. "You can use all the help you can get."

Drennan poked his foot into the eye of a raccoon, sending it yelping into the darkness. With the temporary lull, he loosened the rope and released Drack. Drennan returned his attention to a raccoon circling him. It lurched for him. He dodged to his right and tripped the off-balanced raccoon as he ran by. Then he pounced on the fallen raccoon's back and bit off an ear. He was about to take the other ear from the screeching mammal when Drack attacked Drennan's back.

Drack secured Drennan's wings to restrict his ability to maneuver. The injured raccoon twisted around and bit deeply into Drennan's neck. Drennan looked at Drack with horror, not so much in recognition that he was dying, but at the evil duplicity that befell him. His lifeless body slumped to the ground as the raccoon and Drack looked for another victim.

Meanwhile, at Big Lake's edge, Danielle pecked off another raccoon's nose. Wailing in pain, he released her wing, front paws to his bloody face.

However, as Danielle climbed on to land, Moosta leapt off a large rock, landing on top of her. He snared her neck with sharp teeth and used his greater weight to wrestle her down toward the lake. Moosta's teeth sunk deeper into her neck, weakening her will. He pushed her beneath the churning water with his strong paws while keeping his own head above water. She was losing consciousness. She thought of her unhatched eggs, of the children she would not have. As she cried for them, the water washed away the tears before they could form. Her air was almost gone.

Unexpectedly, Moosta's grip loosened slightly. Revived and enraged, Danielle flapped furiously and pushed her head above the water, sucking in the precious air. Moosta's grip released completely and she pulled away from him, climbing to land once more.

Already, she saw two of her children and many other ducks lying dead or badly injured. Most were bleeding profusely from bite and scratch marks, long scrapes of feathers torn from their bodies. The fewer scattered raccoon casualties gave her momentary hope, but she realized that there was no possibility of victory. The raccoons had the best weapons. Their teeth were sharper than duck beaks, and their claws cut more violently than duck feet. The raccoons outnumbered them twice over, and this time Moosta had them working as one unit.

"But why did that large raccoon let me go," she wondered momentarily, as she sought a new target. "I was beyond any hope of escape."

Suddenly, a bewildering raccoon wail pierced the din of quacking ducks and snarling raccoons. Then another scream reverberated through the swamp. Moments later, a third scream rose, louder than the two preceding. Raccoons paused in their attack to locate the source of the noise, a signal of unexpected danger that was startling them. Heads raised, but no one saw anything alarming. Another scream near the water, stifled by a gurgling sound, drew closer attention. They stared at the swirling lake, their keen eyesight penetrating the darkness. For several seconds, no one moved – not a duck, not a raccoon. The screams had momentarily hypnotized warriors on both sides.

Suddenly, a huge log shot from the water as if catapulted. It was a green log with two enormous eyes and eighty large, glistening, white teeth clenching Moosta tightly. But it was not a log. It was Green Duck! He threw Moosta's lifeless body to the ground, and snatched the nearest raccoon into his mouth, shook his head sharply and thrust the shocked animal into a watery grave. Before others could react, his jaws crushed the body of another mesmerized raccoon unlucky to be near the water's edge.

"Noooo!" erupted a high pitched scream as Drack hurled himself on to Green Duck's back in horrifying understanding that all would be lost. Green Duck did not even notice that a light-weight duck was sliding along his back toward his tail. By the time Green Duck swiped at a fourth raccoon with that violent tail, Drack had slid all the way to the tip. In an instant, both raccoon and duck shot through the air to their instant deaths against the giant cypress tree that had secured Green Duck's egg those many years earlier.

In great disarray, the other raccoons scattered for the meadows beyond the trees, as ducks chased and nipped at their tails. From the look of sheer terror in the eyes of the raccoons, the ducks knew that those evil creatures would never return and would ignore any other attempts to organize them. The war was over. Mallard Village was saved.

CHAPTER I

The Apology

The next morning, Green Duck lay next to Danielle's nest. His dead brothers and sisters had been buried. Millard and the other survivors slept soundly and safely around Green Duck's long, leathery body. Paldine, with bruised feathers matted with blood, looked proudly at Danielle as she sat upon her eggs.

Slowly, all of the other ducks approached, their heads bowed in shame and gratitude, their brown and green face feathers pink with blush. Even those with injured legs pulled themselves forward. "We came to thank you, Green Duck, and to apologize for our past behavior towards you. Our village is saved, and we are alive only because of you. We hope that you will always stay, and we invite you to join our Council of Elders."

275

Green Duck was silent. He looked slowly from duck to duck, forcing each to look into his eyes. When he finished, he said, "Do not apologize to me; apologize to my mother, for without her, I would never have been allowed to live years ago when she adopted my egg. It was she, not I, who truly saved your lives and your village."

Then he paused and again forced eye contact with every one of the apologetic ducks. "And *my* village," he added finally, flashing his endearing smile. Paldine beamed and hugged Danielle.

Cheers rang up from all around. Green Duck had returned in triumph and was staying in the village – his village. "Hooray! Hooray! Long Live Green Duck!"

One by one, the ducks came up to Danielle to offer their apologies. To each she said that she held no bad feelings. "The important thing is not what has passed, but what is to come. Jealousy is a vicious vice. It gains nothing and hurts many. If we treat each other kindly, we will be treated kindly in return."

Paldine added, "You have seen what comes of loyalty. We faced difficulty together, and Green Duck remained true to the village despite the poor treatment he had received. Combining as one, we did not surrender. We did not give up. We were victorious!"

More cheers erupted from the exhausted ducks. Then they retreated to their nests to rest. When everyone was gone, Paldine gave Green Duck a big hug and led the youngsters away so that Danielle could be alone with Green Duck.

With her uninjured wing draped softly over Green Duck's head, she again shed tears, but this time they were tears of joy, not sorrow. Green Duck was silent for a long time. Then he looked up at Danielle and whispered, "Some alligators eat ducks, Momma."

She looked at him for a few moments and asked, "Why did you say that, son?"

Green Duck did not know if he should continue. He gulped, took a deep breath, and confided, "I don't eat ducks Momma, but I am really an alligator, not a duck. My new name is Montooth, for the one large tooth that sticks out from my mouth."

She pulled him close. "I know that you are an alligator, Green Duck. I've known for a long time. Your daddy is the best flight instructor in the history of Big Lake. When you could not learn from him how to fly, I knew that there had to be a reason. After thinking about it for a while, I remembered that after a terrible storm, I found an egg near the big cypress tree. At the time, I thought that it was one of mine. I brought it back to our nest, and helped it hatch just like the eggs of your brothers and sisters.

"A short time before that, your father and I had been swimming near that cypress tree. A very large alligator frightened us there. We never saw her after the storm, so

I believe that the egg was probably hers. That is how I figured out that you were an alligator." She paused for a few moments to allow Green Duck to think about what she had just said.

"And I know that you wouldn't eat ducks," she continued. "Moreover, I don't care if some call you Montooth now. You will always be Green Duck to me."

Green Duck smiled his biggest smile ever.

CHAPTER 17

The Strike

Resistance to criminal rashness comes better late than never.
Titus Livius (Livy)

Zeller had returned early in the morning before The Crew passed by. First he hid the truck in the shed where it would be out of view. The Rex Seafood signage on the sides would be a helpful disguise once they were well on their way, but if a potential witness saw the truck around the Hostetter Cutoff, authorities might be led to them.

For lunch, he fried some pork chops with a salsa sauce, boiled potatoes and green beans, and tossed another vinegar salad. The two residents were again so grateful for the tasty meal that they did not object to cleaning the kitchen afterward. Not that either of them would have had the temerity to complain if Zeller had prepared kidney gruel with butterscotch gravy.

"We have had a small change of plans," Cruz advised over coffee. "The four kids showed up again."

Dredman and Hostetter looked at each other in surprise. Even Zeller was taken aback.

"I saw them walk past the house while we ate. They didn't pay us any attention, and I don't think they will cause us trouble. You were right about the girl's bow, Carey. I had a good look. It's a modern recurve longbow. It looks to have a lot of tension, so it can't be a toy. I'm no expert in bows, but she must be a strong girl if she is actually able to use that thing.

"So it's Plan A. Dredman, off to the bike park; flatten the tires to be safe. If a kid escapes, bring him back. Don't shoot unless it is absolutely necessary. If all is quiet, just stay put. We'll pick you up after we secure the treasure.

"Hostetter, first you'll get us into the house as we discussed. Help us to secure the witch and the kids. Then take your position on the southeast path past the chicken coop. If anyone goes for help to the east, he'll take that route. We can be confident that no one will use the lengthy north fork to head east. Any questions?"

There were none.

Zeller took the Ford and drove Dredman to the end of the cutoff. There the two deflated the bike tires. Then Zeller found good cover where Dredman could spring out if anyone went for a bike. The location had a good view up the cutoff so Dredman would have plenty of warning if anyone came along. Dredman released the safety on his gun. Zeller rolled his eyes and hoped that Dredman would avoid shooting himself in the foot before anyone arrived.

"Don't panic," he admonished. "Just stay alert so you don't have to fire that thing."

Zeller returned the Ford to its parking place next to the house and reported back. The three loaded their weapons. Cruz had the knife that he had retained from his Sierra Maestra days, a .44 under his belt, and a .38 in an ankle holster beneath his pants leg. Both Zeller and Hostetter carried .38s and extra ammo. All of the weapons were in perfect condition. They did not take rifles, as they were not planning for any long distance action.

Zeller wore the bulletproof vest that he took from the Japanese soldier. He never forgot the incident that had taken his comrade in the Pacific fighting, and had been committed to bulletproof protection ever since.

When they neared the Canfield house, Hostetter was told to stay in place under cover. Cruz circled the house looking for stragglers outside while Zeller made sure no one was using the outhouse. He did not bother to boost himself up to look into one of the high windows, as the nearly opaque shears would obstruct his view. The three neared the door just as Sally finished *The Legend of Montooth*.

She had closed the small book softly, and Hale returned it to the bookshelf where he was glancing through a few of the many volumes. The others were talking about the story when a knock on the door startled everyone. Sally sat bolt upright in her chair. Outside of the four current visitors, no one had been at her door in nearly a decade. She looked inquisitively at Carty.

"I don't think it is anyone we know, Miss Canfield," she said, understanding the unexpressed question.

The pounding became more insistent, followed by a squeaky voice. "Miss Canfield, this is Clemens Hostetter, your neighbor. I fell and hurt my arm. I think it is broken. Can you help me?"

"I don't like this," Sally whispered. She sprinted to the side of the door and climbed atop a step. From this vantage point, she was able to peer out of a small crack in the planks, positioned to provide her with a partial view outside the door.

Returning quickly to the table, she said, "I can't see them too well, but there are at least three men. Clemens shows no sign of any problem with his arm. Carty, you and Blake go up those stairs. Take the second bedroom and leave by the window. You can actually use the stone wall outside as a primitive ladder."

Pointing to the west wall, she said to the other boys, "See that large cupboard? Climb into it and look for a hinged latch on the outside wall. Pull down to release. That's an escape route. Two of the outside cypress boards will swing upward and allow you to leave.

Blake protested in a hushed voice, "Miss Canfield, if there is any danger, we'd like to face it together with you. We are not going to run away and leave you alone." The others nodded their heads in agreement.

The knock became even more insistent. "Please, Miss Canfield. I'm in a lot of pain," Clem shouted.

Sally resumed her public persona momentarily and replied in a croaking, raspy voice. "I don't know who you are. I am not a doctor. Go to a doctor if you are injured."

To her visitors, she said softly, "All right, here is what we will do. Carty, go upstairs and listen from behind the door. If there is a problem, it will be good to have someone on the outside. If you sense trouble, climb down the wall. And Carty, take your bow. Boys, who is the fastest runner?"

Hale raised his hand while the others pointed at him. "Hale can beat anyone in the school in a sprint or a long run," Blake added. "No one can come close."

"Then Hale, you get into the cupboard and listen. Pull the latch right away so you won't make noise later. Wait to see if there is trouble, and if there is, go out the escape door and make for Mocking Bird Road. There are plenty of houses there. Ask someone to call the sheriff. Mack, Blake, and I will try to stall them if they are going to cause difficulty. If they just want to talk, stay in the cabinet and be quiet."

Another hearty knock on the door spurred them into action. Carty grabbed her bow and quiver and raced quietly up the stairs. Mack helped Hale into the cupboard and closed him in.

Hale ran into difficulty immediately. He found the latch, but it wouldn't give way to his strong tugs. He tried several times without success. It probably had not been tried in years and was rusted in place from high humidity. He debated climbing out to get Blake's help, because Blake was probably strong enough to break it off if necessary. But he decided that he did not have enough time.

The two remaining boys resumed their seats at the table. Sally hid the cups and plates that Carty and Blake had been using.

"I'm Clem Hostetter, Cora Hostetter's son. I know that you knew her. I live in the farmhouse west of here. I wouldn't bother you, but I am in real pain. Please help me.'

Sally waited for almost another minute to be certain that Carty and Hale were in proper position. Then she approached the door. Resuming her witch voice, she croaked a response. "One moment, young man. I'll open the door."

She unlocked the door and eased it slightly ajar, expecting to engage in conversation with the men. Instead, Cruz and Zeller bull-rushed the door, which threw her back and on to the floor. Mack and Blake jumped from their seats to offer her help, but immediately saw that they were facing two guns. Hostetter then followed, adding a third.

Feigning surprise, but actually so that the hidden pair would know what was occurring, Blake shouted loudly, "Mack, they have guns!"

Both boys came around guardedly to help Sally to her feet while Cruz held his gun on them. "Have a seat, gentlemen. You may help the lady to a chair on the way."

Blake's call reached Carty upstairs. There was no mistaking the urgency in his voice. Carty had already removed the screen from the open window to facilitate a fast escape. She had pushed her bow and quiver through the opening and hung them on the rough rock wall well before Blake yelled. Quickly, she reached out, unhooked the weapon and quiver and dropped them gently to a flowering bush. Then she climbed out and began working herself down.

With the others under control inside the house, Hostetter was already heading for his position near the chicken coop. Carty caught a glimpse of him running for his position and believed that he probably saw her as well when he turned around. Therefore she opted for speed over stealth and ran across the open pasture. She sought the cover of the swamp that she knew rather than the forest that was unfamiliar to her.

As she ran, she remembered that she had gone to church in a white blouse and was grateful that she had changed into a dark green color before setting out for Sally's. She did not need to stand out like an egret while she was hiding in the swamp.

"God must have been looking out for me," she thought. "Please stay with me a little longer," she prayed.

As prearranged, Zeller bounded up the stairs to begin searching the rooms. Because he examined the closest room first, Carty had enough time to escape, and she was well across the pasture when he entered the second room. Carty had taken the few seconds available to her earlier to remove the window screens from the first room too in order to confuse the scene.

After a few minutes, he reported that no one else appeared to be in the house, but that he had noticed that two upstairs windows were open with the screens taken out.

Cruz looked toward the table where the three prisoners were gathered. The boys had helped Sally to a chair by that time. "Before we get started, tell me where the other two are – the Negro and the girl."

Sally presented a confused look and croaked in her stage voice, "There are just three of us here. What do you want?"

Cruz peered at her through his snake-like squint. He was not certain that Carty and Hale had actually gone into Sally's house after passing by the farmhouse, but it was a good guess. Where else could they be? So he bluffed, "You do not want to play with us. We know that the other two came in. We have been watching your house since early this morning."

Recalling the time when he saw them pass in front of the house, he calculated enough time to travel the distance from Hostetter's to Canfield's. "They arrived here just before one o'clock and we saw no one leave since then."

Cruz saw from their eyes that he had guessed correctly. The question remaining was the location of the pair now. He was angered by the silence that followed. Glancing to the side to be certain that his accomplice had his gun aimed at them, he set his own gun on a small end table away from the captives. Always intimidate rather than confront, he reminded himself.

In one swift move, he grabbed Mack by the shirt collar and yanked him to his feet. He drew his knife, and without warning, and with minimal effort, used the expertly honed blade to slice off an inch long piece from the top of Mack's ear, which he dropped to a thud on the table. Mack's hand shot to the damaged ear that was bleeding, but Cruz was impressed that the boy did not make a sound.

Fortunately, the ear has relatively weak nerves, and the pain was tolerable and blood minimal. More to the point, Mack had already faced a lifetime of harrowing escapes from Nazis and had lost many family members to them. A little physical pain was hardly unbearable.

The impact on Sally was dramatic, however. All pretense of resistance vanished. "The others left when you arrived," she immediately responded. "Your man already noticed the missing screens upstairs. If you examine the outside wall, you can see that it is easy to climb down."

Believing that Hale was already on his way for help, Sally wanted the invaders to focus their attention to the east of the house to give Hale a greater head start in the opposite direction.

Seeing the consequences of lying to this man, she determined to avoid a repeat. However, she thought that if he discovered some misdirection on her part, he might be willing to tolerate that.

Unfortunately, unknown to Sally, Hale was still trapped in the cabinet. He no longer tried to pull the spring latch, because the noise would give him away even if it loosened. He found that he could twist the latch slightly without noise, though, so he continued to work the latch in that manner, trying to weaken years of rust with small, nearly silent movements.

Cruz pushed Mack into a chair at the table and retrieved his gun. He gave a flick of his head to Zeller, who strode through the still open front door. Zeller returned about two minutes later. "She's right. A nimble person could climb down the wall easily. There are several recent marks on the stone. I'd say they were from someone on the wall. There is stone on the ground underneath the wall, so I had no way to tell how many came down that way. I'll look through the house more carefully in case one of them is hiding."

Sally asked if she could make a bandage for Mack's ear while the second search was going on. Cruz did not answer, but as he did not object, she got up to retrieve gauze, tape, and a pair of scissors from a drawer.

"I trust that you won't get careless with the scissors. Miss Canfield, is it?"

Sally nodded and patched up Mack's ear. "You seem to know me," she said, "May I know your name?"

Cruz had no intention of leaving any witnesses, but it paid to be careful. "You may call me Mr. Smith. My friend there," pointing up the stairs with his free hand, "is Mr. Jones. You already know your neighbor,

Mr. Hostetter." Hostetter's name didn't matter. The plan did not include his survival.

When she was finished tending to Mack, she returned the scissors to the drawer and closed it while standing to the side, satisfying Cruz with the process.

"Nothing, Mr. Smith," Zeller reported when he returned. "There is no one up there. I even checked the attic. No one has been up there in years," he said, brushing dust from his jacket in emphasis.

"Should we search down here, Mr. Smith?"

"No, Mr. Jones. I believe that Miss Canfield will tell us what happened." With that, he grabbed Mack's shirt collar and reached for his knife.

Sally thrust her hands forward with the fingers splayed out in a symbol for restraint. "Wait. I'll tell you what I know." She was a good storyteller and hoped to gain additional time by holding their interest. Still maintaining her witch voice, she explained that the first Canfields came to this untamed wilderness when only volatile Spanish authorities and unpredictable Indians inhabited it.

"This house is not a medieval fort, but my ancestors built it strong so that they could hold off a small assault for a short time and give the family time to seek an escape. The idea was to have unanticipated exits in three compass directions that could be accessed if the need arose. The ladder-like stone wall to the east allows escape in that direction.

Addressing Cruz, she complimented him. "Mr. Smith, you appear to be competent at this line of work. I assume that you have noticed that we have but the one door. There is no other apparent entry or exit. Our lower windows are too small for an adult person to climb through. However, one of the windows in the south wall has a removable top section that expands the opening. A person could squeeze through the larger hole."

She paused while Zeller went into the back room and examined the windows. After a few minutes, he returned with the report. "It is as she says. It's a clever design. But it hasn't been used for years. The surrounding area is unmarked. No one went out that way."

Sally continued, becoming slightly unnerved that her rendition seemed to be amusing Cruz rather than concerning him. "The small window in the west wall does not expand. As you can see, it is too small for anyone to squeeze through. The west escape route is through that cabinet against the wall. It opens a section of the outside wall."

When Hale heard Sally describing the first escape routes, he realized he was in trouble. Sally believed that he was already gone, and she would soon disclose his location. If he yanked the latch free while the men were in the room, it would make enough noise that his capture was certain even if he got outside.

In the dark, he strained his eyes, looking for a solution. The cabinet ran the full height of the high wall, almost a full twelve feet. He was kneeling on the floor in a cavity behind the actual shelves. There was barely enough room for him to stand, but he quietly got to his feet. Bracing his hands and feet tightly against opposite walls, Hale slowly inched himself upward. By the time Zeller opened the cabinet door, Hale was perched precariously against the ceiling.

Zeller peered into the dark cabinet and crawled forward. In the dim light filtering in from the room, he could see that the latch was still intact. With more light, he might have seen that some of the rust had recently been worked loose, but the opening to the room was too small to illuminate the latch adequately. "The latch seems rusted in place," he called out.

Hale was straining with every ounce of his strength to maintain his position hovering high above Zeller. The heat at the top of his enclosed cavity exceeded 100 degrees. Sweat dripped from Hale's nose on to Zeller's back, but he could not risk taking a supporting hand away from the wall to wipe his face. Only Zeller's thick, bullet-proof covering under his shirt prevented him from noticing the faint drips.

With a final strong tug, Zeller pulled the latch loose. He swung the door up and outward and looked out at the soft ground. "No one got out this way," he yelled to Cruz. "That latch hasn't been opened in years, and there are no footprints outside." Zeller pulled the door in, slammed the latch pin back into place, and crawled out of the cabinet.

Fortunately, Cruz did not notice the momentary confused looks on the faces of his captives. Now they were less sure of Hale's whereabouts than Cruz, who assumed that Carty and Hale had scaled the wall together.

"Well then, Miss Canfield, that was not too difficult, was it? You did so well with that explanation. Perhaps you can tell us a little about the Canfield Treasure now."

She was tempted to claim she had nothing of value but realized that this "Mr. Smith" would not react well to any obvious lies. Her only hope came from possible help that the two escapees might bring. She decided to employ delaying tactics by sprinkling them with dollops of truth.

"WHEN my ancestors arrived in this territory, there were no banks or other places to store valuables. In the early days, everything was kept

buried on the land here or in the house. Some of it came in the original wagon train. Most came in later years when the family was more established here. Over the years, about half of the wealth had been converted to gold, though Morgan Canfield retained ownership of New Orleans and Savannah real estate. I still hold deeds to valuable properties there and here in Florida.

"As civilization began emerging, later descendants became active behind the scenes as principals in several banks, including the local Ensign Bank. Much of the family valuables are stored in the Ensign Bank vault. All the stocks are kept there and the deeds are in other banks in Florida, Georgia, and Louisiana, depending on the location of the property.

"Here at the house, we've always kept only a small amount of cash along with the bonds that require us to clip quarterly coupons to present for collection. Nearly all of our tangible valuables, though – mostly jewels and artifacts – are at the Ensign Bank."

"In the earliest days, the family buried a modest amount of gold here on the property. Gold was the motivation for bringing in so much granite for building the house. The gold bars in the wagons were hidden with piles of rock. If anyone had known about the gold being moved, the wagon trains would have been under constant attack.

"During the Depression in the Thirties, citizens were supposed to turn in their gold to the government for paper money, but ours just stayed buried in the ground. The family figured that someday Americans would be allowed to own gold again."

Cruz stared intently at her eyes until he was satisfied that she was telling the truth. The idea of using Hostetter and Dredman to go into town with Sally to try to withdraw valuables from the bank vault did not appeal to him, especially because hauling them would require several trucks. The chance of that pair messing up was high. Maybe she had enough valuables on the property to make the venture worthwhile.

He asked, "About how much of the 'modest amount' of gold do you have buried on the property, and what is the face value of the bonds that are here?

"There are about 750 gold bars of about 27 pounds each. The bonds are worth about $400,000."

Along with the two criminals, Mack and Blake gasped at the enormity of what she was describing. Mack realized that Sally's valuables were many times more than the entire value of the Sebring Airport property where his dad was building the racetrack.

Cruz went through some quick mental calculations. "At $35 per ounce, that makes the gold you have buried worth well over eleven million dollars, assuming it can be moved out of the country where its possession is legal. I'm sure that you won't mind sharing some of your wealth with Mr. Jones and me. How about showing us the bonds first?"

Sally noted that Mr. Smith did not include Clem in the sharing.

Sally led them into the first floor bedroom. Zeller prodded the boys along for safekeeping. She approached the fireplace and knelt down to lift a heavy slate slab from the hearth. They could see the top of a large metal box. Taking a key from a hook behind the mantle, she offered it to Cruz.

"No," Cruz said, alert to a possible booby trap, "You go right ahead. I'll be watching closely that you don't have a gun in there, though. So move slowly as you open the box and make sure that I can see what you are doing."

Sally happily complied with the last order. The longer she stalled, the more likely Hale and Carty would be bringing help, though she was still confused about what happened to Hale. She had a momentary feeling that Mr. Smith seemed thoroughly unconcerned about the two escapees. She wondered if the prospect of the enormous wealth had distracted him from thinking clearly, though she doubted that.

WHEN Zeller left the cabinet earlier, Hale worked his way back down the wall and waited for an opportunity to retry his escape. When he heard everyone moving out of the large room, he tugged at the latch pin. It was still tight. Zeller had opened it, but he had slammed it back tightly when he closed the latch. Using two hands, Hale found that the twisting became easier, and in less than a minute, a final strong tug pulled it down. He held his breath, waiting to see if the minimal noise brought a reaction from the men.

ABOUT THAT TIME, Sally opened the lock on the storage bin and pulled back the heavy lid. Making certain that Cruz could see into the container, she lifted out a stack of bearer bonds and set them on the bed, then returned for more.

"Give her a hand, boys," Cruz ordered. "It's not nice to make ladies do all the work." Immediately, Mack and Blake knelt down and added to the extraction effort.

When they had stacked the entire cache on the bed, Cruz said, "How about tallying that up, Mr. Jones?"

After about half an hour, Zeller finished. "Four hundred forty-two thousand, six hundred dollars of face value, Mr. Smith," he said. "Even if she isn't telling the truth about the gold, this is an amazing haul."

"Do you have some large bags that would hold all of these bonds, Miss Canfield?"

"No, Mr. Smith, I'm not accustomed to moving large amounts of documents," she replied coldly.

Eventually, Zeller found twine and directed the boys to tie the bonds into neat square stacks that could be carried easily.

"Don't worry about doing too good a job. We'll have to risk bringing the truck out here anyway. We can't haul ten tons of gold by hand, even with the help of these two strong young lads."

When the bundling was complete, Cruz ordered the captives into a corner of the room. "Just sit there on the floor quietly. Mr. Jones and I need to confer."

While keeping his gun trained on them, he discussed with Zeller how they would have to modify their plan. "Assuming that she really has 750 bars of gold, the weight will be about 20,000 pounds. It'll take a sustained effort to move it. The truck can handle no more than two tons at a time. Making four or five trips out here is asking for trouble. We'll have to eliminate the witch and the kids along with Dredman and Hostetter. The kids are certain to be missed by tonight, so we can't just keep them captive.

"We'll march all of them out into the swamp and bury them there. We can dump their bikes between here and Tampa. We've got to assume that the parents know they are here or in the general vicinity, so there is bound to be a major search around the property. We can't bury them too close.

"Everyone will blame the witch for the disappearances, as she will be gone too, but it'll take a long while for things to die down.

"Eventually, this property and Hostetter's will go for sale. I'll buy the two properties and we'll wait around a few years. It'll be perfectly normal for me to have a truck – not the Rex Seafood truck, but an unmarked truck – on farm property.

"When everything has quieted, I'll move the gold to one of my fishing boats and on to Cuba. We'll split it there. In the meantime, we divide the bonds 60-40 as we agreed earlier."

"One thing is very important. We cannot go digging up the yard to find the gold now. When the search parties arrive looking for the kids, the first place they will look will be any recently disturbed earth to see if the witch buried the kids. If we've gone digging at the gold site, that location will be the first place they figure the kids are buried. They won't find the bodies, of course, but they would find our gold."

Zeller was not fully confident that he would be included in the split of the gold in Cuba, but almost $200,000 from the bonds would set him up for life. He was not about to challenge Cruz about the plan to move the gold to Cuba after several years of waiting. Besides, he didn't have a better idea.

"So we will have to bluff the witch into showing us where the gold is buried and then trust that she is telling us the truth. If she believes that we are planning to actually dig for the gold now, she will lead us to the right place. She will not risk our ire by inducing us to dig an empty hole. So make a big fuss about getting shovels for the boys to solidify the idea in her head."

Since Hostetter had not brought Carty and Hale back into the house by this time, Cruz assumed that they had chosen to hide in the swamp or to run for help toward Dredman's position. Leaving Zeller in charge, he first went to check on Hostetter.

He was pleasantly surprised to see Hostetter alert and prepared. "No one tried to get out along this path?"

"No, Señor. I saw someone near the house, but he ran toward the swamp. You told me not to worry about anyone who went in that direction, just to keep them from escaping down this path."

"You've done well. Anyone running for the swamp is planning to hide at least long enough for our purposes. Were there one or two?"

"Just one that I saw. But there could have been another before I got into position."

"Was it a girl or a boy?"

Clem thought for a moment. "You know, it might have been a girl. It's pretty far from here, but, now that you mention it, I think I noticed a ponytail."

"If they had intended to run for it, they would have done so by now, so I think we can abandon your post. Come along to the house to give Zeller some help while I go see about Dredman."

CHAPTER 18

Running for Help

A white lie is always pardonable.

KARL KRAUS

Once Hale pulled down the latch, he found that it operated much like the pet door – with hinges on top – that his family had for their dog at home. For a few seconds, he remained prone on the ground outside the house, looking in all directions until he was satisfied that no others were watching.

He crept carefully to the driveway that was the extension of the Hostetter Cutoff and moved into the heavy vegetation paralleling it. Once he went around the curve and moved out of sight of the Canfield house, he came back to the cutoff and took off at a brisk but measured speed. He had quite a way to run and needed to pace himself so he could continue without stopping.

He gave the Hostetter house the slightest glance, hoping that no one was posted there who might stop him. He had contemplated ducking into the brush and bypassing the house slowly so that he could not be spotted. In the end, he decided that too much time had already been wasted, so he continued past the house at a slightly faster run, hoping that he would not be seen. If someone did come out after him, he could charge into the forest and hope to evade the pursuer.

Fortunately, no one appeared, and he kept running. A short time later, he saw Mocking Bird Road in the distance and a car passing by. "Darn," he thought. "There isn't much traffic on that road on a Sunday afternoon. That car's driver might have been my only easy chance at quick help." He continued forward at an intensified pace.

EARLIER, Dredman was alert and poised to strike if anyone approached the bikes, but he knew that Cruz didn't have much faith in his abilities. So he rightly concluded that Cruz didn't expect anyone to actually escape the house and get this far. He almost wondered if this posting were designed to get him out of the way. If that were the case, he was more than a little worried about Cruz's next step. For a moment, he considered returning to the house to grab the old Ford and leave, but greed overcame fear.

Initially, his senses were on edge, when it was too early for an escapee to actually reach the bikes. That was his first mistake. Because he did not relax when he could have, the unnecessary anxiety exhausted him as the day moved along. While the branches overhead kept the bright sun from beating on him, the day was hot and the humidity brutal this near to the black asphalt of the road. He was getting bored and sleepy.

Passing cars were few; in fact, only two passed since he arrived. Bored, he began walking around to stay awake, confident that no motorist would spot him. Eventually, he tired of that modest exercise and looked longingly at a beckoning patch of soft grass. He eased himself down and rested his back against a tree. He reclined only a few feet from the bikes, so even in a drowsy state, he was confident that he could nab anyone approaching them.

His new position was more comfortable, but it did not provide a good sightline up the Hostetter Cutoff, so he failed to see Hale approaching on the run. The soft Florida sand that made up the dirt road impeded Hale's progress, grasping at every footfall. But the cushy substance also provided a quiet surface for Hale's churning feet.

When Hale first started his run, he had planned to grab his bike and pedal to the right, toward town. He recalled that the first house was about a mile distant. As he neared the bike stand, though, he remembered that there was a house trailer in the opposite direction less than a hundred feet past the cutoff. It had a long sandy drive that made a bike useless. So when Hale reached the end of Hostetter Cutoff, he kept running into a left turn, spurning his bicycle.

Dredman had barely come to his feet as Hale flashed by, heading in the wrong direction away from the bikes where Dredman could have caught him. Dredman was not a marksman. He couldn't shoot well enough with a pistol at that distance, especially at a moving target, to accomplish anything except making noise.

He was at a loss. "Maybe," he said aloud, grasping at a straw, "the kid left before the action took place. If he needed help, why wouldn't he take his bike?" Dredman decided that he should just wait. He didn't want to tell Cruz that the kid had slipped by – that was certain. He thought again about making an escape, but settled for inaction.

HALE reached the door of the ramshackle trailer about the time that Dredman had decided a do-nothing approach was called for. He knocked on the door loudly and pushed the bell button without hearing a sound. Soon a plump, middle-aged woman with fluffed blond hair answered. She was dressed in a well-worn, navy blue dress too tight for her build, and was trying unsuccessfully with excessive make-up to hide a black eye and puffy lip.

Hale rushed his words in his excitement. "Hello, Ma'am. My name is Hale Wending. Some men are trying to break into the Canfield house. Could I use your phone to call the sheriff, please?"

She looked at Hale with a wide-open mouth and confused look on her face, as though he were speaking in a foreign language.

"Who is it, Bertha?" boomed a slurred voice from inside the house.

"It's some colored kid. He wants to use our phone."

"What? Tell him we didn't put in no phone so Negroes could help themselves. Never mind, I'll tell him in a way he'll understand. He's probably trying to rob the place. Where's my shotgun?"

"Kid," she said quietly, "If I was you, I'd be skedaddling. Clyde don't like coloreds even when he's sober, and he ain't been sober since Friday at breakfast."

Hale knew there was no value to arguing his case here. He took off down the two stairs and ran for the road before Clyde could get a hold of his shotgun and likely blow off his own leg. At the road, he turned left again and ran for the next residence, still disappointed that no cars passed by.

This effort was even less successful. By the time he negotiated around the dogs snapping at his legs and lost more precious time conversing with the unsympathetic and suspicious residents, he was despairing.

As he searched for the next house, he figured he needed a different approach here outside of Winter Free. He had to stop and catch his breath and think. The run up and down the last driveway had been at a dead sprint, so his breathing was labored.

Getting a second wind by slowing to a jog, he moved up to a better speed. He was looking for a third house without knowing how far away it was. After quite a distance, he was about to give up and retreat for his bike and a trip toward town when he came to a driveway.

This house sat a quarter mile back from the road on a winding drive. Hale could see that it was in excellent condition, with well-tended landscaping, raising his spirits a little. The mailbox read "Novotny."

Hale's rapid knocking brought a tall, smiling man in his fifties to the door. The belly beneath his clean white buttoned shirt hung just a little over his belt, and his bushy white eyebrows added to a Santa impression. This fellow appeared sober, a refreshing change.

Hale was ready with his revised approach. "Hello, Mr. Novotny," Hale began, wringing his hands and making himself teary eyed. "It's a terrible thing, a terrible thing. My three brothers is a beatin' a white boy silly. I thinks deys a gonta kill him. He's owed them money for der moonshine and he cain't pay. Now Jimmy and Larese and Bobby saying deys takin' it out of da white boy's hide. Please call da sheriff, Mister. If 'n my brothers kills him, dey all gonta get da chair fo' sure."

"Where's this going on, son?"

"About half mile fuddah den da old Hostetter farmhouse on da cut-off, nears da Canfield house. Oh, please, Mister, hurry and call da sheriff."

"OK, calm down, son." Swinging the door open, he directed Hale to a nearby chair. "Have a seat, young man, while I ring up the sheriff." As Novotny left the room for the phone in the kitchen, he called back to Hale, "What'd you say your name was, young fella?"

"Hale, Mister. Please hurry. Dat white boy's good as dead if 'n da sheriff don't git dere soon."

Hale tried listening through the doorway to make sure that the man reached the sheriff and that he had the story straight. After quite a long wait, he heard a few muffled words. Then Novotny said a little louder, "Hail. Yeah, I'm sure, like the frozen rain up north, I guess. That's an unusual name. I wouldn't get it wrong."

After a pause, he heard more. "A Negro boy. Fourteen or fifteen maybe. Not quite six feet; skinny as a rail; butch haircut; broad nose; a half inch vertical scar on the right side of his forehead; small ears; light blemish on his left thumb; dressed well; polite."

Hale was impressed at the man's ability to recall so detailed a description from no more than a few seconds exposure.

Novotny yelled at Hale from the kitchen, "Is your last name Wending, son?"

"Yassah, Hale Wending."

The man spoke again into the phone, "Yep. Hail Wending. OK then, good. Hail says to hurry or his brothers are going to kill the white fellow. Pardon me? What was that? OK, Sheriff. I'll tell him."

The man returned to the door and said to Hale, "Sheriff Elsmore says he knows you and will be on the way as soon as he can get a deputy to bring in a car from out in the county. The sheriff's car is on a lift at the Fleet Wing getting an oil change. They had to send out for the filter. He said to tell you that your four-, six-, and seven-year-old brothers must pack quite a wallop to warrant his attention."

"Thank you, sir," Hale responded to the confused man. No longer speaking in dialect, he added, "You've been a big help. I can't thank you enough."

VOSMIK Novotny was retired from government service. During the War, he served in the OSS in central Europe under the noses of the Nazis. Though the United States had employed war-time spies dating back to George Washington in the Revolutionary War, the OSS in WWII became the country's first organized spy operation.

Novotny was fluent in Slavic languages. Born in Hungary shortly before coming to the United States as a toddler, his Hungarian and Czech parents mixed enough of those two languages with English to make him effortlessly multilingual. Growing up in New York City, he heard enough of the myriad of other languages there to pick up pieces of them as well.

After earning a law degree from Columbia, he went to work for the U.S. Attorneys office in New York where he came to the attention of William Donovan. When President Franklin Roosevelt tapped Donovan to start up the OSS, Novotny was one of Donovan's first hires.

Donovan sent him to central Europe to link up with the Resistance. The many dangerous escapades of those years wore heavily on Novotny, so he was happy to invest his modest retirement money in a quiet Florida home. He never married and expected to be content to live out his life in the warm climate. However, he tired quickly of the daily golf game and solitude of his isolated house, so the unusual encounter with his visitor was a welcome diversion.

Besides possessing unusual language abilities, Novotny was a sharp and capable lawyer. He realized that this young lad had scammed him, though he didn't know why. Novotny smiled as Hale retreated down the stairs with a brief wave. "Hmm," he murmured to himself, "Sharp kid."

THE task of calling for the sheriff finally accomplished, Hale retreated toward the cutoff. He hoped to get back to Sally's house to see if he could offer some help. By the time he got around the corner at the cutoff, he was thoroughly winded and barely making a slow jog. For a moment, he stopped, placed his hands on his knees, and breathed deeply. He was about to start up the cutoff when Dredman's voice jolted him from behind.

"Hey kid, I didn't expect you back. Where have you been?"

Hale looked into Dredman's gun and decided to play his cards carefully. "Up the street. I've been trying to get help, but the people around here don't think much of coloreds. I was heading back to see what I could do. I assume that you're part of the gang that attacked Miss Canfield's house."

"You assume correctly, but we prefer to think of ourselves as professional treasure hunters rather than gang members." Waving his gun up the cutoff, he ordered, "Let's go see how everyone is doing up there, shall we? Just keep your mouth shut when we get to the house unless I authorize you to speak. No talking without my permission, got it?" Dredman emphasized the point by jabbing the gun into Hale's side.

"Yes, sir, I'm not to say anything unless you give the word." Hale tried to figure out why this gunman did not want him to speak, but he came up short of answers.

As they walked, Hale feigned more exhaustion than he felt to slow their progress and give the sheriff more time to get there. Fortunately, Dredman was not a man of high energy, so he was content to allow their progress to continue at a slow trudge. Besides, Dredman dreaded facing the prospect that Cruz might discover that the kid had slipped past him originally.

CHAPTER 19

Getting Together Again

A cunning fox cannot outsmart a skilled hunter.
CHINESE PROVERB

As Cruz and Hostetter neared the door of the house, they saw Dredman and Hale walking toward them well in the distance.

"Ah, it appears that I do not have to make that long walk to visit Dredman after all. Our intrepid sentry approaches with his catch." Cruz waved his arm for them to hurry the pace and went inside with Hostetter to wait. Cruz nodded Clem to a chair and sat on the steps that led upstairs.

He announced to his captives, "We will be having a surprise visitor in a few moments," adding in a sarcastic voice, "If my speedy associate ever gets here, that is."

The captives looked to one another, wondering who the new arrival

306

would be and what his appearance would mean.

After several minutes, Cruz looked through the open door and announced, "Ah, here are the two we have been waiting for."

Cruz was amused at the looks of despair on the faces of Sally and the boys when they saw Hale enter the room in front of a gun-wielding Dredman. "It seems," Cruz said, "that one half of your rescue squad failed to make it. And since the young lady is no doubt still nearby watching the house, you may rest assured that there is no help on the way.

"So, here is what we will be doing. I will go out into the swamp and bring her back. In the meantime, Mr. Jones will lead the rest of you out into the yard where Miss Canfield will show us exactly where the cache of gold is located. You three boys will dig for the gold. If it is not precisely where she says it is, you will be digging your graves. Do you understand what I am saying, Miss Canfield?"

"Yes, I do, Mr. Smith," she replied, though confident that Mr. Smith had no plans to allow any of them to survive the day either way.

CARTY continued watching the house with increasing dismay. She was shocked to see Hale leave the house nearly an hour after she had reached the swamp. She had expected to see the sheriff responding to Hale's call for help when it turned out he was still inside the house all that time. With Hale's late start, there appeared to be no chance of help arriving soon.

She was positioned behind a large oak when Hale first escaped from the house. From there she could see the front and two sides of the house and well down the dirt road. She watched Hale's initial progress as he moved through the brush along the road and was relieved when he made it around the curve and out of view of the house. From her location, she could see him running almost as far as the Hostetter property.

She felt confident that, though late, he would bring help. In the meantime, it was up to her to try to delay the criminals, whatever their intent. She wondered if she should let fly with an arrow into the manor house door – just to let those men know that she was armed and on the loose.

Then she saw the apparent leader go outside and retrieve a sentry who was positioned on the farm path leading to the south fork. Apparently, they were no longer worried about anyone leaving by that route.

After that, when she saw Dredman pushing Hale toward the house, she began feeling desperate. For a moment, she contemplated running through the swamp to Aunt Lilly's, but she figured that choice was too late now. She decided to stay to see what help she could offer from her current vantage point and thought that she would approach the house and initiate her own rescue operation if no other idea soon came to mind.

Meanwhile, leaving Zeller in charge, Cruz went to the back of the house where he found the window escape mechanism that Sally had described. He raised it to its maximum height and quickly squeezed through. Once out, he ran for the adjoining woods. Under cover, he tracked westward in the general direction of the Hostetter farm. Near the farm, he raced across the untilled field northward into the swamp. Carty could not see Cruz leave the rear of the house or circle around to flank her position from Hostetter's.

He chose to take the more circuitous route because he wanted to get into the swamp unnoticed. The girl did, after all, have a weapon. Though he doubted that she posed a serious threat, he was not a man to take unnecessary chances.

After a short wait, Carty watched three of the criminals emerge with Sally and the three boys. One man and Blake split off and entered a small building that was apparently a tool shed. When they emerged, Blake was carrying a pickaxe and two shovels. The latter two tools he handed to Hale and Mack.

Carty moved along the woods line to stay as close as possible to the group without exposing her position. She was too far from them to hear what was going on.

With Sally in the lead, the group moved away from the house and nearer to the east end of the property where it met a spur of Duck Lake. As Carty paralleled their eastward move, she saw Hale and Mack in brief conversation, and then Dredman hitting Hale in the head with the butt of his gun.

Hale went down in a heap and sat, stunned, his forehead bleeding profusely from the blow. Carty took an arrow from the quiver and readied herself to fire if the situation got further out of hand.

Then Dredman pointed his gun at Hale and began yelling at him. From the distance between Carty and Dredman, an arrow from her bow would arrive in about a half a second – not as fast as a bullet, but easily too fast for anyone to seek cover even if they could hear the sound of the bowstring and recognize what it was.

It was a nearly windless day, which would help her accuracy. Though the humidity would affect her light-weight arrow, she had more than enough experience in damp conditions to mentally adjust.

Normally, she sought a deadly strike on an animal when she hunted for food, but she had no desire to kill this man. Him she wanted to only wound. She anticipated correctly that Dredman would probably not hear the sound of her bow, nor quickly react deer-like to its sound, if he did.

So the arrow found its target precisely as aimed. The gun flew from Dredman's hand as the arrow penetrated his gun arm just below the elbow, shattering bone. Everyone reflexively flinched when Dredman let out a loud scream.

Zeller instinctively calculated the approximate location of the archer from the angle of the impact on Dredman's arm. He grabbed Dredman under the armpits and dragged him behind a large water trough while simultaneously ordering everyone else to join them. The three boys sized up the situation immediately and were not afraid of the archer, but they were compelled to comply with the instruction since Zeller and Hostetter still were armed.

Dredman was wailing in pain when everyone was gathered. "Shut up, you fool," Zeller ordered. "Let me see the arm. It's not so bad. No broken bone that I can see," he lied. "Another few inches, though, and she would have hit you in the chest instead and killed you."

Blake interjected, "If she had wanted to kill him, he'd be dead. You can be sure she went after his arm because that's what was holding the gun. She hits what she aims at – exactly what she aims at. I've been to some competitions where she won every event. Some of the competitors have told her that if female archers were allowed in the Olympics, she would be on the U.S. team."

"Nobody asked you, kid," Zeller said, "but it doesn't matter anyway.

That arrow gave away her position to Mr. Smith. No doubt he got her already, or she's too preoccupied to be a further threat."

Then to Dredman he asked, "What did you hit the kid for?"

Between moans, Dredman answered, "I told him earlier to keep his mouth shut, but I saw him talking to the other kid."

"So what? Let them talk. They aren't going anywhere."

Suddenly, Hale realized Dredman's problem, so he spoke up. "He probably doesn't want you to know that I made it past him the first time and got a neighbor to call the sheriff for help."

All eyes went to Dredman. Sally and the boys saw his fear as hope. Hostetter was as bewildered as ever. Zeller pictured their project unfolding in the sagging features of Dredman's face.

No one who had heard Zeller speak before would have described his voice as friendly. When he spoke this time, though, it sounded deadly. "What is the boy saying, Dredman? Did he get past you before you caught him?"

Dredman refused to answer. He moaned as if in too much pain to speak and concentrated on holding his throbbing arm.

Zeller looked to Hale. "Boy, tell me precisely what happened."

Hale explained how he had bypassed his bike and run to a house where he found a resident to call the sheriff. He omitted recounting the two failed efforts. When he returned to see if he could offer any help in the meantime, Dredman captured him.

"Then why isn't the sheriff here by now?" Zeller asked skeptically.

"His car was in the garage, and he needed to wait for a deputy to come in with another vehicle. This is a big county. I don't know where the deputy was, but it could have been fifty miles away or more or less. But the sheriff will be here soon – you can count on that."

Zeller turned his attention to Dredman, but Dredman had already bounded to his feet and was running toward the lake. Zeller gave chase firing his gun. With both men running at full speed, Zeller's first shot was remarkably accurate, but it barely missed. The shot whizzed past Dredman's neck causing him to duck. When Dredman heard the second shot buzz past, he dived forward into the tall grass.

Before he hit the ground, he saw that he was diving through what appeared to be rows of white fence slats above and below. Only when he hit the rough wet tongue and slid deeply into Montooth's throat did he realize that he was a dead man. Fortunately, he fainted and lost consciousness before he felt Montooth's teeth snap his body in half. Montooth swallowed Dredman's top half in one large gulp and discarded the remainder for a later meal.

Zeller skidded to a stop only a few yards short of Montooth and briefly lost his balance, dropping to one knee. He quickly regained his feet and ran to the left. With Montooth in pursuit, Zeller reached a full gallop after a few steps. Nevertheless, he knew he could not outrun the gator, and a .38 would have limited immediate effect on a beast of that size, even if he could target it moving at such a pace. He vaulted a split log fence in a strong leap.

Two steps later, he crashed through a mat of sticks, straw, and leaves into a deep, squared-off pit. When he splashed to the bottom, his forward momentum carried him crashing into the far wall. He bounced and fell backward into two feet of mud and water. The pit had four sheer walls of slippery mud rising ten feet above. Zeller saw nothing to grab that would enable him to climb out.

Regardless, he wasted no time. He jumped up, grasped a large stick, and began gouging footholds into the side of the prison. Seconds later, from above, he heard a hissing sound like that of a leaky air hose. He looked up and saw Montooth. Montooth looked down at him. The two paused momentarily assessing their situations.

Then Montooth placed his front legs on the edge of the pit and reached his enormous head downward. He snapped at Zeller, who backed to the farthest wall. He held the largest stick in his hand, but it was useless as a weapon. His gun was somewhere underfoot in the water. He dropped to his knees and searched with both hands, dodging Montooth's increasingly frenzied snapping.

The gun would probably not kill the beast, but enough bullets might make it back off. Otherwise he would have to get lucky and penetrate its brain through an eye.

Hostetter stood immobile until Blake took charge and yelled to him, "Your man needs help! Use your gun! Get that gator!" As Hostetter took a few tentative steps toward the gator, Montooth dropped headfirst into the pit. Blake herded the others toward the house in a run. He half lifted Hale, who was still woozy from the gun butt blow.

By the time Hostetter realized that they were running for the house, they had too big a lead for him to shoot at them accurately. He stood in place first, and then stepped toward the house, then back toward the pit, then back to the house. Then he stopped to think.

After a few more moments of hesitation, he decided to ignore

Zeller's plight and chase after the escaping prisoners instead. They got to the house ahead of him and slammed the door, locking the latch securely. They shuttered the windows that were too small for Hostetter to climb through but large enough to extend an arm through and fire his weapon.

Sally helped Hale to a chair and ordered, "Mack, latch Hale's escape route in case Clem tries to get in that way. I'll check the back window. Blake, get the rifle mounted above the fireplace. It hasn't been fired in so long that I don't know if it is in workable condition, so let's hope we don't need to find out. There are shells in the drawer on the left of the fireplace."

She retrieved the old pistol from a drawer but then realized that it had never been reloaded since Cora Hostetter's visit long ago. She had no ammunition for it.

As everyone scattered to the assigned task, Clem began pounding on the door. "Open up," he shouted. With atypical resolve, he did not wait for a reply, but began firing at the door latch. The hardware was strong enough to hold for a while, but not forever. Bullets clanged and ricocheted with slight but increasing progress. Clem had all the extra rounds that he needed to break through eventually.

Sally spoke to Blake, gesturing rapidly, and sent him to the attic. She seated Mack midway up the stairs where he could relax but still see Sally and be heard by Blake.

IN THE SWAMP, Carty had watched the scene unfold as if it were a movie. Her arrow hit Dredman within an inch of where she aimed, and that imprecision occurred only because he was waving the gun. She wanted him to drop the gun and have a useless arm to restrict any further violence. She had no idea why Zeller had chased him into Montooth's gaping mouth.

Seeing the reptile in bright daylight for the first time, she was amazed at its size. To think that she was within feet of Montooth a few days earlier made her brow perspire. She watched Montooth drop into the pit and saw neither him nor the man climb out.

She was grateful to see the scramble for the house, but dismayed at Hostetter's firing into the door. She was about to reposition for a second arrow when it occurred to her that she had lost contact with the fourth man. When the three men emerged from the house, she assumed that the fourth had remained inside, but she knew better now. Surely Sally and the others would not have run for the house if the fourth man were still inside. That meant he had left and was probably looking for her.

With her consciousness alerted, she saw ever so briefly enough movement in the distance to her right to know that she was right. He was coming after her. She tucked the bow to her side and began moving deeper into the swamp.

For a moment, she felt how her prey might feel when she was on the hunt, but she quickly recovered her confidence. "This is my terrain," she thought. "If he wants to play my game, let him try. At least our odds have improved. Two of the bad guys are gone, and the house should be safe for a while. I saw a rifle over the mantle, so if needed, Sally has some fire power. She must know how to shoot, but if not, Hale and Blake are good marksmen."

From a hundred yards away, Cruz had seen Carty's arrow hit, and he was able to approximate Carty's position of attack. He carefully and quietly worked his way to the spot she had since vacated.

After he was certain that she did not have a clean sight line on him from elsewhere, he examined where she had stood and where she had rested her left shoulder against a tree for additional steadiness. He saw from two impressions of her feet, slightly deeper than the others, that she had apparently sprung quickly about fifteen feet to the east after firing.

"That was an experienced move. A novice would have stayed in the same place."

Carty was able to observe the man examining her previous position, but there were too many trees and vines between them to give her any clear target. She retreated deeper for about ten minutes. She was impressed that he had located her position so quickly. This one was no Fedora-wearing amateur. If the encounter were not so potentially deadly, she would have enjoyed the challenge. Nevertheless, the adrenalin rush heightened her senses.

When she found a suitable large cypress in a high dry spot, she removed one of her walking shoes. She scanned the area around to be certain she was not about to step on anything dangerous. Cruz was to her southwest, so she placed the shoe with the toe ever so slightly exposed to an approach from that direction. She was careful not to show too much leather, as something obvious would be a give-away to an experienced tracker. Then she cautiously backed away, covering her tracks with natural debris as she moved.

A short time later, Cruz darted from in front of a nearby tree, gun drawn, expecting to find her standing there. Carty was startled at the speed with which he materialized, but she was ready and let go with another arrow. The distance was well short of when she targeted Dredman, so Cruz had no time to react to the sound of the bow string. The arrow struck his right arm, in nearly an identical place to the one that hit Dredman earlier – this time precisely where she aimed.

"Wow," she thought briefly to herself, "I'm really in a zone today."

Cruz dropped the gun when his arm was hit. He dived to the ground and retrieved it. He retreated, using the tree as cover. He broke off the back of the arrow and, grabbing the arrowhead, pulled most of the remainder of the shaft, minus some splinters, through his arm.

He could shoot with his left hand with accuracy nearly as deadly as his right, so the functional loss of one arm was merely a painful inconvenience. In fact, he could still use the injured right arm for a close-in shot if necessary.

The shoe gambit was more than he had expected from a young girl. He probably would not have fallen for it if he had been tracking a man. Had he been more alert for such expertise, he chastised himself, he would not be dragging a painful right arm. It gave him a grudging respect for her.

After Carty retreated, she moved generally back toward Sally's house, figuring she might eventually be able to help there if she could shake this stalker. She looked for an appropriately mid-sized tree and found an oak with high branches. It suited her needs.

Scanning quickly to make sure her pursuer was not yet nearby, she put down her bow and shinnied up the tree. When she reached the lowest branch, about twenty feet up, she shinnied back down. Retrieving the bow, she backed slowly away for about ten yards, carefully scattering leaves and other loose material as she went. Then she moved farther away briskly until she reached a place of good cover and sight line from where she could keep her eyes on the tree.

Though she expected him to go near the oak, she continued to scan in all directions to avoid an unpleasant surprise. Within ten minutes, her wait was rewarded. He appeared almost from nowhere, but exactly where she had expected, about fifteen feet from the oak. She was startled again, though, that she had not seen or heard him approach beforehand.

He looked around and then glanced upward with a quick scan. Seeing nothing unexpected, he eyed the scuff marks she had left on the bark from climbing. As he looked up more intensely toward the lower branches, he aimed his pistol upward. He followed the marks on the bark with his eyes until he saw that they stopped at the first branches without purpose. Recognition that she had tricked him again hit him a fraction of a second before an arrow cut deeply into his thigh.

The blow knocked him down, and he used the momentum to continue to roll away from her firing position. The back part of the arrow broke off as he rolled. Confident that he was safe for a moment, he tried to pull the arrow through, but it held fast; his leg had much more meat than his arm. So he broke off the protruding arrow head and left the center shaft in his leg. Though the pain was sharp, leaving the shaft in place at least minimized the bleeding.

His hamstring ached, and blood oozed down the back of his pant leg. He knew immediately that there were no arteries involved and that the blood loss would be tolerable. He was not a typical man; he would still be able to walk with nearly normal speed.

This young girl had entirely gained his respect by this point, but he was wasting too much time with her, especially with Hostetter blasting away with enough shots to arouse the curious and nearly awaken the dead. He scolded himself for being so overconfident. Twice she caught him being too cocky. That would not happen again.

As soon as Carty shot the arrow, she again left her position. She had no desire to kill this man, no matter how evil he and his companions were. By aiming for his leg, she expected to disable him. Now she wanted to get to the house to see how she could help there.

Cruz anticipated Carty's move toward the house. He recognized earlier that she was circling in that direction. He found an opening devoid of low branches and Spanish moss. He lofted a small rock through that gap into the direction ahead of where he expected her to go.

Carty could differentiate a thrown rock from someone's footsteps. Her dad had taught her that ploy early in her training. So instead of moving away from the sound as the thrower would expect, she moved toward the direction where the stone landed, confident that it was the safest place in the swamp.

Immediately after hurling the rock, Cruz circled around. His movements would have been slow and deliberate to remain undetected anyway, so the hole in his leg did not hinder his progress significantly. Having belatedly realized that Carty was an experienced tracker, he changed his approach.

Obviously, she was too smart and well-trained to succumb to his ruse of the thrown rock. He anticipated that she would recognize his trick and move toward the noise instead of away from it, and maneuvered himself accordingly. The growing respect that he had for her was rewarded.

As Carty emerged from the hip-high, water-filled swale to make her way toward the house, Cruz lurched at her from behind a tree. He grabbed her around the throat with his good arm and put his gun to her head with the damaged but still usable injured limb.

"Young lady, that effort was the best display of woodsmanship that I have ever experienced, except for my own, of course. If you possessed more of a killer instinct, I would be a dead man. Under different circumstances, I might be inviting you to join my team instead of killing you."

He said this with a deadly calm as if he were commenting on the weather or the color of a shoe.

"By the way, what is your name?"

"Carty, and yours?"

"You may call me Mr. Smith, Carty. It's a pleasure – of sorts – to meet you."

With that said, Carty put a move on him that had flipped Dolder in the third grade. Long hours of archery practice had developed strong arms and shoulders. She may have been the strongest student in Cross Creek except for Blake, the Danner twins, and Billy Young, the school's wrestling champion. However, her effort did not budge Cruz in the slightest.

"Now don't get carried away with my compliment," he admonished. "That move would work on the weak or unsuspecting, but I have humbly and belatedly acknowledged your extreme competence.

"The only question is whether to kill you here or take you back to the house first. Given that we will be burying all of you out here in the swamp regardless," he reflected, "There is no reason to take you out of here.

"I'm not a religious man, but I see by the cross around your neck that you are a believer. You earned enough of my respect that I'll give you thirty seconds to say a final prayer. Use the time well; it is not something I normally offer."

Instead, she asked in a voice surprising to him for its composure, "Why are you doing this?"

With anyone else, Cruz would have replied with a bullet to the head or a snap of the neck, but this plucky girl deserved an answer. "You were not there to hear the witch's story. It seems that she has conjured up a fortune, which I believe would be better held in my custody. Unfortunately for all of you, witnesses are an inconvenience that I cannot allow.

"As you can see, witch or not, she hasn't been able to cast a protective spell on herself or the others. At this point, she and your friends are barricaded inside of the house under the incompetent onslaught of my cohort, Hostetter. It is his ineptitude that requires your swift demise so that I can supervise the final part of the plan."

His calm manner of speech, as if lecturing to a classroom of students, was more frightening than the gun at her head.

"Unfortunately, the more able of my colleagues seems to have visited one of the witch's pits that I discovered in my earlier visits to her homestead. He too would have seen it had he been walking and not otherwise occupied. I should have warned him, but I did not expect him to be evading reptiles and hurdling fences."

Carty had no ideas how she could get away. He was too strong for her and had a gun under her jaw. She decided to take his offer and, with barely audible words, began reciting the Lord's Prayer.

BACK at the house, Hostetter was making progress. The metal was nearly blasted away. Sally remembered that Cora Hostetter had mentioned Sally's witch persona to Clem so often that he apparently believed it. It may have been the excitement that came with the shooting and chasing that erased his memory of her supposed supernatural abilities. She tried to resurrect his fears.

She croaked at him in a loud voice, "Clem Hostetter. A person who attacks a witch exposes himself to spells that normally do not apply to humans. However, you have crossed the mystical barrier. I offer you one chance to leave now. Or you will suffer the consequences."

Momentarily, her speech had the intended effect. Suddenly, Clem remembered that he was attacking a witch. With a trembling voice, he yelled though the door, "If you are so powerful, why haven't you done anything yet?"

"Haven't done anything? Fool, lummox, oaf. Have you not seen what happened to your two friends? Do you know how difficult it is to conjure up a twenty-foot alligator? Sally glanced at Mack with a look that wondered if she could get away with this bluff.

For nearly a full minute, Clem thought over what she had said. He was almost a believer, but in the end, the gun gave him new-found confidence. He fired three new shots into the metal in rapid succession.

Immediately, Sally began chanting loudly in indecipherable language, "Mochtar, Halbar, Avalange – Mochtar, Halbar, Avalange – Mochtar, Halbar, Avalange." With each phrase, she increased the volume of her voice. "Mochtar, Halbar, Avalange – Mochtar, Halbar, Avalange – Mochtar, Halbar, Avalange." "Mochtar, Halbar, Avalange," she repeated again even louder.

Hostetter stopped firing when she began the chant. His gun was empty, so he reloaded while listening. The words meant nothing to him, but he was worried. He looked around as if expecting Montooth and was relieved to discover he remained alone. Reloaded, he moved closer to the door and resumed firing.

At that point, Sally signaled to Mack on the stairs. He in turn waved to Blake, who was staring down from the attic. Blake scrambled back and reached for a thick chain that hung from the ceiling and pulled it with all of his weight, as one would a large bell in a church tower.

As the chain let loose and descended, it reverberated like a large ship's anchor dropping into the sea. Blake darted to the side to avoid the cascading metal clanging to a pile upon the attic floor and shaking centuries of dust from the ceiling on the floor below. In the meantime, a louder sound began rumbling on the roof.

Blake's chain had pulled down and flattened a wide gate on the high pitched roof. That metal barricade held back hundreds of pounds of moss-covered granite stone slabs and rocks. As the stones rolled, slid, and cascaded from the roof to the ground in front of the house, they buried Clem so deeply that only an up-thrust arm appeared from the pile when the barrage ceased.

His gun was lost at the bottom of the mound of rock. Whether he survived the avalanche or not, he posed no further threat.

When Sally eased the door open, several large rocks and small boulders bounded into the house. Quickly the boys moved them away from the door in case they needed to close it again. Then they looked in all directions. They knew that Mr. Smith was unaccounted for, but they saw no one. A soft moan emerged from the pile. Amazingly, Clem was alive.

The boys began removing the rocks from where his arm stuck out. Hale joined in, apparently recovered from his head wound. They were careful to avoid causing Clem any additional damage. Several minutes passed before they fully unburied him. He was semi-conscious. Miraculously, damage to his head seemed minimal.

The rest of his body was a mangled mess, however. The bones from a compound fracture of his buried arm jutted through his skin above the elbow. One foot was at a ninety degree angle to his leg. Blood oozed from countless places, including his mouth, suggesting internal injuries.

Sally asked several times if he could move his legs, arms, and neck. On the fourth request, he coughed a "Yes." He looked at Sally with stark fear in his eyes. Though in severe pain, he responded to her instructions and moved all of his appendages except the broken arm.

She concluded that it would be safe to remove him from the rock pile and take him into the house. As carefully as possible, they lifted Clem as he screamed in pain. They laid him on a bear rug in front of the fireplace and covered him with a blanket. Despite the warm temperature, Sally was worried about shock setting in.

She was grateful to note that he was not coughing up blood. His earlier cough apparently was expelling dust that slid down the roof along with the rocks. The blood from his mouth came from where several teeth had been knocked out.

"Keep him warm and hold him down so I can set his broken ankle and look for other broken bones. I don't want to tackle the compound fracture, though. He needs a doctor for that and for any internal injuries we cannot see. We will have to hope that the sheriff gets here soon – both for Clem's sake and because Mr. Smith is somewhere outside.

"Maybe I can find Hostetter's gun," Blake countered. He raced for the door and searched through the rubble, but was disappointed to find that the boulders had ruined the weapon.

He displayed the damaged gun to Sally, who commented, "If Smith shows up before the sheriff, we will be in trouble with no more than that old rifle for protection. She added, "I am afraid that I have run out of Canfield surprises."

Blake secured the door with what remained of the lock when Sally mentioned the missing Mr. Smith. Blake was confused as he briefly thought of the piles of rock. The immense quantity appeared to vastly exceed the amount he had seen on the roof earlier. "Where did it all come from?" he wondered momentarily. Then he forgot his bewilderment as more important issues took his attention.

AS Carty was finishing her prayer, "... deliver us from evil," she and Cruz heard the rumble from the house. Cruz dragged her toward the pasture to see what had happened. When he saw the pile of rubble and circling dust in front of the door, he realized what that strange shape was that he had seen on the roof. Some ancestral Canfield had stored stone there after the completion of the house. It was rigged as a booby trap like the several deep pits fenced in around the yard.

"Hmm. It seems that I might be the last one standing. I am afraid it is time for decisive action, Carty. It was an intellectual pleasure – though a bit painful – making your acquaintance, but I must get to the house, take what is readily available, and finish this job."

He was then startled to hear a voice not thirty-five feet away.

"If you fire that pistol, you are a dead man."

"Dad!" Carty exclaimed. She couldn't see Michael, but she recognized his voice. Her heartfelt prayer had been answered.

Cruz slowly turned and looked into an old but well maintained Army .45 pointing between his eyes. "Ah, this young lady's father. I don't know how you managed to get this close to me without being seen, so I assume that you are her mentor. You are to be complimented. She was remarkable in this swamp. You may note these two rather pronounced holes in my body resulting from her efforts."

"I'm sorry I didn't get here sooner, Carty," Michael said, while maintaining his concentration on Cruz. "Sheriff Elsmore called me when neither of his deputies could reach him promptly. I had returned from my trip a few hours early and was just coming in the door when he called.

"James wasn't sure what was going on, but he has been aware of potential problems out here since Aunt Lilly tipped him off several weeks ago. When he heard of Hale's plea for help, he figured I might be able to assist until he could get out here. It appears that he was right."

"I'm sure that your sheriff is a fine gentleman," Cruz interjected, "but he is not someone I wish to meet. Now how do you propose we solve all of our problems? You can't shoot me and risk that this hair trigger blows your daughter's head off. I assume that is why you didn't shoot earlier. On the other hand, if I shoot her first, you might get me at this close range no matter how fast I duck."

"I can assure you that there is no possibility of your getting one step away if you pull that trigger."

"A forty-five is a notoriously inaccurate weapon. You must know that."

"Not in my hand it isn't."

"No, I suspect not," Cruz conceded. "You managed to sneak up on me. It is likely you are equally as competent with the firearm. So, I repeat the question, how do we resolve the dilemma?"

"Well," Michael suggested, "We could continue motionless in this Mexican standoff until the sheriff eventually gets here. How does that sound?"

"You surprise me, sir. You must know that I would prefer to chance being shot by you than to give up to the sheriff. Indeed, if I see the sheriff or his men arrive and start for the swamp, I will shoot Carty first and hope for the best with you."

Michael stared at Cruz's eyes. He saw enough malevolence through those squints to believe what Cruz had stated.

"There is another possibility," Michael offered reluctantly. "You could turn your gun toward me, let Carty go, and begin backing away. I'll allow you to go. I would enjoy tracking after you, as I saw enough to realize it would be a fascinating challenge. However, Carty and I need to get to Sally Canfield's house to see what help we can offer there."

Cruz thought for only a moment. Then he turned Carty toward her father and moved his gun along the side of her jaw until it was pointed at Michael instead of Carty. Ever so slowly, he withdrew his arm from around her neck and turned the gun toward Michael.

As he released her, to his disappointment, she avoided the temptation to run to her father, which would spoil Michael's aim and doom the both of them. Instead, she moved calmly and steadily to the side and knelt down behind a tree, out of the line of fire.

With both guns aimed at one another's heads, Cruz began taking small steps backward. He was sufficiently aware of his surroundings and possessed enough of a sixth sense to avoid tripping on a log or stumbling into a gator or other problem creature. The farther back he went, the more trees and other obstructions came between the two men.

Eventually, Cruz disappeared, and then Carty ran to her dad. He kept his eyes and gun forward, but he squeezed her hard with his free arm.

"Oh, Dad. I love you so much. All I thought of when Smith was getting ready to kill me was that I would not have the chance to say goodbye to you and Mom." At that point, Carty broke down and cried as she had never cried before.

Michael continued holding her for a minute. Then he gave her a quick kiss and said, "That is some evil man. We should get to the house. Tell me what has been going on as we go."

They paced briskly across the pasture toward the house, arm in arm, when they saw the red flashing lights of the sheriff's car heading there as well.

CHAPTER 20

Wrapping Up

A victory is twice itself when the achiever brings home full numbers.
WILLIAM SHAKESPEARE, *MUCH ADO ABOUT NOTHING*

The medical business appeared to be picking up. Doc Brannigan was climbing into his shiny new Chrysler Crown Imperial as the ambulance carried away the battered criminal and a deputy guard from the sheriff's office.

The doctor had already attended to the nicks, cuts, bumps, and bruises that the boys suffered from their ordeal. Hale had recovered quickly from the bash on the head and did not appear to have a concussion – just a bad bump and a mass of dried blood that made things look worse than they were. Nevertheless, he had an appointment with Doc Brannigan tomorrow after school for a follow-up exam.

"It's too bad I didn't get here sooner, Mack," the doctor had concluded earlier. "I might have had a chance at sewing that ear back together."

"That's OK. It doesn't really hurt that much. Maybe hair styles will be longer someday and I can cover it up."

"I don't know, Mack," Blake interrupted, "I think you should flaunt it. It gives you a speedy, aerodynamic look."

Carty was glad to see a little humor creeping back. She sat at the table with the boys, who were gorging themselves on the fresh bread Sally had set to baking since the ordeal ended.

Sally poured the last of the hot tea into Sheriff Elsmore's cup. He and Michael stood at the fireplace, their cups resting on the mantle. The unfired rifle was remounted in its familiar place above them.

The sheriff resumed talking. "We bailed out enough of the water from the pit to be certain that Mr. Jones, whose real name is apparently Carey Zeller, is not in the bottom. The marks on the sides of the pit are consistent with the probability that a very large alligator – maybe your Montooth, Miss Canfield – lifted a human from the pit and dragged the body into Duck Lake."

Sally, no longer using her witch voice, asked him to call her by her first name instead of Miss Canfield. "You've been here twice now, Sheriff. I feel that we are old friends."

"Actually, Sally, I've been *inside* your house twice, but I've been here on a number of other occasions. Lilly Andersson alerted me to Clem Hostetter's return and asked me to keep an eye on your place. I've driven out here at night several times in the last few weeks, but it always appeared that Clem was home and not disturbing you.

"After I told Lilly that my hands were tied unless Clem made a threatening move, she told me that she would come up with a discreet way for Carty to observe things. She agreed to keep Carty's involvement low key to avoid alarming everyone needlessly. She promised to instruct Carty to stay away from the Canfield house.

"She has great confidence in you, Carty, but I know that she would have told you more and handled things a lot differently had she suspected the potential for violence. That was partly my fault, as I told her that Clem seemed as harmless as he was stupid. Evidently, Clem learned more in Detroit than I gave him credit for; unfortunately, those were all bad lessons.

"In any event, Sally, it appears that your gator grabbed Zeller across his body to lift him from the pit and set him down on top. Somehow the gator managed to crawl out of the ten foot deep pit. Gators can use their strong tail for support, so he probably managed to push himself up and out. You can see quite a bit of erosion and scrape marks on one side of the pit. That would have been something to watch.

"Then it grabbed a hold of Zeller's head and upper torso and waddled backward to Duck Lake, dragging the body. The zigzagging drag marks of Zeller's two legs are unmistakable. I hope he was dead by that time. It would have been horrible – even for an evil man like that – to be dragged into a watery grave while still alive and aware.

"We found a gun in the pit under the water. It was so full of mud that it might not have been operable – not that he would have been able stop a gator that size with that small caliber.

"Can you explain what these pits are for, Sally?"

"Yes, Sheriff..."

"Make that 'James,' Sally," the sheriff interrupted.

Sally smiled at the offer. "Yes, James. We have had several pits around the yard since shortly after the family first arrived. They were designed to capture predators that preyed on the domestic livestock. In the early days, there was an abundance of bear, coyote, wolf, and panther enjoying the easy meals our isolated farm was serving up. Apparently, we lost quite a few hogs, sheep, and cattle the first year.

"The family couldn't be on the alert twenty-four hours a day, so they decided to dig a series of deep pits to provide a protective screen. You can see how the pattern of fencing kept our animals from falling into the pits. The predators, on the other hand, easily scaled or crawled under the rails, and when they did, they fell into the pits and were captured. Some, like the bears, made good food, and all were usable for their fur.

"Evidently, the system worked so well that we didn't have to do much hunting for years. Not only were our domestic animals safe, but we were capturing a goodly supply of wild meat.

"Small predators like fox and weasels were too light to crash through the pit ceilings, so enclosing the chickens in a coop at night proved more effective against them.

"Periodically, we had to rebuild the false floors above the pits whenever the wood rotted away. That is a lot of work, especially now that I am alone. Nowadays, the number of large predators is down to almost nil, though, so I was actually contemplating filling in the pits when it next came time to do the repairs. Under the circumstances, I'm grateful that I hadn't already done so."

"So how did you convince Zeller to jump into a pit?"

"Fortunately, he did that on his own. I knew that was going to be the hardest part of the plan, but it became the easiest part, thanks to Carty and Hale.

"It was apparent to me that Smith and Jones-Zeller were not going to leave any witnesses. They had made no effort to hide their faces, and, of course, I already knew who Clem Hostetter was. From various things that were said, it seemed probable that Clem and the man that Clem called Damon were on the list for elimination as well. If Smith and Jones-Zeller were planning to kill their own partners, it seemed unlikely that they would allow us to survive.

"They had already seen the financial bonds that I keep in the house, so the idea of additional loot seemed plausible to them. I created a story about buried treasure that they were already predisposed to believe. I hoped to maneuver one or two of them to fall into a pit and then, with help from the boys, overpower anyone left. It was high risk, and actually unlikely to succeed, but I saw no alternative, especially when they brought Hale back.

"When I saw Hale walk through the door with a gun at his back, it seemed to mean that there was no prospect of help arriving."

"Then what happened?"

"Hale was our quick-witted hero. Unknown to any of us at that time, he had already alerted you that we needed help. More importantly, as it turned out, he recognized that he was in a position to cause dissension among the criminals by disclosing to Zeller that he had made the call to you. Up to that time, Zeller thought that Damon had made a clean capture.

"When Zeller realized that Damon had misled him, he went berserk and chased Damon toward the lake. Zeller let go with several shots – two or three as I recall – but didn't hit him.

"That's when Montooth entered the picture. I don't think Damon ever saw Montooth. It looked like Damon dived headfirst into Montooth's gaping mouth. Normally, seeing a gator eat a human would be horrible to witness, even with such a miserable criminal. But in this instance, it happened so quickly, we didn't even have time to feel empathy."

Sally reflected. "Over the past few hours, I couldn't help but think that my father probably died much the same way that Damon and Zeller did. That's what really makes me sad. Damon and Zeller may have deserved an end like that, but my father surely did not."

While she paused to regain her composure, Mack offered a comment. "Zeller was running so fast after Damon, he was barely able to stop in front of the alligator. In retrospect," Mack's choice of the five-dollar word drawing smiles from his three companions, "He looked like the cue ball following a solid into the same pocket for a scratch shot. Zeller stopped maybe ten to twelve feet from that gaping mouth.

"Amazingly, he retained his balance like a pop-up slide into second base and ran to the side where the closest fence was located. He probably figured that the alligator couldn't climb over the fence as rapidly, so he could get enough of a head start to be safe. He took the fence in one leap like a hurdler, but when he landed, he kept going down and disappeared. We heard a splash and never saw him come up.

"When Montooth approached the pit, Blake shouted at Hostetter to help his partner. While Hostetter was confused and distracted, Blake maintained his calm and got us moving for the house before Hostetter recovered from the shock. We didn't stay long enough to see what happened to Zeller."

It was Carty's turn to add to the story. "Dad, I encountered that gator, Montooth, last week in the swamp. In the twilight, I had him pegged as a seventeen footer, the largest I'd ever heard of. But Miss Canfield says she has measured his imprint at over twenty feet. I saw Montooth draw to the edge of the pit and peer in at Zeller."

Hale added, "Carty, you forgot the part where you played Robin Hood. Mr. Andersson, you should have seen those guys when her arrow hit Damon's arm. He had already clobbered me for squealing on him, and I think he was about to shoot me when his gun went flying and the man let out a soulful howl. Carty's arrow did the damage that got things moving." Carty blushed at the compliment while Michael beamed in pride.

Carty continued with her part of the saga. "As everyone ran to the house, Clem chased after them. When he pounded on the door and started firing his gun, it dawned on me that I had lost track of one of the men, the one who called himself Smith.

"I knew that they wouldn't have run for the safety of the house if he were still inside, unless he was injured or dead. Neither made much sense, so I guessed that he had decided to come after me. That realization alerted my senses just quickly enough for me to notice unexpected movement in the distance. That is when I retreated into the swamp and started employing the evasion techniques you taught me.

"He was an unbelievable tracker, Sheriff, and I could not bring him down. I hit him with two arrows, one in the arm like I did with Damon, and one through his thigh. He just broke off my arrows and kept coming after me as if I'd smacked him in the nose with a fly swatter. If Dad hadn't showed up when he did, I would not be talking to you now."

"That's the one thing I haven't taught you, Carty, because I had no reason to believe that it was a lesson you needed. Obviously I was wrong. Aiming to wound another human instead of to kill has its place, but when the difference is your life or the lives of your friends or family, you have to be as deadly as your opponent. That realization was the worst part of the War for me. I am saddened that it is still true back home.

"This Smith was a little better than you, I have to admit. He might not be better when you get another five years of experience, but he was better today. Still, you surprised him with your skill, and you could have stopped him twice before he realized you were a serious threat. That's when he began to concentrate, and you lost your advantage.

"As I turned on the cutoff following James' call and noticed the bikes, I stopped to see if one was yours. The eight flat tires alerted me that the sheriff's fears were real. I left the car and jogged up the cutoff, catching just the slightest glimpse of Smith as he passed the Hostetter property and made his way into the cover of the swamp.

"It was his furtive demeanor that enticed me to follow him instead of continuing toward the house. It did not take long to realize that he was tracking someone, and, given the difficulty he was having, you seemed the likely quarry.

"Carty, you risked everything opting for delaying tactics instead of a deadly strike. As it turned out, I'm glad that you don't have his death on your conscience, deserving as it may have been, but I would have preferred that to Mom and me mourning your death."

Blake took up the narrative. "Clem started shooting at the door latch." Pointing to the re-mounted rifle, "Miss Canfield told us that the rifle hadn't been fired or cleaned in years, so we couldn't fully rely on using it against Clem and – if he got back – Smith.

"That's when Miss Canfield began yelling 'witch spells' to scare Damon. Her chants stopped him for a few moments, but then he resumed shooting. When he moved close to the house again, Mack signaled me to release the rock pile from the roof. It's a miracle that he survived that avalanche."

The sheriff offered, "Evidently, he was close enough to the door to benefit from a small amount of protection that the overhang provides. With all the broken bones and bruised lung, not to mention the prison sentence he faces, I doubt that he will be anyone to fear for a long time."

Hale mentioned Sally's incantations against Clem. "I know that those 'spells' you cast, Miss Canfield, had no influence on the rocks that Blake released. Were you simply trying to intimidate Clem Hostetter so that he never returns?"

Returning for a moment to her witch persona, Sally paused and stared at him coldly, rasping, "So you don't believe that I can cast such spells, sonny? Have you ever considered how a life on a lily pad eating insects might suit you? Ha, ha, haaa."

Even the adults were momentarily taken aback. Then everyone broke into sustained laughter led by Sally. "Clem was susceptible to such thoughts before," she said, returning to a normal pleasant voice. "My hope then was that he would stop shooting. Now I hope that he has given up ever trying this again."

Michael suggested that she was probably right. "However, it is Smith I would be more concerned about. He is not the type to worry about myths or the mystical. I doubt that he even believes in God. He could be a real threat in the future."

Sally added, "I've been thinking about that since this ended. Keeping the bonds here made clipping the quarterly interest coupons more convenient, but I'm going to move them to the Ensign Bank vault and haul my scissors there in the future. I don't want to face this again, because I can't count on having so many young helpers next time." She seemed to lose a year of age every time she smiled. This smile wiped out a decade.

The sheriff brought them back on target. "Tell us about the rocks on your roof."

"Unlike the pit that luckily caught Zeller, the rocks were used exactly as intended – just a hundred years late," Sally explained. "When the family finished building the house, they found that they had a large supply of granite left. They'd used it for some of the walks and the foundations of all of the farm buildings. Then they just piled the excess into a big heap, where it sat undisturbed for 150 years or so.

"Over those years, security concerns waned and nothing was added. We left everyone alone and everyone left us 'witches' alone. Then the War Between the States started up, and the family realized that they might have problems from both sides.

"Florida was not the hotbed of Johnny Rebs like some of the states to the north of us, and the family had no interest in the outcome, one way or the other. We just wanted to stay out of it.

"Nevertheless, the family believed that the state militia would want every able bodied man for the Army, and at the time, we had several young men living here – so we expected to be pressured or forced to help the cause.

"The Canfields have a long history dating back to Europe fighting for King and Country and were knowledgeable military tacticians. That's how they earned the Canfield ancestral plaid. Though we never used that prowess in America, the knowledge was passed on like much of our other education.

"Isaiah Canfield, the family head at the time, realized that Florida was poorly positioned to hold off the North, no matter the eventual outcome of the war. The North had vast naval superiority, and Florida has hundreds of miles of coastline. He surmised that the family might have to resist the Confederate recruiters initially, but that Yankee invaders would be the next threat.

"I explained this earlier to the boys. In the 1700s, our family built into the house several escape routes in case they were attacked by the Spaniards or Indians. Ninety years ago, they were concerned about fallout from the War Between the States.

"Around that time, one of the small children, Jedidiah, was playing on the rock pile when he was bitten fatally by a large rattler that had nested in the granite rocks. That, together with the newly intensified concern for security, spurred them to action. They figured that the longer they could hold out inside the house, the better choice of escape route they could use. So they built the rock enclosure on the roof to come crashing down on anyone trying to break in.

"It would have been a back-breaking job hauling the rocks up there. So they designed quite an impressive crane-like structure. The plans are in one of the family log books. The release mechanism is based on a similar design they used in the Scottish castle the family owned before they ran afoul of the English and departed for Massachusetts in the 1600s.

"In this Florida climate, it did not take long for the north facing rock pile to be covered with an amorphous blanket of moss that obscured its granite base. It came to look more like a poorly designed or damaged roof, all the better for our purposes.

"As it turned out, this part of Florida was so isolated that no one from the state militia approached us on a recruiting mission, and the Union Army never came near either. During Reconstruction, the witch rumors re-emerged and we encouraged them to flourish, so the carpet-baggers paid us no attention either."

A knock on the door caught everyone's attention. A sheriff's deputy stepped into the room. "Sheriff, we're about to wrap up the search for the elusive Mr. Smith. We couldn't find any footprints, even in the softest part of the swamp. It's like the guy is a spirit. If the Anderssons hadn't seen him out there, we would not have known he existed.

"We did find these, though." He held out Carty's shoe and parts of her bloodied arrows to the sheriff.

"Sam," the sheriff admonished, "We might have been able to get finger-prints from these arrows if they had been handled more carefully."

"Oh, right. Sorry, Sheriff."

"At least we'll be able to get a blood type that might help if we find a suspect, so put those in an evidence bag."

James sighed softly to himself. He had a long way to go with up-graded training.

James handed the shoe to Carty as the deputy continued. "The only useful thing we found was in a shed at the Hostetter farmhouse. The old

Ford parked next to the house has Michigan tags and is registered to Clemens Hostetter – no surprise there.

"However, at least two other vehicles have been parked in the shed recently. Neither set of tire tracks matches the Ford's. Actually, both sets are from large tires, either big luxury cars or medium sized trucks. We've taken plaster casts of the tracks. Maybe this guy Smith drove away after we passed by."

The sheriff had considered blockading the cutoff when he first arrived, but he was accompanied by only one deputy. He opted that a show of force at the Canfield house to save lives was more important than catching a potential escapee.

Dusk had already passed, so the deputies had no interest in traipsing around the woods in the rapidly darkening evening. The sheriff told them to call off the search until morning, and he scheduled a deputy to keep watch on the house until he returned at noon the next day. He made a mental note to search the Hostetter house tomorrow in the daylight.

Clem had told them that the missing Mr. Smith was called "The Cuban," but he didn't know his actual name. He remembered that the first and last names were the same, like Smith Smith, but Spanish sounding. He was unable to offer any other clues. According to Hostetter, both Smith and Zeller were from Detroit. That's where he had met Damon Dredman as well.

The sheriff committed to asking for help from the Detroit police, but sensed that he would have little hope of finding Mr. Smith in Michigan.

"Sally, I'm leaving a deputy with you tonight. Please don't scare him, even as a joke. I've managed to defuse a lot of that speculation in these men, but you could easily undo it. I'll be going through Hostetter's place tomorrow, and I'll stop in to see you afterward to make sure everything is OK here. You know, you really need to get a phone out here."

"I think you are right. This experience has me thinking that I need to join the Twentieth Century. Maybe I can get electricity in the house too. We never had anything against modernizing. We simply did not want installers and repairmen roaming around. Too much familiarity might weaken the community's witch fears."

Within twenty minutes, everyone was leaving. Michael had piled Carty and the boys into his car. At the end of the cutoff, they managed to tie the useless bikes inside the trunk. The first stop was Fred's Fleet Wing, where Fred's air hose took care of the tires. Fortunately, Dredman and Zeller had only let the air out rather than slashing the tires.

Michael dropped Hale and Mack at their homes and to relieved families. The sheriff's office had called earlier with reports they received by radio from the Canfield farm. Mr. Stein cancelled his appointment in Sebring and waited with his hand-wringing wife for Mack. Both boys had exciting stories to tell well into the night.

Blake went back to the Andersson house for a belated meal after relating a short version of the story to his dad by telephone. "Mrs. Andersson," he commented, "The long wait was well worth it. This is the best food I have eaten since... since... well, since the last time I was here."

Everyone laughed at Blake's enthusiasm for food, and Bay beamed at his compliment. "I am baking my orange cake for the town Easter Party next Saturday night. I will be sure to save a piece for you, Blake. You are my favorite customer.

"This may be the last town-sponsored Easter Party," Bay said, "So we want to make it special."

"How did that start up again?" Carty asked.

"You remember Mr. Toth, the principal who left a few years ago?" Mr. Andersson said. "He started things off, professing the idea that religion and public facilities did not go together. He thought it might hurt the feelings of anyone who wasn't a Christian. He even wanted to stop the students from reciting the Lord's Prayer in school each morning.

"Thankfully, those ideas died when he left. However, a few of our political leaders have brought this issue up again. It seems that there was a Supreme Court decision about a year ago that held that the state of Illinois could not allow a voluntary prayer in school – something about the Constitution preventing the Government from establishing a religion. They think it won't be long before someone forces the issue in Winter Free."

Carty responded, "Even Mack, who is Jewish, thinks that's stupid. He said that only a dummkopf would come up with it, and if we were in school in Israel, we would be saying Jewish prayers and celebrating Jewish holidays. He says he isn't likely to become a Christian just because he attends the town's Easter Party and is in the classroom where the Lord's Prayer is recited.

"Besides, we have learned enough about the Constitution in school to know that the article specifically says, 'Congress shall make no law.' If the Founders meant to keep the states out of it, they would have written, 'Neither Congress nor the States shall make a law.' None of the other nine articles singles out Congress, so it should be obvious to anyone, especially a judge, that only Congress is restricted. What silly judge can't tell the difference? I think the judges spend too much time in law school and too little time in reading class.

"The only ones who will be happy are Haywood Dolder and his motley group, who are usually laughing and horsing around during prayers. The best way to turn other students into Dolder disciples is to remove religion from the classroom and from the town. It's hard to believe that anyone in power would be that short-sighted."

"Let's hope that you are right, Carty," her mom said, a little amused by Carty's passion.

CHAPTER 21

Back at School

Lies and perfidy are the refuge of fools and cowards.

PHILIP DORMER STANHOPE, 4TH EARL OF CHESTERFIELD

Monday arrived as a perfect day. Central Florida's reliably warm April is its driest month. The only clouds today were marshmallow puffs drifting in robin's egg blue sky. The day's high temperature forecast called for the low eighties, and a slight breeze already stirring promised to keep the warm temperature pleasantly comfortable.

Michael offered to drive Carty to school that morning. He sensed that she wanted to cling to him as long as possible, and he missed her as much. She and the boys thought of their ordeal as a grand adventure, but he knew that some stress would press on them as they thought more about it. He learned that from his combat experience, and he wanted her to feel the

345

comfort that his presence brought.

When she got out of the car, a small crowd began to gather around her. That was her first realization that the school was abuzz about the attack on the Canfield house and the part that four of Cross Creek's students played in the skirmish.

Rumor had already exploded reality into rapidly expanding myth. Some heard that Sally Canfield lured the four students to her house for foul purposes. Others believed that she called up ghosts and spirits to battle Yankee invaders.

Fortunately, no rumors of "treasure" floated around. The sheriff had admonished them to keep that part of the story to a minimum. He even kept it from his own deputies.

When Sally told the sheriff about the deep pits, Mack, Blake, and Hale had noted that Sally's rendition of her conversation with Smith omitted mentioning gold bars. She had referred to a more general "treasure" instead, implying moreover that the story she told the invaders was untrue.

Whether the gold existed or not, the boys decided among themselves to keep that quiet. If even a whiff of a rumor of buried gold got out, Sally could be invaded with shovel-toting treasure seekers at any time, greed overcoming fears of witchcraft.

They committed to avoid talking about it even with their families or Carty. They truly trusted her to keep the confidence, but saw no reason to expand the circle of knowledge. Mr. Andersson and the sheriff knew of the bonds, but only generally of a "treasure."

IN FACT, it was Mr. Andersson who had some time ago impressed upon Carty, Blake, and Hale the difficult but important concept of keeping a secret. He explained that there is a big difference between "need to know" and "nice to know." As D-Day approached in 1944, and the Allied troops were in England poised for the Normandy Invasion of the European mainland, the plan was kept secret.

He related that it would have been nice for them to know where they would be landing. But they had no "need to know," and had they all known, the invasion probably would have failed, and many more men would have perished.

"The basis of the invasion," Mr. Andersson went on, "was to convince Hitler that our initial thrust would be across the English Channel where it is narrowest to Calais, France, instead of farther south to Normandy where we actually struck. Ike and the Brits came up with an enormous ruse with fake troop concentrations, tents, plywood mock-ups of tanks and artillery pieces – anything that would look real to a German reconnaissance plane. Even our best general, George Patton, was 'commanding' our fake army supposedly stationed across the channel from Calais.

"In the meantime, the actual invasion site was kept from almost all of the Allied troops as well. Only a few generals and critical lower ranking people were in the know. I had no idea where we were headed, nor was I aware of the plan to trick the Germans. On the one hand, I would have felt better knowing the entire plan, but had I and thousands of my colleagues all known, the ruse would doubtless have been discovered by the Germans. Then the invasion might have failed, and surely it would have been bloodier. Not knowing saved many of our lives.

"Days after the actual invasion started on the several beaches of Normandy, Hitler was still so convinced that Normandy was a mere diversion that he refused to allow reinforcement troops to be rushed from Calais to help. That has been credited by most historians as a critical factor in our gaining a foothold in France and the eventual downfall of Hitler.

"So, boys and Carty, if you learn a secret, keep it to yourself. It may be fun and satisfying to tell others, and they may promise to keep the secret. But remember, you just gave up the secret, so why do you think that they will behave more honorably than you?"

The boys passed on the logic to Mack, and he understood. They could not do anything about what Hostetter or the enigma, Mr. Smith, might know, but the three would contribute their part to maintaining Sally Canfield's peace. It was a matter of honor.

MACK was already at Cross Creek Elementary when Carty arrived. She smiled at the group of girls chattering around him as if he were Frank Sinatra. The ear that Blake had dubbed "aerodynamic" proved to be a girl magnet. Mack tried to pull away from the crowd of new-found female admirers when he saw Carty walk up.

"Sorry, girls, the true heroine arrives. She put three arrows into the criminals from a hundred yards away."

"Less than sixty, Mack, and with no wind, but thanks for the compliment." With a wave, she gestured Mack back to his fans. "We'll talk at lunch."

A few boys neared her, anxious to talk about the experience, but a bit too intimidated to initiate conversation with this almost mythic girl. It wasn't until Hale and Blake joined her, walking from the school yard into the classroom, that a growing crowd of boys peppered the trio with questions. The hubbub continued even as Mrs. Tryon came into the room.

"All right, class. Let's take our seats.

"I understand that Carty, Blake, Hale, and Mack collected more than flora samples this weekend. I doubt that we will get much done today unless you learn their story first hand."

Besides, Mrs. Tryon was as curious as the students to know what had occurred. "Why don't the four of you come up front where you can tell us what happened?"

Mack, still basking in his new found glory, strode to the front with Prussian bearing. The others walked up more slowly, self-conscious at the attention coming their way.

For over an hour, they explained how the quest for the specimens led them near Miss Canfield's house when she invited them in. They omitted finding Chapmann's rhododendron there, though, as they did not want the entire class invading her yard after school. Moreover, they sought to maintain their competitive edge.

Instead, they concentrated the discussion on their second visit and the subsequent invasion by criminals, including Miss Canfield's neighbor, Clem Hostetter. Most of the time was spent answering questions.

"Is Sally Canfield a witch?"

"No, but she does seem to have the power to keep well-armed criminals at bay."

"What were they looking for?"

"Miss Canfield has always kept some valuable stocks and bonds in her house, but she has decided to put them into the Ensign Bank for safe keeping. She wants to make sure there isn't a repeat of this attack."

"Is it true one criminal escaped?"

"No one knows for certain. He was wounded with two of Carty's arrows, but he was not found despite a wide search by the sheriff's deputies. He could have been eaten by a gator, but the sheriff believes that he escaped."

"How large is the gator that ate the other two?"

"Some time ago, Miss Canfield measured the length of his outline in the mud at twenty and a half feet. That's three feet longer than any gator on the state's records. It lends credibility to the theory that the Whorton disappearances of years ago were gator related."

"What is going to happen to Clem Hostetter?"

"The sheriff says he will be tried when he recovers from his injuries and will likely be sent away for most of his remaining life."

Giving Hostetter more credit than he deserved, Billy Wilson asked, "Where did Hostetter get his gang?"

"That's still a matter of conjecture, but the understanding is that they came from Detroit. Sheriff Elsmore is concentrating his investigation in that city."

Dolder bristled at the attention the four were getting and the admiration that was building for them. He spoke up with the first thing that popped into his head, trying to divert attention from their achievement.

"I heard that this is just the first wave of criminals that are coming here from the North. The Canfield woman brought them down to work for her, but this first group of hers mutinied and turned against her."

Blake rolled his eyes, while Hale and Mack stared at him dumbfounded. Carty reacted smoothly to Dolder's latest stupidity.

"Actually, you are on the right track, Haywood. There is a reason these guys came from Detroit. It has nothing to do with Miss Canfield, though. They were sent by General Motors. GM is canceling all of its Chevrolet dealership agreements. The company is sending its own sales people to take over all Chevy sales in the southern states.

"Oops, I wasn't supposed to let that slip. I'm really sorry that your dad will be losing his business, Haywood." Carty gazed at him with as solemn a facial expression as her prevailing smile could allow.

A few of the slower-witted students believed her absurd tale and turned questioning eyes toward Dolder. Dolder started stammering as his hands trembled. "Wait, wait, we, we haven't heard that. Wait, my dad would have told me. He would have. That can't be true. How can they do that? My dad will sue them. They'll never get away with that."

By this time, most of the class got the joke and started snickering. The Crew tried to hold in the laughs that were poised to burst forth. Finally, an explosion of laughter erupted from almost everyone. Even Dolder's cronies let go. Dolder was engulfed in a torrent of derision.

When he realized the fool he had made of himself, his face got red and he appeared ready to burst from the room. Mrs. Tryon rescued him from further embarrassment with a change of direction.

"All right, class, settle down. I think that we have spent enough time on our new celebrities today. Let's get to work.

"Remember, your lab work is due in tomorrow morning. I would like a status report on it from each group. Veronica, you first, then the other twelve."

"Our group has done very well, Mrs. Tryon. We are down to three missing items, including one that doesn't appear to grow this far south. We are going out again as soon as school lets out."

"Good, Veronica. Haywood, how are you boys doing?"

Dolder puffed himself up as well as he could, not yet recovered from Carty's earlier repartee. "My dad – who is not going to lose his dealership by the way – helped us out with a few items that we couldn't find. So we have twenty-four of the specimens, missing one found only up in the Panhandle. He couldn't find a nursery that carried that item."

With that last comment, Mrs. Tryon thought that Mr. Dolder's "few" might more accurately have been described as "most," but those were the rules she set out.

"Eddie, how is your group doing?"

"Almost as well, Mrs. Tryon. I have to admit that we have collected a couple of specimens that we're not sure about. But I know that you will tell us if we have the wrong ones. Including those, we'll be in the twenties at least. And we're going out this afternoon too. By the way, we want to thank Carty's group for their help. With the reference books gone from the library, we would have been lost without their assistance."

Veronica added, "Oh, I'm sorry, guys. Our group wanted me to thank you too, but I forgot with all the excitement today."

There were several more expressions of gratitude from others that left Mrs. Tryon looking confused. "I'm not sure that I follow you, Eddie. What is this about the reference books?"

Eddie continued. "When Bill and Mary got to the library to research the plants for our group late that first evening, they found that every one of the reference books had been checked out earlier in the afternoon. We were in a panic until Mrs. Andersson called to let us know that Carty's group had made a list to share with all the rest of us. That was a life saver."

"Why did your group do that, Carty?" Mrs. Tryon asked.

"Oh, well, immediately after school the day you gave us the assignment, Mack and Blake went to the library and developed our list. Shortly afterward, we heard that someone had checked out the very same books they had used. We realized that the other groups would be at a real disadvantage if they couldn't do the necessary research. So we wrote out a copy of our list to share, and my mom called someone from each group to let them know they could come to my house to copy it.

Carty scrupulously avoided identifying Dolder and his cohorts as the guilty party.

Suddenly concerned, she added, "We didn't do anything wrong, did we, Mrs. Tryon?"

Dolder interrupted, looking smug. "It looks like you did, Carty. The rules did not allow groups to help each other. That will mean a disqualification, won't it, Mrs. Tryon?" he asked hopefully.

At that point, Mrs. Tryon realized what had happened to the reference books. The boys in Dolder's group were the only students not expressing thanks for the shared list. It was apparent that Dolder's group had attempted to sabotage the competition by removing the reference materials.

"Actually, Carty, since the groups are competing with each other, it did not occur to me that one group might help another, so I never thought to establish a rule about it. However, my rules clearly allowed any of you to ask for and accept help, so I can't see anything wrong with offering assistance as well."

Dolder shot eye darts at both Carty and Mrs. Tryon.

"Since you have the floor, Carty, how is your group doing?"

Pointing to the group's specimen book on Mack's desk, she said, "We finished with all twenty-five on Saturday. There were a couple of tough ones deep in the swamp, but we got them.

Hale added, "Mack was really in tune with this project. He even spotted a Chapmann's rhododendron from fifty yards away."

"But on that, we aren't giving help," Carty said with a little chuckle. "The rest of you have to figure out that one on your own."

"I am impressed with your effort," Mrs. Tryon praised. "The Chapmann's was supposed to be my little joke. I never expected anyone to find that specimen."

The remaining groups gave their reports. No group was doing as well as Carty's and Dolder's, but Mrs. Tryon was more than pleased at the effort that everyone had devoted to the project. Though it was a difficult challenge, they had all shown remarkable interest and initiative. She was too modest to realize that it was her dedication that inspired the students.

AS the students continued making their reports, she thought wistfully about next year's class. For the past twenty-two years, she had taught every eighth grader at Cross Creek. This year's class of fifty-one students was her largest, and the student population continued to grow.

Next year, the eighth grade was being split into two classes for the first time, and a new teacher was being hired to take one class. Though Mrs. Tryon looked forward to the reduced work load, her heart wanted all sixty-four of the seventh graders to come under her capable tutelage.

When the last report was made, she said, "All right then, you still have this afternoon to finish your search. Remember to turn in the assignment tomorrow morning."

Around their favorite outdoor lunch table at noon, The Crew continued fielding questions. They managed to keep Sally out of the discussion for the most part and never mentioned buried treasure, real or imagined.

At one point, when the questioning moved too close to the part that Sally had played, Mack and Hale diverted attention to Carty. They paced off the approximate distance that Carty's first arrow traveled. The audience of boys seemed suitably more impressed than the girls. Carty stood nearby, a little embarrassed at the renewed attention, while Blake smiled at her unaccustomed shyness.

Mack had left their specimen book on the picnic table. Dolder eased up to it. With the crowd's attention focused on the arrow's simulated path, Dolder sent his followers to stand shoulder to shoulder in front of the table. With them serving as a visual barrier, no one noticed Dolder removing the page with the Chapmann's rhododendron. Then he returned the book precisely to the location where Mack had left it.

Dolder laughed with his fellow conspirators as they headed back to the school building. "So, it looks like Carty was doing a little too much bragging. Her group has only twenty-four specimens now, and no Chapmann's. On the other hand," developing the cover story in his mind as he tucked the page away, "It appears that good old Dad came through for us with a last minute ride up to the Panhandle."

His cronies slapped him on the back and clenched their fists in triumph. He and they had finally bested that nemesis Carty and her friends.

Then he realized that Mack's detailed drawing would be a give away if he inserted the unaltered page into his group's book. So he removed the specimen from its wax paper and threw the shredded remainder of the page into the trash can. Later, at home, he added the specimen to a page that matched the style of the others in his group's book.

"I'd love to see her face after she turns in her book and Old Lady Tryon tells her that there were only twenty-four specimens. Let that be a lesson to her. Don't cross Haywood Dolder." Every time he thought about it, he laughed until his belly hurt, almost too much to eat dinner – almost.

That night about eight, Bay knocked on Carty's door. "You have a phone call. It's Mack. He says it is very important."

Carty descended the stairs rapidly. It was odd for Mack to call, especially this late at night.

As soon as Carty said hello, Mack began rambling half in German and half in English. Carty could not follow him.

"Slow down, Mack. I can't tell what you are saying. Take a deep breath."

Mack restarted at a more measured pace. "Tonight I was thinking that I did not do a good enough sketch of the Curtiss milkweed, so I took out the book to draw an improved version. The Curtiss page is alphabetically in the book right after the Chapmann page. As I was paging through to the Curtiss page, I saw that the Chapmann page was missing."

"Missing?"

"Yes, missing – gone. I carefully looked through the entire book to make sure it hadn't been mixed up somehow. It did no good. The page is gone."

"When was the last time you saw the page? Do you remember?"

"Oh, yes. When we were in class and you were giving Mrs. Tryon our progress report, I turned to the Chapmann page as you spoke about that specimen. It was exactly where it was supposed to be. After that, I never opened the book again."

"Well, I can't envision the page falling out or disappearing on its own, Mack. Do you have any ideas?"

"Do you think it might have had a spell attached to it, Carty?"

"Mack, stop that! There was no spell. The only plausible explanation is that someone removed the page. Where was the book from the time it was on your desk until you got it home?"

"It was with me the entire time that I was in the classroom. When we went to lunch, I brought a couple of books with me to our table, including the specimen book.

"After that, it was back on my desk until I put it into my bag and rode my bike home. I didn't stop anywhere on the way. It has been here ever since."

"No one in class asked to see it?

"No. Even if they had, I wouldn't have passed it around. It would have been in my control the whole time. Anyway, no one asked for it."

"How about at lunch?

"Same thing. No one asked to see it, and I was always with it." He paused, "Except when …"

"'Except when,' Mack?"

"Do you remember at lunch when discussion got too close to Miss Canfield's stocks and bonds? Blake and I changed the subject by marching off the distance your arrows traveled. I left the book unattended back on the table when we were doing that, but it couldn't have been longer than five minutes."

"Hmm. That's good enough of a clue for me, but it doesn't solve our problem. Who is the one student in the class who wasn't showing any interest in our adventure, and who would be especially disinterested in anything I did with a bow, and who was not clustered around when you were measuring the distance?"

"Haywood Dolder, Carty. What until I get my hands on him. I'll get our page back."

"Much as I would like to go along with throttling Haywood, that won't do. We can't prove that he took our page. He is surely shrewd enough to disguise your work to look like his, so we cannot complain to Mrs. Tryon about him. Unless we can think of something, we might have to accept that he has found the missing twenty-fifth specimen – thanks to us."

"But to lose to a cheat like Haywood Dolder is unacceptable, Carty."

"We aren't going to lose, Mack. We are still in a position to tie at least. Dad's gone until late tonight on business, or I'd ask him to drive me to Miss Canfield's. I'll bike out there and ask her for another specimen. I don't like biking on Mocking Bird Road at night, but I'll be careful. While I'm doing that, can you do another sketch from memory?"

"Sure thing. I remember that one very well. I'll leave it a little rough until I get the actual specimen from you. Then it'll take just a minute to finish. We can meet before school tomorrow morning for the touch-up."

Carty explained the problem to Bay and got permission to go out to Sally Canfield's. Traffic was very light and posed no difficulty. Carty parked her bike at the usual corner and jogged the bumpy dirt road to Sally's. She could not help feeling anxious as she passed the Hostetter house, though she knew that no one was inside and there was nothing to fear. She noted that the old Ford was gone, apparently towed to the county impound lot at Fred's Fleet Wing, and the house appeared deserted.

She made it to Sally's a little before nine o'clock. Lantern light shone through the open door. As Carty approached, she could not help but notice the beautiful woman standing in front of a mirror.

For a brief second, Carty thought Miss Canfield had a visitor. Then she realized that she was looking at Sally. At that moment, Sally glanced out of the door and saw Carty staring back. A look of resignation came over Sally's face. She walked to the door and invited Carty in with an exaggerated bow.

The image was almost beyond belief. Carty saw Sally hatless for the first time. Sally's hair cascaded as a flow of red wisps curling atop her shoulders. Instead of the usual shapeless black dress, she wore a thin-strapped, otherwise bare-shouldered, fitted, calf-length, white, cotton sundress. Pink piping offered a touch of color. Sally capped it with a lacey off-white shawl.

Sally said nothing. She beckoned Carty in and motioned her to a nearby chair. She picked up her old black pointed hat and handed it to Carty. Carty saw that stringy black hairs were sewn to the inside hat band so that they would drape from the wearer's head. Carty put the hat back on the table.

"Gosh, Miss Canfield, you are beautiful. There were times when you were talking with us, when you started to warm up to us, that you seemed to grow younger, and now look at you. You didn't cast a 'young' spell on yourself, did you?" she laughed, trying to lighten the atmosphere.

"You know my secret now. The only way I know how to make myself into a witch is to don that hat, those Spartan black clothes, and tall-laced shoes. After all the events of the last several days, I have been thinking of entering the world of real people. This isolation worked well for the family when it was larger, but it is too lonely for one person.

"I read books about real people, about other places, and feel that I am missing so much. I read the Bible, but long to hear a minister tell me what so much of it means. I have even taught myself foreign languages, but have no way to use them.

"What do you think I should do, Carty?"

"Oh, Miss Canfield. I'm just a kid. I don't know what to tell you. I know that your life would be too lonely for me. I love being around people – well, people unlike our recent visitors, of course."

"The deputy has left, so Sheriff Elsmore said he would be checking on me tonight after work on his way to his apartment. How do you think he would react tonight seeing me this way instead of dressed in my witch's outfit?"

Carty smiled broadly. "Now that I can answer. I think that the sheriff was smitten with you even when you looked like a witch. He looked at you differently than at the rest of us, and not in a bad way. If he sees you like this, he'll propose marriage and whisk you away to a preacher with lights flashing and sirens wailing, without waiting for your answer."

"Carty, you make me laugh. I would have liked having you as a younger sister."

"I'm an only child, Miss Canfield, and I have always wanted a sister. I'll be your younger sister, if you'll be my older sister."

Sally smiled at those earnest eyes. "Then you had better start calling me 'Sally.' Who ever called her sister, 'Miss Canfield?'" With that, she embraced Carty and they held each other tightly.

"So, Sis, what brings you here so late at night?"

"Gee, Sally, I'd almost forgotten why I came. Someone stole the page from our report that contained your Chapmann's rhododendron. I came to ask for another cutting."

"That's easy enough to solve. Let's go." Sally took a small knife from a drawer and preceded Carty out of the front door.

As she selected a piece of the plant to cut, she asked, "Do you have any idea who stole your cutting?"

"A very good idea, Sally, but no way to prove it. One of the other students, Haywood Dolder, had the opportunity and is one of the few students in the school who is dishonest enough to do it."

Carty explained how her group dropped from first place to second by losing the specimen, but how they would be tied for first with the new cutting.

"Is he any relation to the Dolder Chevrolet dealership?"

"Oh, sure. Haywood is Mr. Dolder's oldest child. I hope that he sells cars more honestly than his son handles his life."

Outside, the sky was dark from high clouds, but there was enough light for Sally to cut a good specimen from the bush. Carty tucked it into her bag and declined an offer for a cup of tea.

"Mom was nervous with me biking on Mocking Bird Road at night. I'd better get home.

"Goodbye, Sally, and thanks for the cutting. I can't wait to hear what the sheriff's reaction is going to be."

Both of Carty's parents were waiting for her when she came home. Waving the specimen bag, she ran into the house in high spirits, "I've got the specimen, but have I got some happy news to tell you while I wax it."

CHAPTER 22

Leaving the Scene

Let no guilty man escape, if it can be avoided.

ULYSSES S. GRANT

After the attack on Sally's house the night before, Cruz had worked himself away from Carty and her father. He reached the woods behind the Hostetter house when he saw the second sheriff's car tear past his position heading toward the Canfield property. As he fled to the shed and into the truck, he was encouraged that no additional vehicles followed.

Zeller had the truck's keys in his pocket when he jumped into the pit, but Cruz was not concerned. Rex Seafood policy was to keep a second key in a magnet case under the bumper. Drivers losing keys had caused too many lost man hours, so Cruz had implemented the simple fallback measure of the hidden key.

363

Cruz could have hot-wired the vehicle, but he'd have a difficult time trying to explain driving without a key if he got pulled over. So he knelt painfully in front of the truck and retrieved the case.

There was no hesitation. He knew that the riskiest part of his escape plan appeared immediately before him. If he encountered an officer on the cutoff, he could give no reasonable explanation for a Rex Seafood truck being there. The faster he got to Mocking Bird Road, the safer he would be. He charged along the cutoff at speeds stretching the capacity of the truck. The springs were put to the test, and he almost lost control at the deepest chuckhole.

Once he skidded from the cutoff to the road, he knew that his chances at escape had improved markedly. If he passed an officer at this point, he would be considered just another commercial truck on a public road.

As Cruz drove toward Tampa in those early hours before sunrise, he scanned the sides of the road for a pay phone. He passed a drug store that was open, but he did not want to attract attention to his bloody condition while seeking out the phone inside of a building.

He sought an isolated phone booth outside, but the only one he found so far was out of order.

He stopped at a small Standard Oil station on State Route 70, southeast of Bradenton. The gauge read above half of a tank, more than enough to get back to Rex Seafood, but Cruz had noted the sign advertising a telephone inside. The station was manned by one attendant this early in the morning. "Fill it up, Elmer," Cruz said from the driver's window after reading the man's name tag, "and check the oil, please. I've heard a little tapping in the engine the last few miles. Restroom inside?"

In the back of the truck, Cruz had found an old Rex Seafood uniform shirt that he put on over his. A long sleeve covered his injured arm. The truck held nothing to use to hide his bloody pants leg though, so he had to rely on the early dark hours for concealment. He had swung the truck around into a u-turn when he pulled next to the pump so that he could walk to the station with the least exposure to the attendant.

Elmer nodded at Cruz's question. "Yep. Key's hanging just inside the door. Help yourself."

Cruz didn't need the restroom. He needed a phone. Fortunately, Rex Seafood would be staffed at this time in the early morning. He dialed the local operator and she connected the collect call to his dockside business.

"Andy? Cruz here," he began without preamble. "Is the Cuba Sea Reef still tied up?" After receiving an affirmative answer, Cruz gave the orders to pass on to Capt. Luna.

Returning to the truck, he saw that Elmer was too efficient for his own good. He had finished filling the tank, checking the oil, and washing the windshield.

"Oil is good. If you'd like, I could take a look at that engine."

"No. That's the company's problem. They can get on it when I get back. I'm just told not to let the oil run down."

"Suit yourself. That's a buck sixty for the gas. Noticed you're limpin' pretty bad on that leg. Look's kind of bloody too."

"Yeah," Cruz answered. "Caught myself on a rusty spike on the loading dock in Venice. Would've gone to the doctor down there, but if I don't get this fish to Tampa on time, I won't have a job tomorrow."

"Kind of odd going all the way down to Venice for fish when most of the commercial boats is out of Tampa. Knows a little bit about it, 'cuz I used to do some commercial fishing when I was younger," he explained.

Elmer was a former fisherman getting very close to being a former gas station attendant too, Cruz was thinking. The man talked too much, was way too observant, and displayed a disturbing curiosity capacity.

Cruz weighed the pros and cons of a quick kill. He contemplated making it look like a robbery attempt. However, there must have been half a dozen cars that had passed by the station since he drove in. A murder would bring attention and even a hick sheriff might connect two nearby felonies within twenty-four hours in the same general area where jaywalking was probably a noteworthy crime. He did not want to risk that some witness might recall seeing the Rex Seafood truck in the area.

He could make Elmer disappear; the fish around the docks would make short work of a weighed-down body. Cruz could force him to write a note that he was quitting and moving out west. But he didn't know anything about Elmer's life. Maybe Elmer had a wife and three kids that he would be unlikely to leave. Cruz didn't have enough time to learn Elmer's life story in order to concoct a plausible resignation letter.

So Cruz handed him the money and answered. "They got word of a big grouper catch and sent me down. More than the locals could take. Got a real good price. Well, look, I got to get going. You take care, Elmer.

"Sure 'nuf, buddy. What did you say your name was?"

"Why it's Elmer, just like yours," Cruz replied as he drove away, with a tight smile and a wave of his hand.

"That boy'd better take care of his leg," Elmer thought, as he followed the unnoticed trail of blood drops into the station, not realizing how close he came to littering the pavement with a supply of his own.

A few minutes later, aboard the Cuba Sea Reef, Capt. Luna checked on his first mate's progress. "We will be shoving off early. Have you rounded up the crew yet?

"I sent the three men from the boiler room to track down everyone. Most are back already."

"Good. If you can't find some, they will be left behind. Is the owner's stateroom ready?"

"Yes, sir. We readied it as soon as you gave the order. Will Sr. Cruz be with us for the entire voyage?"

"He disembarks in Havana." Luna's terse reply and baleful glare told the first mate to avoid further questions.

Capt. Luna received the call from Rex Seafood while he was eating an early breakfast. Sr. Cruz was driving to Tampa and would be coming aboard immediately upon arrival at the dock. He ordered the ship surgeon to be aboard and wanted the ship to cast off as soon as possible after his arrival.

Capt. Luna could think of any number of reasons for his new orders, but he knew it best to avoid dwelling on any of them. Traveling to Havana with one passenger and no cargo was hardly a plan for financial success, but what Sr. Cruz wanted, Sr. Cruz received. Questions were not part of Capt. Luna's arrangement.

When Cruz reached Rex Seafood off of East Adamo Drive, he was light-headed and a lot weaker than he expected. The loss of blood was catching up with him. "I'm not twenty anymore," he chided himself.

He pulled the truck around to the back of the building as near to the dock as possible. After scanning for potential witnesses and finding the dock area empty, he left the keys in the ignition and dropped heavily from the truck. He struggled up the gangplank and found a helpful assist aboard when the first mate noticed his plight. Once in sick bay, the ship's doctor put him under and removed the remaining arrow part and splinters from his arm and leg.

Dr. Penticost was not a great surgeon. He was not even a good surgeon. A fair surgeon might be inflated praise. Otherwise, why would he be on this ship instead of in a successful practice with a nice house, pretty wife, and cute kids, he thought many times. Fortunately for Cruz, this doctor did have one specialty that he practiced frequently: removing barbed hooks, spars, and other pointed objects from various body parts of fishermen. Extracting a thin arrow and fragments and sewing muscle back together were simple by comparison.

The doctor too knew better than to question Cruz on the circumstances of his wounds. Cruz could not have answered any question by that time in any event. He did not regain full consciousness until the day after the Cuba Sea Reef docked in Havana. Then, loaded with penicillin and fortified with compatible blood from two of the ship's sailors, he sat as a subdued passenger as his plantation foreman drove him to the Sierra Maestra and safety. As Cruz began to come out of his haze, he thought about the ordeal.

"I've covered my tracks, but not as well as I would have under less stressed circumstances. Hostetter is definitely a loose end. I'm not sure if he knows my name or not, but Dredman himself didn't know about Rex Seafood, so Hostetter is in the dark there in any event. I didn't like sparing nosey Elmer, but there was no better alternative at the time.

"There are several witnesses who could identify me in a lineup: the witch, the boys, the girl, and her father. That pair was something. I'm not sure I'd want to take on those two ever again. One at a time might be interesting, but together – I don't think so.

"In any event, I'm safe here in Cuba as long as no one suspects me."

But the investigation would get closer before long.

CHAPTER 23

Night Visit

The witch that came (the withered hag)
To wash the steps with pail and rag
Was once the beauty Abishag

ROBERT FROST

Carty's prediction of Sheriff James Elsmore's reaction to Sally's new persona was not far off the mark. He did not propose marriage or whisk Sally away, but he began the night nearly tongue tied. By the time he got around to telling Sally his news, he knew that he had made the right decision.

"Before you were like a tasty cake, perfect in shape, color, and texture. Now the beautiful cake has been covered with rich icing. I liked looking at you even before the transformation. Now you have reached a perfect state."

He had Sally blushing at more compliments through their second cup of tea. She was beginning to believe that Carty was right.

As James finished off another scone and jam, he said to her, "Actually I came tonight to introduce myself as your new neighbor."

Sally looked at him confusedly. "Neighbor? What do you mean?"

"The Hostetter place has been in arrears for back taxes for so many years, it was available from the county to anyone who paid to bring them current. I emptied most of my savings account and bought the place by paying the overdue taxes. Clem has a period of time to pay the taxes himself and void the transfer of ownership, but I'm sure that he doesn't have the money to make the payment himself. And since he doesn't know that the witch next door has transformed herself into a gorgeous angel, he probably has no interest.

"So now I can keep an eye out for unsavory types who might want to trespass on your property. They'll have to pass by me first."

Then he half apologetically asked, "I hope that you don't mind that I did this."

"Mind, James? I am delighted. That first night years ago – when you came to question my grandmother and me about the missing Whorton boy – you looked like a Greek god to me. I'd never been that close to a uniformed man in all my life." She laughed, "I mean, we don't even get a mailman out here.

"Maybe I should act coy with you, but I don't have any experience in that way. Besides, I'm too old for that. If I am going to change my way of life, I'm not going to fool around. James, I want you to take me to the town Easter Party on Saturday. Unless I have entirely misunderstood your intentions, I am assuming that your answer is yes."

"Your assumption is right on mark, Sally. I would be delighted to be your escort."

She beamed the brightest smile she had ever allowed herself to wear. "Now, it's getting late, and since you are no longer here on official business, it is time for you to leave. What would the neighbors think?" she added with a big grin.

"Neighbors? Who, the owls?"

Reluctantly, he began backing toward the door as she placed her hands on his chest and gently pushed him in that direction.

Sally would have enjoyed talking with him into the wee hours of the morning, but she had one more task to perform before she gave up the witch aura for good.

She couldn't discuss her plan with James. He might regard it as a little bit illegal – and way too crazy.

CHAPTER 24

Final Witching

Ding-dong! The witch is dead.

Munchkins in "The Wizard of Oz"

James had been gone for about thirty minutes, and Sally's mind concentrated totally on another matter.

Outfitted in a black cape, full-length black satin dress, and calf-length, laced, black boots with medium heels, Sally rubbed greenish gloss around her eyelids and white on her high cheekbones and the backs of her exposed hands and wrists. She added a small piece of blackened candle wax to an upper front tooth to give the impression of a gap and glued a brown piece to her nose to look like an ugly wart.

Long strands of black hair cascaded from under the pointed hat atop her head. She arranged the stringy, greasy hair in a haphazard, scraggly manner along her shoulders. A few strands she strung down her face. She attached long fake fingernails, some that were stained black. Finally, she wiped a light mixture of camphor and ground garlic on her neck and to the sleeves and shoulders of her dress – not enough to be overwhelming, but the right amount to cast an unpleasant odor for anyone nearby.

With one last look in the mirror, Sally smiled a wry grin, satisfied that she had achieved the desired look. She departed the house in good spirits that defied the effect of her appearance.

A red kerosene lantern shone brightly from the back of her wagon. She placed a rope, some hardware, tools, a ladder, and her large broom inside. Earlier she had pulled down a brown, dying branch from a palm tree and picked up a large dead branch that had fallen from an oak. These she added to the wagon's modest load. She climbed aboard and flicked the reins lightly on the black horse's back. The dark pair headed at a determined pace for Mocking Bird Road and the outskirts of town.

The lantern provided adequate warning to the two cars that passed the wagon on Mocking Bird Road. Both drivers weaved a bit after doing a double take when coming abreast.

At a closed Sunoco station near town, Sally pulled up to the lighted booth and paged through the white pages of the phone book. She found the address of the only Dolder in the book and recognized the Polk Street location as the wealthy part of town where houses were typically built on five to ten acre wooded estates. That was good. The more isolated the Dolder house was, the better it molded into her plan.

At nearly midnight, she approached the sprawling Dolder one-story ranch. In the distance, she saw that there were no palm trees near the house, but she was pleased to see that it was surrounded with large sprawling oaks. It had been a good guess on her part, because most Florida houses rely on the shade of tall trees for relief from the hot summer sun.

Sally tied her horse to a fence post well off the street and walked quietly to the house. She circled it methodically. For her purposes, there was sufficient light from interior night lights and the half moon outside. She ignored windows of large rooms like the living room and concentrated on bedrooms. The first was too frilly for a boy's room, and the second piled with toys too young for a teenager.

The next room was obviously the master bedroom. It also had the only room air conditioner while the other rooms relied on open windows, fans, and screens for circulating the muggy, warm night air.

At the fourth window, she believed that she found what she was looking for. To be certain, she continued around the house to look at other rooms. After completing a full circuit, she was confident that the fourth window belonged to Haywood's room.

Sally looked above his window and was disappointed that no well-positioned overhanging tree limbs were strong enough to support her weight. However, she found that the sturdy window frame was suitable for the requirements of her fall-back position. She retreated to the wagon and retrieved her supplies, abandoning only the palm branch which was useless for her plan, since only oaks were in evidence.

She placed the ladder along one side of Haywood's window and climbed a few steps so that she could reach the top of the window frame. She secured a sturdy hook apparatus to the top of the frame. Then she moved to the other side of the window and repeated the procedure. She tied a rope between the two hooks.

With thin but strong strands of wire, she connected the front and rear of her broom to the rope so that it swung horizontally at a mid-window height. The wires would be invisible in the dim night light. Carefully, she climbed aboard and straddled the broom. The contraption held her weight and allowed her to swing gently back and forth in front of the window as if she were floating.

She tapped lightly on the window frame and scratched her nails on the screen. She could barely make out the dark, lumpy form on the bed across the room. It did not stir. She tapped more insistently. Still no reaction.

She waited and listened for the room air conditioner in the master bedroom. It had cycled off during her walk around the house. She continued tapping without effect. After a few minutes, the air conditioner kicked on and the masking noise gave Sally the cover she needed for more aggressive efforts.

"Haywood Dolllllder," she began to chant in her eerie witch's voice. "Haywood Dolllllder," she continued even louder.

After she added several additional chants, Haywood rolled over and looked toward the window from where the sound came. "Haywood Dolllllder," Sally continued as she rocked gently above ground.

Dolder sat upright in shocked silence. He pulled the covers around his chin and stared. At first he thought he was dreaming.

"Do not make a sound, Haywood Dolllllder, if you value your life," Sally ordered. "I am Sally Canfield, and you have stolen property of mine. I need it for my midnight enchantment and if you do not return it, you will regret your perfidy as long as you are allowed to live. Do you understand what I am saying, Haywood Dollllder?"

"No," barely emerged from his trembling voice, "I did not take anything from you. You have made a terrible mistake. Please leave me alone."

"You have stolen my Chapmann's rhododendron. You have it here. You cannot hide it for I can smell it. You must return it or face the worst. Where have you put it?"

"No, I did not take it from you. I found it at school."

"There are no Chapmann's rhododendron growing at your school. They only grow in my plot. They only grow for my purposes. It was stolen and I intend to get it back one way or another. It is your choice. You may return my property or you will live to regret it.

"WHAT IS YOUR DECISION?!"

Dolder had given up trying to hang on to the specimen, but his devious mind grasped for a way to salvage something out of the dire situation. He hopped from the bed and raced for the specimen book.

"Look, I have the specimen in this book. Let me get it out for you."

As he removed the page, he said, "I did not steal this from you, but I know who did."

"Bring it to me, Sonny, and tell me what you know. If your information is valuable I give you my word that I will reduce your punishment. But the information must be true. Now give me the Chapmann's."

Dolder lifted the screen from the window frame. Standing as far back as possible, he reached the page toward Sally. She snatched it from his hand with a strong jerk and uttered a wicked laugh. Dolder stepped back and held his breath.

"Now what do you have to tell me?"

"The person who stole this from you is Carty Andersson. She bragged to us at school how she snuck on to your farm. She had her friends distract you while she searched your property. When you weren't looking, she made off with it. I only took it from her because I was trying to figure out a way to get it back to you."

"I can smell your lies and I can smell a Rudbeckia nitida and a Drosera intermedia in your room as well." Sally had remembered Carty mentioning those two items. "I need those. Give them to me. That will be adequate punishment for your falsehoods."

"I can't give those to you. I need them for my project. They are not yours."

"They are mine now, because you will give them to me. Your lies have brought this upon you. Give those two items to me, and I will not have to enter your room."

Sally grasped the window frame and feinted toward the open window, bluffing that she was going to climb through.

"No, no, stay there. I will get them for you."

Dolder rushed through his book and extracted the two pages of specimens that Sally asked for. He held them out to her, far from his body. Again, she snatched them with vehemence and a shrill laugh.

"You have cooperated well. Not all do. You will survive the night. Not all do. Now return to your bed and cover your head with the blanket. Remain quiet for the remainder of the night, and I may not have to do more."

As soon as Dolder was under the blanket, Sally dismounted the broom and stepped on the ladder. She removed the two hooks from above. She used a small gardening shovel to fill in the holes on the ground that the ladder had made. Then she covered the entire area with loose oak leaves to mask any footprints. Finally, she leaned the large oak branch against the window frame.

The horse took Sally home without incident. She thought as she rode, "Carty is a delightful young lady and the boys are equally gallant. They deserved my help as much as Dolder deserved the punishment."

She was satisfied that this final witch act was for a noble cause. By moonlight in those early hours, Sally buried all of her witch outfits in the pit that had captured Zeller. Though rumors of the Canfield witches persisted for many years, Sally no longer encouraged them.

Back at the Dolder house, Haywood remained shivering under the useless protection of his blanket. His racing heartbeat kept him awake for an hour until, exhausted, he fell into a fitful sleep. In the morning, he awoke with a start and spied the large branch against the window. For a moment he thought that he had experienced a terrible nightmare. He reasoned that the branch crashing into the window had initiated the bad dream.

He eased out of bed and saw that the screen was on the floor where he remembered placing it in his dream. Cautiously, he pushed the branch away from the window and looked around, seeing nothing unusual.

Then he thought about the specimen book. Quickly, he grabbed the book and scanned the pages. Three were missing – the three he remembered giving away during the dream. He ran to his parents' room with a wild story.

After calming Haywood down, his father examined the area around the window and saw nothing unusual, except for the large, dead branch that appeared to have fallen from the tree and had scratched the window frame. "Haywood," he rebuked, "You had a bad dream. That's all. Now stop all this nonsense about witches, or the town will think I am raising an idiot."

"What about the missing pages from my specimen book?" Haywood whined.

"If you lost some of your specimens, you won't get any sympathy from me with stupid excuses about flying witches. Why would a witch or anyone else want your specimens anyway?"

"She said she was making an enchantment or spell or something. I don't know. I only know that the witch came last night and took my specimens."

"Look, that's it. One more word about witches and you'll spend the next week in the house each night – and that includes the town Easter Party. Do you understand?"

Haywood wanted to press his case more fervently, but not at the expense of missing the Easter Party, so he dropped his head and remained silent.

At school that morning, the members of Dolder's class-project group – Gore, Folger, and Stanton – couldn't believe their ears. "A witch flew up to your window last night and demanded that you give her three of our specimens? Are you crazy?" Gore questioned.

Patiently, Haywood repeated his story. He had no other way to explain the missing pages from his group's specimen book.

"Did the witch threaten you?" Stanton asked.

"She said I would regret not giving up the specimens. She said that the extra two were punishment for stealing the Chapmann's."

"But what did she threaten you with?"

"Well, nothing specific, but I knew it would be something serious.

You can count on that with a witch."

The three shook their heads and looked at one another in bewilderment and disappointment as the bell rang. They rushed in to class.

Mrs. Tryon greeted the students. "All right, everyone. Turn in your specimen books."

One by one, the leader of each group handed a book to her. She asked each representative for a total number. Carty's group was the only one turning in all twenty-five, but the other groups had rallied strongly. Except for Dolder's, each had reached twenty-three or twenty-four.

When Dolder announced sheepishly that his group had collected only twenty-two specimens, Carty and Mack gave each other confused shrugs.

After lunch, Mrs. Tryon reported the final results. One of the specimens from Eddie's group proved to be misidentified, dropping that group to a twenty-three. Otherwise everyone had classified the specimens properly. The twenty-fours were awarded As and the twenty-threes received Bs. Dolder's group, in last place, received a C. Carty's group received the only A+.

Then Mrs. Tryon offered an additional announcement. "For aiding fellow students well beyond necessity, and even to the potential detriment of their own results, I am awarding Carty, Blake, Hale, and Mack a bonus of twenty points each on their final written exam next month.

"You four showed an exemplary sense of fair play. I am more proud of that than I am of your actual results."

Later that afternoon, as The Crew met before heading home, the boys thanked Carty for her idea to help the other students. "If it hadn't been for you, Carty, we would not have those extra points," Mack said. "But even without the bonus, you taught us a good lesson."

"I'm still baffled about Dolder's group," Carty commented. "If they had only twenty-one collected, why nip our Chapmann's simply to get to twenty-two? That one extra specimen wouldn't really help them very much. You'd think they would have grabbed several from our book instead of only the single rarest.

"Sometimes Haywood confuses me so much that he makes my head hurt."

CHAPTER 25

Cruz Cruz Investigation

It is a riddle wrapped in a mystery inside an enigma.
WINSTON CHURCHILL

Detective Leland of the Detroit Police Department and Sheriff Elsmore concluded their otherwise disappointing phone call on a positive note.

"That's all we have been able to come up with since you inquired several weeks ago, Sheriff. Hostetter had two drunk and disorderly arrests, Dredman a public intoxication and an aggravated assault. Hostetter got probation on all of his charges. Dredman served thirty days on the assault charge. There was a shoplifting arrest from a liquor store for both of them, but charges were dropped for insufficient evidence.

"We had nothing negative on Carey Zeller. He's ex-Army. Did a good job in the Pacific apparently. He shows up as a legitimate manager in a wholesale food and cigarette business here in Detroit. There is a connection to your part of the country that you might find interesting, though. Apparently the business up here is related to a company in Tampa, Rex Seafood, which is owned by a Cuban American.

"There is no telling if that Cuban is the same fellow you are looking for, but maybe this will give you something to go on."

"Thanks a lot, Detective. You've given me more of a lead than anything else we have been able to develop. If you ever make it down to Florida, give me a head's up and I'll show you some Gulf fishing."

"That sounds like a good offer. I'll keep it in mind. The most edible thing I ever fished out of Lake Michigan was an old Uniroyal tire."

The next day, James spoke with Sgt. Vasquez of the Tampa Police Department about the Cuban owner of Rex Seafood. James and Sgt. Vazquez had been in the Navy at the same base, but their assignment timing did not overlap. Nonetheless, they had a common bond that accelerated the sergeant's responding to the sheriff's inquiry.

"James, this Cuban fellow you asked about is an interesting character. He's a former U.S. Marine from before WWI. He was born in Tampa, but is a dual Cuban-American citizen as his parents were Cubans. As a young man, he was one of our cigar kings between the Wars. He sold out for a fortune in the Twenties and has kept a low profile since. He owns a small business, Rex Seafood, a fish wholesaler – more as a hobby than a real business, according to local businessmen. Apparently, he is well to do. He has quite an estate on the bay in Ruskin, south of Tampa.

"There were a few rumors from about twenty years ago of strong-arming restaurants to sole source their fish from him, but nothing ever came of that. Witnesses always seemed to lose interest shortly after filing complaints. Aside from that, we hear nothing negative.

In fact, this Cruz Cruz is a modest contributor to various charitable organizations promoted by local political leaders, so he is well connected. What is odd is that we cannot seem to get a good physical description of him. Apparently, he seldom attends any functions but offers his gifts through intermediaries.

"We found a grainy photo from a January 1917 story in an old Spanish language newspaper. It talked about him coming back from the army and joining his father's company. Cruz Cruz is standing in the background behind his father, showing only a fuzzy profile. I doubt that you could identify anyone from a shot like that.

"We haven't been able to find any photographs more recent or of useful quality. Apparently, he is camera-shy, which is a bit incongruous for a person of some social standing.

"Ramon, did you say this Cuban's name is Cruz Cruz?"

"Yeah, kind of odd, isn't it, the same given and family name?"

"I'll say. More to the point, the only other surviving member of the attackers identified his leader as a man with two identical Spanish sounding names. This may be the break I've been looking for."

"Well, maybe not, James. I checked with Rex Seafood and was told that Cruz seldom comes in anymore. He spends most of his time semi-retired in Cuba. In fact, the manager says that Cruz hasn't been in the States in over four months. If that is true, he wasn't here at the time of the attack. Of course, the manager could be lying."

"Ramon, I'd like a chance to meet Cruz. The company manager

could be covering for him. Would you mind if I accompany you for an interview the next time Cruz is in town?"

"I'm already on it, James. The Rex Seafood manager, Andy Gilbert, was very cooperative. He said that Cruz was scheduled to be visiting the business in about three weeks. He said he would try to arrange a suitable time for us to meet. I'll set it up and give you a time."

Immediately after Vasquez's first visit a week ago, Gilbert had phoned Cruz to warn him about the inquiry. At the time, Cruz told him not to worry, and to schedule an interview with the police in about three weeks if they called back.

BACK at the Andersson home, Michael hung up the phone and turned to Carty. "It looks like the sheriff will be able to let us get a look at a suspect, a man named Cruz Cruz, Carty, but he may not be the right man."

"I know, Dad. From listening to your part of the conversation, Cruz Cruz sounds like someone who would have a Spanish accent. Our Mr. Smith didn't have one that I could tell, so this Cruz Cruz doesn't seem like a good prospect. Clem Hostetter may be leading us down the wrong trail. He did not strike me as a truthful or reliable witness. Maybe Cruz is connected in some other way, though."

"I agree, Carty. I detected no Spanish accent either. In fact, I would have pegged the guy as a Midwesterner. Of course, growing up here on the coast, he probably wouldn't sound Spanish.

"Perhaps if our conversation in the swamp had lasted longer, we could have noticed something along those lines, but none of us was seeking a long talk. Anyway, James says the guy is coming back to Florida soon. He'd like us to accompany him to Tampa, unofficially, to see if Cruz is our man. He'll try to arrange it on a Saturday so you don't have to miss school."

Twenty days later, Vasquez was on the phone with Andy Gilbert, firming up the meeting with Cruz.

"So the day after tomorrow at three in the afternoon is good for Mr. Cruz?"

"Yes, Sergeant. He says he is very curious how his name became mixed up in such a wild tale."

"You said he was flying into Tampa, Mr. Gilbert?"

"That's right, Sergeant. Tomorrow morning from Havana."

The only Thursday morning flight from Havana was a Pan Am that originated in Rio de Janeiro. Vasquez stationed two of his undercover men in the customs area. Since Cruz was a dual citizen, he could come through either the line for foreign visitors or for U.S. citizens, depending on the passport he used.

When a man with the name Cruz Cruz came through the immigration line, the agent took a little longer than normal to peruse the Cuban passport. He added his official stamp to the many that cluttered Cruz's passport and sent him through.

For a Federal agency, U.S. Customs had a good reputation for working with local police officials, and the Tampa connection was strong. As Cruz passed by, the agent nodded to Vasquez's undercover officer to pass on the prearranged signal that the Cuban passport was genuine, government-issued.

Vasquez wanted to make certain that Cruz did not pull a switch with another man for the meeting. This officer accompanied Vasquez and Sheriff Elsmore on Saturday to ensure that they met with this same man and not a substitute.

The next day, Cruz, a slight, middle-aged, silver-haired man, sat behind an old cherry-wood desk at Rex Seafood. He put down the company's monthly financial figures and greeted Sheriff Elsmore, Sgt. Vasquez, and the officer who confirmed with a subtle hand signal that no switch had taken place.

James explained that Cruz's former Detroit manager was identified as one of the assailants in an armed robbery and kidnapping in Winter Free. They were following up with Cruz to see if he could add any information. The conversation was pleasant and fruitless. Cruz provided no useful information and offered no idea why Zeller had come to Tampa.

Cruz mentioned that he had discussed the possibility of closing his Detroit operation and wondered if the potential loss of Zeller's job might have pressured him into an illegal act. Cruz appeared genuinely distraught that he might have indirectly contributed to the crime in that way.

"Carey Zeller did a good job for me. The business has changed and it wasn't making sense for us to keep that Detroit branch running any longer. I could have found something else for him if I had known that he was taking a possible closure so hard."

"We're sorry to have bothered you, Sr. Cruz," Ramon concluded. "It doesn't look like you are able to help us with the investigation. Unfortunately, our contact in Detroit was not able to develop any additional information."

As the police officers drove away in the sergeant's car, Michael and

Carty waited in the DeSoto across the street. A few minutes later, the sheriff darted through an alley from where Vasquez dropped him. He climbed into the back seat.

"That interview was useless. Either Cruz doesn't know anything about this, or he is a really good liar. We'll wait here until he comes out, and you can look him over and determine if this is the guy you met in the woods. If he is, I'll have Ramon take him in for some tougher questioning."

They waited until shortly after five in the sweltering heat engulfing a car without air conditioning. Northerners would be surprised to learn that the U.S. Weather Bureau had never recorded an official triple digit temperature for the city of Tampa. The city's proximity to cooler Gulf breezes kept the hottest days from exceeding the nineties. But high nineties with high humidity made miserable conditions for the patient trio.

About ten after five, Gilbert and the Cruz whom James met came out the side door of Rex Seafood and got into the manager's Nash.

Michael awakened Carty, who had dozed off. He shook his head and said to the sheriff, "No, James. Neither of those two comes close to resembling Mr. Smith. They are both too slender. Their faces are oval, not squared off like our guy."

"Carty, what do you think?"

"I agree with Dad. The man in the swamp was built like a fire hydrant, had black hair, and seemed way stronger than those guys. And he had really unusual slitted eyes like a snake's – but horizontal instead of vertical. Is there any chance that he has pulled a switch?"

"Sgt. Vazquez had a man at airport Customs when Cruz came through with a Cuban passport. If he had a different name or didn't match the photo, the sergeant's man would have been tipped. Our Customs contact says that Cruz was traveling on a legitimate government passport with the name Cruz Cruz. It's is not likely that there are two people with that oddball name.

"That was our last real shot. This case will have to go into the 'unsolved' file for the time being," grumped the frustrated sheriff.

"After this disappointment, I think we need a good dinner. I'm buying, James. Would you care to join Carty and me?" Ironically, they dined at The Columbia – now transformed from its modest beginnings into a great restaurant – where much of the Cruz saga originated.

One week later, the visitor from Cuba departed Tampa by plane. He had arranged completion of the sale of Rex Seafood to its former manager, Andy Gilbert. Without the cigarette smuggling, it was only a marginally profitable business, but it generated a fair cash flow. When Gilbert was given a chance to buy the entire operation for a nominal price of one hundred dollars, he jumped at it. Of course, it did not hurt his chances when he agreed earlier in the month to go along with Cruz's plan.

Cruz's accountant in Havana, Miguel Maldonado, was always helpful. With Cruz's contacts in the Cuban government, it was not difficult to get an official passport for Maldonado in the name of Cruz Cruz. Several bogus entry and exit stamps for a number of other countries added authenticity that cost only little more.

Traveling as Cruz Cruz, Maldonado acted as and was accepted by Gilbert outwardly as the president of Rex Seafood for the ten days it took to satisfy the two law officers. As Cruz's accountant, Maldonado had no difficulty handling the paperwork to transfer ownership of Rex Seafood to Gilbert, a fair enough reward to Gilbert for years of faithful service.

It was not foolproof, and there were loose ends. With Rex Seafood implicated, that nosey sheriff might find someone who remembered seeing the truck in the vicinity of Winter Free. Hostetter might regain his memory for a reduced sentence. That sheriff might find a recent photo of Cruz to show around – there weren't many, but there were a handful. Gilbert or Maldonado could get greedy and blackmail him, and there was still the Elmer problem.

Overall, though, Cruz was content. Although he didn't have enough influence with the current regime in Havana to head off extradition action if Uncle Sam put up a strong fuss, at least the heat was off for a while. Moreover, his situation would improve if he used the time prudently to get Batista into power.

CHAPTER 26

The Easter Party

*Dating at least from ancient Rome, the holiday was a time of public
and communal celebration, a time to commemorate some event of civic
or religious significance that all citizens participated in equally.*
BARRY SCHWARTZ

The town Easter Party was always on the Saturday immediately before Easter, giving students a great start to their vacation the following week. The weather nearly always cooperated that time of year. Townsfolk enjoyed renewing friendships with former residents who returned for the festivities. Students relished the opportunity to relax and get together outside of school. This year it came on April 8, only a few days before Carty's fourteenth birthday.

The town turned out in whites and pastels for Easter Week. Blooms, primarily lilies, graced the porches and flower boxes of all the houses in the downtown area. Colorful bunting with printed Scripture on banners draped from city light poles. Residents tidied front yards, and store fronts were cleaned and freshly painted.

The evening was reserved for a dance and buffet in front of the gazebo that served as the bandstand and stage. The town strung lights above and supplied the ham, turkey, potatoes, and salads. Members of local churches and civic organizations staffed cooking and serving crews.

Residents brought favorite breads and other baked goods as well as cooked dishes, especially casseroles and desserts. The latter of these were the best part of the food offerings, because the women sought to outdo each other to win the town's award.

Most of the daylight hours were devoted to games and contests for the youngsters. The highlight event was the annual baseball game between graduates of the area high schools, known as the "Old Team," and an all-star roster of current high school players and a few Cross Creek Elementary players, dubbed the "Young Team." Mack and the Danner twins were Cross Creek subs on the team this year with Dolder in the bullpen.

Blake, at shortstop and batting cleanup, and Hale, at second, were the only Cross Creek starters on the Young Team. The youngsters were led by Bill Normand, the coach at Winter Free High. Normand normally favored his more experienced high school players, but he kept an eye out for talent on the Cross Creek Elementary team. He was salivating at the prospect of bringing in Blake next year and wished that he could position Hale across at second base as well.

With those two added to the holdovers on his current roster, he envisioned a state championship. Unfortunately for Normand, Hale was slated for the Negro high school in the adjoining city.

The Old Team was on a six-year winning streak, usually prevailing by a large margin, so prospects were not good for the student athletes. "Age and cunning trump youth and inexperience every time," was the motto of the increasingly cocky senior group, led by Michael Andersson on the mound, James Elsmore in center field, and Harrison Wending at third.

Blake laughed when he heard the motto, because it reminded him that the older ducks in Sally's fable made the same claim. "Some day I'll be old and try it out on the kids," he thought.

Hale's father, Harrison, had given up a potential career in a Negro League when he chose to marry and stay in Florida instead. Nevertheless, he still possessed the slick fielding skills and lightning quick reflexes of a third baseman that had attracted a scout for the Kansas City Monarchs many years earlier.

This year, the younger players held their own through six innings. With the score tied at one in the top of the seventh and none out, the sheriff lined a double to the wall in left. A grounder to Hale at second moved him over to third, and Michael's sacrifice fly to deep center plated the go-ahead run. But in the bottom of the inning, Blake crushed a solo home run off Michael's curve ball to tie the game.

Through nine innings, the score remained tied. No one could remember an extra inning game in the series. Both teams tore through their pitching staffs as the innings mounted. The game almost came to an end in the fifteenth when Blake lined a two-out blast into right center with runners on second and third. But the sheriff laid out a dart-like dive and snared the ball inches from the ground just short of the fence. Even the players on the Young Team applauded as James jogged into the infield sporting a grassy green stripe from his chest to his belt buckle.

Often a long game loses some of the fans, but not today. In fact, the opposite occurred. Additional spectators continued arriving as the innings mounted, drawn by increasingly loud cheering and curiosity that the game did not end in the normal time. By the seventeenth inning, the stands were filled and late arriving fans crammed the areas along the foul lines and behind the outfield fence.

The advantage was gradually moving in the Old Team's direction. Except for pitchers, they were still playing most of their starters. After pitching the first ten innings, Michael moved to first base, but his was the only position substitution.

In the meantime, Normand had used the Young Team roster aggressively trying with pinch runners and pinch hitters to push across a winning run. By the seventeenth, the Young Team was down to using all of its Cross Creek players. Hale was smooth in the field, and Blake was the team's hitting star, but the other elementary school teammates were not their peer, nor the peer of the high school players that they had gradually replaced.

Dolder, pitching in the top of the eighteenth to the first three hitters, loaded the bases on two walks and a sharp single to left, and the situation looked grim. However, Blake started a slick bases loaded 6-4-3 double play on a one hopper in the hole, as Hale turned a sharp pivot. It was key to preventing a big inning, but the go-ahead run did score on the play.

Normand thought to himself, "I've got to get both those two kids next year."

Relieving the ineffective Dolder, Hale came in from his second base position to face Sheriff Elsmore with a runner on third. Hale had no fastball to speak of, but he was a master of a curve that he threw slow, slower, and slowest. In fact, he threw his only three pitches of the game in exactly that sequence. The sheriff let the first pitch go by for a called strike, and swung futilely at the next two tantalizing floaters to the laughter of the fans, opposition, and even his own teammates.

As James took the field, he raced over to Hale, who was leaving the mound and said good naturedly, "Good job, Hale. I still can't figure out how gravity failed to attract those five-mile per hour pitches of yours."

"Shucks, Sheriff. I'm good for an inning, but if you faced me again, you'd have the timing down to destroy my pitches."

The sheriff laughed and gave Hale a swat on the rear as he raced out to center field. The fans, including a few who were fearful that the meeting portended a confrontation, joined in the laughter.

Hale led off the bottom of the inning with a slow chopper to short that just eluded his dad's frantic dive from where he was guarding the third base line against a double. Thanks to Hale's speed, he beat out the infield single without a throw to the frenzied delight of the Wending family, taking up most of the top row of the third base stands.

For only the second time since the twelfth inning, the Young Team had a base runner. On the first pitch, Hale stole second standing up. Normand shook his head in awe. Three pitches later, Hale took third easily on a medium fly to right.

Mack came up with a chance to drive in the tying run with a fly ball. Chances for a nineteenth inning looked promising. He was hoping for a low pitch that he could loft far enough to get Hale home. High pitches were his weak spot, but the opposition didn't know it.

Dolder recalled the time when Mack had embarrassed him with a home run on a low pitch. The idea that Mack might become a hero this afternoon irked him. From the bench, he shouted out to the opposing pitcher, "Pitch him high. He can't hit a high pitch."

Most of the Young Team's members didn't know Mack or his pitch preferences, but they were struck by the strange situation. Dolder yelled it out again.

The Cross Creek contingent fumed silently as Dolder continued to rant. Blake got up from the bench and headed over to Dolder to shut him up, but the Old Team pitcher was ready to pitch before Blake reached Dolder.

The pitcher then made a logical mistake. He assumed that Dolder was trying to help Mack and the team. Naturally, the pitcher thought that Mack's strength must be the high pitch, and that Dolder was trying to trick him into throwing it there. So he threw the same type of low curve that Dolder had pitched that first day of practice. It broke into Mack's wheelhouse, and his long arching swing took it deep into right center field.

Hale waited at third to tag up after the catch. He would score the tying run without difficulty on a ball hit that far. James went back like a fleet gazelle seeming to outrun the ball. But the ball gained a little loft in the slight breeze that had picked up later in the day. The ball kept going and going.

James ran out of room. He stopped at the fence and watched as the ball sailed five feet beyond for a game winning home run. The Young Team had won the game, the first in seven years, and the Cross Creek kids were the saviors.

Mack's team mobbed him at home, barely seconds before the fans cleared the stands to join in. Only Dolder was lost in the cheer. "It was my idea," he implored. "I'm the one who tricked their pitcher. I'm the real hero." No one paid him any attention.

AFTER THE LONG GAME, players had to rush home to get cleaned up for the evening festivities. Carty jumped into Michael's DeSoto and they drove home quickly. "Mom, you should have seen Dad. He was the star pitcher and knocked in what was almost the winning run."

"Bay, Carty is the perfect daughter. She thinks I can do no wrong. In reality, Blake and Mack were the stars, and Hale came up big as well. The Young Team won with key contributions from the youngest part of their team, the Cross Creek contingent. There are going to be some good ball players representing this town for several years to come."

"Well, you two can tell me all about it when we drive to town this evening. Right now you need to get cleaned up, and I need to get Carty prepared to be a lady for a change."

"Aw, Mom, can't I just wear my peddle pushers and a white blouse?"

"Not tonight, Carty. We've discussed this. Tonight, I am in charge. I have everything already set out, so get going. I'll meet you in your room in twenty minutes."

Carty refused to admit it, even to herself, but she was actually pleased at the prospect of dressing up for the big event. She still clung to her tomboy image publicly, but over the past few months, she was beginning to feel that sometimes she might want to act differently than a boy.

Bay knew how to make herself look glamorous. Carty secretly hoped that her mother could use that talent to transform her. Bay could, and for tonight, she had every intention of doing so.

On Carty's bed, Bay spread out a new dress from Tampa's most exclusive women's shop. When Carty came in from the shower and saw it, she surprised Bay with a squeal of delight and a big hug. Carty was easy to shop for, since she had the tall slim figure of a model that dress makers seemed to design for. Her bust was developing a bit slowly, but that was just as well in Bay's opinion.

"Sit down here," Bay directed. "We are going to do wonders for your hair." Carty's patience during the styling process was as unexpected as it was pleasing for Bay. She thought to herself, "I guess that Michael was right when he told me that Carty would be ready when she was ready."

When Bay and Carty met Michael at the door in preparation for the trip to town, he stared in awe. The two beauties looked like sisters, Bay appearing years younger than her age and Carty years older. They were remarkably similar in appearance, a resemblance that he had not noticed before, except in a general way. His smile said everything.

"Ladies, I could not be more proud, chauffeuring Florida's most beautiful women to this event." He wrapped an arm around each of them as he escorted them to the car.

THE tax sale for the Hostetter place was not yet official, so James was still living in his small apartment. After the game, he raced there to clean up, and then to Sally's house to bring her to town. This would be the first appearance of a Canfield at a public function, and he did not want to make Sally wait or to give her additional time to get cold feet. He need not have worried. She was ready at the door as he pulled up in his sheriff's vehicle.

She greeted him with an enormous smile when he knocked on the door and pleased him with a gentle embrace when he commented on her striking dress and matching necklace. "Sally, you'd make the town take notice just showing up. Wait until they see you like this.

"Come in a moment, I want your help," she said. "I am going to surprise Carty with a necklace tonight. I've already discussed it with her mother, so Carty will not be wearing one when she arrives."

Holding two elaborate jeweled necklaces before him, she said, "Bay Andersson told me that Carty will be wearing yellow this evening with a slightly scooped neckline, so either of these will do, but tell me which one you like the best."

He looked at them closely. They were nearly identical diamond necklaces, except for the center jewels. One had red garnets and the other glistening opals.

"The opals are my choice. When Carty flashes that smile of hers, the room sparkles. The highlights of opals would be a perfect complement, don't you think?"

"That was my thought too, but I'm glad that you agree. Both belonged to my great grandmother. I remembered them from the photographs I showed Carty and the boys recently. Even in the old photographs, either necklace looked like it would be perfect for Carty. I'll be right back."

She slipped the opal necklace into her small purse and returned the other jewels to the first floor bedroom. When she returned, she took his arm and walked toward the door. "I trust that you will drive this automobile carefully. I've never been in one before, and I know that they travel a lot faster than my wagon."

"You've never been in a car?"

"No, not even parked. Father's old car is under a canvas tarp in the barn. It hasn't been driven since the day he died. He had purchased it that very morning. I have never wanted to see what it looked like.

"I did touch a red car outside of the Ensign Bank a few years ago. It looked so much like a giant ruby, so bright and red and shiny, that I was drawn to it. I thought the poor man inside the car was going to faint. When I moved away, he gritted his teeth in fear as he started the car.

"Occasionally, I liked to tease nasty people to see their reactions, but that time it was not intentional, and I felt bad. He wasn't being mean and didn't deserve to be frightened."

"I remember that well," James joshed, "I was the terrified driver of that car."

"You were not, you silly man. You were one of the few people I met who wasn't at all afraid of the scary Canfields."

ONCE in the car, of course, James could not resist the temptation. So on a sparsely traveled section of Mocking Bird Road, he switched on the siren and took the Ford up to 80mph for a short run. Surprising both of them, Sally was not intimidated. Actually, she enjoyed the wind rushing through the open windows. "This is even better than my broom," she exclaimed with a long laugh.

James was still shaking his head at this unpredictable lady as he switched off the noise and slowed down nearing town.

A discernable hush came over the crowd as the couple walked from James' car. At first, no one recognized the beautiful woman on the sheriff's arm.

Sally was dressed in a full-length, emerald green, slim, satin dress with a scooped neckline. The gown emphasized her narrow waist and hips and lifted her bosom. Matching green slippers peeked from beneath a thin slip. A diamond necklace with a large center emerald draped below her neck and was set off by wispy red hair. Sally's dazzling green eyes finished the picture brightly. Contrasting with the pastels that were in vogue at the festivities, she stood out brilliantly.

Gardner Ensign was the first to recognize her, though he was amazed at the transformation. He had been told by his vice president that Sally appeared in the bank yesterday looking remarkably different. Now he saw for himself what the man meant.

When he and Homer discussed the unexpected sight, others leaned their ears toward them for more information. Slowly, word began circulating that the striking woman was the witch, Sally Canfield. No one knew how to react. Everyone stood and stared in silence as the pair continued to walk toward the dance area in front of the bandstand.

There, Lilly Andersson noticed them and walked up to Sally and embraced her warmly.

"My, Sally, I remembered you as a pretty young girl, but I had no idea you looked like this as a grown woman."

Sally's blush added to her attractiveness, and she hugged Lilly tightly. "This is so intimidating for me," she whispered, "even with James as my armed protector. Thank you for coming up to greet me."

"I see someone else who will want to say hello," Lilly replied, stepping back and waving toward the other Anderssons. Carty broke away and ran up to them.

"Hello, Aunt Lilly. I see that you have met my new sister.

"Hi, Sally," Carty beamed. "You are so beautiful, even more than the last time I saw you."

"Look who's talking, Sis. This is quite a change for you too. You are not even carrying a weapon, unless you consider the effect that this look will have on the boys in town."

It was Carty's turn to blush. "Thanks, Sally, but I don't think I'd know how to use that kind of weapon."

"Oh, you will. It's instinctive. I figured it out, and I had no experience with men."

"It's good to see you so happy, Carty," James added. "That is an attractive dress, and your hair is different. I like the way it swirls around and piles up on top."

Sally chuckled at his clumsy but accurate description. "That's a French twist, James, and on Carty, it's as nice as I have ever seen," Sally said. Among the many books in Sally's library were fashion texts from several eras and countries. Part of Sally's fashion sense came from fantasizing over those books, and the rest was intuitive.

"I have something for you, Carty, and it looks like James and I chose wisely." From her purse, she extracted the thick silver necklace with a display of six fiery opals strung nearly four inches wide. A string of diamonds set off each side of the opals.

"Turn around so I can put it on you."

Sally fixed the clasp at the back of Carty's neck while James held the small purse with awkward self-consciousness. The necklace was a perfect complement to Carty's outfit. Though Carty had initially resisted Bay's choice of hairstyle, Sally's compliment made her glad that she had relented. The necklace added to a change in Carty's appearance that was only slightly less striking than Sally's.

Indeed, Carty's hair pulled atop her head emphasized her height, long neck, and sharp jaw line. Her tightly-waisted dress was a smooth yellow silk with a lacey outer overlay of white and yellow daisies, silver dollar size. The neckline grasped precariously to the edges of her strong Florida tanned shoulders, with just enough modest dip in front to display the necklace in perfect detail. With her slightly raised heels, she stood several inches taller than Sally in flat slippers.

Carty was almost speechless, but forced out sincere thanks. Before she could elaborate, Michael and Bay arrived. Michael introduced Bay and Sally to one another.

"We spoke yesterday by phone, Michael. Sally called from the Ensign Bank offices to see what color and style of dress Carty would be wearing. She told me that she was planning a little gift, but I expected nothing as elaborate or expensive as this," she said, fingering the necklace on Carty's neck. "Sally, I'm not sure we can let Carty accept it."

"It is easy to see where Carty got her beauty and her good manners," Sally replied. "Bay, I have jewels upon jewels locked up and hidden in bank vaults. From now onward, I plan to wear them whenever appropriate, but it gives me great pleasure to give this one to Carty. She looks delightful tonight, and the necklace is a perfect finishing accessory. Please don't refuse my gift."

Michael gave Bay a slight nod to signify his willingness. Bay smiled and said, "All right, I can't argue with that. Gift accepted. Thank you."

Now Carty embraced Sally emphatically. "Thank you so much, Sally. I've never owned anything so beautiful. Well, to be honest, I've never cared to before tonight, but now that it is draped around my neck, I may not ever take it off. I love it, and I love you."

After several minutes, Carty spotted Blake and Mack at the punch table and excused herself from the adults. Mack, with his back turned, was refilling his cup as she approached.

Carty's brightest smile glistened in the sharply angled late afternoon sun. Blake turned and stared at her, envisioning a graceful long-necked swan emerging from a spray of dew-dropped spring flowers. He stood mesmerized as she came close, and then began stammering when she arrived.

After a moment of staring, all he was able to get out was, "Carty, you, ah, you have a neck."

She scowled a nasty look at him. "I have a neck?! I have a neck?! What's that supposed to mean? Of course I have a neck. How do you think my head stays attached? Ooh, you make me so mad sometimes, Blake Holmes."

Before he could recover, she spun on a toe and marched back to the adults in a huff, leaving Blake red-faced, bewildered, and speechless.

"That was real Cary Grant[24], Blake," teased Mack, who caught the end of the byplay. "You've never noticed that Carty had a neck before, or that she was pretty?

"Oh, man, I blew that. When did that happen? She didn't look like that yesterday. She sure didn't look like that in the stands at the ball game this afternoon. I know she is a girl, but not a *girl*. I mean Betty Rose Hawkins and Mary Kelsey are *girls*. Carty has always been a pal, not that gorgeous creature who just fluttered in, glared at me, and flew back out.

"What am I going to do now? She didn't look like she ever wanted to speak to me again."

"Well, I wouldn't count on melting the ice anytime soon, suave man. But you'll have the whole summer to make up while working with her at Mr. Andersson's mine. I'd be careful not to let her get behind me with a bulldozer, though, if you I were."

"'If I were you,' Mack," Blake corrected absently.

REV. Father Nicholas Monaghan of St. Charles Catholic Church was about to give the invocation from the bandstand. It was a tradition to rotate the honor among local churches. Fr. Monaghan first expressed thanks to Pastor Selby Bullock of First Baptist for a special kindness.

Taking into consideration the increasing number of Catholics moving into the area, Pastor Selby suggested changing the starting time for the annual baseball game from eleven AM to noon. For Winter Free's Catholics in 1950, Lenten observance ended on Easter Saturday at noon, so the hour's delay was appreciated.

After the crowd issued its amen, Mayor Gitmoure took over the microphone. First he announced the winners of the tastiest dessert, fanciest lady's hat, best pickle, and other awards. Then he spoke about the recent attack on the home of one of Winter Free's residents, Miss Sally Canfield.

"At this annual Easter Party, we award our Citizenship Medal to a citizen who contributed greatly or displayed extraordinary courage in making Winter Free a better place to live. On this day, we are breaking with tradition by awarding four medals instead of one. Four of our Cross Creek Elementary students played a prominent and critical role in fighting off three invaders from Detroit and sadly one of our own.

"Accordingly, I am proud to present the Winter Free Citizenship Medal for 1950 to Catherine Andersson, Blake Holmes, Maximilian Stein, and Hale Wending. If you four will come up to the stage, I would like to personally hand these awards to you."

The four quickly climbed the steps to generous applause. Carty and Blake stood at opposite ends of the stage, she still casting severe glances at him, and he acting thoroughly befuddled.

They thanked the mayor and examined the medals in the velvet-lined boxes. Then Hale asked the mayor if he could say something. The mayor backed away from the microphone so that Hale could approach it.

"There is an unsung hero who needs to be recognized. I saw him at the dessert table a few minutes ago, so I know that he is here. Ah, there you are, Mr. Novotny," Hale continued, pointing at him. "Would you please come on to the stage?"

Novotny was not accustomed to drawing notice, nor was he a gregarious individual. Though he enjoyed the day's festivities, he had not expected to be a center of attention.

He really did not want to go on the stage, but with everyone in the crowd staring, he had no choice. He climbed the steps to the stage and shook hands with the mayor and The Crew. Hale resumed speaking.

"When I was running from house to house seeking assistance to reach the sheriff, only Mr. Novotny was willing to help. If he had not called the sheriff, who got Mr. Andersson involved, we probably would not be here today. I chose to tell him a little fib at the time to convince him of the urgency of our plight, but in retrospect, I believe that he would have assisted me regardless. I am embarrassed about my trick and wanted to apologize to him in the best way that I know. Mr. Novotny, please accept my medal."

Hale handed his medal to Novotny as the crowd cheered and applauded. Novotny was speechless as he wiped his eyes with the back of his hand. The mayor led Novotny and the four heroes from the stage to rejoin their families. Hale insisted that Novotny meet his family, especially his three little brothers who were supposedly going to be "beatin' a white boy silly."

THE band began playing, and a few couples danced, but most eyes continued to gaze on the group clustered around the former witch turned fairy princess. Folger, Gore, and Stanton were especially interested. They could not stop staring.

"So she's the ugly witch on the broomstick who stole our specimens from you?" Gore asked Dolder incredulously. "What do you take us for, fools? Admit it. Somehow you lost the pages and cost us that C grade."

"Yeah," Folger agreed, before adding lasciviously, "She could bewitch me anytime."

Stanton motioned them around a corner of the town hall. They continued to watch Sally from that hidden vantage as she danced with Michael and a few others, but mostly James. She smiled a lot. Her bright white teeth belied the missing tooth that Dolder had described. They saw nothing to allow themselves to believe that they were looking at anyone other than the best-looking woman whom they had ever seen, not Dolder's foul-smelling, black-haired, old crone.

Folger continued, "That knock-out 'movie star' is Sally Canfield? You told us that Sally Canfield is an ugly old witch with warts and a missing tooth, who flew to your house and made you hand over our specimens. You must be out of your mind if you think we are going to believe that the gorgeous woman dancing over there is a hideous witch."

Dolder was as confused as they, even more so since he had experienced Sally's visit and they had not. Poor light at night or not, there was no way that the witch he saw looked anything like this beauty.

Every attempt at a plausible theory failed before he got it out. He must have said, "What about...?" half a dozen times, stopping moments afterward at each effort, as he realized the absurdity of what he was about to propose. He saw that they were not going to give him an opportunity to escape. He pleaded, "Just give me a few minutes to sort this out in my mind."

After fifteen minutes or so, Folger placed a fist against Dolder's nose and threatened, "OK, that's long enough. You tell us the truth. Admit you lied, or we are going to pound you until you do, and then we'll pound you some more anyway."

Dolder was desperate. Then it came to him. "Wait, I think I do know what happened. Just give me one more minute to think it through.

After a few moments, he began. "You remember what I told you. She flew to my window and demanded the Chapmann's rhododendron. She wouldn't believe me when I told her that we did not steal it from her – which is true, as you know, since we actually took it from Carty's group.

I tried to convince the witch that Carty's group had stolen it and that we were trying to find a way to return it to her.

"Anyway, the witch claimed that she needed the specimen for a 'midnight enchantment.' Then she insisted on the other two specimens as well – two that we hadn't nipped from Carty. Don't you see? She needed those specimens to brew into her potion. She needed them to change herself from being a witch into a princess."

The boys looked at each other and at him skeptically, but there was just enough consistency in his rendition, and it played sufficiently on their own beliefs in the witch rumors to make them pause.

Sensing their hesitancy, Dolder continued on. "Look, she called it a 'midnight enchantment.' I told you that before, right? That probably means she changes back into a witch at midnight. What's more, have you noticed that she has been hanging around Carty? Doesn't that look suspicious? We nipped Carty's specimen and the witch knows that it got inserted into our specimen book."

The three boys looked to one another. Then Folger spoke, "OK, how about we hold off and keep her in sight until midnight? If she turns into a witch, you are off the hook, Dolder. If she stays looking like a princess, you are dead meat."

Gore and Stanton nodded their agreement. Dolder knew he was grasping at straws, but anything to postpone a beating was worth trying, and he had almost convinced himself that he was right. The rest of the evening, as the townsfolk were enjoying the party, Dolder and his pack lurked in the shadows, keeping Sally in sight.

SALLY noted a solitary Blake away from the crowd and excused herself to speak with him. "Blake, you do not appear to be enjoying yourself. What is the matter?"

"Gee, Miss Canfield, I really goofed up. When Carty came up to me, I was so flummoxed by how beautiful she looked, my attempt at a compliment came out as an insult. I don't know what to do. She may never speak to me again."

"Blake, Carty is not going to allow one slip of the tongue wipe out a lifetime of friendship. Relax, be yourself, and give her a chance to get over it. Anyway, I heard Mack talking with her when they were dancing to 'Stardust.' It appeared that he was putting in a good word for you."

"Oh, I hope so, Miss Canfield. Miss Canfield, may I ask you a question?"

"Certainly, Blake."

"I've been thinking about that pile of rocks that descended on Hostetter. I know that there was quite a volume up on the roof. I was confused about it when I walked across your pasture the first day we visited you, and kind of mapped it out in my head. I don't understand how, but the avalanche that fell on Hostetter appeared to be a quantity well greater than what I saw on your roof."

"So what is your question, Blake?"

"Uh, how could more rocks fall on him than were on the roof to begin with?"

Sally smiled at him warmly. "Why, Blake, you are a very perceptive young man. Why don't we go and see if Mack solved your Carty problem." With that said, she took the arm of a confused young man and led him back to the crowd.

Indeed, Mack had smoothed the waters. "Blake was just shocked at how gorgeous you are, Carty," he had told her. "You grew up when he wasn't looking."

"Why, Mack, that's the nicest thing you've ever said to me. Do you really think I look grown up – that I'm gorgeous?"

"You look like an angel on a Christmas tree. Now, just don't tell Blake that I vouched for him, Carty. Anyway, for awhile let him stew. It'll do him a little good. But don't leave tonight without letting him off the hook."

By evening's end, Carty and Blake had made up, and she saved the last dance for him. In Blake's euphoria, he forgot about mundane things like rocks.

Sally emerged as the highlight of the party and the town's primary item of gossip well into summer. She had studied books on dancing for years. That, and frequently trying out solitary dance steps with imaginary Prince Charmings in front of a mirror, proved successful in practice that night.

She spent most of her evening with James, but managed to get in a dance with a few of the men she knew from her previous persona. Surprisingly, elderly Gardner Ensign proved to be quite light on his feet. Homer, on the other hand, nearly crushed her toes in those soft slipper-like shoes. Michael Andersson mercifully cut in on Homer before any bones were broken.

AS the time moved closer to midnight, Dolder was becoming increasingly tense. Sally showed no signs of reverting to an old hag or fearing the onward movement of the clock. His escorts seemed to be closing in on him inch by inch as each hour passed. They had no intentions of providing an opportunity for him to run off.

A little after eleven-thirty, the crowd had dwindled slightly, but most people were hanging on for the fireworks display – not a Fourth of July standard, but enough rocketry to retain interest. It was to be a ten-minute event ending precisely at midnight. Most people had secured places on the public square lawn well away from tree branches that would obstruct good views.

Sally and James stood in a patch of grass farther away than other spectators, out near the parking area, so James could check his radio for distress calls. Although he was not on duty tonight, one of the conditions of driving the county car for personal use was to be available for emergencies during off hours.

James hadn't been to the car for several hours, so just before the fireworks were about to start, he excused himself from Sally and checked the car radio. He had not yet returned when the first rockets spewed red and white into the night sky to the oohs and aahs of the spectators.

Dolder's captors were sufficiently distracted by the sight that they did not notice James return to her side and help her to her feet. "I'm sorry, Sally, I have to go. There has been a bad accident on State Road 70. Apparently a gas station blew up. The fire department's already on site. You can come with me, or I can ask the Anderssons to take you home."

"Oh, no, you don't. You're not getting rid of me that easily on our first date," she said, smiling. "Besides, it sounds exciting, and I'll probably get a longer speedy car ride this time."

"You can count on that. Let's go."

They rushed to the car while Folger, Gore, and Stanton had their eyes glued to the sparkly sky. Only Dolder noticed the race for the sheriff's car. He had more at stake than the other three boys, so he had more reason to pay attention. Once the car pulled out of sight, Dolder shrunk back with a violent jerk. He let out a loud cry in mock surprise and fear, and pointed to the area that Sally and the sheriff had just vacated, "Holy cow. Have you ever seen anything like it?"

The other three boys looked in vain for anything unusual. "What? What is it?" Gore yelled, over the bursting rockets, noting that Sally was gone.

"The witch. She just disappeared in a puff of smoke. I don't know what happened to the sheriff. He was with her and then she pointed for him to go away. As soon as the sheriff left, she waived her left arm in a wide arc and poof, she was gone. Weren't you guys watching?"

They didn't know what to say or do. It was their own fault for being distracted. They did not believe him entirely, but Sally and the sheriff were definitely gone. She was there moments ago watching the fireworks as they were. Where else could she be? Reluctantly, they left Dolder off the hook. Only then did the four of them realize that they had wasted their entire evening. Aside from the fireworks show, they had missed out on all of the festivities throughout the evening.

SALLY was not disappointed at the fast ride. Though James drove at top speed, the trip took over an hour to get to the accident site. Chief Fireside, appropriately his real name, briefed James on what they had found.

"We got the call about ten and rushed over. A passing motorist phoned it in from a mile south of here. We have his contact information for you, but he probably can't add much. He heard the explosion only moments before he passed by, and the fire was well on its way by that time. It was out of control and too hot for him to offer any help.

"This is an isolated location that would normally take us over an hour to get to, but we made it in only six minutes and got things under control fast. Fortunately, we were returning from a small grass fire and were nearby when the call came in. The van and the whole gas pump area were ablaze. It's a good thing they paved with cement instead of asphalt or we'd be up to our ankles in melted tar.

"The explosion blew out the glass in the station, but we were able to save the building. Fortunately, a light breeze was coming from the right direction to keep the flames away from the structure. The only damage there is soot and smoke.

"It looks like a hose from the gas pump malfunctioned and spewed gas all over the place. Then a spark or cigarette or something similar must have set it off. The explosion was heard ten miles away. We had a dozen calls from all over the area.

"We've located two dead men, and we're reasonably sure that will be all. We think one was Elmer Morris, the station attendant. The other appears to be the driver of the seafood truck that was buying the gas."

At this last statement, James arched his eyebrows. "Seafood truck? What company?"

"I really haven't looked that closely," the chief replied. "The writing is probably burned off the sides of the truck. I'm not sure if you can read anything on them or not. Let's take a look. The fire's out now, but watch for hot metal and sharp debris, Sheriff."

As they walked over to the burned out hulk, it smelled like a fish fry marinated in gasoline. The chief was right about the signage. The intensity of the heat had destroyed any identifying marks on the sides of the vehicle, and the license tags had melted from the heat. However, the volunteer fire department's fortuitous quick arrival saved part of the front of the truck, so James held hopes of getting identification numbers from the engine block in order to track down ownership.

The back door to the boxed part of the truck was hanging askew by one lower hinge. Careful to avoid touching it as the heat radiated from the vehicle, they peered inside and saw a charred victim sprawled on piles of still smoldering fish.

"Your men didn't move the fellow into that position, did they?" James asked.

"No. We could not have gone in there if we had wanted to. The heat was too intense. You seem distracted, Sheriff, what's up?"

"It strikes me odd that the driver is in the back sitting on the fish. You think he would have been in the driver's seat while the attendant filled his tank. There is no access from the driver's area into the cargo area.

"Surely he wouldn't have rushed out of his seat into the back of the truck when the fire broke out. There is no way he could have expected to unload the cargo fast enough to save it. Even if he did believe it possible, he should have been found near the back door, not situated all the way forward like he is."

"I see what you mean."

"Where did you find the attendant?"

"He was charred beyond recognition too. You probably saw us pulling him away as you drove up. His body is over in the grass under that blanket if you want to examine it. We couldn't read the name tag on his uniform because most of his clothes had burned away. For now, we're assuming that he was Elmer Morris because the time sheet inside the station shows a man with that name to be on duty. The station manager is on the way, so we can get confirmation when he arrives.

James walked over and gently removed the blanket. The corpse was unidentifiable as anything but a vaguely human body. James reverently put the blanket back and paused to say a silent prayer for the man. The body reminded him of some of the casualties he helped to unload from a torpedoed Navy ship that had limped back to port early in the War.

When James returned, the chief continued. Pointing to an area between the pump and the truck, he said, "We found his body crumpled up next to the pump right here."

"Was there any indication that he had died from anything other than the fire?" James asked.

"Nothing that I could pinpoint. Usually in violent events like this we would expect to see the victim spread eagled from the explosion or splayed out where he had succumbed running away. Being crumpled in a fetal position is unusual, but maybe he hit his head on the pump when the blast came, and he fell into a ball."

"Looks like Doc Brannigan will be earning his county coroner's salary on this one," James remarked.

When the metal had cooled sufficiently, one of the firemen retrieved the vehicle identification number for James. He radioed it into headquarters and went back with the chief to examine the area for anything unusual. By the time they finished, the report was radioed back to his car:

Rex Seafood of Tampa owned the truck. "Why did I think that was going to be the case?" he thought to himself.

A deputy arrived and James put him in charge. "This is considered a crime scene until I can check out a few things. Keep everyone away except the fire officials," he instructed. "Ask them to refrain from moving anything that isn't involved with their fire fighting duties. I'll get you some relief on the next shift."

Back in the car, James asked Sally, "Are you sure that you want to be involved with someone who has to make runs like this in the middle of the night?"

"It seemed exciting when we were racing to the site, and even more so at first glance when we drove up to the inferno. But then the reality of the firemen hauling a dead person away hit me, and I realized how serious your work is. It is not a responsibility that I would relish, but I admire you for taking it on.

"I heard from several people at the party tonight that you have held the county together like no previous sheriff or politician. Mrs. Wending told me that you were the best friend that the Negro community ever had. She said she hoped that everyone would be like you someday.

"So do I want to be involved with someone who has to make night visits like this? I can't think of anyone I'd rather be involved with, James."

"Then you'll have to get used to some late night abandonment too. I'm going to drop you off at home and then go into the office. It is almost daybreak, and I recall that Rex Seafood – the company that owns the burned-out truck – opens at six. I want to get an early start.

"I just want to look at a map before we get going. Could you help me hold it down in this breeze?"

James unfolded a large road map and placed it on the hood of his car. Pointing to a spot on the map, he said, "Here is about where your place is located, Sally, just off Mocking Bird Road. And here is where Rex Seafood is, on the docks in Tampa on State Route 60, also named East Adamo Drive.

Tracing light blue and bold red lines on the map with his finger, he continued, "You may recall that we suspected that Rex Seafood was in some way related to the attack on your place. If someone drove from near your house to Rex Seafood in Tampa, he would most likely take this route."

His finger came to a rest on a red State Route 70 line which he tapped a few times. "This is where we are right now. You can see that the driver would have passed right by the gas station where we are standing now."

"So you think that there is a connection between the men at my house and this fire. But what could it be?"

"I try not to come up with any theories too early in the game, Sally. Guessing wrong tends to put blinders on when conflicting evidence comes in. Instead of looking at the new developments objectively, you try to bend them to fit your pre-conceived ideas. I don't know what is going on, but there are too many coincidences to ignore. And Rex Seafood seems to be the common factor for many of them."

Back at headquarters later, he called Rex Seafood and introduced himself to the man who answered. "I would like to speak with Mr. Gilbert."

"I'm sorry, sir, but Mr. Gilbert is not here. We had a large delivery called in late yesterday afternoon, and he decided to make it himself. He hasn't returned yet, but he probably got in late and had to sleep in.

To James's next question he replied, "No, that is very unusual, but the customer insisted in dealing directly with Mr. Gilbert.

"No, now that you ask, I can't recall him ever making a delivery before. What seems to be the problem, sir?"

James advised him about the fire involving the company's truck, and that a man perished inside the vehicle. He cautioned the employee that the victim had not been identified yet and said that he would ask Sgt. Vasquez of the Tampa Police Department to stop over when they had more information.

CHAPTER 27

Sarasota Preparatory Academy

Life... is not simply a series of exciting new ventures. The future is not always a whole new ball game. There tends to be unfinished business.

ANITA BROOKNER

Aunt Lilly, Bay, and Carty chatted away excitedly as Michael concentrated on navigating through the busy downtown Sarasota streets.

"Turn left on Palm, Michael. It's the next street," Lilly instructed. "That's where the academy is located. The city is a lot more built up than when I went to school here," she marveled.

The academy's open house had drawn prospective students from around the country and from several countries south of the United States. Throughout their tour of the campus, Lilly pointed out classrooms where she had spent time and introduced Carty to two of her former teachers who were still on staff, well past normal retirement age. Carty was impressed that both of them remembered her great aunt.

AS they moved into the auditorium to hear the headmistress give her welcoming remarks, Michael stopped in front of a handsome man of similar age to his. He had a head of thick wavy hair – black without a hint of the gray that sprinkled Michael's.

They embraced in Latin style for a long moment to the astonishment of the Andersson women, who had never seen Michael behave in such an emotional way publicly. Both men fought tears. They stepped back from one another.

"Captain Rafferty," Michael said respectfully.

"Captain Andersson," the other man replied.

Carty detected a pleasant and readily apparent Spanish accent, despite the Irish sounding surname.

After introductions, Michael added, "You are probably confused by Rafael's family name. His father, Tim Rafferty, was a young banker from New York City when Teddy Roosevelt was looking for volunteers to fight the Spaniards in Cuba in 1898. When the Spanish American War ended, Tim Rafferty stayed in Cuba. That is why one of Cuba's biggest and better-run banks, Banco Rafferty, has a Celtic name."

Rafael was accompanied by his wife, Margarite, and daughter, Elena. Elena was remarkably blond for one of mostly Spanish ancestry. But Tim Rafferty's genes had flowed generously through to her and to her younger brother, Roberto. Perhaps that was why Elena felt closer to Roberto than to their six dark-haired siblings who favored Margarite's French and

Spanish ancestry.

Elena was visiting the academy for the same reason as Carty. She was planning to begin classes in September as well.

On occasion, two people meet and instantly dislike each other for no apparent reason. Other times, the opposite occurs. This was an instance of the latter.

The two girls, similar in disposition and personality, looked sufficiently alike to be mistaken for sisters. They were tall, athletic, and blond. Both smiled easily, though Carty's was partly because of her natural facial structure and Elena's was by her nature. Within minutes, they were giggling and chattering at top speed, oblivious to the adults – until Michael and Rafael started talking about the War.

"Rafael is a dual citizen by virtue of his father's U.S. citizenship. He joined the U.S. Army from a cadet training program at Harvard in 1942.

"We met unexpectedly during the Battle of the Bulge. Three of my men and I got caught in the German offensive. We were pinned down behind German lines and taking fire from all sides. After Rafael got his own men headed back to safety, he worked his way behind a machine gun nest and took it out by himself. Then he led us back to our lines."

Rafael interjected, "Michael forgets to mention who the real hero was. On the way back, as we reached our lines, a lone German surprised us with a hand grenade – one of those grenades that looks like a dynamite stick. It came to rest right in the middle of our group of five. It appeared that we were all seconds from being dead men. Instantaneously, Michael dived for the grenade and covered it with his body to protect the rest of us as we hit the dirt. It was certain death for him to save us."

Lilly, Bay, and Carty stood open-mouthed, staring at an embarrassed Michael, who was rocking back and forth on his heels. He had never spoken of this.

"What happened?" Bay gasped, her hand covering her mouth in shock.

"The ugly German grenade was a dud," Michael said quietly.

"After a few moments longer than it would take for the fool thing to explode," Rafael went on, "I realized that it wasn't going to. So I jumped up and grabbed Michael's arm and began pulling him away. It took two of his men and me to get him away from it, because he was sure it was still a threat, and he kept trying to shield us. Once we moved out of range, his sergeant shot it with his M1 and blew it up.

"Needless to say, Michael is high on the hero list of four ex-soldiers, including me."

Michael eyed him sternly, "You really didn't need to get into any of that, you know."

The three Andersson and two Rafferty women stood in awe of both of these humble men, and everyone remained speechless.

MICHAEL was rescued from further comment when the headmistress, Mrs. Tutwiler, tapped the microphone lightly to signify that she was ready to speak.

"Welcome, prospective students and families," she began. "In a few short months, many of you girls will be coming together here in Sarasota to take a large step forward in your lives. For the first time, most of you will be living away from your families for an extended period of time. You will make friendships that may be life changing and will last your entire lives."

"We at Sarasota Preparatory Academy are here to teach academics, but also to be a temporary substitute for your parents. You may count on us to help you when you need us, to laugh with you when you are happy, to console you when times are difficult, and," she added with a stern look capped by a slight, tight smile, "to keep you on the straight and narrow."

Carty smiled knowingly at Elena. Now they knew why one of the student guides had confided in them earlier that Mrs. Tutwiler was known by the students as "Mrs. Tut-tut."

Mrs. Tutwiler continued in this vein for another fifteen minutes, eventually outlining the rigorous academic challenges ahead and introducing key members of the faculty.

Finally, the outgoing senior class president spoke about her four years at SPA. That she shed a tear or two at the prospect of leaving the institution in a few short weeks said more than her words about the fondness that alumnae held for the institution.

Cake, cookies, coffee, and punch were served in the gymnasium. Teachers attended tables where printed materials explaining the subject matter to be taught sought the attention of the students. The two academic tracks were science and liberal arts, both designed to prepare students for success at a four-year university. The scientific track was relatively new, developing after the War as more girls were entering medical colleges.

THAT evening, the Anderssons and the Raffertys enjoyed a joyful and boisterous dinner at an Italian restaurant. Michael and Rafael told many non-combat stories of their time in the Army, omitting or altering those unsuitable for mixed or under-age company. Nevertheless, the tales kept those at the table and a few eavesdropping nearby entertained all evening.

Michael was particularly interested in hearing about Rafael's two years in Germany after the War ended. Newspapers were not covering how the Army was helping with rebuilding while fighting off remnants of the German army and gangs of displaced former slave laborers who had melted into the hills.

Normally, SPA accommodated requests of girls who wanted to be roommates. By evening's end, the two girls had decided to make that request before they left for home. Whatever hesitancy Carty felt about living away from home for the next four years had dissipated with the prospects of the budding friendship.

In the morning, the Raffertys returned to Havana by air, and Michael drove his family back to Winter Free.

IN MID-JUNE, Cross Creek Elementary conducted its graduation ceremony for the eighth graders. Afterward, The Crew and their families met at the Andersson's house for a small party and buffet.

Hale had the biggest news of the day. He would be joining Blake and Mack at Winter Free High. Coach Normand, the baseball coach, had convinced the school board to allow Hale to attend Winter Free instead of forcing him into the Negro high school in the adjoining town. The fact that Hale graduated from Cross Creek with the highest grades played a part, but it was Sam Normand who made the difference.

Sam really wanted to team Hale and Blake at his keystone next year. Three state championship awards residing in the school trophy case and two former players in the major leagues during his twenty-year reign gave him plenty of influence.

The news gave Carty momentary pause in her enthusiasm for SPA. She thought of how enjoyable high school would be for the next four years with The Crew intact. But she was excited about teaming up with Elena and experiencing the freedom she would have at the Academy.

The Crew and their families joined together for a toast of orange-dosed Lilly Lemonade to a future that looked bright and promising for the eighth grade graduates.

At that moment, not one of them had any idea that the same president who ended World War II with a big bang would that summer be involved in a new hot war with Communist forces on the Korean Peninsula. The world would be changing, and events would overtake The Crew in ways they could not anticipate in the years and decades ahead.

THE END

POSTSCRIPT

Hiding places there are innumerable, escape is only one, but possibilities of escape, again, are as many as hiding places.

FRANZ KAFKA

The spectacular fire and explosion of the Standard Oil station attracted widespread newspaper interest, so Cruz Cruz was able to read about the coroner's report in a Tampa newspaper. The paper always arrived a few days late in Havana, but he felt compelled to stay abreast of the news from his original home city, even belatedly.

In his favorite coffee shop across from the University of Havana, he sprinkled a second spoonful of sugar into his cup and read with particular interest what Dr. Brannigan had to say.

"Dr. Brannigan's coroner's report was sufficiently vague to leave several questions open," the story continued. "From dental records, the victim in the truck was positively identified as Andrew Gilbert, a Tampa business owner, and the station attendant as Elmer Morris. Neither identification surprised authorities.

"The severity of the fire masked any definitive evidence about the cause of death," Brannigan stated. "Mr. Gilbert had suffered a severe blow to the head, but I am unable to determine if the injury occurred before the fire or concurrent with it.

"The explosion could have thrown Mr. Gilbert's head against the metal walls of the truck, or he could have been hit by someone wielding a blunt object shortly prior to the blast. There is no way to tell. There were several heavy items loose in the cargo area, including tools and wooden pallets. These dented the metal walls in several places. Any of these objects could have struck Mr. Gilbert's head as well.

"Elmer Morris, the station attendant, suffered a number of bruises, including a blunt trauma to the head. Some or all could have been incurred by being thrown against the gas pump by the force of the explosion. Some or all could have been inflicted by unknown causes or persons shortly prior to the blast as well. There is no way to tell.

"Absent any compelling evidence to the contrary, I am calling both of these deaths accidental, with the possibility of reviewing the determination should new facts come to light."

The article went on to say that Sheriff Elsmore and Chief Fireside were continuing their investigations into the blaze. The sheriff was quoted as saying that robbery was eliminated as a motive. The day's receipts for the station were found in the cash register. They tallied exactly to the total on the machine's tape.

The paper reported that a group that called itself the "Society Against Greed and Excess" urged the governor to send in a team of investigators to "determine why Standard Oil was allowing its gas hoses to leak and cause terrible fires." A Hollywood actress with ties to Florida, Miss Sara Ann Dan, was quoted as saying, "Standard Oil doesn't care about safety – only about profits."

"Standard Oil," reported the paper, "Had no comment." Of course, Standard Oil might have had a comment if the reporter had bothered to ask for one.

Cruz loved this new group, SAGE. He laughed to himself, "The formerly comely Miss Dan apparently thinks that Standard Oil profits rise when its stations blow up. Really shrewd planning by company management. Think how much more money they would make if the company's CEO destroyed all of its stations."

Cruz realized that the reporter was as brain befuddled as Miss Dan. He put that concept into his memory bank. "Find a washed-up publicity seeker to lead the fight and a gullible reporter as media mouthpiece and use them for propaganda purposes. How grand," he chuckled.

To the point at hand, Cruz had hoped for a more definitive ending. But at least Cruz's brief return to Florida tied two loose ends into one nice knot. Cruz had flown into Atlanta, Georgia from Havana in case the police were monitoring the Tampa airport for the return of someone with his now well-known name.

The round trip drive to meet Gilbert at the Standard Oil station proved successful. Just prior to setting the fire, Cruz bashed Elmer's head and, moments later, knocked-out Gilbert who had sought refuge in the back of the truck. Cruz had planned for the intensity and duration of the gasoline fire to mask the identifying features of the Rex Seafood truck.

However, that part of the plan obviously fell short, evidently due to the unexpectedly prompt arrival of fire fighting equipment.

There was always Maldonado to be concerned about, but he was still useful, both as an accountant and for special projects. He would spare Maldonado – for now anyway.

Cruz longed to solve his Hostetter problem, but he could not afford to bring additional attention to the situation right now, especially with that nosey sheriff still inclined to keep investigating. If Hostetter died so soon after these deaths at the Standard Oil station, the sheriff might be further energized. Cruz did not want that; he wanted the sheriff concentrating on unrelated matters, say one of those jaywalking outbreaks.

Cruz finished his small, sweetened coffee in a large gulp and walked to his car. It was time for his meeting with Batista.

AROUND THE SAME TIME, in the little town of Clewiston, Florida on the south side of Lake Okeechobee, a Mexican sugar cane picker returned to her one room shack after another back-breaking day in the fields. Since her husband, Martino, died of cancer two years before, Easter Huerto lived day to day on barely enough money to survive. So when she happened upon the unconscious man on the side of US Highway 27 several weeks earlier, she was really not in a position to help.

Nevertheless, she gave him water from the canteen she always carried and brought him back to partial consciousness. Then she half dragged him to her nearby one room shack. From that time, she had not been happier despite the hardship of giving him almost constant care. Easter attended to him every woken hour when she was not laboring in the cane fields. The burden of the extra effort paled compared with the desperate loneliness she felt since Martino passed away.

Today, for the first time, the injured man spoke his first few logical words, mostly mumbling but somewhat understandable. He tried to get out of his bed, but she pushed his shoulders gently back and admonished him to remain in place. The sharp pains in his chest helped to convince him, but he seemed to recall that those pains were worse not too long ago.

He pointed to a small mirror and motioned for Easter to bring it close. He looked at himself for the first time in weeks, with eyes that had cleared considerably. His face was marred and scabbed. His hair was a perfect white. He almost cried when he saw his horrible condition, and he had not cried since he was in the first grade at St. Stanislaus School decades before.

He did not recognize the shirt he wore. His pants were strange as well. The lower pant legs were a different color than the upper portion. Easter had sewn the extra cloth on to an old pair of her husband's pants to make them fit her patient's taller frame.

When Easter noticed him looking at his attire, she recalled the strange clothes she had removed from the man that first day. Torn, more like shredded, and bloody beyond anything she had ever seen, the clothes nearly matched the condition of the man's flayed skin when she found him.

He appeared to have been snagged by some large machine or to have been stabbed repeatedly with a short knife. His body showed hundreds of shallow open wounds. In dozens of places, his flesh had been gouged and stripped away. His face was scraped raw as if someone had rubbed it forcefully with sandpaper.

His inner garment, a long shirt of sorts, intrigued her. She had tried to mend it, but broke two of her scarce needles in the attempt. Like his skin and flesh, it bore countless scrape marks, but because it was made of a thick, woven, multi-layered, hard substance, it had not shred. Indeed, the durable material had protected the crucial torso of the man's body from the puncture wounds that appeared nearly everywhere else. The strange shirt that had resisted her needles had withstood most of the gouges and stab wounds as well.

The man attempted to ask, "Where am I?" Even in his weakened and dazed condition, he could tell that he spoke in slow motion as if playing a record at the wrong speed. He did not recognize his own whispered voice, nor could he comprehend what the woman answered, though her Spanish-accented English was competent.

He realized that he had gained a little strength, but he sensed that he was not going to be healthy for a long time. After eating nearly a bowlful of soup, more food than he had taken from Easter in all of the previous days with her, he fell back to sleep, exhausted with the minimal effort that mere eating required.

She was pleased to hear him ask where he was. Those were the first intelligible words that he had spoken. Previously, his only phrase made no sense, though he repeated it over and over, often when semi-conscious. She thought it must be important to him, but she wondered what meaning she could piece together from words that sounded like, "carry seller, carry seller, carry seller."

ENDNOTES

1) *Brylcreem* – hair gel for the "slicked-back" look to men's hair; popular in the Fifties.

2) *Comstock Lode* – major silver mining area around Virginia City, Nevada.

3) *DeSoto* – automobile model sold by Chrysler Corporation; discontinued in 1961.

4) *Pan Am* – Pan American World Airways; the primary international airline in the United States from the Twenties through the Seventies; misguided mergers and Government deregulation policies that favored other carriers sent Pan Am into decline in the Eighties; the company went out of business in 1991.

5) *Andrew Carnegie* (1835-1919) – founded Carnegie Steel Company, the world's most profitable company at the turn of the Twentieth Century; sold it to J. P. Morgan in 1901, who turned it into United States Steel Corporation; willed nearly all of his fortune to construct libraries and other public enterprises.

6) *Cross Creek* – title of a 1942 memoir by Marjorie Kinnan Rawlings (1896-1953), author of The Yearling, a 1938 coming of age novel set in the Nineteenth Century wilds of Florida.

7) *Graham* – automobile popular in the Twenties and early Thirties; ceased production in 1940.

8) *Bowie Knife* – large knife; generally between six inches and twelve inches in length; originally designed by Col. James Bowie (1796-

1836), adventurer and explorer who was among those who perished defending the Alamo.

9) *Hoover* – first vacuum cleaner to combine the vacuum with a rotating brush to loosen dirt; due to the market dominance of The Hoover Company in the early and mid-Twentieth Century, "Hoover" became synonymous with "vacuum cleaner" in that era.

10) *Penny and Jody Baxter* – father and son characters in Marjorie Kinnan Rawlings' The Yearling, a 1938 coming of age novel set in the Nineteenth Century wilds of Florida.

11) *Old Slewfoot* – rampaging bear; a character in Marjorie Kinnan Rawlings' The Yearling, a 1938 coming of age novel set in the Nineteenth Century wilds of Florida.

12) *Glinda* – the "Good Witch of the North" in the 1939 movie version of the novel by L. Frank Baum (1856-1919), The Wonderful Wizard of Oz.

13) *Mercurochrome* – popular antiseptic used for topical treatment of minor injuries to the skin; the FDA effectively removed it from distribution in the United States in 1998 because of its mercury content; still popular outside of the United States.

14) *Moon Pie* – a pastry of the Chattanooga Bakery, Inc.; a graham cracker, marshmallow sandwich dipped into chocolate or other flavor; about the size of a hockey puck; especially popular in the South.

15) *Barq's* – soft drink brand; most frequently root beer; company acquired by The Coca Cola Company in 1995.

16) *Toll House* – county inn near Whitman, Massachusetts, where in the

Thirties the owner created the chocolate chip cookie by slicing chocolate slivers from a Nestlé chocolate bar into cookie dough; she later teamed up with Nestlé to promote the popular cookie.

17) *Lederhosen* – traditional knee length Bavarian leather pants worn by men; shorter length versions worn by boys; typically accessorized with tall knee socks.

18) *Frigidaire* – first self-contained refrigerator; company name adopted in 1919 and continued through various owners since; due to the market dominance in the early and mid-Twentieth Century, the trademarked name became synonymous with "refrigerator" in that era.

19) *Tropical Golden* – beer brand sold by the Florida Brewing Company from the Eighteen Hundreds until Prohibition; continued under Tampa Florida Brewery, Inc. from 1933 until 1961.

20) *Crosley Radio* – first low priced radio; created in the Twenties by Cincinnati businessman, Powel Crosley, Jr. (1886-1961), who went on to invent the first push button radio and to pioneer many innovations in radio broadcasting, including the first soap opera.

21) *Edward Hopper's diner* – subject of the most well-known painting (*Nighthawks*, 1942) of American artist, Hopper (1882-1967); it depicts a lonely all-night city diner occupied by a counterman and three customers – two men and a woman; the male customers are shown wearing fedoras, in the style of the Forties.

22) *Bab-O* – scouring cleanser; popular in the Fifties; still available from Fitzpatrick Bros. of Chicago.

23) *Charles Atlas* (1893-1972) – one of the first body builders to

capitalize on his physique to amass a fortune; mass marketed his strength system in comic books and other light reading fare popular with young men.

24) *Cary Grant* (1904 - 1986) – stage name of a movie star from the Thirties through the mid-Sixties. Exemplified the suave, debonair leading man who always had the right quip and wooed women with his impeccable taste and style.

AUTHOR'S NOTES

With this book, I have tried to capture an uncomplicated era where good and evil were clearly understood.

In immediate Post WWII, nearly all Americans believed in the fundamental goodness of their country and awesome competence of its citizens. Political bickering stopped at the borders, because the party out of power stressed the "loyal" in loyal opposition, instead of seeking partisan advantage at every foreign policy turn.

It was a time before television was widespread, when kids had fun outside, and when most parents, especially those in Winter Free, could let them go without fear of gang violence, illicit encounters, drugs, or drive-by shootings.

It was a time when society expected women to be ladies, and men to respect them for it. It was a time when public schools were effective teachers of academic subjects, civic duty, and respect for institutions. The best and the brightest women flooded the schools as highly competent teachers

439

instead of seeking careers as business executives, journalists, and doctors. While those latter professions now benefit greatly from the influx of talent, today's students suffer as many highly skilled women have chosen fields away from the schools.

It was a time when religion continued a nearly 160-year tradition of being readily accepted in America's public square and in public schools, a time when most people shunned rather than celebrated those who displayed bad behavior, and a time when people relied on themselves, relatives, organized charities, and neighbors rather than on a government handout or a fast-buck lawyer.

There were faults in the era, like those of any time and any place, and I happily admit to glossing over them for the sake of a fun read. This is a book of fiction, after all.

Speaking of which, some may believe 1950 Winter Free to have been a fictitious place. I hope it was real. If it were not, it surely should have been.

Ybor (pronounced "ee-bore") City cigar rolling did take place in large rooms where Readers were an important part of the production process. Cigarettes did begin to supplant cigars after WWI. Smuggling cigarettes between states to avoid taxes takes place even today, but it likely never occurred to the degree employed by Cruz.

The Columbia was founded in 1905 in modest circumstances, and today, descendants of the founder continue in the management of the world class restaurant that remains an Ybor City landmark. It has expanded to several other Florida locations as well.

The Sebring Race Course was "built" in 1950, although in that year, its construction involved little more than sectioning off part of the airport on whose tarmac the race was run. The first race took place on New Year's Eve of that year.

References to Cuba's political situation are based on historical people and events, except for the involvement of Cruz.

The Japanese Army experimented with bullet proof vests during WWII, but they were not used extensively.

Despite Carty's coming attendance at Sarasota Prep, where she will be separated from the boys in The Crew, the four members will continue their adventures during the high school years and beyond.

If you enjoyed Carty's first book and would like to be advised when the second is finished, go to the official book website, www.montoothbook.com. There, through free membership in Montooth Members, you can sign up to receive updates on the second book, and you can discover an assortment of additional information about the first book.

I hope that you liked reading about Carty and her friends as much as I did learning about them as I wrote.

Robert Jay

CONTEST

An astute reader can win a one-of-a-kind, leather-bound copy of the second book in the Carty Andersson series by solving "**The Mystery of the Names**" from Montooth and the Canfield Witch.

Go to the book's official website, www.montoothbook.com, and click "**The Mystery of the Names**" to give us your answer. All entries must be received by May 31, 2010 to be eligible.

SECOND BOOK IN
THE CARTY ANDERSSON SERIES

If you enjoyed <u>Montooth and the Canfield Witch</u>, you may be interested in the second book that chronicles some of Carty's adventures with Elena Rafferty at Sarasota Preparatory Academy. The Crew comes together for another encounter with evil, and Cruz Cruz returns with his menacing presence.

Sally will relate another swamp parable to The Crew that impacts the lives of some of the characters.

On the official book website, www.montoothbook.com, you can sign up for a free membership in Montooth Members. This will enable you to read even more about the first book, as well as to receive updates on the second book, scheduled for release in late summer of 2010.

To receive an update by mail on the next book in the Carty Andersson series, provide your contact information in the following form:

Your name and age
Your street address
Your city, state and zip code

Add the statement:
"Please notify me when the sequel to <u>Montooth and the Canfield Witch</u> is published."

Send to:

Montooth Press
1916 South Tamiami Trail
Ruskin, FL 33570